William Wetmore Story, Giovanni Duprè, E. M Peruzzi

Thoughts on Art and Autobiographical Memoirs

William Wetmore Story, Giovanni Duprè, E. M Peruzzi

Thoughts on Art and Autobiographical Memoirs

ISBN/EAN: 9783337028497

Printed in Europe, USA, Canada, Australia, Japan

Cover: Foto ©Raphael Reischuk / pixelio.de

More available books at **www.hansebooks.com**

Thoughts on Art

and

Autobiographical Memoirs

of

Giovanni Duprè

TRANSLATED FROM THE ITALIAN BY

E. M. PERUZZI

WITH AN INTRODUCTION BY W. W. STORY

BOSTON

ROBERTS BROTHERS

1886

INTRODUCTION TO NEW EDITION.

THIS book contains the record of the life and thoughts upon Art of Giovanni Duprè, one of the most eminent sculptors of the present century in Italy. It was written by him from time to time, during the latter years of his life, in the intervals of work in his studio, and given to the public about three years before his death. Those three years, of which it contains no account, were assiduously devoted to his art. Every day had its work, and it was done faithfully and joyously even to the last. "*Nulla dies sine linea.*" Within these years, among other works of less importance, he successively executed a basso-relievo of the Baptism of our Lord, a portrait statue of Pius IX. for the Cathedral of Piacenza, one of Victor Emmanuel for the public square at Trapani, one of Raimondo Lullo for a chapel in the island of Majorca, and one of St Francis of Assisi which now adorns the front of the Cathedral at Assisi. This was the last statue which he ever made. The model he had completed in clay and cast in plaster, and had somewhat advanced in executing it in marble, when death arrested his hand. It was finished by his daughter Amalia, who had for years been his loving and faithful pupil, and who had already won distinction for herself as a sculptor. In this his last work he found a peculiar attractiveness, and his heart and hand were earnestly given to it. "I am most happy," he says in his reply to the authorities of Assisi, who gave him this order, "that the Commission has thought of me,— not so much on account of what little talent I may possess, as for the love I bear to religious art." The statue itself is very simple, and informed by a deep religious sentiment. It is clothed in the dress of the order which St Francis founded, the hands crossed over the breast, the cowl falling behind, the head bent, and the eyes cast down in an attitude of submission and devotion.

The statue had not only deeply interested all his feelings and sympathies, but in its treatment and sentiment he seems to have been satisfied. A singular presentiment, however, came over him as he was showing it to a friend upon its completion. "It will be a triumph to you and a glory to Assisi," said his friend. "Ah," he answered, "who knows that it may not be the last!" So indeed it proved. But a few days after this conversation he was seized by an attack of peritonitis. From this, however, he recovered, as well as from a second attack, which shortly afterwards followed. As he was recovering from this second attack he wrote to Monsignore Andrea Ulli: "The doctor has no doubt that I shall get well, and in a few days I hope he will allow me to return to my studio. But how I have suffered!—doubly suffered from having been deprived of the occupation that most delights me. This is my joy and my life. What a happy day it will be when I am permitted to put my foot again into my studio, and to resume my work and my St Francis."

His hopes, however, were fated to be disappointed. Although he sufficiently recovered to go to his studio, he was able to do but little work; and shortly afterwards—on the 1st of January—he was again prostrated by a third attack of the same disease. His death, he felt, was now certain; but he met its approach with the courage, resignation, and piety that had always characterised him, looking forward with certainty to a reunion with the dear ones who had gone before him—Luisina, his daughter, whose loss he had so bitterly felt, and his wife Marina, his steadfast help and loving companion for so many years, who had died seven years previously. One regret constantly possessed him during these last days, that he should not be able, as he had projected, to model the statue of the Madonna for the Duomo at Florence, upon which he had set his heart. One day when he gave expression to this feeling, his daughter Amalia sought to console him by saying, "But you have already made her statue, and it is so

beautiful—the *addolorata* for Santa Croce." "Ah!"
he answered, "but I desired to model her as Queen
of Florence." This apparently was the only desire
that haunted him during his last attack. In regard to all other things he was resigned ; and after
lingering in almost constant pain for ten days, he
expired on the 10th of January 1882, at the age of
sixty-five.

The announcement of his death was received
everywhere in Italy with the warmest expressions
of sorrow. It was felt to be a national loss. His
life had been so pure, so conscientious, and so
animated by high purpose—his temper and character had been so blameless and free from envy
and stain of any kind—he had been so generous
and kindly in all the varied relations of life, as a
son, as a husband, as a father, as a friend,—and he
had so greatly distinguished himself as a sculptor,
that over his grave the carping voice of criticism
was hushed, and a universal voice of praise and
sorrow went up everywhere. All classes united to
do him reverence, from the highest to the lowest.
Funeral ceremonies were celebrated in his honour,
not only in Florence, where a great procession
accompanied his remains to the church where the
last rites were performed, but also in Siena, his
birthplace, in Fiesole, where he was buried in the
family chapel, and in Antella and Agnone. The
press of his native country gave expression to high
eulogiums on him as an artist and as a man.
Public honours were decreed to him. In front of

the house where he was born in Siena, the municipality placed this inscription: "This humble abode, in which was born Giovanni Duprè, honour of Art and Italy, may teach the sons of the people what height can be reached by the force of genius and will." In the Parrocchial Church dell' Onda (in Siena) was placed a bust of the artist executed by his daughter Amalia ; and in Florence, over the house where he had passed a large portion of his life, a tablet is inserted, on which is inscribed these words: "The Municipality of Florence, in whose council sat Giovanni Duprè, has placed this memorial on the house where for twenty years lived the great sculptor, glory of Italy and of Art, and in which he died on the 10th day of 1882."

During his life honours had been showered upon him at home and abroad—honours well deserved and meekly borne, without vanity or pretension. He had been made a knight and counsellor of the Civil Order of Savoy, a member of the Institute of France, a knight of the Tuscan Order of Merit and of the Legion of Honour in France, an officer of the Brazilian Order of the Rose, a commander of the Order of the Corona d'Italia, Mexico and Guadaloupe, an associate of the Academy of St Luke, and of various other academies in Italy and elsewhere. The Municipal Council of Siena also commissioned his friend and pupil, Tito Sarrocchi, to execute for it a bust of his master in marble during his lifetime, on which was this inscription : " To Giovanni Duprè of Siena, who to

the glories of Italian Art has added, by the wonders of his chisel, new and immortal glories. The
city of Siena—xii. July 1867."

His life was a busy and an earnest one. During
his forty years of patient labour he executed
about a hundred works in the round and in relief,
including a considerable number of busts and
statuettes. Of these, perhaps the most important
are: The statues of Cain and Abel, the original
bronzes of which are in the Pitti Palace in Florence, and by which he leaped at once to fame as a
sculptor; the group of the Pietà in the cemetery of
Siena; the large bas-relief of the Triumph of the
Cross on the façade of the Church of Santa Croce in
Florence; the monument to Cavour at Milan; the
Ferrari monument in San Lorenzo, with the angel
of the resurrection; the Sappho; the pedestal for
the colossal Egyptian Tazza, with its alto-reliefs,
representing Thebes, Imperial Rome, Papal Rome,
and Tuscany, each with its accompanying genius;
the portrait statue of Giotto; the ideal statue of St
Francis; and the Risen Christ.

The Tazza, the Pietà, the Triumph of the Cross,
and the Risen Christ, were selected by him out of
all his works to send to the French Exposition of
1867, and it may therefore be supposed that he
considered them as the best representatives of his
genius and power. Indeed, in a letter to Professor Pietro Dotto (1866) he mentions particularly
these last three as the statues which in conception he considers to be the most worthy of praise

of all his works. This selection also indicates the religious character of his mind and his works. At this Exposition he was one of the jury on Sculpture, and though he gave his own vote in favour of the eminent sculptor Signor Vela of Milan, who exhibited on that occasion his celebrated statue of the Last Hours of Napoleon I., to his surprise the grand medal of honour was awarded to himself. He had scarcely dared to hope for this ; and in his letters to his family he wrote that he considered it certain that the distinction would be conferred upon Signor Vela. When the award was made to him, he wrote a most characteristic letter to his daughter, announcing the result. " Mia cara Beppina," he says, " I have just returned from the sitting of the jury, and hasten at once to answer your dear letter. It is true that the Napoleon I. of Vela is a beautiful statue. There is always a crowd about it, and consequently every one thought it would receive the first prize. I have given him my vote ; but the public and I and you, Beppina, were wrong. The first prize has come to me, your father ! Vela received two votes with mine. You see, my dear, how the Holy Virgin has answered your and our prayer. Let us seek to render ourselves worthy of her powerful protection."

It was toward the close of his life, as has already been said, that he wrote his ' Biographical Reminiscences and Thoughts upon Art,' of which the present book is a translation. It was at once received by the Italian public with great favour, and is by no means the least remarkable of his works. It would be difficult for any autobiography to be more simple, honest, frank, and fearless. The whole character of the man is in it. It is an unaffected and un-pretending record of his life and thoughts. He has no concealment to make, no glosses to put upon the real facts. He speaks to the public as if he were talking to a friend, never posing for effect, never boasting of his successes, never exaggerating his powers, never assailing his enemies and detrac-tors, never depreciating his fellow-artists, but ever striving to be generous and just to all. There is no bitterness, no envy, no arrogance to deform a single page; but, on the contrary, a simplicity, a *naïveté*, a sincerity of utterance, which are remark-able. The history of his early struggles and pov-erty, the pictures of his childhood and youth, are eminently interesting; and the story of his love, courtship, and early married life is a pure Italian idyl of the middle class of society in Florence, which could scarcely be surpassed for its truth to nature and its rare delicacy and gentleness of feel-ing. If the 'Thoughts upon Art' do not exhibit any great profundity of thinking, they are earnest, instructive, and characteristic. His descriptions of his travels in France and England; his criti-cisms and anecdotes of artists and persons in Florence; his account of his daily life in his studio and at his home,—are lively and amusing. Altogether, the book has a special charm which it is not easy to define. In reading it, we feel that we are in the presence and taken into the confidence of a person of great simplicity and purity of character, of admirable instincts and perceptions, of true kindness of heart, and of a certain childlike *naïveté* of feeling and expression, which is scarcely to be found out of Italy.

In respect of style, this autobiography resembles more the spoken than the written literary language of Italy. It is free, natural, unstudied, and often careless. But its very carelessness has a charm. Duprè was not a scholar nor a literary man. He was not bound by the rigid forms of what is called in Italy "*lo stile*," which but too often is the enemy of natural utterance. Undoubtedly this book needs compression ; but no exactness of style and form could compensate for the absence of that unstudied natural ease and familiarity which are among its greatest charms. The writer, fortunately for the reader, is as unconscious of elaborated style as Monsieur Jourdain was that he was talking prose. The character of Duprè's writing has been admirably caught and reproduced by Madame Peruzzi, in the translation to which these few words may serve as preface.

As an artist, Duprè was not endowed with a great creative or imaginative power. His spirit never broke out of the Roman Church in which he was brought up, and all that he did and thought was coloured by its influence. The subjects which he chose in preference to all others were of a religious character, and his works are animated by a spirit of humility and devotion, rather than of power and intensity. His piety—and he was a truly pious man—narrowed the field of his imagination, and restricted the flights of his genius. "But even his failings leaned to virtue's side," and what he lacked in breadth of conception, was compensated by his deep sincerity of purpose and religious feeling. He was not a daring creator—not an originator of ideas—not a bold discoverer. He hugged the shore of his Church. He wanted the passion and overplus of nature that might have borne him to new heights, and new continents of thought and feeling. His Cain, almost alone of all his works, breathes a spirit of defiance and rebellion, and breaks through the limitations of his usual conceptions. But it was not in harmony with his genius; and in natural expression it falls so far below his previous statue of Abel, that it was epigrammatically said that his Abel killed his Cain. There was undoubtedly a certain truth in this criticism, for though the Cain is vigorously conceived and admirably executed, the heart of the man was not in it, as it was in the gentle and placid figure of Abel. In mastery of modelling and truth to nature, this latter statue could scarcely be surpassed. Indeed, so remarkable was it for these qualities, that it gave rise in Florence to the scandalous calumny that it had been cast, not modelled, from nature,—a calumny which, it is scarcely necessary to add, was as false in fact as it was inconsistent with the honest and lofty spirit

of Duprè; and which, though intended as a reproach, proved to be the highest testimonial to
the extraordinary skill of the artist.

Within the bounded domain of thought and conception which his religious faith had set for him,
he worked with great earnestness and devotion of
spirit. Though he created no works which are
stamped by the audacity of genius, or intensified
by passion, or characterised by bold originality
and reach of power, yet the work he did do is
eminently faithful, admirably executed, and informed by knowledge as well as feeling. His
artistic honesty cannot be too highly praised.
He spared no pains to make his work as perfect as
his powers would permit. He had an accurate eye,
a remarkable talent for modelling from nature, and
an indefatigable perseverance. He never lent his
hand to low, paltry, and unworthy work. Art and
religion went hand in hand in all he did. He
sought for the beautiful and the noble—sought it
everywhere with an inquiring and susceptible spirit;
despised the brutal, the low, and the trifling;
never truckled to popularity, or sought for fame
unworthily; and scorned to degrade his art by sensuality. As the man was, so his work was—pure,
refined, faithful to nature and to his own nature.
He pandered to no low passions; he modelled no
form, he drew no line, that dying he could wish to
blot; and the world of Art is better that he has
lived. While he bent his head to Nature, the whole
stress of his life as an artist was to realise his fa-

vourite motto, *"Il vero nel bello"*—the true in the beautiful.

His last letter, written only three days before his final attack, was addressed to his friend Professor Giambattista Giuliani, and as it breathes the whole spirit of the man, it may form a fit conclusion to these few words: "My excellent friend,—We also, Amalia and I, wish you truly from our hearts, now and always, every good from our blessed God—perfect health, elevation of spirit; serene affections, peace of heart in the contemplation of the beautiful and the good, and the immortal hope of a future life, that supreme good that the modern Sadducees deny — unhappy beings!"

W. W. STORY.

PREFACE.

"Do you know," I said to a friend six months ago, while I was looking over the rough draft of my memoirs, "that I have decided to print them?" "You will do well," he answered; "but you must write a preface—a bit of a preface is necessary." "I do not think so," I said. "In my opinion the few words on the first page will suffice." My friend read over the first page and replied, "That's enough."

Now, however, a couple of words do not seem to me superfluous,—first, in order that I may express my surprise and pleasure that my book, written just as it came to me, has been received with so much kindness; and then to explain that this second edition has been enlarged by some additions and necessary notes. The additions do not form an appendix, but are inserted in the chapters, each in its proper place.

It did not seem advisable to me, as it did to some other persons, to enlarge this book by letters, documents, and other writings of mine. I thought this would interfere with the simplicity and brevity of my first plan.

In re-reading this book, I admit that I have found passages here and there which I felt tempted to correct, or rather to polish and improve in style, but I have let them go. Who knows that I should not have made them worse? It seems to me (perhaps I am wrong) not to perceive in good writers the labour, the smoothing, and the transposition of words, and so on, but a rapid and broad embodiment of the idea in the words that were born with it.

One last and most essential word I have reserved for the end as a *bonne bouche.* Some persons have excusably and pleasantly observed that to write a book about one's self while the author is living is both very difficult and rather immodest. I replied to them, both by word of mouth and through the press, that although on account of my life and works I had studied to be as temperate and unpretentious as the truth and the facts would allow, still here and there my narrative with regard to some persons might not be agreeable, and therefore after my death it might be discredited or denied. No, this must not be, I said, and say again. I am alive, and am here to correct everything at variance with the truth, and also (I wish to be just) what is wanting in chivalrousness.

NOTE BY TRANSLATOR.

IN making the present translation of the Memoirs of Giovanni Duprè, one of two courses had to be taken—either to turn the whole into pure idiomatic English, or to follow, with a certain degree of literalness, the peculiar forms of expression, and the characteristic style, or absence of style, of the original. I have chosen the latter course, in order, as far as in me lay, to convey the individuality of the author, and the local colour and character of his book. This would to a great degree have been lost had I attempted to render into purely English idiom a work that is not only written in a careless, familiar, and conversational form, and abounds in turns of expression which are essentially Florentine, but derives its interest, in part at least, from this very peculiarity.

E. M. P.

CONTENTS.

CHAPTER I.

CHAPTER II.

CHAPTER III.

CHAPTER IV.

CHAPTER V.

CONTENTS. XV

AUTOBIOGRAPHICAL MEMOIRS

OF

GIOVANNI DUPRÈ.

CHAPTER I.

MY MOTIVE FOR WRITING THESE MEMOIRS—MY FATHER'S FAMILY—REMOVAL
OF THE FAMILY TO FLORENCE—MY CHILDHOOD—MY FATHER TAKES ME TO
PISTOIA, BUT I RUN AWAY FROM HIS HOUSE TO RETURN TO MY MOTHER—
FROM PISTOIA I GO WITH MY FATHER TO PRATO—MY FIRST STUDY IN
DRAWING—STRONG IMPRESSION MADE UPON ME BY AN OLD PRINT—MY
FATHER'S OPPOSITION TO MY STUDIES—MY SORROW AT BEING SO FAR
FROM MY MOTHER—I RUN THE RISK OF BEING BURNT—HAVING GROWN
TALL, FEARS ARE ENTERTAINED FOR MY HEALTH—I RETURN TO MY
MOTHER AT FLORENCE AND WORK WITH AMMANATI—I GO TO SIENA AND
STUDY ORNATE DESIGN IN THE ACADEMY—CARLO PINI GIVES ME LESSONS
IN DRAWING THE HUMAN FIGURE—SIGNOR ANGELO BARDETTI'S PROPHECY
—I RUN AWAY FROM SIENA, AND ON FOOT GO TO MY MOTHER AT FLORENCE
—SIGNOR PAOLO SANI—DEATH OF MY SISTER CLEMENTINA—MY MOTHER'S
INFIRMITY OF EYESIGHT—MY BROTHER LORENZO GOES TO THE POORHOUSE
—MY AVERSION TO LEARN READING AND WRITING—MY FIRST LIBRARY,
AND INEXPERIENCE OF BOOKS.

 HAVE often thought that perhaps it would
be well for me to leave some written me-
moirs of my life—not only for the sake of
my family, but also for the young artists of
the future; but I have hitherto been deterred from
so doing by the fear lest I might seem to have been
prompted by pride and vanity. Since, however, various

A

notices of my life and my doings in art have been made
public, it may not be either without interest, or indeed
without a certain utility, if I venture now to speak at
length on these subjects; for it seems to me that these
memoirs may not only serve as an encouragement to
timid but well-disposed youths, but may at the same
time be a severe admonition to those who, presuming
too much on themselves, imagine that with little study
and great boldness they can wing their way up the steps
of Art instead of laboriously climbing them.

My father was Francesco Duprè, the youngest son of
Lorenzo Duprè, who came to Siena with the princes of
Lorraine.   My grandfather kept a draper's shop in the
Piazza del Campo, where at first, through his activity and
honesty, his business so prospered that he was able to
give his family a good education; and my father was just
entering on the course of studies that his brothers had
already finished, when my grandfather, through the
ignorance and bad faith of his debtors and his own determination to be honest himself, was reduced to poverty.
In consequence of this, my father was obliged to discon-
tinue his studies, and to set to work to learn a trade, in
order that he might earn his bread as soon as possible;
and thinking to derive some advantage from the studies
he had already made in drawing, he apprenticed himself
to a wood-carver.   Later he married Victoria Lombardi
of Siena, and she was my mother.   I was born on the
1st of March 1817, in Via San Salvadore, in the Con-
trada dell' Onda, and lived in Siena until I was four
years old.   My family then removed to Florence, where
my father went, at the request of the wood-carver, Signor
Paolo Sani, to help him in the execution of some *intaglio*
decorations in the Palazzo Borghese, which the Prince
was anxious to have finished within the shortest possible

time.　My recollections of those early days are not worth recording.　I grew up from a little boy going with my father to the shop.　I had a few lessons in the Catechism and in reading from a schoolmistress who lodged in our house.　In the evening my *babbo*[1] used to read and explain some Latin book (I do not remember what it was), perhaps for the innocent satisfaction of letting us know that he had studied that language, but certainly with no profit to me, who understood nothing and was greatly bored.　When, however, he gave me some of his designs of ornamentation, such as leaves, arabesques, and friezes, to copy, I was very happy.　The time passed without my knowing it ; and such was my delight in this occupation, that I often put off the hour of supper or sleep and gave up any amusement for it.　At home we lived very poorly.　My father earned little, for his work was badly paid, and by nature he was slow.　This poverty of our daily life began to disturb the relations between my father and mother.　The family had increased, and besides my eldest sister Clementina, who died soon after-wards, were born Lorenzo and Maddalena.　I remember the sharpness of the tones, but not the sense of the words that passed between my parents ; and the tears of my mother and sullen silence of my father frightened us little ones, and filled us with sadness.

It was impossible that such a state of things could last long, and my father decided to leave Florence and go to Pistoia, where he thought he could earn more money.　I was destined to follow him, while the others remained with my mother.　For more than three years I stayed with him.　My life was sad for me here, as the distance from my mother made it almost unbearable ; and all the more so because my father, whenever he went to Florence

[1] " Babbo " is the familiar word for father in Tuscany.

to see her, as he sometimes did, always left me behind him, alone, at Pistoia. Once, when I was barely seven years old, I ran away from the house, and went on foot to Florence, although I knew for a certainty that I should have to pay dearly for the kisses and caresses of my mother by a thrashing from the *babbo*. Nor was I mistaken : I got the thrashing, and was brought back.

About this time there awoke in me a certain sentiment and longing to try to draw the human figure — leaves and *grumoli* had begun to weary me ; and this desire was developed in an odd way. There was in Pistoia, in the house of a certain gilder named Canini, a little theatre for puppets, and one of the characters, which was wanted for a certain performance, happened to be missing. Canini, who was a friend of my father, was much put out by this loss, and came to beg my father to make the head and hands for the puppet. He answered that he could not do this, as he had never attempted anything in the way of figures ; and the poor gilder, who was director and proprietor of the company, was at a loss to know where to turn. I, with the utmost effrontery, then offered to make the head and hands myself ; and as Canini was hopeful as well as incredulous, and my father gave a sort of half consent, I set to work, and succeeded so well that my puppet turned out to be the most beautiful " personage " of the company. The happy result encouraged me to go on, and I remade almost all the puppets. I also made some small ducks in cork, that were to appear in a pond, and were moved about here and there by silk threads. It was a pleasure to see the little creatures—they turned out so well, and had such a look of reality ; and this I was enabled to give them because in the court of our house there were some ducks which I could copy from life. Ah, Nature ! not only

is it a great help, but it is the principal foundation of
Art !

From Pistoia the *babbo* took me to Prato, where he
had been requested to go by the gilder Signor Stefano
Mazzoni. There we took up our abode in a street and
court called Il Giuggiolo. In the same house, and
almost with us, lived a man from Lucca, who made little
plaster-images, and was one of the many who go about
the streets selling little coloured figures for a few sous.
This connection, ridiculous as it may appear, inspired me
more and more with a desire for the study of figures. It
is true these figures and parrots and clowns were ugly ;
but, at the same time, their innocent ugliness attracted
me, and filled me with a longing, not indeed to imitate
them, but to do something better. In turning over my
father's papers and designs, I found a quantity of prints,
fashion-plates of dresses, landscapes, and animals, and
particularly (I remember it so well that I could draw
it now) a large print representing the building of the
Temple of Jerusalem. In the distance you saw the
building just begun, and rising a little above its foun-
dations. Carts loaded with heavy materials and tall
straight timber (the cedars of Lebanon) were dragged
along by a great many oxen and camels, amid a vast number of people and things. On all sides were workmen of
every kind, some carving the columns, some putting up
a jamb and squaring it, some sawing timber, and some
busied in making ditches ; others were talking, or listening, or admiring : and all the scene was animated with
a truly marvellous life. In the foreground you saw the
majestic figure of Solomon, surrounded by his ministers
and soldiers, showing his architect (with his scholars)
the designs of the Temple. In fact, it was a wonderful
thing to behold, and I was so enchanted that I could

not sleep for thinking of it, for it seemed to me impossible that any man could imagine and execute anything so marvellous. My little head seemed on fire, it was so full of these figures. I tried at first to copy in part this print, which, above all the others, had taken my fancy; but I did not succeed, and I was so discouraged that I sat down and cried. And not for this only I cried, but also because my father looked with so unfavourable eye on these efforts of mine—they seeming to him quite unnecessary for an *intagliatore*—that, in order to go on with these studies, I was obliged to hide myself almost, and to work in spare moments. Finding this print so complicated that I could in no way copy it, I then undertook to copy the little costume-figures that I found amongst the prints. These, one by one, I drew during the evening, after my father had gone to bed and was asleep; and sometimes it happened that I fell asleep over my drawing, and on waking found myself in the dark, with the little lamp gone out. This constant exercise, to which I gave myself every day with great ardour, so trained my hand and practised my eye, that my last drawings were made with little or no erasures.

But though I derived a good deal of satisfaction from these small drawings, my heart was still oppressed at being so far from my mother. I longed to see her, and have her near me, and begged my father to take me to her, or at least to send me to her by the carrier; but wishes and prayers were useless. My father went sometimes, it is true, to see her; but although I was only seven or eight years of age, I had to remain behind at Prato to look after the house. I do not wish to blame my father, but neither then nor since have I been able to understand his notions of things; and certainly, to keep a little boy alone by himself in a house, and often for several days together, is not to be recommended. One evening I remember, when, having fallen asleep while reading at the table, with my head bent near the lamp, my little cap caught on fire, and I woke up with my hair in flames. But this adventurous life—beaten about, thwarted in all my wishes and in all my affections—formed my character. I became accustomed to suffer, to persevere, and to obey, while I always kept alive those desires and affections which my conscience assured me were good.

About this time, what with continuous study, hardish work in my father's shop, and the melancholy that weighed upon me because I could not see my mother, my health began to fail. Even before this, and indeed from my birth, I had always been delicate, but now I became so pale and weak that every one called me *il morticino* (the little dead fellow). A physician who examined me about this time talked seriously to my father about me on the subject, telling him that I ought to rest longer in the mornings (my father rose very early, and I had to get up to go with him to the shop), and eat more nourishing food; and he explained what it should be. Amongst other things, I remember he ordered me to drink goat's milk, milked and drunk on the spot, as soon as I got out of bed, before leaving my room. This treatment succeeded marvellously. Every day I gained strength, colour, and flesh. The little goat that came every morning to my room to pay me a visit, and brought me her milk, sweet, warm, and light, will be always remembered by me; and I still have a feeling for the little creature, even after half a century, which I cannot well define.

Restored to health, I was taken to see my mother in Florence. My own great joy, as well as her caresses and

petitions that I might be left with her, it is impossible to
describe. She insisted that she would find me a shop
where I could go and continue to learn the art of wood-
carving. Thank God, this time my mother's tenderness
overcame my father's tenacity (loving though it was),
and I was allowed to remain with her. They both looked
about to find me a shop, and I was finally placed
in Borgo Sant' Jacopo, with the wood-carvers Gaetano
Ammanati and Luigi Pieraccini, who worked together.
They were both very able men, certainly much more so
than my father, who, poor man, owing to the constant
requirements of the family, had never been able to perfect
himself in his art. In this shop figures were carved, so
that I had before me models and teachers, as well as in-
citement to work. My principals liked me, and I them;
and I should have remained with them who knows how
long, had I not been carried off by another *intagliatore.*
And the way in which it happened was this: Signor Paolo
Sani, a carver in wood who sometimes came on business
or for other reasons to Ammanati's, seeing that my work
was fairly good, and that I worked with goodwill, determined, if possible, to take me away to work for him.
He wrote, therefore, to my father, who had returned to
Siena, asking him to remove me from Ammanati's shop,
and send me to him, binding himself to pay me double
the salary that I was then receiving. As he did not wish,
however, to appear to act underhandedly (though this
was really the case), he persuaded my father to take me
to Siena, and place me at the Academy of Fine Arts, to
study drawing; and he promised, after I had passed
some months there, to take me to work in his own shop.
My father accepted the offer, and I was obliged to go to
Siena, where I studied in the Academy at the school of
"Ornato," which was then under the direction of Pro-

fessor Dei. Out of school hours my father let me work upon anything I liked—such as children's heads, angels, and even crucifixes. God knows what rubbish they were! I also took lessons, in drawing the human figure, of Signor Carlo Pini, then the *custode* of the Academy, and afterwards one of the most distinguished annotators of Vasari, and keeper of the drawings by the old masters in the Royal Gallery of the Uffizi.

At that time Signor Angelo Barbetti, a very skilful wood-carver, was at Siena, and my father wished to place me in his shop, which was in the Piazza di San Giovanni. But Signor Angelo was as irascible and fault-finding as he was intelligent; and one day, when I had not succeeded in executing some work that he had given me, he struck me on the head, accompanying the blow with these words, which hurt me more than the blow itself—" You will always be an ass, harnessed and shod, even when the beard is on your chin." Afterwards I was sent to Signor Antonio Manetti, who not only carved ornaments and figures in wood, but also worked in marble, and was occupied in restoring the façade of the cathedral. Signor Manetti was a man of no common genius—he designed and sculptured ornaments and figures with much facility and cleverness. But even with him I was not fortunate. He gave me a little Napoleonic eagle with thunderbolts in his claws to execute. For what it was intended I do not remember, but apparently I did not succeed in satisfying him. In this case, however, there were neither blows on the head nor bitter words, but, with a certain haughty dignity, he took my poor little eaglet in his hand, and dashed it to the ground, breaking it to atoms in spite of the thunderbolts. Viewed from this long distance of time, this scene has a somewhat comic character, and must seem especially so to one who hears it described. But for me, a poor little boy, anxious to learn and get on, so as to lighten, as far as possible, the burden on my father —who, poor man, earned little, and of that little was obliged to send a portion to his family in Florence—it was quite another thing; and though I felt within myself that I was not a complete donkey, still to see my work thrown thus brutally on the ground was so painful to me that it took away all my little strength. I wept in secret; and as the time assigned by Signor Paolo Sani and my father for my return had arrived, I begged my father to send me back to Florence. He wished, however, to keep me with him still longer, and so I occupied myself in making angels and seraphim heads for churches.

I begged and begged my father to take me to Florence, to see my mother. He promised to do so at Easter. Meanwhile, I contented myself with this hope; but on the eve of Easter he told me he could not go, on account of his engagements, which would detain him at Siena, and also for many other reasons that I could not and would not understand. Now, however, my patience gave way before my loving desire to see my mother; and without saying a word, I rose early and ran away from the house. Passing out of the Porta Camollia, I set off on my walk with only a bit of bread in my pocket, in the boyish hope of reaching my destination the same day, and so passing my Easter with my mother, without reflecting that, by so doing, I should pass it neither with my father nor my mother. I was about nine years old, and walked on with courage beyond my strength. So great was my desire to get to Florence, that I passed Staggia and Poggibonsi without feeling tired; but near Barberino—which is about twenty miles from Siena, and half-way to Florence — my mind misgave me that I should not be able to arrive in Florence that evening;

and then my strength abandoned me, and I was so
overcome with fatigue that I could not get up from a
little wall on which I had seated myself to rest. I had
not a penny. No carts or carriages were passing that way.
It was Easter, and every one was at home resting for
his holiday; and I, there I was alone in the middle of
the road, oppressed with weariness and remorse for having
left my father in such anxiety. At times I hoped that
he might come after me with a carriage to take me up,
and I quite resigned myself to a sound beating; but even
this hope was vain, and I had to continue my walk.
How many sad thoughts passed one after another
through my little tired head! What will my mother, who
is expecting us, do or say? What will my *babbo* think,
left alone, and not knowing where I am? He will be
certainly looking for me, and asking after me from every
one in Siena. What will become of me in the middle of
the road if night overtakes me? This thought gave
strength and energy to my will, and on I went. I don't
think that I was frightened. At length my strength
was exhausted; the sun began to set; I was seven or
eight miles from San Casciano, and I could not be certain of arriving even there to pass the night. I stopped
at a wretched little house to rest, and asked for a glass
of water. A man, a woman, and several children were
eating. They asked me where I came from, and I told
them. With expressions of compassion, especially from
the woman, they gathered round me, gave me some
bread, a hard-boiled egg, and a little wine, and I thanked
them with emotion. They wanted me to stay with them
until the next day—and tired out as I was, I should have
stayed and accepted their kindly offer; but at this moment a *vettura* for Florence passed by, and with my
eyes full of tears I told them how infinitely grateful I

should be if I could be allowed to fasten myself in any
way on to the carriage. The driver, who had stopped
to get a glass of wine, seeing the state I was in, and
hearing my story from these good country people, took
me up on the box by his side, and carried me to Florence,
where we arrived in less than three-quarters of an hour,
an hour after nightfall. As my mother and the other
children lived in Via Toscanelli, when we were near the
Sdrucciolo de' Pitti the good driver set me down there.
I descended from the box and ran—no, I could not run,
for my feet were swollen, and my sides numb, but my
heart was glad, exultant, and throbbing. I knocked; my
mother came to the window and saw me, but she did not
recognise me until I spoke, and then she gave a scream
and came down. What followed I cannot recount. Those
who have a heart will imagine it better than I can tell it.
Neither the good family who welcomed and refreshed me,
nor the honest humane carrier, have I ever seen, for I
remained in Florence, and did not return to Siena until
many years after. Then I made all possible researches
to find both the one and the other, but I could never
find them. Not, indeed, that I wished to remunerate
them with money (the price of charity has not yet been
named), but I wished to express to them my gratitude;
and this is the only recompense acceptable to charitable
hearts.

The day after, as I hoped and feared, the *babbo*
arrived, and as soon as he saw me, his expression,
anxious and grieved as it was, became threatening. His
few ill-repressed words were the sure sign of the blows
to come, and he was just going to strike me when my
mother, with indescribable tenderness, caught me in her
arms and pressed me to her, with her face and eyes
turned towards my father, without uttering a word.

Softened by this, he then began a long speech on the
obedience and submission due from children to the holy
parental authority, not omitting to censure my mother's
indulgence and petting. After this I begged his pardon,
and all was at an end. My father returned to Siena, and
I went to Signor Sani's shop (built with his own money),
in the Piazza di San Biagio, under the Piatti printing-
office. Signor Paolo Sani was a man of about fifty, thin,
pale, and exceedingly active. He had a great deal of
work to do, and was employed by the Court and first
houses in Florence. His taste was not exquisite, but he
understood effects and proportions, so that his decora-
tive carving, either in the way of furniture, caskets,
frames, chandeliers, or ornamental work for churches,
was greatly in demand. He had many men, and the
works succeeded each other with great rapidity. In
his house he had portfolios full of designs, and the walls
of his shop were covered with plaster casts, bas-reliefs
of figures, and ornaments, animals, arabesques, flowers,
angels, &c., making a strange fantastic medley full of
attraction for me. When the master was not there, the
men at their work used to talk and sing; but when any
one saw him coming, the scene changed, and there was
perfect silence. I came into the shop as an apprentice
and errand-boy; so that although I had my little bench,
with my tools and work, yet, if there was any glue to
be heated or made, or the tools were to be taken to the
grinder, or the breakfast to be brought for the men, this
duty always fell upon me. But I did not in the least
complain. It is true that amongst these duties there,
was one for which I had a dislike, although I did not
show it, and this was carrying a basket full of shavings on
my back to the master's house in the Borgo Sant' Jacopo.
To go there I had to pass through the Mercato Nuovo

and over Ponte Vecchio, which is much frequented at
all hours, as every one knows ; and during this year I
went there with the basket of shavings on my back.
Notwithstanding this, I was well off in the shop, and was
light-hearted from being near my mother and sisters.
One of my sisters—my elder by a year—died soon after
my return from my wanderings with my father. Poor
Clementina! she was so good, delicate in health, and
suffering. Indeed, we all suffered because of our
poverty. Father sent us little, for he earned little, and
our bread was often wet with tears because we could not
help our mother as we wished. Added to this, she could
do almost nothing herself on account of her infirmity
of eyesight, which little by little so increased, that at last
she was no longer able to see us ; and as I have already
said, Clementina died. God willed it so—to shorten her
road, which was too full of thorns and danger, to one
pretty as she was, artless, away from the father's watch-
ful eye, and with her mother blind. My other smaller
sister Maddalena accompanied her mother when she went
out, as she did in the endeavour to earn something by
buying and selling women's old clothes. My brother
Lorenzo (perhaps because he was too quick-tempered)
was obliged to go to the poorhouse, and here he learnt
the art of carpet-maker. After a short time, however, he
came out and returned to Parenti, who had a carpet
manufactory in the ancient refectory of the monks of
Santa Croce, where he remained for some time.

But all these difficulties and sorrows one feels less in
early years, and in spite of them I was light-hearted. I
had the master's goodwill, and the men in the shop
treated me with the open cordial heartiness belonging to
that class in those days. My love for the study of design
increased, and in the off-hours of work I used to stay be-

hind in the shop and eat a bit of bread there, and draw
from some of the casts hanging on the walls, without
taking them down or even dusting them. I began with
little things such as leaves, branches, small figures, cap-
itals of columns, heads of animals, and so on and so
on, until I got to figures. In the shop there were two
beautiful bas-reliefs from the pulpit in Santa Croce, two
from the doors of the sacristy of the Duomo by Luca della
Robbia, and several of those little figures by Ghiberti
which surround the principal door of San Giovanni. All
these casts I drew during this period—badly, as one may
imagine, and without guide or method; but still, this
served to occupy me pleasantly, and also to keep alive
within me the craving to learn and advance myself, so
as to be able to do other and more important work in
the shop, and thus gain distinction.

This desire of distinguishing myself has always been
very strong in me; and through all my privations, dis-
comforts, loss of sleep, harsh corrections, irony, and
scorn, I was borne up by this desire to do myself credit,
and see my father and mother rejoice in me and for me;
and also, I must confess, by the hope of seeing the rage
of those who had treated me with irony and scorn. But
if I learned, more and more every day, how to design and
to carve in wood—for this was very attractive to me—in
everything else I was perfectly ignorant. I had not even
learned to read well, and could not write at all. My
father had tried placing me at a public school, but I
learned absolutely nothing there. The rudiments of
writing and arithmetic were so irksome to me that the
master in despair sent me home again, and would have
nothing to do with such a little dunce. For all this, I had
my little library at home, which I kept with great care
locked up in a small box in my room, and it was com-

posed of seven or eight books. These I had bought in
the streets from book-stalls set against old walls, and
they were as follows: A volume of the ' Capitoli of Berni,'
'Paul and Virginia,' and 'Atala and Chatta' (translations
of course), a volume of the comedies of Alberto Nota,
and the 'Jerusalem Liberated,' 'Guerrino Meschino agli
Alberi del Sole,' 'Oreste,' and the ' Pazzi Conspiracy.' At
first I understood almost nothing excepting some of the
adventures of Guerrino. Afterwards ' Atala and Chatta '
and 'Paul and Virginia' became my favourite reading; and
so much did I like them, and so often did I read them,
that whole pages remained in my memory. Then I fell in
love with the 'Jerusalem,' and this my memory more easily
retained. Some of the verses I tried to write from memory,
in a little running hand, copying the letters from my
father's writing, for, as I have said before, I never learnt
the rudiments of writing ; and those pot-hooks, and big
letters between two lines, never were to my taste. As to
other things, I had the innocence and good faith belonging to my age and the imperfect education I had received. I thought all books good—good because they
were printed—and not only good at home, but good
everywhere else; and so I used to take my books to
read in church during the Mass. One day (it was Sunday) at mid-day Mass in Sant' Jacopo, while I was reading
the 'Conspiracy of the Pazzi,' my master, Signor Sani,
who lived opposite the church, and was also at Mass, observed me, and suspecting that the book I was reading
was not a proper one to take to church, stopped me as
he was going out and asked to see it, and finding what
it was, told me that I was not to bring it again to church,
as it was not a book of prayers. More also he added
that I did not understand, especially when he wanted to
explain to me the verses—

" Il putrido
Annoso tronco, a cui s' appoggia fraude." [1]

I obeyed, however, and never took this or any of my other books to church; and so I learnt that books you can read at home you cannot read in church.   Later I learnt there are others not to be read anywhere.

[1] " The rotten knotted trunk on which fraud leans."

CHAPTER II.

WITHOUT KNOWING IT, I WAS DOING WHAT LEONARDO ADVISES—NEW WAY OF DECORATING THE WALLS OF ONE'S HOUSE—I WISH TO STUDY DESIGN AT THE ACADEMY, BUT CANNOT CARRY THIS INTO EFFECT—A BOTTLE OF ANISE-SEED CORDIAL—INTELLIGENT PEOPLE ARE BENEVOLENT, NOT SO THOSE OF MEDIOCRE MINDS—THE STATUES IN THE PIAZZA DELLA SIGNORIA AND ALABASTER FIGURES—THE DISCOVERY OF A HIDDEN WELL—MY FATHER RETURNS HOME WITHOUT WORK, AND LEAVES FOR ROME—YOUNG SIGNOR EMILIO DEL TABRIS—SEA-BATHS AND CHOLERA AT LEGHORN—WITH HELP I SAVE A WOMAN FROM DROWNING—I GO TO SAN PIERO DI BAGNO—MY UNCLE THE PROVOST DIES—MY FATHER RETURNS FROM ROME, AND SETTLES IN FLORENCE—MY WORK, A GROUP OF A HOLY FAMILY, IS STOLEN—DESCRIPTION OF THIS GROUP.

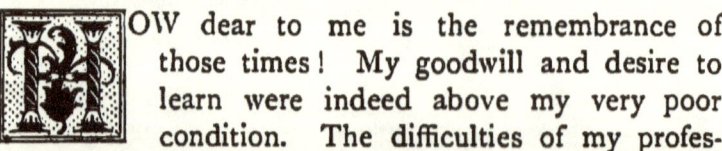

OW dear to me is the remembrance of those times! My goodwill and desire to learn were indeed above my very poor condition. The difficulties of my profession did not discourage me; on the contrary, I felt a pleasurable though distant hope of surpassing my companions in figure-work that they did so badly and laboriously. For this purpose, from that time I gave all my efforts to the study of the human figure. I bought an album and kept it always with me, begged my friends to stand as models, and drew their portraits. At first my attempts were not happy; but I was never tired, and after a time I acquired so much freedom that with a few strokes I could make a fair likeness. I was always at work, and the walls of our kitchen and dining-room were all smudged over with charcoal. Naturally, there was no one to scold me for this unusual way of adorning the walls, for the mother, poor dear, was blind, my father was not there, and as I was the eldest, I was, as it were, the head of the family. Besides, though my mother could not see, she still knew of this strange practice of mine, and thought it better for me thus to occupy myself than to be playing with the boys in the street.

In the meantime, however, many doubts and self-questionings arose within me. I knew that there was a school where one could really learn to draw and paint and make statues. Heavens, how delightful it would be to know how to make statues ! In fact, I understood there was the Academy of Fine Arts, for so I had been told, and some of the fortunate young men who frequented this Academy were my acquaintances, and had shown me their designs, which seemed to me, as my friend Dotti would say, *most stupendous !* I was no longer happy. The Academy appeared to me in the most splendid and glowing colours; it seemed to me the haven, the landmark, the temple of glory, the throne of my golden dreams.

I spoke of it to my mother with tears in my eyes. She mingled her tears with mine, but not, perhaps, so much from being persuaded of the necessity of such studies as from a desire to soothe me. She spoke about it to Signor Sani, who, I shall always remember, with his eyes fixed fiercely on me, made even more formidable under his silver spectacles, replied, that to do all that was to be done in his shop, it was enough to remain in the shop and have the wish to learn — of this he was certain ; but as to the work in the Academy, he did not feel so sure, for, on the contrary, that would fill me

with desires and cravings that I could not satisfy, owing
to the poverty of my family, even admitting that I had
the disposition to enable me to master these studies;
and finally, he hinted at the danger there was of my
being contaminated by my companions. My mother
did not answer him. She said good-bye to me, and in
her sightless eyes I saw the sadness within. She went
out, and I set myself to work.

I resigned myself, but continued always to study by
myself. As Luigi, the master's eldest son, was studying
design at Professor Gaspero Martellini's school, which
was in the Fondacci di Santo Spirito, he gave me some
of his designs to copy. Not only did Professor Martellini give him lessons in drawing, but also in modelling
in clay, and Sani was one of the most assiduous of his
scholars. I remember to have pounded his clay for
him many times, in a room on the ground-floor in his
house in Borgo Sant' Jacopo. This little room was
used as a storehouse for all sorts of odds and ends, and
amongst these I once found a flask of anise-seed
cordial, that (to confess the truth) I tasted sometimes.
One morning, having finished what I had to do, and
having gone up-stairs to take the key of the room, one
of the master's daughters (he had four) smelt in my
breath the odour of anise-seed, and said to me—

" Who has given you anise-seed ? "

" No one," I answered.

" You smell of anise-seed ; who has given it to you ?
Mind, don't tell lies."

Then I told everything.

" I don't believe you. You are a liar."

" No ; come and see."

" Certainly I wish to see."

She then came down, and taking the flask in her

hand, looked at it, smelled it, and tasted it. Apparently she must have drunk a little, for as soon as she had put down the flask and shut up the room, she began to totter, and could not stand on her feet. With difficulty I succeeded in getting her up-stairs, where, as soon as her mother saw her in that state, there ensued a serious scene. They all talked and scolded at once—the three girls who had not drank the anise-seed, as well as the mamma ; and when I tried to explain how the thing had happened, I felt two slaps in the face, which were given with such force that I was stunned. My ideas became so confused that I was not able to say anything. Fortunately the girl spoke, and said—

" Nanni is not at fault."

At these words the mistress said—

"Go at once to the shop. Master shall know everything this evening."

I did not breathe a word, and even she said nothing about it to the master, nor was I scolded by him, or by the Signora Carolina (the mistress). Some days after I returned to knead the clay, but the flask of cordial had disappeared.

About this time there was a *residenza*[1] to be made in the shop for some church, where, in the midst of the clouds that supported the *ostensorio*, were a quantity of seraphim. This work was required to be done at once without delay ; and as Bartolommeo Bianciardi, who did this kind of work in the shop, could not alone do all that was required of him, I proposed to the master to make one of the seraphim myself, and I succeeded so well that he was entirely satisfied. After that I made others, and always better and better. From that time, when similar

[1] The throne on which the monstrance is placed when exposition of the sacrament takes place.

work came to the shop, I was always employed on it together with the other workman, and sometimes in preference to him. In the meantime I continued to make progress in the art of wood-carving, and the best and most skilful workmen flattered me and helped me with their advice, but the others looked upon me with an evil eye. I could not understand this difference, nor can I understand it now; but as I have since met with this, and felt it always at every time and everywhere, it must be in the natural order of bad things.

But there was always a thorn in my heart. The seraphim were not enough to satisfy me, nor even the large masks and heads of Medusa with all their serpents. And when I passed through the Piazza della Signoria and saw the David, the Perseus, and the Group of the Sabines, I thought that by going to the Academy of Fine Arts one might learn how to make such works!

Heavens, how grand a thing it would be to be able to go to the Academy! But it was useless even to think of this, for my father had declared himself opposed to it. Therefore peace be to it, and let me have patience. At least those pretty little alabaster figures that are shown in the shop windows of Pisani on the Prato, and Bazzanti on the Lung' Arno, those I should be able to do with time and study and a firm will. For after all, it is only a question of changing the material, of substituting alabaster for wood, a seraphim or an angel for a little Venus or Apollo—there is nothing to create. Those who make these figures, also copy them from others in alabaster, plaster, or bronze, as I do; and even now I invent my little seraphim, and no longer look at Flammingo's little boys as I did at first—I do them from memory, making them either leaner or fatter, or more smiling or more sad, as best I feel inclined. So I reasoned and persuaded

myself that in the end, one day or other, I also should
be able to make one of those graceful little statuettes.

In this way I consoled myself, and went on with
courage and hopefulness. Here some one may say, this
artist in his old age gives us a picture of himself as a
boy where there is too much fancy. The portrait is
beautiful, but is it a likeness? Has not the love of
beauty seduced him? What is the truth? Who ever
saw a boy who was always obedient, studious, patient,
constant, &c. &c. ?

Slowly, my good sirs—slowly; have a little patience.
Some scrapes even I have got into, and for the love of
truth I must not pass them by in silence. But everything has its place, and here, for instance, *is* the place
for one of these scrapes. In the shop where I was
employed, close to my bench there was a great plaster
pillar rising from the floor to the ceiling. Neither
I nor any one had ever thought or inquired for what
purpose it had been made. In this pillar was a sort of
little niche, into which was walled up a phial of oil kept
for sharpening our tools. Now it happened that this
phial got broken, and in consequence it became necessary to knock down the rest of the little niche in order to
put in a new one; but in performing this operation, I
perceived that the wall was thin under the hammer, as if
it were hollow, so I began to think what this could
mean. The others also wondered, and some said one
thing, and some said another. In the meantime, as I
continued to hammer on the wall in the interior of the
niche, a brick fell down, the wall gave way, and we
looked into a hollow space. Taking a stick to measure
the depth, we found it was considerable; but we could
not understand what the meaning of this could be. I
have already said, in the beginning of these memoirs,

that our shop was under the Piatti printing-office—and
so it is, for the printing-office is on the first floor over it;
but the building is very high, and above that floor are
others occupied by lodgers.   Suddenly, as we stood still,
perplexed and wondering what could be the use of this
hollow pillar, I, being nearest the spot, heard a noise
within like a rustling or rubbing of something which we
could not explain.

For a while I stood still, thinking, when suddenly I
guessed what it was, and said to my companions—

"In a moment, if I succeed, you will witness a scene
that will make you laugh."

"What do you mean to do?"

"You will see."   Taking a long piece of beaten iron
wire, I bent it into the form of a mark of interrogation,
and fastening the straight end of it firmly to a bit of wood,
when I heard the noise again I thrust it to the opposite
side of the hole, and again and again tried if I could
catch hold of anything within.   At last, when I thought
I had grappled hold of something, I pulled it up, and
found it to be a rope.   As soon as the rope was caught,
we heard several voices scolding, calling, and disputing—
amongst others, a woman's voice shouting, "No, I tell
you there are no other lodgers; pull away, the bucket
must have got into some hole."   Then the poor woman
pulled, and every time she pulled I gave a loud groan.
At last, apparently the woman's strength failed, the mistress herself or some one else pulled at it, for I could
feel she had no more strength to pull, and then cried
out with an impertinent voice, worthy of greater success,
"Who is there?"   "The souls of purgatory," I shouted
out lugubriously, and instantly felt the rope fall down.

To say the truth, I was then a little alarmed through
fear of being discovered, so I pushed forward the iron

hook, and the rope fell, bucket and all, into the well. My companions laughed at the scene, but I did not ; and thinking the joke might be found out, I hastened to close up again the hole with a brick, set the little bottle of oil into it, restore the niche as it was, smudge it over well that it might appear old and as if it had never been touched, sweep away all traces of the plaster that had been used, straighten out the instrument I had used, and apply myself to my work in serious rather than hilarious mood.

About this time my father, failing to get work, came to Florence, hoping to find something to do; but his hopes proved vain. He stayed there a little while, but at last determined to go away, and this time for a more distant place. My mother and all of us tried to dissuade him, telling him to have patience, that some way would be found, that we would do all we could to help, and although we were very poor, still we should all be together. But it seemed to him that we could not get on in this way, and accordingly he left for Rome. So long as he was at Siena and wrote to us, and sometimes sent us a few *sous*, it was not so bad, and we were accustomed to it ; but now, who could say how we should get on? So far away, without any one to help him, without acquaintances, and with so imperious a character, what would become of him? Fortunately, however, he found employment, and he wrote that he was well, and hoped in a short time to be able to send us something. God knows there was need of it.

Meanwhile I had become tolerably skilful. I was no longer a boy ; I earned about three *pauls* a-day, and nearly all this I gave to my mother, reserving for myself only a few *sous* to buy paper, pencils, and books. Beyond these things I wanted nothing, for my mother took care to keep me cleanly and decently dressed.

As my face, my way of speaking, and my manners were not vulgar, many of the customers who came to our shop took me for the son of the principal instead of an apprentice. They readily addressed themselves to me; I took their messages, and sometimes their orders for the work, and the older and more skilful workmen showed no ill-feeling about it. Amongst other customers who had a liking for me, I remember Signor Emilio de Fabris, who at that time was the head workman in Baccani's studio. He used to come to direct and urge on the work. He used to talk with me, and to make his observations on the work; and as he even then had an easy and graceful way of talking, I listened to him with attention. He was a thin, tall, refined young man, admirably educated, and courteous in his manners. To-day he is one of the most famous masters of architecture, President of our Academy of Fine Arts, and my good friend.

But although I had many reasons for being contented, —for at home, thanks to the small wages of my brother Lorenzo, the few *sous* that came from Rome, and the earnings, meagre though they were, of my mother, we were able, by putting all together, to live tolerably though poorly, and in the shop I was liked and esteemed by my master, by the men, by all,—still I was not contented. I felt there was a void, a feeling of uneasiness, and a melancholy that I could neither explain to myself, nor could others explain to me except by jestingly calling me "the poet."

And this was the truth, for the poet is eminently a dreamer whose dreams are more joyous and smiling than any reality, and I dreamed—yes, but not of a smiling future when I should be rich and famous, but of any sort of way by which I could find vent for that inward longing to distinguish myself above others, and to distinguish myself especially in figure-work, though it should be only in wood; but it was not possible for me to satisfy this longing in the shop. Here I was obliged to work at all sorts of things—chandeliers, frames, mask-heads, everything; and I not only felt unhappy, but was unhappy, and my health began to fail. I was advised to take sea-baths; but in Leghorn the cholera was raging, and it would have been imprudent to go there, and so another year passed in the midst of desires and hopes and fears and ill-health. But at last I went to the baths. I had scarcely arrived there, however, when that terrible disease reappeared and raged furiously: the inhabitants and strangers hastened to fly from it; all business was suspended; movement and gaiety almost entirely disappeared; the shops were shut; and in a short time Leghorn became deserted, sad, and oppressed with fear.

My mother wrote to me from Florence urging my immediate return; but I—I know not why—felt myself, as it were, riveted to Leghorn. It may have been perhaps on account of the effect of the sea air, the novelty of the life, and the excitement produced in me by the danger to which my life was exposed, which I not only did not fear, but even felt strong enough almost to challenge, and more than all, the notable improvement that I daily felt in my health, which decided me to remain. I had found some friends even gayer and more thoughtless than myself. We went to the fish-market and bought the best fish for almost nothing—fresh red mullet for two or three *soldi* a pound—for there were no purchasers. It was generally believed that the disease came from the sea, and was brought on by eating fish; but we ate and drank and smoked merrily.

In a few days I recovered my health, got a good colour, gained strength, and melancholy went to the

devil. I also found some work to do. The few *soldi*
that I had brought with me rapidly disappeared. I
worked but little, only doing so much day by day as
would enable me to live merrily. By one o'clock my
day of work was over, and then began that of amusement
—which consisted of dinner, walks in the country sometimes as far as Montenero, towards evening a good swim
in the sea, then to the *café*, and late to bed. Leading
as I did this happy life, one can readily imagine that
my letters home breathed trust, courage, and tranquillity
of spirit, so that my mother, although she never ceased
to beg me to return, did so in less pressing terms and
with gentler expressions.

One day when I had gone with my friends on board
one of those small vessels which are stationed at the
"Anelli," and while we were eating a dish of fresh fish
called *cacciucco*, which the sailors excel in making,
a woman who was walking by the shore fell or threw herself into the sea. For a short time she floated, sustained by her clothes, which puffed up into a sort of
bell; then she began to waver to and fro, and down
she went. We looked at each other, and then about
us to see if any of the sailors on the neighbouring ships
had seen the woman and were moving to the rescue, and
those on board our boat only shrugged their shoulders
as if she were a dog.

" Down with you! throw yourself in! you know how
to swim!"

" I, of course; but don't you swim better than I?"

" I! no; but yes——"

And at this one of us, a fellow nicknamed Braccio di
Ferro—I don't remember his real name—taking off
jacket and boots, shouted out, "Hold your tongues,
cowards!" and plunged in head first with his hands above

his head. At the word cowards, made even more telling by the brave act of the man, I felt my face suffused with shame ; and although I was not such an expert swimmer as Braccio di Ferro, I also took off my jacket and shoes, and gathering my loins tightly together, with my hands under my feet, jumped in. Under water one could see quite as clearly as above, for the rays of the sun penetrated obliquely and lighted up all the space about me. I saw my friend diving down to touch bottom, which meant that he had seen that poor woman, but I had to come up to the surface to take breath. As soon as I had done so once or twice, I made a somersault, and away I went, striking out with my hands in the water. My friend, however, had found the woman, and had seized hold of her by her foot. Swimming around, I caught hold of her skirts,—and just in time ; for poor Braccio di Ferro was blown, and who knows how much water he would have drunk if I had not come. Leaving the woman to me, he made a curve in the water, and went to the surface to breathe, plunging his head under again to look after us. The two boats that had come to get the poor woman were ready. Braccio di Ferro mounted into one to help me pull her in. With one hand I caught hold of the boat, and with the other I clung on to the woman's dress, who was at once dragged out, placed on her face that she might throw up the water she had swallowed, taken to land, and escorted to her house, which was not far off. We mounted upon our vessel amidst the applause of the people and of our friends who were waiting for us ; they took off some of their clothes to cover us as best they could, and we hung ours out to dry on one of the cords of the ship. We drank some *pipiona* wine, finished our repast, and each of us returned home.

I remained about a month longer in Leghorn ; and if it

had not been for my mother, who pressed me to return, I should have stayed who knows how long. I found also something to do which was to my taste; I made three heads of Medusa to ornament the panels of a chemist's bench. It was a new chemist's shop that was to be opened in those days. Who knows what they have done with those poor heads of mine !

I have just said that when we returned to the ship after having got hold of the woman who was drowning, we drank some *pipiona* wine; and now I must stop and put others who may intend to drink of this *pipiona* on their guard. It is wretched wine, or perhaps we drank a drop too much, for we, who might have had the medal awarded to courage, went home almost drunk. And whereas an hour before we had been honoured and applauded, on our return we ran the risk of being scorned. So it is; a drop of wine too much may serve one such a turn that I, as a good Christian, warn my equals, and especially inexperienced young men who find themselves in the company of merry companions, against it.

I returned to Florence, and never heard anything more of my Livornese friends. Part of them were in Magagnini's shop, who was then a cabinet-maker, and is now a much - esteemed architect. Others — and amongst these Braccio di Ferro—were with Ricciardelli, cabinet-maker in Via dell' Angiolo. I returned home, therefore, and found the mother always dear and loving, who clasped me in her arms. The day following, I went back to the shop so brisk and well that the principal and all the men were rejoiced.

About this time my uncle, on my father's side, Atanasio Duprè, provost at San Piero di Bagno, died. They wrote to us from there to bring my father to take posses-

sion of the inheritance of his brother ; and as he was in
Rome, by my mother's advice I left at once for Bagno.
According to my habit, and also to save a few *soldi*, I
left towards evening on foot, and walked all night. It
was winter, beautiful weather, cold, and with clear
moonlight. In the middle of the night I met no one,
and only towards daybreak some few carts passed me
near Borgo alla Collina and Bibbiena, where I stopped
at the inn, as I could not go on any farther, having come
thirty-six miles without halting. I rested there some
hours ; but in order to pursue my journey, I hired a
mount and guide, because it was necessary to go along
the dry river-bed of the Corsalone for some miles, and
cross it several times. Through this plain, which was
flooded over at times, the river ordinarily kept to a
narrow tortuous channel, which, seen from the heights of
Bibbiena, produced a wonderful effect. It looked like an
enormous serpent with golden scales when lighted up by
the rays of the sun. Having gone over this strange and
fatiguing road, leaving to the right La Vernia, abode and
sanctuary of the "poor one" of Assisi, I mounted the
Apennines, and descended again, arriving towards evening at San Piero di Bagno. I went at once to my poor
uncle's residence, where I found a woman and some priests,
who showed me our inheritance. It was little enough, to
speak truly—some modest furniture, a little linen, and a
little money. What was really of value was the library ; but
this he had left to the Eremo of Camaldoli, from whence
it originally came, as, at the time of the suppression of
convents, he had taken it to save it from the thieving
hands of the governors and partisans of Napoleon I.

In order to understand how my uncle was able to
save a great part of the books and precious manuscripts
belonging to the library at Camaldoli, it is enough to

know that he was one of the fathers of that hermitage, and when at the suppression they were all expelled, my uncle became a priest, and was made provost of San Piero di Bagno, where he remained until his death.

My father hastened at once to Florence, where I found him at home, after I had stopped a few days at San Piero. He went there and took possession of those few things, and afterwards returned to Florence, and from that time forward never left it. He opened a little shop himself, and I used to help him in spare moments with certain kinds of work that he was unable to do,—such as little figures, animals, and other things. It is a great comfort to me to remember those days. I had the will and the ability to help my father to do work that was appreciated and liked as if it were really his, and so increase his reputation and obtain his affection. It happened once, however, that a most miserable man took advantage of my father's good faith about a piece of work that had cost me not a little time and study. This was what occurred :—

One day a man presented himself to my father, and said that he had a commission to have a group made in wood of not very large dimensions, that should represent the Sacred Family—the Virgin Mary, St Joseph, the Infant Jesus, and St John—and that it had come into his head to come to him, whom he knew to be so clever at figure-work. My father tried in some way to excuse himself, feeling that the work would be a long one, and not wishing to take too much advantage of my hours of rest and study. But there was no way of avoiding it, and he had to yield and take the order for this work, without even speaking of the price, "for" (so said this man) "the person who gives the order is both intelligent and rich, and will not question the price." Having pledged himself in this way, he spoke to me about it, and said, "Here is a fine opportunity. It is true you will have to work hard, but you will be recompensed. The money for this will belong entirely to you, as I can do absolutely nothing on it." I said yes, to satisfy him; but in reality I intended to leave the gain to him, only taking something not to humiliate him.

The work was begun: I made a little model in clay, gave it a great deal of study, and took much interest in it. I got on with it very well, but slowly, as is natural; and the man in question came almost every week to see it and hurry on the work, saying the person who had given the commission was most desirous of seeing it, and that we·must let him know when it would be in a condition to be seen,—in brief, when the little group would be nearly finished. To say the truth, it was entirely finished; but as then a doubt came up as to whether, in order to finish it entirely, it would be well to put the lamb at St John's feet, and as he would not decide upon so important a matter, he proposed to my father—I was not present—to show it to the person who had commissioned it at his house, as he could not come to see it at the shop; and he also congratulated my father on his work, which he felt sure was most praiseworthy. "The house is not far off —a mere step or two for me there and back—and so the question about the lamb will be decided." So saying, he took the little group, wrapped it up in a handkerchief, and begging my father not to move from the shop, that on his return he might not be kept outside waiting with the group, he went away, and never more was seen.

I need not say how my father felt: as for me, for more than a year my fixed·idea was, could I but only meet the man who had robbed me! I looked for him in the

c

streets, in the market-places, in the churches—yes, even
in the churches. For had he not stolen a Holy Family
from me? He might also steal a lamp or a candle hung
before some image. The ardent desire I felt to find the
thief, was not to put him into the hands of justice—for,
more than the actual loss of the money, I felt roused by
the insult and mockery of it. I wanted to teach him
what a lamb was! I! yes indeed; for although I was
young then, I was not at all weak, and there was more
than enough strength in me to break his nose and give
him a black eye. I foresaw all the consequences, even
to my imprisonment, which would undoubtedly have followed, for I was fully aware that one cannot administer
justice on one's own account. It did not matter to me;
I felt I must break his nose with my own fists! As
these were my thoughts then, I am obliged to narrate
them as they are, though God forgive me! All this,
however, was useless, for I never saw him again.

As wood is not wax, this group must be somewhere
now, and will last for some time to come; so I leave the
description of it, that he who is the present owner may
know that its first possessor was a thief.

The little group is a little more than a palm in height;
it is of linden wood, and is composed of four figures in
high relief. The Madonna is seated, with the infant
Jesus in her arms, who, with both His arms around the
Virgin's neck, is in the act of reaching up to kiss her, and
she presses Him to her bosom with one hand, whilst the
other hangs down on her left side. St Joseph is bent
forward and kneeling, with an expression of love and
adoration; and little St John, also on his knees, behind the Virgin, is pulling aside her mantle that he may
see this touching scene. St Joseph is at the right and
St John on the left of the Virgin.

CHAPTER III.

A PUNISHMENT WELL DESERVED, AND MY SATISFACTION—DIFFERENT TIMES,
DIFFERENT CUSTOMS—THE USE OF THE BIRCH GIVEN UP IN SCHOOLS—A
PORTRAIT—COMPANIONS AND BAD HABITS—HOW I BECAME ACQUAINTED
WITH MY DEAR MARINA—MY FIRST TIME OF SPEAKING WITH HER—DIF·
FICULTY TO OBTAIN MY MOTHER'S CONSENT TO OUR MARRIAGE—SHE
MAKES TROUBLE, THINKING TO DO WELL—I AM SENT AWAY FROM MY
BETROTHED, AND RETURN TO BAD HABITS—AN ESCAPADE—THE PUBLIC
BATHS OF YAGA-LOGGIA—MY CLOTHES STOLEN.

ERHAPS some one may think, "How is it
that, after so many years, you have been able
to remember the composition of your work?"
To say the truth, even I am surprised; but it
must be taken into consideration that, besides being
gifted with a most tenacious memory, the first efforts of
the mind remain more firmly engraved thereon, being
produced by the workings of one's whole soul. So it is
with one's affections and one's hopes. Add, therefore, to
this, the brutality of the offence, and it will be seen that
I could not forget it in any way.

In the meantime, in Sani's shop I had made for myself
an almost enviable position. All the works of a certain
importance were given to me. The principal placed entire
confidence in my judgment and skill—so much so, that
he put me at the head of the young men in the shop,
and delegated to me the direction of the great works
that were being executed at that time for the approaching

nuptials of the Grand Duke Leopold II. with the Prin‑
cess Antoinetta of Naples.   I had even the satisfaction
of directing a certain Saladini, a young Sienese who had
come to help us, and whom I had known at Siena at the
Academy of Fine Arts.   There we had been companions
and fellow-students, sharing the same desk; but to say
the truth, he drew better than I did, which irritated me,
and one day we came to words, and I said boastfully that
I defied him to draw with me, and could easily beat him.

It appears that the master heard loud words, and from
the glass bull's-eye in the door of the room from which
he dominated the whole school, he saw me standing by
the desk with one leg in the air, my arm passed under
my thigh, making a drawing of a Corinthian capital.   I
could not see the master, as my back was turned to him;
neither did I perceive how silent the school was, nor the
singular attention my rival was devoting to his work. ·

The reason of it all, however, I soon discovered, or
rather felt, from a sharp switch on my back, and before
I could put my leg down, three or four good blows, ac‑
companied with these words, "And this is the prize for
those who are skilful in drawing from under their legs."
These words were accompanied by the general ill-re‑
pressed hilarity of the school, and especially of my rival
Saladini.   I confess the blows, and even the laughter of
my companions which made them more stinging, were
well merited; but I remember that I took it in bad part,
especially as my friend Saladini, who certainly had seen
the master, had not warned me, as I felt I should have
done in his place.   For this reason I rejoiced when he
came to Florence to work in our shop, and was put by
the principal under my direction, when I could and was
obliged to correct him and say, " No, it is not right in
this way; you must do so and so."   I must add, how‑

ever, that I did not make any abuse of my power, that Saladini had no reason to complain, and that we became good friends. •

It now occurs to me to make an observation. I had a switching, therefore the "birch" existed in our schools. The master could administer it and the scholar receive it *coram populo* officially, according to the natural order of things, as a legitimate correction ; but I ask, if to-day a master in our Academy, or in fact in any academy in Italy, gave four blows on the back of a young man, be his fault even much greater than mine, what would happen? The heavens would fall ; there would be a revolution in the school and shouts without, and a scandal for the master. The ill-advised master would be reprimanded by the head-master ; a report made to the Minister of Public Instruction ; the master dismissed altogether or sent elsewhere ; and perhaps even, if the Ministry be *Progressista*, all would lose their places.

So it is. " *O tempora ! O mores !* " But is it, after all, a bad thing to administer a good whipping to a rascal who, instead of studying himself, annoys those who are really working, instigates them to leave school, and leads them to do wrong by using bad and obscene words, swearing, and drawing and writing improper things on the Academy walls? They can be sent away from school, but they must not be beaten, is the answer. But the fact is, that though they ought to be sent away, they are always allowed to remain. Would it not, therefore, be better to administer a little corporal punishment with the "birch" before arriving at this finale? Where is the harm of it? I have had it myself, and at fifty years of age am well and strong. But enough of this.

The good Saladini, therefore, was placed under me. He endured and even appeared to enjoy my corrections.

In fact, he had a character and temperament that prevented his feeling anything. He was a young fellow
about eighteen or nineteen, older than I was, small, fat,
with good colouring, chestnut hair, and light eyes which
never grew animated and moved slowly, seeing little and
being surprised at nothing. He never got angry, and
laughed in the same way when he heard of an accident
as when he heard a joke. It was not that he was stupid,
for his words, though few, were not devoid of sense. He
ate more than I did, and drank more too, and retired to
bed early, being an enemy of walks, of discussions, and
merrymaking even of the most discreet and proper kind.
He lived but a short time, and died as soon as he returned to Siena, I don't know of what malady. Not of
disease of the heart, however; for although his heart was
not bad, yet it seemed a useless part of him, never beating with any feeling of emotion or passion : there it was,
quite stock-still, seeming even dead, like the hearts of
stoics or stupid people, which are about the same thing.
Those, however, who have the misfortune to be made in
this way, live a long time, eat much, drink much, and
sleep—above all things sleep—profoundly ; and so did
he, though only for a short time, because he died. It
was better so, for who knows whether his heart would
not have waked up some day, repented the time lost
in sleeping, and quickened its beat? Therefore it was
better so. May the earth weigh lightly on you, my
friend, and the peace of the Lord rejoice your spirit !

By this time I had grown to be a young man beloved
by my friends, who were not many, and not all of them
excellent. Some were a little too full of life, like myself,
and these gay young fellows used sometimes to drag me
to places where young men of good repute should never
go—I mean to *osterias* and billiard-rooms. In such places

there is loss of time, loss of health, and loss of morals. Vaguely I felt, even then, the impropriety of such places, and an internal sense of dissatisfaction warned me to break off from these habits and to avoid these friends. Indeed at home I was no longer like the same person. I was restless, intolerant, despising the naturally frugal meals of the family; and my mother, my poor mother, suffered for this, but my father was angry, and sometimes with loving words and sometimes with severe ones he reproached me for my crabbedness and caprices, and I then felt sincere regret, and my heart softened, and quite overcome I embraced my mother. For all this, the road that I had taken was a slippery one. I no longer studied anything or drew as I had always done before. I read very little, and that little was rubbish. Praised and cajoled by my companions, quite satisfied with the kind of superiority I had acquired amongst them in the shop, I might have fallen very low, and have become a good-for-nothing man, and perhaps a despicable one ; but God willed it otherwise. And now that I must begin to speak of her who saved me and loved me, and whom I loved and esteemed always, because she was so rich in all true virtues, I feel my hand tremble, and ·the fulness of my love confuses my ideas. One day as I was standing by my work-bench, I saw a young girl pass with quick short footsteps, quite concentrated in herself. It was but a fugitive impression, but so vivid that every now and then that vision came back to me and seemed to comfort me. I had not seen the features of her face, nor her eyes, which she kept on the ground ; and yet that upright modest little figure, those quick little footsteps, had taken my fancy. I desired to see her again. Every now and then I looked up from my work, in the hope of seeing the person that I had been so struck by ; but I did

not see her again during that day or the following
ones.

The second *festa* of Easter I was at Mass in the
Church of the Santi Apostoli near by. Suddenly lifting
my eyes, I saw facing me the dear young girl on her
knees. Her face was in shadow, as it was bent down,
and the church was rather dark, but the features and
general expression were chaste and sweet. I stayed
there enchanted. That figure in her modest dress
and humble attitude, so still, so serene, enraptured
me. When Mass was finished, the people began to go
away, but she still remained on her knees. At last
she rose and went out, and I followed her from afar.
She stopped at a house on the door of which I saw
the sign of "laundress." I could not believe that such
a modest serious young girl could be so employed;
for as a general thing, laundresses are rather frisky and
provocative, turning their heads and glancing about, and
sometimes very slovenly in their dress—in fact, the opposite of all that dear good creature was. From the first
moment that I saw her I felt for her a respectful admiration, a tranquil serene brotherly affection and trust. I
was seized with an irresistible desire to love her, to possess her, and to have my love returned. Often without
her knowing it, I followed her at a distance, to assure
myself of her bearing and her ways, and always observed
in her a chaste, serious, and modest nature. At last I
attempted to follow her nearer; and when she became
aware of it, she hastened her steps and crossed to the
other side of the street. I was disconcerted, but at the
same time felt contented. One day, however, I decided
at any cost to speak to her, and to open my heart to her;
and as I knew the hour when she was in the habit of
passing by the Piazza di San Biagio, where I was at work,

I held myself in readiness, and as soon as I saw her, went out and followed her, that I might draw this thorn out of my heart. Yes, I somehow thought she would not take my offer amiss. She crossed the Loggia del Mercato and took the Via di Baccano and Condotta, and turned into the Piazzetta de' Giuochi, and I always followed her nearer and nearer. At last she became aware of this, stopped suddenly, turned, and without looking me in the face, said, " I want no one to follow me."

I stammered a few words, but with so much emotion in my voice, that she again stopped, looked at me a moment, and said, " Go home to your mother, and do not stop me again in the streets."

I gave her a grateful look, and we parted. I returned to the shop with my heart overflowing with love and hope.

From that day a great change took place in me: companions, rioting, and billiards disappeared as by enchantment from my life. That same evening I went to the laundry. I saw the mistress of it, and with an excuse of having some work to give her, I spoke to her casually, and in a general way, of the young girl (whose name I did not know) ; but she being very sharp, smiled and said—

" Ah yes; Marina — certainly — I understand. But take care and mind what I say ; Marina is such a well-conducted girl that she will not give heed to you."

" But I did not say that I wanted to make love to her."

" I know ; but I understood it, and I repeat that she will not listen to you,—and if you want to do well, you will never come here again. Here there is work and not love-making to be done. But if you like, you might go to her house and speak with her mother. Perhaps then — who knows ? But I should say that nothing would come of it, and it would be better so. You are

too young, and so is she.   Now you understand.   So go
away, and good-bye."

"Thank you, I understand; but where is Marina's
house?"

"It is in the Via dell' Ulivo, near San Piero."

"Good-bye, Signora maestra."

"Your servant."

The day after this.I went to Marina's house and
found her mother Regina. The house was a small one,
but very clean.   In a few words I opened my heart to
her and told her all, even of my having stopped Marina
in the Piazzetta de' Giuochi.   Regina was a woman of
about forty years of age, and a widow.   She listened
quietly to me until I got to the end, and then only
blamed me for having stopped her daughter in the street.
She added that she would think about it; but she did
not conceal from me that she thought me too young.   I
hastened to tell her how much I made by my day's work,
and that I had a settled occupation.   She then wished
to hear about my family, and showed a desire to know
my mother; and after having spoken to Marina, she said
she would allow me to come to the house of an evening
two or three times a-week.   So far· things went well;
but at home I had as yet said nothing, and this I was
obliged to do, as it was the first condition made before I could go to the girl's house.   I was not afraid
of my father, because, single or married, it was the same
to him, as long as I continued to help him in the work
he required of me; but as regards my mother, it was
quite another "pair of sleeves."   As soon as I had
opened my mouth I saw a frown on her beautiful
forehead, and she would not let me go on to the end,
saying that I was doing wrong, that I was too young,
that I ought to think of the shop, of my family, and

make for myself a standing. Not without tears she made
me feel that she looked upon this determination of mine
as a sign of want of love for her. I attempted in every
way to persuade her that I always cared the same for
her, and that this new affection would in no wise diminish
my love for her; that the young girl was an angel; that
she would be pleased by her, and love her like a daughter.
I embraced her, and wept, and she took pity on me, poor
mother! She condescended to make the girl's acquaintance, and so we went to her house. The two mothers
talked a long time together, whilst Marina put some
things in order here and there about the room, without
going away; and you could see the embarrassment of the
poor girl. I held one of my mother's hands in mine, and
kept my eyes on Marina, who never looked at me once.

It was settled that I could go to the house two or
three times a-week without speaking of the time that was
to elapse before the day of the wedding. Yes, I really
was too young, as I was only eighteen.

All these particulars may seem superfluous, and for
most people they certainly are so; but I meant, and I
said so from the first, that these memoirs should be destined for my family and for young artists, to whom I desire
to show myself such as I am, even in all the truth and
purity of the most tender of affections. Then it is with
a feeling of tender gratitude and painful sadness that I
go back in memory to those days of my meeting with
her, the difficulties that arose to prevent our union, and
the very great influence she had over me. From these
pictures interpolated now and then amongst these papers,
young men of good intentions will feel the charm that
surrounds the sanctity of domestic affections. Every
other evening I saw the good and charming girl. I remained for only about an hour or so—such was her

mother's desire. Whilst both of them worked — the
mother spinning and the daughter sewing together their
long braids of straw—I talked to them of my work in
the shop, of my studies, and of my hopes. Again returned to me stronger than ever the desire to do figure-
work, and a vague, persistent, and fierce hope to become
a sculptor in marble. When in various forms I expressed
these my thoughts, Marina, who was listening to me with
her eyes on her work, looked up to me and seemed to
search in mine for the meaning of my words. Poor
Marina, you did not then understand what agitated the
heart of your young friend. Later you understood;
and although full of fears, you did not discourage him.
But enough—do not let us anticipate.

Although my poor mother had yielded to my prayers,
and had convinced herself that Marina was a well-conducted girl, industrious, docile, and honest, yet she could
not, as she said, be persuaded that she would have to
lose me; and every evening when I returned home and
tried to speak to her of Marina, she would be troubled,
and break off the conversation as if it annoyed her.
Already, unknown to me, she had gone several times to
the mother of the young girl, and said that I was too
young—that I ought to think more of my studies than
taking to myself a wife, of whom in the end I should
tire; and poor little Marina would be sure to suffer,
in the first place because she cared for me, and in the
second place because, if abandoned by me, she would
find it hard to get a husband. All these things were said
by my poor mother for love for me and through the fear
of losing me. I knew it some time after. But now let
us see what were the fruits of these words of hers.

One morning—it was Sunday—I went to Marina's
house feeling more light-hearted than usual. It was

about one o'clock, after Mass. I went up-stairs, knocked, and Regina opened the door to me; but as I entered I heard a rustling sound, and saw Marina retiring into her little room. Her mother was more serious than usual, but seemed not to wish to show it. I perceived at once that there must be something the matter, and wished to clear it up. So I began—

"Marina—where is she? Is she not at home?"

"Yes; she is in her room."

"Does she feel ill? I hope not."

"She has nothing the matter with her, thank God; but as I have something to say to you, and as she knows what it is I want to say, she would not remain, and has retired to her room."

After this preamble, although there was nothing that I could reproach myself with, I felt quite frozen up.

"What is it then that you have to say to me?"

"Listen, and don't take it ill; in fact, I have already told you from the first that you are too young, and who knows when you will be able to marry my daughter? From now until then some time must elapse, and I have no wish that you should occupy that time sitting about on my chairs. *Then*, too, you may change—your companions may put you up to this; and we are poor people but honest, and I don't want my Marina to be courted by one who——"

"Enough, Regina—enough. It is true I am too young, but you knew it when you allowed me to come to the house. My earnings seemed then sufficient; and if no date was fixed for the marriage, it was because it was not asked. I am decided, if it so pleases Marina, to take her home in a year or a year and a half's time. Your words are the result of the tittle-tattle of people who wish us ill."

"No," Regina hastened to say—"no, they are not ill wishes of you or of us. But you understand me quite well, that if I speak in this manner to you, it is for the good name of my daughter. Nothing is damaged by it. For the present you will be so good as not to come to the house. If it is a rose, as they say, it will blossom; and when you return and say, next month, I want to marry Marina, you need have no fears; she will wait for you."

I remained silent and sad, and then said—"Is this also Marina's wish?"

"It is."

"Will you allow me to say one word to her before going?"

"Say it, certainly."

I went to her door and pushed it open a little. She was standing with one hand leaning on the back of a chair; her eyes were cast down, but the expression of her face seemed tranquil. "Marina," I said, "your mother has sent me away, and she has told me that this is also your wish." She lifted her eyes and moved a little. "I therefore obey, but be sure that I will never look into the face of another young girl until I come to claim you for mine. Do you accept my promise willingly?"

"Yes," she answered, with a steadfast quiet voice. Then I stepped nearer to her and put out my hand. First she looked towards her mother, and then she put her hand in mine, and we looked at each other, and in her eyes I saw a little tear, and her faith in my promise.

I went away pierced to the heart, but firm in my resolve. Neither at home nor at the shop could they understand what was the matter with me, for my whole character had so changed. I think my mother understood what it was, for she caressed me more than usual, and asked me no questions; and I set my heart at rest, because I trusted in the strength of character and true nature of the girl. Although it was prohibited me to go to her house, yet I made it a study how to meet her out of doors, and, without being seen, to see her, and even follow her from a distance. I was not at peace, however—not because I had any fears as regards her, but I was afraid of myself. I felt an aching void within me that nothing would fill. I saw smiling dreams of fame and honour vanish little by little. I heard a voice whispering within me—" Put an end, poor fool, to your melancholy; you were born poor and ignorant, and so you will die. Qualities are required to lift one's self above others that you are entirely wanting in. Genius is necessary, and you cannot say that you have it. Education is necessary, and you have none. Money is necessary, and you have not a farthing. Above all, a strong will is needed, and yours is most variable, transient, and weak, bending to the slightest breath of a contrary wind. Put an end to it all, and do as I say : enjoy day by day whatever is given to you to enjoy. Amuse yourself with friends your equals, and whenever any of these thoughts oppress you, drown them in a glass of wine. As to your young girl, remember it is as her mother has said, 'If it is a rose, it will blossom.' Up! up ! *Viva !* and keep a light heart." I already felt myself half yielding to these suggestions. I was down-hearted, and had not the strength to shake myself free from this strait of discouragement and desolation.

I had but little religion in me, which alone could have comforted my soul with constancy and faith in these first ebullitions of life; so it is not to be wondered at if, in this state of languor and discontent, I again turned to the amusements of my friends, losing not a few hours in the public billiard-rooms. I returned to one of the worst

of habits, for him who has a home—that of going to the
osteria; and I remember to have felt humiliatéd on finding myself in the midst of that noisy, vulgar merriment,
and hearing the coarse words uttered in those taverns,
where the air was heavy with wine, food, and cigar-smoke.
The chaste image and simple gentle words of my good
Marina came back to me, and I felt troubled, and,
shaking myself, I used to rise abruptly and go away.

Yes, truly the image of that gentle being aroused me,
and made me return to myself with a feeling of shame,
and a determination to put an end to all this. It was
providential, however, that not only her image but she
herself appeared to arrest me on the brink where I had
allowed myself to be dragged, and my meeting with her
deserves to be narrated.

Months had passed since I had been sent away from
my Marina's house. It happened one day, it being a
festa, that I had promised to go out of the Porta San
Miniato to meet some friends and eat a fresh plate of
salad ; and when I was near the Church of San Niccolo,
I could not cross the street on account of the procession
that was just coming out of the church. I think it was
during the Octave of Corpus Domini : there were many
people, and I waited until the procession had passed ;
then, perhaps because I was in such a hurry to overtake
my friends, in passing by I inadvertently knocked against
two women who were in the company of a young man.
They took it in ill part, and the young man, thinking
perhaps that I had knocked against them on purpose,
said—

" Has the boor passed by ? "

" You are a boor yourself," I answered.

" Pass on, if you want to." And he gave me a push.
I turned around on him and hit him a blow in the face,

and from that instant I had all three, the youth and the girls, down on me. But they got little good out of it: the young fellow, who was rather slight than otherwise, was put at once out of fighting condition by two blows of my fist in the face ; and I freed myself from the girls, who seemed like infuriated harpies. In an instant lace, ribbon, and feathers flew in the air like dry leaves scattered by the wind.

A space was cleared around me, and some said, " Oh, what a scandal!" others, "*Bravo!*" Some ran away, some laughed, and the soldiers came to clear the place and quell the tumult, and the *sbirri* (for there were *sbirri* then) to make arrests.

A mounted dragoon stationed himself in front of the church. A strong-built young man, then practitioner at the hospital, and now a distinguished physician—Doctor Gozzini—seeing the bad plight I was in, and having been one of those who had called out "Bravo!" came quickly to me, and taking me by the arm, hid me amongst the crowd, and took me with him behind the mounted dragoon. There we stood quite still, and saw them arrest the poor young fellow with his broken nose, and the girls with their crushed hats. I was not discovered that evening. They found me, however, easily enough next morning at the shop; but I will speak of this later. And now I feel in duty bound to assert that that was the last escapade of that kind that I was guilty of. I feel strong enough (or, as some may think, weak enough) now to bear quietly similar words and acts that so outraged me then. Ah! indeed age and experience are, as one may say, like the grindstone that rounds and softens down the asperities and impetuosities of early youth to form the character.

Not to excuse the affair nor the violence of my ways,

but for the love of truth, I feel bound to narrate another
adventure that happened to me on the morning of that
same day, which had perhaps served to exasperate my
already irritable state of mind. About mid-day I had
betaken myself to the public baths of Vaga-Loggia, a
bathing-place which was formed out of that part of the
canal called the Macinante running between the Fran-
zoni Palace and the palace belonging to the Baroness
Favard. It was covered in by a framework of wood,
with awnings, and the entrance was by a little door and
through a narrow corridor that went along the side of the
canal. At the end of this passage was a sort of stand,
and a room that was used for undressing, and where, for
a few *soldi*, an *employé* of the municipality was stationed,
who furnished towels, and took charge of the clothes and
other effects belonging to the bathers. For those also
who could not or would not pay, below the steps leading to the baths there was a sort of small amphitheatre
with a little wall around it, and in this wall niches to
put one's clothes in. It seems to me that I have seen
a something of the same kind that was used for a
similar purpose at Pompeii, only there they were hot
baths.

I chose this second-named place, which was more
economical certainly, but not so safe, as you will see.
After having bathed, on coming out of the water I went
to my little niche and found it empty. I looked about,
inquired, and swore. No one knew anything about my
clothes. At first I thought it was a joke, to keep me
some time naked ; but at last I was convinced, and the
other bathers as well, that my things had all been stolen.

What was there then to do? Nothing had been
left—they had taken everything ; and to say the truth,
it did not seem at all comic to me, however others

might laugh. A friend relieved me from my embarrassment. He dressed himself in haste, went home to his house, which was on the Prato, and brought me all I required, from my shoes to my hat. I dressed myself, went home in the worst of tempers, and I have already described what followed.

CHAPTER IV.

RETURN TO THE HOUSE OF MY BETROTHED, AND PUT AN END TO MY
THOUGHTLESS WAYS—A TALKING PARROT—HE WHO DOES NOT WISH TO
READ THESE PAGES KNOWS WHAT HE HAS TO DO—HOW I WENT TO PRISON,
AND HOW I PASSED MY TIME THERE—"THE DEATH OF FERRUCCIO," BY THE
PAINTER BERTOLI—SIGNOR LUIGI MAGI, THE SCULPTOR—HOW I LEARNT
TO BECOME ECONOMICAL—SHIRTS WITH PLAITED WRIST-BANDS—THE FIRST
LOVE-KISS, AND A LITTLE BUNCH OF LEMON-VERBENA—MY MARRIAGE—MY
WIFE HAS DOUBTS AS TO MY RESOLUTION OF STUDYING SCULPTURE—PA-
CETTI'S SHOP IN PALAZZO BORGHESE—I SELL THE "SANTA FILOMENA" TO
A RUSSIAN, WHO RE-CHRISTENS HER "HOPE"—I BEGIN TO WORK ON MARBLE
—I MAKE A LITTLE CRUCIFIX IN BOXWOOD, WHICH IS BOUGHT BY CAV.
EMANUEL FENZI—VERSES BY GIOVANNI BATTISTA NICCOLINI.

AND now to return to my unfortunate escapade, which, so to speak, was the cause of
my good fortune. Whilst they were looking for me, hidden in the crowd, I got away
by slow degrees to the Porta San Miniato, and, keeping
close to the walls up the hillside, escaped the observation
of the police; and then, on thinking over the danger I
had run, and the scandal I had created by my folly,
I resolved to mend my ways. Here the remembrance
of the dear gentle maiden came over me, and I thought
if I had been with her and had not been driven away,
this disturbance would never have taken place. Her
presence, her words, the desire of possessing her, and
being loved and esteemed by her, were necessary to
me. At last I returned to town by the same road, and,

going up by the Renai, I crossed the Ponte alle Grazie, and near there I saw Marina and her mother walking before me. My heart leaped within me! Had they been to the procession? Did they know what had happened, and had they seen me? What a start it gave me! To appear such a poor creature in her eyes was intolerable: what others might say was nothing compared to her condemnation; and, let alone condemnation, what I feared was the loss of her esteem. Under the influence of this fear, I had not the courage to address her; but at last, this uncertainty seeming too bitter to bear, I went up to her mother's side and said, "Good evening, Regina."

"Oh, see who is here! Good evening," she replied, with a joyful face.

I felt a new life come to me.

"What! have you been to the procession?" she said.

I looked both straight in the face and answered, "I come from that direction. I have been out of the gate of San Miniato."

"Have you heard that there has been a disturbance in the Piazza di San Niccolò?"

"I believe so; but it was a mere nothing."

"Ah, not so much of a mere nothing. They came to blows; there were some women among them; the soldiers came—the dragoons. I tell you it was a great row. Besides, some have been arrested, and will be taken to prison; and it serves them right. Pretty business, such a scandal as this!"

After a pause, I began again, turning to Marina—

"Where were you when you saw the procession?"

"We!" answered Marina—"we were in the church. We saw it go out, and a little after the disturbance occurred. I had such a fright!"

Having ascertained that they knew nothing of my doings, I was consoled, changed the conversation, and accompanied them down from Santa Croce to their house. When we were on the threshold I sadly said good-night; but Regina, to my great surprise and pleasure, said to me, " Won't you come up for a little while?"

" Well, if you will permit me, I will stop a little while with the greatest pleasure." And looking into the face of my good Marina, her eyes seemed to say, " Yes, I am most happy." We then went up-stairs, and I remained there only a short time, so as not to appear to presume upon their kindness; but in taking leave, I told the mother that I should return the next day, for I had something to say to her. My resolution was taken.

Have you done at last with all your childish follies, your tiresome tirades, your colourless love, fit only for collegians? You promised to give us your memoirs, and we supposed that you had something of importance and interest to tell us. Are these, then, your memoirs? and do you really and seriously think that such things as this are of the least interest to anybody?

Listen, dear reader. You have a thousand good reasons to think so, after your mode of viewing things; but I have quite as many on my side, as I will now prove to you. But first let me tell you a little story. There was once a parrot trained to put together certain words and make a little speech, almost as if it was his own. One day the servant (who was new to the house where the parrot was, and had never seen such a bird before) was struck with astonishment at hearing him, and was so delighted that he stretched out his hand to touch him. As he did this, the bold and loquacious bird opened his beak and said, " What do you want?" The astonished servant at once withdrew his hand, and, lifting his cap, answered, "Excuse me, sir, but I took you for a beast!"

I find myself now in the opposite case, and say to you, "Excuse me, I took you for a man"—that is to say, I imagined that you sympathised with me, and even appreciated a man who promises to tell the truth, and to narrate things just as they really were and are; and this I am doing, and mean to do to the end, without caring who likes great effects of light and shade, fearful shadows, and mere inventions, more or less romantic. If you don't like my way of doing this, you know very well what to do—shut the book and lay it aside, or skip what bores you, and perhaps you may find here and there something which pleases you. But I wish to give you fair warning, that these memoirs refer to and describe in part that very love which, though it may seem to you perfectly colourless, was none the less living, deep, and holy, and that retained its warmth and vividness of light for forty years, until she who was its object disappeared from this earth, leaving in my heart the memory of her rare virtues, a love which is ever alive, and the hope that I may again see her.

And now again I take up the thread of my narrative. Truly, when I said to Regina that I should return the next day to speak with her, I counted without my host, as the saying goes. The next day I found myself in "quod"—for but a short time, if you please, but still in prison for fourteen hours from morning to evening. But I was very well off there, as I shall now explain.

The morning after, on Monday—I was at my post, the first bench in Sani's shop—a person, after walking for some time up and down before the shop windows, came in and said, "Be so kind as to come with me to the Commissary of Santo Spirito, and—— Do not be

alarmed; it is nothing. The Signor Commissario wishes
to learn from you something about the disturbance that
occurred yesterday at San Niccolò after the procession."

" But I—be assured——"

" Don't stop to deny anything. The Signor Commissario knows all. Your name is Giovanni Duprè. You
live in Via del Gelsomino, which is precisely in our
quarter; and I did not go to look for you at your house,
in order not to disturb the family. But I can assure you
that it is a matter of no importance—perhaps a scolding, but nothing more."

I resigned myself, and went with him. This person
was not absolutely a *sbirro*, but something of that kind ;
and out of a sense of delicacy, and divining my thoughts,
he said to me—

" Go on before me. You know the way. I will
keep behind you in the distance, and no one will perceive
that we are together."

This I did, and arriving at the Commissariato, was immediately introduced to the Commissario. The Commissario was in those days a sort of justice of the peace,
who possessed certain attributes and powers, by which
he was enabled to adjudge by himself certain causes, and
to punish by one day's imprisonment in the Commissariato itself. If the affair after the interrogatory required a
longer punishment, the accused party was conducted to
the Bargello.

The interrogatory then took place ; and after severely
blaming me for my conduct, he told me that the matter
in itself was very grave, both on account of the assault
and the injuries done by me to these persons, and also
of the tumult which had been occasioned on a *fête* which
was not only public but sacred, and that therefore it
was beyond his power to deal with such an offence. I

felt myself grow cold, and had scarcely breath to speak,
so completely had the idea of being sent to the Bargello
overwhelmed me. But the good magistrate hastened to
add, "However, do not fear. The single deposition of only
one of the *corrisanti* is not in itself sufficient, and therefore it may be assumed that the provocation came from
their side, and that you acted in legitimate self-defence.
But as there was disorder, and injuries were received,
you must be content to pass the day shut up in one of
our cells." Thus saying, he rang his bell, and said to a
sbirro who appeared at the door, "Conduct this gentleman out, and lock him up;" and as I went out he
added, "Another time be cautious, and remember that
you might fall into the hands of some one whose name
is not entered here;" and he laid his hand upon a large
book which he had on the table. I bowed, went out, and
the *sbirro* opened a door in the court of the Commissariato, made a gesture to me to enter, and shut me in.

The room in which I found myself was tolerably large,
with a fair amount of light, which came in from a high
iron-barred window. In one corner was a heap of charcoal; and from this, perhaps, the room had received the
name of the Carbonaia. The walls were dirty, and
covered with obscene inscriptions. There was a bench
to sit upon, a closet, and nothing else. I remained
standing and looking about, but I saw nothing. My
thoughts were wandering sadly and confusedly from one
thing to another, and fixed themselves with fear and
sorrow upon my mother and Marina, who, in the state in
which I found myself, seemed to me more than ever dear
and worthy of honour. I thought of their grief, and felt
a shudder of emotion come over me. But the assurance
that I should soon be free, and should not pass the night
there, strengthened me and gave me courage, and I

walked up and down the room humming to myself.
Then, not knowing what to do, and how to occupy the
time, which is always so long and tedious when one has
nothing to do, I caught sight of the charcoal, and my
spirits rose, and I said, " Now I have nothing to fear,
for here is an occupation which will last me as long as
there is light ;" and I began to draw upon the wall a
composition of figures almost as large as life, the subject of which was the death of Ferruccio.   This was
a composition which I had seen at about that time
in the exhibition of the Academy of Fine Arts, in a
picture which had struck my fancy.   It represented
Ferruccio lying on the ground mortally wounded, and
wrapped in the flag of the Commune.   With a fierce
and scornful look he seemed to be saying to Mara-
maldo, who was giving orders to finish killing him,
" You kill a dead man."   The author of this picture
was the painter Bertoli, a young man of great promise, and who unhappily died not long afterwards in
the insane asylum.   The drawing that I made upon
the wall was a reminiscence of that composition, and
there was nothing of mine in it beyond an effort of
memory.

My poor mother, having been informed by the people
of the shop, came to the Commissario, in the hope of
obtaining my liberation, but she could not even obtain
permission to see me.   The only thing allowed to her
was permission to bring me my dinner—that is, to give
it to some one to bring in to me, all but the wine ; and
this she did.   Oh, my sweet mother, may God grant thee
the reward of thy love !

In the meantime the evening drew nigh; the walls
were covered with my poor drawings, and my hands and
face and handkerchief were all black.   I would willing-

ly have remained in prison till another day in order to finish a little less badly the Ferruccio ; but to stay there for long hours in the dark, and with nothing to do, so irritated and disquieted me, that I began to cry out, and beat on the door, asking for a light at my own expense. But no one heeded me ; and as I continued to drum loudly on the door, and had even taken the bench to hammer with, a voice different from the others called out to me, " Sir, for your own good I pray you to stop. The rules forbid lights ; and if you go on in this way, I promise you that you shall sleep to-night in the Bargello." Never did so short a speech produce the desired effect like this. I hastened to answer that I would be absolutely quiet. I put back my bench in its place, and seated myself upon it, in the attitude perhaps of Marius sitting on the ruins of Carthage ; and there I remained until eleven o'clock at night. The door was then opened, and I was told to go to the Signor Commissario to thank him. This I did, and he repeated to me the sermon of the morning, and added that I owed to him the mildness of my sentence. I renewed my thanks to him, and ran home, where I found my mother and father awaiting me—he with a severe face, and she with tears in her eyes.

The day after, I went to the house of Marina—for I invented some sort of lie to explain why I had not come the day before, as I had promised—and taking aside Regina (as Marina had established a school in the house), I expressed to her my desire to be married as soon as possible. It was rather soon, I confess ; but for me there was no other safety. With her—with my good Marina—I felt that I should cut short the too excited kind of life I was then leading, and which carried me into company and into gambling, and down that decline which leads every one knows where. That very

evening I returned and insisted on acquainting the dear
girl with my determination, at which she showed herself
modestly happy. The true affection that I felt for that
good creature, and the solemn pledge that I then took,
put an absolute end to the thoughtless life which I had
been leading. Stronger than ever came back to me my
love for study, and I began to turn over in my mind
how to occupy myself in marble work, even though it
should be as a simple workman. At that time I made
the acquaintance of Signor Luigi Magi, who was in the
Studio Ricci, in Via S. Leopoldo, now Via Cavour, and
I opened my mind to him, and he did not dissuade me
from my purpose. But he advised me first to learn
how to draw well and to model, and after going through
a certain course of these studies, then to attempt to work
in marble. He offered to procure for me copies to draw
from; and then, as he intended to set up a studio for
himself, he offered to give me lessons in modelling in
clay. This being agreed upon, I returned home happy
in the hope of carrying out this plan. But the many
little things that I had to think of, and not the least of
which was to save all the time I could in order to pro-
vide for the unusual expenses of my marriage, upset entirely for several months this ambitious project.

The ideas of wise economy which have up to the present
time always accompanied me, I owe to my most excellent Marina. One day she said to me, " You make four
pauls a-day, and two you spend on the house. What do
you do with the other two?"

"I dress, buy cigars, and I don't know what else."

"See," she answered, " on your dress it is evident that
you don't spend much; your cigars are a small matter;
so it seems to me that you might put a part aside to
supply what we most need."

" The fact is, that I cannot keep the money."

" If you like, I will keep it for you."

I accepted with pleasure, and every week brought her the surplus ; and I strove that it should not be small, for she knew pretty well what I had over. At the end of a few weeks I found that I had a package of six or eight beautiful shirts with plaited cuffs, such as I had always worn ever since I was a boy. An intelligent economy saves us from need, and even in narrow circumstances makes life easy. I owe to this wise woman the exact and judicious regulation of my family, as well in the first years of our marriage—when we were very much restricted in means—as in those which came after.

My eagerness to see her every evening, my exactness in carrying her all my savings, and the respect which I showed her by my words and acts, made me dearer to her eyes than I ever was before. One evening we were standing at the window of our little parlour, which over-looked a garden which was not ours. On its ledge were some pots of flowers reaching out over the windows, and among the flowers was a plant of verbena, which she liked above all things. I talked to her of my studies, of my hopes, of the happiness I felt in being near her ; and all the time I was so close to her, that our two breathings were mingled together.

She was silent, her face and eyes lifted to the starry heavens. The perfume of the flowers, the silence of the evening, and her sweet and chaste ecstasy so touched me, that, impelled by an irresistible force, I reached my lips towards hers. My movement was instantaneous, but I failed to carry out my purpose ; she turned away her face, and my lips only brushed against a lock of her hair, and then she immediately moved away and seated herself beside her mother. After forty years this comes back to

me as if it had just happened. Her face had an expression neither of displeasure nor of joy; but a certain
somewhat of sorrow was there, which seemed an answer
to all that I had been saying. When she perceived that
I was serious and a little mortified, she said with calm
benignity—

"Do you like verbena?"

"Oh yes ; I like it so much."

Then quickly rising, she cut off a sprig, put it in the
buttonhole of my coat, and said—

"There, that looks well!"

I took my leave, and on going away said to her *addio*,
and not *a rivederla*.

The 7th of December 1836, on the Vigil of the Imma-
culate Conception of the Virgin Mary, I married my
good Marina in the Church of St Ambrogio. This was, in
truth, the great event of my life, and that which exercised
the most salutary influence over my studies, over my peace,
and over the prosperity and morality of my family. We
were married in the evening, not only to screen ourselves
from the curious, but also because our joy was as secret
as it was great. Our witnesses were Luigi Sani, son of
my chief—he for whom (as I hope my reader has not forgotten) I used when a boy to prepare his clay—and Bar-
tolomeo Bianciardi, who was a workman in the shop of
Sani. At our modest supper, besides the witnesses, were
my father and mother.

My new existence being thus assured, I began to think
seriously how to carry out and give real form to the
dream of all my life, which resolved itself into this—*to
be a sculptor*. My young wife was timid, and sought to
persuade me that I was very well as I was. My father
openly blamed me, and kept repeating in his beloved
Latin, "Multi sunt vocati pauci vero electi" (Many are

called but few chosen). This I knew as well as he; but he referred it to my desire to be an artist, and my ambition did not reach further than merely to be a workman in marble. My mother listened to me kindly, and half sympathised with me in my bold hope of becoming a workman in some sculptor's studio. To my dear wife (for she above all others was nearest my heart, and on her account it behoved me to take care what I was doing) I kept repeating—

" My good Marina, listen. I risk nothing. I do not lose my skill as a wood-carver, and if I only study sculpture in the off-hours of my work, this very study may be useful to me as a carver; and if I succeed in becoming a sculptor, I shall be able to earn more, and acquire reputation, and enable you to live well and to give up your trade. Say, would not this be a good thing? "

And she would look at me sadly, and gently smiling would say—

" But we are very well off as we are."

In the meantime, in view of an offer of Signor Magi to give me some drawings and designs to copy, I went, according to our agreement, to his studio in the Licei di Candeli, and begged him to fulfil his promise; and a few days after he gave me some heads in light and dark from the " Transfiguration " of Raphael, which I copied, working at them early in the morning and in the evenings. Having finished these rapidly and to his satisfaction, he gave me plate by plate the whole course of anatomy of Professor Sabatelli, done in red chalk. In this task I was so interested that I worked till very late at night, until I had attained such facility and knowledge, that after sketching in the general outlines, I at once finished them without requiring to make a rough copy. Magi was surprised that I was able so easily to turn off every day a copy of one of these drawings of legs, arms, and *torsi*, which were of life size. Afterwards he gave me a number of the so-called *Accademie*, which are nude studies of the entire figure—and these, too, I drew rapidly and with increasing taste; and so enamoured was I of them, that I afterwards repeated them at the shop upon any fragment of paper or wood, drawing them in all their attitudes from memory.

I made, as I was well aware, very rapid progress, and I longed for the moment when the master should say to me that it was time to begin to model. In fact, he soon suggested this. However, as it was necessary to have a certain apparatus and help, I could only begin to model in the studio of Magi. It was therefore arranged that I should go to him during all the off-hours of my work; and this I did. I will not stop to note the number of hands, feet, and heads that he made me copy; I will only say that my life was most exhausting, and my wife, poor dear, had to suffer for it. She had to wait for dinner, and I was often so late, that I had only time to swallow a little soup and a piece of bread, and then to rush back to the shop.

When I remember this life of mine, with its painful anxieties and struggles, it makes me angry to see some of the youths of to-day, with every opportunity and all their time, and without a care in the world, either for their family or any thing or person, who rot in idleness, assume airs of scorn for others, even for their masters, and then swear out against adverse fortune, and deplore their genius crushed and unrecognised, and similar insipidities. My two hours of rest during the day, which were from one to three o'clock, were thus occupied : one hour was given to study, and the other was but just sufficient to enable me to go from my shop in the Piazza di San

Biagio to the Liceo di Candeli, and there take my dinner, and then return to the shop. I was punctual too, for I was determined to do my duty, and to keep my promise to my wife never to allow my study of sculpture to interfere with my regular occupation.

It was indeed a life full of agitations, anxieties, fears, and privations, but animated with what joyous hopes ! Every evening when I came back from my work, I devoted myself at home to making anatomical drawings from casts, while my wife did her ironing in the same room ; and I drew until the hour of supper came. It was a pure sweet pleasure to me to see that strong and lively creature coming and going with her flat-irons from the fireplace to the table, and gaily ironing, and singing

" Muskets and broadswords ; fire—fire—poum !"[1]

as she smoothed and beat with the flat-iron on the linen, while her mother sat silently spinning in the corner. Truly that blessed woman was right when she said, " We are so happy as we are "—for one of the purest joys that cheers my present life is the memory of those days. No joy is purer than that which comes from the memory of that past time of work, of study, and of domestic peace. Those days of narrow means and agitations now shine upon me with a serene and lovely light ; and I bless the Lord, who softens by His grace the bitterness of poverty and the harshness of fatigue, and so preserves this sweetness of remembrance in the heart, that neither time nor fortune has the power to extinguish it, or even to diminish it.

In the opinion of my master, Signor Magi, I had arrived at that point in my studies that I could be permitted to make portraits from life. Accordingly he

[1] " Schioppi, sciabola ; fuoco—puhm !"

E

proposed that I should find some friend who had time and patience to stand for me as a model. I soon found one, and his was the first bust I modelled. The likeness was good, and Magi and the others began to have a strong faith in my future. Encouraged by this trial from life, I determined to make a statuette of small dimensions. The subject which was given to me by Magi was Santa Filomena standing with her head and eyes turned to heaven, one hand on her breast and the other holding a bunch of lilies, while the anchor, the sign of her martyrdom, lay at her feet. The statuette was liked; and I pleased myself with executing it in wood, and finished it with great care of handling and delicacy of detail. It was exhibited at the Accademia delle Belle Arti in 1838; was praised by distinguished artists, such as Benvenuti and Bartolini; and the latter recalled it to me when, some time afterwards, I went to ask for work in his studio, and said—

"Believe me, my dear sir, if I had any work to give you to do, I would give it with pleasure, for I have seen that statuette of yours, which shows that you have intelligence and love."

My Santa Filomena was liked—liked by artists and by those who were not artists; but no purchaser presented himself, and I was anxious to sell it, not only for the sake of a little money, which would have been very opportune, but still more for the satisfaction of my *amore proprio* as an artist. But the purchaser did not come, and I was obliged to place my statuette in the magazine of antiquities of the Brothers Pacetti, on the ground-floor of the Borghese Palace in the Via del Palagio. It did not long remain here, however. It was frequented by many strangers, who found there a great number of things which were curious, and some of which were really beautiful. In this magazine there were, first of all, old pictures of our Florentine school: whence they had been excavated I know not, but the exportation of them out of the country was not as difficult as it now is. There were also *terre cotte* of the school of Luca della Robbia, statuettes in bronze, marble busts of the Roman school, to ornament halls or staircases in palaces; chests of ebony inlaid with *pietra dura*, ivory, tortoise-shell, &c. Specially rich was it in Venetian glass, antique plates, enamels, laces, &c., &c. There, among all these anti-quities, figured my Santa Filomena, which seemed more pure and white from contrast with all the chests of drawers, and stuffs, and tapestries which formed its background.

A Russian gentleman asked the price; and it being stated to him, without refusing to take it, he made a strange condition of purchase. He would not have it a saint, and in consequence he exacted that all the attributes which belonged to Santa Filomena should be removed. I took great pains to make him see that this could not be done, and that the statuette would in so doing lose much of its artistic value. If the lilies were taken from the hand, it would be perfectly meaningless and idle, and would injure the expression of the figure. He seemed to a certain extent persuaded, but he still persisted that he would not have it as a saint; and after thinking for a long time how he could change the name, and seeing that there was an anchor at her feet, he said that it might be called Hope. I remained between yes and no, and only observed to him that Hope ought to hold the anchor in her hand, and not leave it on the ground as if she had forgotten it.

"No matter," he answered, "I insist on calling it Hope; but the lilies must be removed."

I answered that they would rather help the subject, and it might be called The Virgin, Hope.

" *Oh! c'est très-bien,*" he replied.

There remained the crown of roses on her head, but in regard to this everything was easy. Roses are the symbol of joy, and Hope in the purity of its aspirations is crowned with joy. Truly that day I was a more eloquent orator than artist.

The Russian, quite content (and I more than he), counted me out the price of the statuette in golden napoleons, and before it was boxed up, had inscribed on the base of the Filomena these words—*La Vera Speranza.*

After this work, Magi advised me to begin to work in marble. This cost me little trouble, practised as I was in carving wood, which, though it is a softer material, is more ungrateful and irresponsive. After a few weeks' practice, I was able to execute some works, and to assure myself that henceforward, whenever I wished, I could go from one material to the other. Remember, however, that I then did not even dream of becoming an artist. I only hoped to succeed as a workman in marble, as I then was in wood. The idea of being an artist came to me afterwards, slowly and by degrees—the appetite growing, as the saying is, by eating; or I should rather say, I was driven and drawn to it, out of pique and self-assertion (*punto d' onore*). But let us proceed regularly.

About this time Signor Sani received an order from certain nuns—I do not now remember whom—to make a Christ upon the cross, which was to be of small size and executed in boxwood. Naturally Sani thought of me, and gave it to me to execute. I set to work upon it with such love and such a desire to do well, that I neglected nothing. After making studies of parts from life, and pilfering here and there, I succeeded in making an *ensemble*, movement, character, and expression appropriate to the subject, and this I executed with patience and intelligence. But the excellence of the work was superior to the importance of the commission. Let me explain myself. The time it cost me, and consequently the price I was paid by my principal for my weeks of labour, far exceeded that which had been agreed upon by the persons giving the commission. Sani, a little grudgingly, but still feeling that it did honour to his shop, showed himself half pleased and half annoyed; and when other persons afterwards came to urge forward the work on which he was engaged for them, and praised this Christ of mine, Sani took all the praise to himself as if it belonged to him. Nor was he to blame for this. The Christ, however, on account of the difference of price, remained in his shop shut up in his chest. But as it had been somewhat noised about, many came expressly to see it. Among these was the Cavaliere Professore Giuseppe Martelli, who lately died, and who having seen it, told Sani that he hoped to induce the Cavaliere Priore Emanuel Fenzi to buy it. He was then putting in order the principal suite of rooms in the palace of the Via San Gallo for the wedding of the Cavaliere Fenzi's eldest son, Orazio, with the noble Lady Emilia de' Conte della Gherardesca, and he hoped to place this Christ at the head of the bed of this young couple. And this in fact happened. The Christ was seen and bought, and I believe that it is still in that house. I saw it there myself when poor Orazio, who honoured me with his friendship, was alive.

I shall again refer to this Christ; but for the present, let us go on. I had a great desire to give up once for

all this working in wood—not because I thought that
material less worthy than marble, for the excellence of a
work depends upon the skill and knowledge of the artist,
and not upon the material which he has used. Very
worthless statues have been seen, and still may be seen,
in beautiful marble, and, *vice versâ*, beautiful statues in
simple *terra cotta* or wood.

"You will be noble if you are virtuous," answered
D'Azeglio to his son, when the latter asked him, with
the ingenuousness of a child, if their family was noble.

Let us then understand that the nobility of any one
is founded upon his deeds, and the excellence of a work
depends upon the work itself, and not upon the material.
We shall return to this consideration hereafter; now let
us proceed. I say that I wished to give up working in
wood, because it was my business at the shop to make
all sorts of little things, such as candlesticks, cornices,
masks, &c. Naturally it fell to me to make them; and
not always—on the contrary, very rarely—it happened
that I had a Christ, an angel, or anything of that kind
to execute: and on this account I was irritable and irascible (except when I was at home) with everybody, and
specially with myself.

At Magi's I had as much work as I wished. I had
already finished for him two busts,—one of the Grand
Duke in Roman drapery, according to the style then
in vogue among the academic sculptors, who dressed in
Roman or Greek costume the portrait of their own uncle
or godfather; the other of an old woman, whom I did
not know. Work enough I had; but naturally I wished
to earn something by it, and this was soon spoken of.
I understand very well that the master has a kind of
right to all the profits of the first works of his pupil; but
with me this went on so long, that at last he saw its

impropriety; and he proposed to engage me to finish the group of Charity which he had made for the Chapel of the Poggio Imperiale, as a substitute for that wonderful work of Bartolini, which is still admired in the Palatine Gallery. But the proposition of Magi was in every way impossible to accept, as he only agreed to pay me when the work was completed—that is to say, I and my family were to go for at least a year without anything to eat.

I tried here and there ; but I could not make a satisfactory arrangement, and I had to resign myself to the making of candlesticks. I had now become a father. My wife had given me a little girl, whom I lost afterwards when she was seven years old; and as I have never made mention of my dear angel, let me embellish the meagreness of my prose with the charming verses of Giovanni Battista Niccolini, who then honoured me with his friendship, and which he wrote with his own hand under the portrait of my little child. They are as follows :—

> Few were the evils that Life brought to thee,
> Dear little one, ere thou from us wast torn,
> Even as a rosebud plucked in early morn.
> Tears thou hast left, and many a memory,
> To those who gave thee birth,
> But thou from Life's short dream on earth
> Hast waked the perfect bliss of heaven to see ;
> And thou art safe in port, and in the tempest we.

> Pochi a te della vita
> Furono i mali, o pargoletta, e mori
> Come rose ch' è colta ai primi albóri.
> Ognor memoria e pianto
> Al genitor sarai, benchè per sempre
> Dal sogno della vita in ciel gia desta.
> Tu stai nel porto e noi siamo in tempesta.

CHAPTER V.

A WARNING TO YOUNG ARTISTS—PROFESSOR CAMBI'S PROPOSITIONS—A FINAN-
CIAL PROBLEM : TO INCREASE GAIN BY DIMINISHING THE MEANS THAT
PRODUCE IT — I LEAVE SANI'S SHOP TO HAVE MORE TIME AND LIBERTY
TO STUDY—AN IMITATION IS NOT SO BAD, BUT A FALSIFICATION IS INDEED
AN UGLY THING—THE MARCHESA POLDI AND A CASKET, SUPPOSED TO BE
AN ANTIQUE—HOW A MASTER SHOULD BE—THE DEATH OF MY MOTHER,
SEPTEMBER 1840—OPINION OF THE ACADEMY—THE "TIPSY BACCHANTE"
—A DIVIDED VOTE—THE "CARIATIDI" OF THE ROSSINI THEATRE AT
LEGHORN.

ET us consider for a moment the state of my
mind at this time. I felt within me an
unconquerable inclination for the study of
sculpture ; and even as a child, I gave vent
to my feeling as well as I was able. As I increased in
years, the more this desire was repressed and opposed,
whether by my poverty or the aversion of my father,
the more it developed into a settled passion. But after
the progress I had made in my studies gave me a right
to hope, and my masters had encouraged me, and I had
acquired some skill in working the marble, no work was
given me to do. Nor was this all. I was humiliated at
last, being told by a workman to whom I applied—who
was the administrator of the studio of a foreign artist—
that there was nothing for me to do there, because the
work in that studio was so difficult as to be beyond my
ability. I swallowed this bitter mouthful, but I did not
despair. Not only did I not despair, but I determined, by

study and force of will, to prove that I was right and they were wrong. Add to this that I was not alone; I had a wife and children. But no matter. Since the first prophecies that I never should be good for anything as a woodcarver had proved false, this also, which was both a humiliation and an insult, might prove to be untrue. My poor wife saw that my mind was greatly disturbed, and, with her sweetness, strove to calm me by representing to me that we were fairly well off and without troubles, and exhorted me to drive from my head a thought which was rendering my life bitter to me. These words, dictated by love, made me still more unhappy; but dissimulating and caressing her, I told her that she was right.

One day, in the studio of Magi, I and another young man were modelling together a man's *torso* which had been cast from nature. A friend of Magi, a painter, as he passed by us paused, and after looking at our two copies, said, turning to my rival and patting him gently on the shoulder, "I am delighted: this is an artist!" Then turning to me with an expression of regret, he said, "*A rivederla.*" My good reader, do you think that made me despair? No, by the Lord! I tell you rather that these words were seared upon my brain as with a red-hot iron, and there they still remain—and they did me a great deal of good. The Professor who spoke them (yes, he was a Professor), three years afterwards embraced me in the Accademia delle Belle Arti before my "Abel." My rival? My rival is perfectly sound in health, and is fatter and more vigorous than I am, but he is not a sculptor. So, my dear young artist, courage! in the face of poverty, and opposition, and abuse, and contempt, and even (remember this) of blandishments and flatteries, which are more destructive than even abuse and contempt.

But be careful to consider well what your vocation really is, and do not allow yourself to be deluded by false appearances. It is absolutely necessary that your calling should be imperious, tenacious, persistent; that it should enter into all your thoughts; that it should give its form and pressure to all your feelings; that it should not abandon you even in your sleep; and that it should drive from your memory your hour of dinner, your appointments, your ease, your pleasures. If, when you take a walk in the country, the hills and groves do not awaken in you in the least the idea that it would be pleasant to own them; but, instead of this, if you feel yourself enamoured by the beautiful harmony of nature, with its varied outlines, and swelling bosoms, and slopes sadly illuminated by the setting sun, and all seems to you an exquisite picture—then hope. If at the theatre you see a drama represented, and you feel impelled to judge within yourself whether this or that character is well played — whether the gestures, the expression of face, and the inflections of voice are such as properly belong to the character, and accord with the affections that move him, or the passions which agitate him—then hope. If, while you are walking along, you see the face of a beautiful woman, and if it does not immediately awaken in you the idea of a statue with its name and expression, but, on the contrary, you idly or improperly admire it—then fear. If in reading of a pathetic incident you feel your heart grow tender; if the triumph of pride and arrogance rouse your scorn—then hope. And if you do not feel your faculties debilitated by the long and thorny path of study, but, on the contrary, tempered and strengthened every day by constant and patient labour, then hope—hope—hope. If you have property, attend to the management of it. If you are poor, learn some trade. It is better to be a good carpenter than a bad artist.

In my own case, I armed myself with stout patience, and pursued my ordinary work of wood-carving; and when I returned home in the evening, I applied myself to study, and, in the simple and frank conversation of my wife, felt a calm come over my agitated mind; and my powers, enervated by ungrateful labour, were thus restored. But the opportunity which was to launch me once and for ever in art was already near, and I seized upon it with all my strength, hope, and love. Many and sad were the first steps against opposition and division; but I pushed on, and I have never stopped since.

Professor Ulisse Cambi, who had seen me modelling in Magi's studio, and who had his own studio close by, now began to talk to me about the triennial competition in sculpture, which took place precisely in this year, and he proposed that I should go in for it, and hoped that I should succeed; but even if I did not, he said, at all events the study incident to it would be no loss to me. Flattered by this suggestion, which showed that he had some confidence in me, I replied that I would think of it, and would speak about it to Magi, who might possibly lend me one of his rooms which he did not use, and also give me his assistance. I spoke to him on the subject, but I did not find him at all disposed to favour the project. In the first place, he told me that he could not give me a room; then that he did not think that I had gone on sufficiently far in my studies to be able to attempt such a competition; and finally, that he would not undertake to direct my work. This answer having been repeated to Cambi, he told me that he was convinced that I should succeed, and that if Magi would

neither give me a room nor superintend my work, he
would do both—and this he did.

The subject of the basso-relievo was "The Judgment
of Paris," and required five figures—Paris, Venus, Minerva, Juno, and Mercury. I made a sketch; but it did
not please Cambi, and taking a piece of paper, he
sketched with a pen a new composition, saying, "That,
I think, will do very well." I then made a new sketch
founded upon this by Cambi. Some one will now say,
"This is not right; you ought to have worked out an idea
of your own, and not one of your master's." Agreed;
but these considerations will come afterwards. For the
present, let us go on.

In the meantime it was necessary to come to a decision, and to take into consideration that the work
required much time, and could not be completed in my
off-hours, as I had hitherto done with my other studies,
and also that money would be required to pay the
models; so that, as it would be necessary to give less
time to my ordinary work, I should earn less, while I
should have need of more money in order to pay the
models. The problem was a difficult one, and at first
sight not easily solved. The reader will remember the
Brothers Pacetti, in whose shop I had sold the Santa
Filomena. One of these, Tonino, had often said to me
that if I would work for them they would give me anything to do that I might prefer—whether cornices rich
with figures and *putti* and arabesques, or coffers and
chests *all' antica*, or whatever I liked with figures, with
the prices agreed upon, and liberty to work when and
how I liked. The offer was excellent, as you see; but
it involved leaving my old master Sani, and I was
affectionately attached to him, and he and all in the
shop were attached to me; and on this account I felt

repugnance to leaving the place and the persons who had helped me on when I was a child. So, thanking Pacetti, I repeatedly refused his offer. But now it was necessary to come to a decision between two alternatives—either to abandon the competition and remain in the shop, or to abandon the shop and accept the offer of the Brothers Pacetti. I spoke of this to my good Marina, who at first did not look upon it at all favourably, fearing that if I left the shop, which had always given me work, I should find myself left in the lurch by the other, in spite of all the fine promises of gain and liberty and the like. But at last, seeing that I was decided, she contented herself with saying, " Do as you think best." O blessed woman, may God reward thee !

When I stated to old Sani my determination to leave his shop, angry as a hornet, he said, " Do as⁄ you like," and spoke to me no more the whole day. The next day, however, more softened, but still severe, he asked me the reason of this strange resolution, and I told him. Then he proposed an increase of salary and a diminution of work, and at last agreed (I must do justice to this good man) to allow me to have all the hours which were necessary for the competition. But I had already made my contract with Pacetti, had decided upon a work after my own choice, arranged the room given me by Pacetti, and which was the Hospital for Horses in the old stable of the Palazzo Borghese, and I could not withdraw from it.

I began to model the basso-relievo for the competition in the studio Cambi, and my *intaglio* work I did in the little studio or stable of the Palazzo Borghese. The work that I had undertaken for Pacetti was curious. It had every recommendation except that of honesty. Let me explain. There was at this time a great passion

among strangers for antique objects: great chests, cornices, and coffers, provided they were old, were sought
for and purchased; but modern works, though of incontestable merit, no one cared for, and they brought very
low prices. It came into the head either of Pacetti or
myself—I do not remember which—to make something
in imitation of the antique (and so far it was all right),
and to sell it for antique, and here was the maggot.

It was settled, then, that I should make a coffer or
chest in the beautiful and rich style of the *Seicento*
—rectangular of form and not high. The cover was
slightly pointed, with various arabesque ornaments, and
in the centre of this cover in the front I carved a Medusa
crying out loudly; and by looking at myself in the mirror,
I succeeded in giving a good deal of truth to the sad
expression of this head—indeed the muscles of the face
and the eyes had such a truth of expression that I would
not promise to do as well again even now. This is the
portion of the work which is really original; all the divi-
sions in panels, and the external faces, were an absolute counterfeit representation of the ornaments on the
bookshelves in the Libreria Laurenziana, which were
carved by Tasso the carver, the friend of Benvenuto
Cellini, and, as some say, were designed by Cellini himself. Every precaution was taken—the wood was antique
but not worm-eaten, so that I could carve with delicacy
all the ornaments, dragons, and chimeræ; and when it
was finished, here and there a worm-hole was counter-
feited and filled up with wax, but so as to be visible.
The hinges and ironwork were also imitations of the
antique, which were first oxidated and then repolished.
In a word, it was a veritable trap, and I give an account
of it for the sake of the truth; and I hope that the first
statement of this falsification does not come from me.

But however this may be, we laughed at it, and it amused me then, though now it displeases me.

This coffer was seen by many persons, some of whom asked the price; but Pacetti set a high value upon it, and he had spread about some sort of story that it was a work of Benvenuto Cellini's. Finally, after some time, the Marchioness Poldi of Milan, who had gone to Florence to urge Bartolini to finish the famous group of Astyanax which he was making for her, saw this coffer, liked it, and took it for an antique; but in regard to the excellence of the work, and above all the name of the artist to whom it was sought to attribute it, she determined to consult Bartolini himself, and if his judgment was favourable, to buy it for the price that was' asked, but which naturally was not what I had been paid. Bartolini decided that it was one of the finest works of Tasso the *intagliatore*, made after the designs of Benvenuto Cellini; and the Marchioness Poldi then bought the coffer, and carried it to Milan.

Four years later, I finished my "Abel" and "Cain." I had made a name, which had been rendered still more attractive by the curious story of my origin; for all of a sudden, while nobody knew who I was, I seemed to be an artist who had been born one morning and grown up before night. The only thing that was reported about me was, that I had never studied, and that I had suddenly leaped from the bench of the *intagliatore* on to that of the sculptor. The reader who has thus far followed me, and who will continue with me up to the completion of my "Abel" and "Cain," will see with what heedlessness these reports were propagated. Let us go on. The Marchioness Poldi came to my studio, and having heard the story of my life, which was in the hands of all, and was written in that easy, attrac-

tive, and poetic style of which Farini is master, told me
that she possessed a magnificent work in *intaglio* by the
famous *intagliatore* Tasso, and said that this work was
imagined and executed with such grace and excellence
that it might truly be called a work of art, and she added
that these were the very words of Bartolini.

The reader may imagine whether I was flattered by
this; and in consequence of this praise, as well as to
pluck out this thorn from my heart by a confession of
my fault, I said, "I beg your pardon, Signora Marchesa,
but that work was made by me."

The Marchioness looked at me with a kind of wonder,
and then said, "No matter—nay, all the better."

I begged her not to tell Bartolini.

But to return to the point where I left off to make
this digression about the Marchioness Poldi. Let me
say, that if in my studio I enjoyed complete liberty of
imagination and action, and if my works met with such
success and were so praised as to give me consolation, matters did not go on so well in the studio Cambi,
where I was modelling for the competition. Scarcely
had I put my foot into that studio when I became timid,
embarrassed, and almost fearful; for the Professor would
not leave me free to see and execute from the life as
I saw it. I do not say that he was wrong; I only say,
that thus feeling my hands bound to the will of another,
rendered me hesitating and discontented. I should
have preferred a studio of my own, and after I had
sketched out as well as I could my own ideas, then to
have my master come in to correct me. But there he
was always; and he was not content with correcting me
by words alone, but he would take the modelling tool
and go on and model what I ought to have modelled
myself. My work might be done with difficulty; but if

I could have done it all myself, as I wished, I should
have been much happier, and my hand would have been
better seen in it—the hand of a youth without skill indeed, but still desirous to do and to learn ; and I should
also have been spared the annoyance of hearing thàt
the work was not done by me, but by Professor Cambi.
Now Cambi is a very dear friend of mine, and I do
not mean in the least to reprove him for what he did ;
but it is my duty to state the facts clearly just as they
are—and I take this occasion to say a few words as to
what I consider a master should do in directing his
young pupils.

Every historical fact, in its manifestations of time,
place, circumstances, and character, presents itself to
the mind of each person who studies it—and far more
to any one who intends to reproduce it—in an entirely
different way from what it would impress another. The
impression each receives depends upon his character,
intelligence, temperament, and education. This being
admitted, it is in the highest degree difficult to assert
with assurance, "I understand and can express the fact
better than you." When certain essential points are
established, such as the age and character of the personages, and the costumes and style of dress, all the
rest depends upon the taste of the artist, and his manner
of viewing and feeling it. As to the composition and
grouping of the figures, in regard to which dogmatic
statements are so often laid down, this should be a free
field to the artist in which he may move about as he
will. The harmony of lines, the balance of parts, the
equality of spaces, are all very fine words ; but above all
and before all, and as the base of all, there should be
clear expression of the fact, truth of action, and living
beauty. It is very true that sometimes, and indeed

F

very often, the young pupil is without much study or much knowledge, and in composing his sketch he makes mistakes in the arrangement of the dresses and the character and truth of the subject he wishes to represent. Then indeed the master should interpose. But how? Not by taking the tool himself and saying, "You should do thus and thus"; but rather by putting his pupil on the right road, and making him clearly appreciate the story he is trying to represent, and showing him that this or that figure ought to have the dress and the character appropriate to it, and to point out the means by which he may attain this result. If after this teaching the youth is dull, he should be counselled not to go on; but if, on the contrary, he improves his sketch, the master should correct it and perfect it in its movement, in its *ensemble*, and in its expression. In this way the youth will take courage and cognisance of his own powers, and improve.

One of the commonest faults with young scholars is their slothfulness in trying to discover for themselves their own way to express their ideas. For the most part, they are completely deficient in this, and prefer to seek among the works of their master, or of some other master, for their subjects, types, and movements—and thus, with little fatigue and less honour, they only succeed in giving a colourless reminiscence of works already known; and one of the faults of the master is this—not only to allow his scholars to imitate and steal from him, but what is worse, to desire to impose upon them his own works as models.

I return to my narrative. In my stable I pursued my artistic life freely and happily, with power to select the work I was to do, to carry out my own designs in whatever style I liked, and almost to fix their prices.

In this way, with only a half-day's work, I was able to carry home my ordinary earnings for the maintenance of my family; and beyond this, I had two francs over to pay my model for the remainder of the day, which I spent on my basso-relievo. My daily life, therefore, was gay and free in my stable, timorous and gloomy in the studio Cambi, and peaceful, glad, and quiet all the evening at home. But for all this, the bitterness had to come. The other competitor, Ludovico Caselli, was already hinting it about that the basso-relievo was not made by me. and that Professor Cambi worked upon it. Caselli was modelling under the direction of Professor Pampaloni; but I never complained that Pampaloni worked upon it, although there were some who affirmed that he did. I kept my peace, and resolved formally in my own mind that whatever should be the issue of this competition, I would again make an attempt the next year. When the time of the exhibition and the decision approached, I began to hear contemptuous and insolent rumours, which, whether I failed or was successful, would equally afflict me. To this is to be added, that my poor mother was suffering from a very severe illness—an illness, indeed, that carried her in a few days to her grave. I remember, as something that still pierces my heart, the interest she showed during that illness for me, for my competition, and for my triumph (as she called it); and it seemed as if this belief of my loving mother gave a certain alleviation to the terrible anguish of her disease, which every day grew worse and worse. This was in the first days of September 1840. On Sunday the 15th the decision was to be given, and my poor mother was at the point of death. . What I felt in my heart may be imagined, it cannot be told. The instant I heard that the prize had been given to me, I ran to my mother—from whom I had of late been somewhat separated—with almost a hope that this good news might bring her back to life again. And in fact, on hearing this news her face became radiant, her cheeks glowed, her eyes, which for a time had seen nothing, became animated and seemed to gaze at me. Then she stretched out her arms, and, pressing me to her, said, "Now I die willingly." She lived a few days longer, and then, comforted by the sacrament of our holy religion, died. She had finished her short life of about fifty years, in the restrictions of poverty and in the bitterness of one of the greatest misfortunes—blindness. God has taken her to the joy of His infinite mercy.

The conflict of judgment among the professors of the Academy at the competition was tempestuous, and the result extraordinary. The votes were divided thus : Ten votes were given for my model, four or five (if I mistake not) to that of my competitor, and there were eleven votes for a division of the prize. I thought that votes for a division could not properly be given ; and at all events, as I received ten and the other four, I considered myself the superior. But no. The legal adviser declared that the number eleven was superior to the number ten, and as eleven had voted for the division, that the prize must be divided. But the matter did not end here. My competitor, not satisfied with his prize, went about saying that it was not I who had competed ; that he did not know who I was, nor where I had studied ; and he threatened to challenge me to I know not what trial in design or modelling. I answered that I intended to continue to study, and that naturally we should be measured against each other often, if he chose to have it so ; and this put an end to it. More than this, we became friends, and still are ;

and I believe he is now employed in the foundry of
Cavaliere Pietro Bonini, as a designer or mechanic, I
don't well know which.   He is a man of talent, and has
made several works of sculpture, among which are
Hagar and Ishmael, Susannah, and the statue of Mas-
cagni which is under the Uffizi.

But in the opinion of the young students at that time
there still remained a doubt whether that work was all
grist from my mill, and in consequence I had a strong
desire to do something by myself in my own studio.   In
order to put an end to all this gossiping, I put up a figure
of life size representing a drunken and youthful Bacchante
leaning against the trunk of a tree as half falling, while
she smiled and held to her lips a goblet.   The difficulty
of the subject was as great as my inexperience.   The
tender age of the model, who could not be made to
stand still, the difficult and fatiguing attitude, my own
total want of practice in setting up the irons and clay,
the smallness of the room, and the deficiency of light,
were obstacles which conquered at last all my poor
capacity, and my figure fell, and I had not the courage
to put it up again ; and it was all the better that I did
not.

After this came new attacks, new gossip, and new
affronts, all carefully covered and veiled, and, as Giusti
says, " *Tramati in regola, alla sordina.*"

I have already spoken of the voting on the competition, and I may as well return to this here—for these
memoirs are not solely a meagre narrative of my life,
but also an examination of principles ; and whenever it
seems to me proper to make this examination, I shall do
so, endeavouring, as usual, to be brief and clear.

And first of all, you must believe that I do not return
to this decision to complain that the prize was divided

between me and my rival; and I wish you to understand
that even had the entire prize been adjudged to me, I
should equally have returned to this question. The
subject I mean to examine is the false principle of a
vote of division.

Whoever undertakes to judge of the comparative merit
of various works, ought, I think, to have sufficient critical
ability to distinguish minutely the smallest differences
between these works on various points—such as, for instance, their composition, character, proportion, movement, expression, refinement, historical accuracy in the
types and fashion of the dresses, truth, style, &c. &c. Now
it is absolutely impossible that in all these particulars two
works can be perfectly equal and of the same value ; and
the conclusion thus far is unavoidable, that the judge
who gives his vote for a division, either has not the
qualities required to discern these delicate differences, or
omits through culpable negligence to make such a rigor-
ous examination as is required to arrive at what is true
and just. Therefore the President should declare formally that the votes for a division will be null ; and as
their absence might invalidate the decision through a
consequent deficiency of votes, he should invite the
judges to declare for one or the other. I conclude (and
with this I shall finish my disquisition on this subject of
division of votes) that whoever feels inclined to give a
vote in this indeterminate way, either is, or thereby de-
clares himself to be, ignorant of the matter in regard
to which he is required to have knowledge and to give
judgment.

The youthful Bacchante fell down ; and, as I have said,
it was well that it did. This I say now; but then I
was much vexed, both on account of the accident itself,
and also for the unpleasant talk that it gave rise to.

But after all, things are what they really are, and not what
we think them to be. I was, however, consoled by a
commission—very small indeed, but it seemed to raise
my depressed spirits—and it was this, to make the four
" Cariatidi " of the Royal Box in the Rossini Theatre in
Leghorn. I should not have mentioned this humble
work did it not give me occasion to note one thing
which the young men of to-day seem to have forgotten.

It is common for the young sculptors of our day to
scorn and sneer at any work that is offered to them
which they think beneath that skill and capacity which
they suppose themselves to possess ; and they will not, as
they say, abase themselves to mere work in plaster. If
any one orders of them a bust or a statue in plaster,
their pretence is so excessive that they deem it an insult.
Now, I say the material counts for nothing; and a plaster
statue merely for decoration, well executed, is worth more
than a statue in marble or bronze which is ill executed.
Undoubtedly, if one could choose, he would reject the
statue in plaster and accept that in marble — always,
however, recognising that the one essential thing is, to
do his work well. But I was not given this choice, and
I accepted this humble commission, and executed it with
zealous love. There was this, too, of good in the commission—it might induce me to believe that I should
have made a far better statue had I been given more
time and more means to make one of my own selection ; and I said, " If I have been able to make these
statues in a month, with thirty or forty lire to pay to
my models, how much better I might do in five or six
months, with much more money ! " The question re-
duces itself, then, to time and money. Let the young
artist consider whether my reasoning is not just ; and let
him also consider what is more important—that if I

had not accepted this commission, I should not have come to the knowledge of the power that was in me, nor have gone through the reasoning which by strict logic induced me to make the " Abel."

This humble work was of great importance to me, and I recommend it to the attention of those young artists who consider themselves humiliated by small commissions. No ; do not let them be alarmed either by the subject or the material, and if they should receive an order even for a great *terra cotta* mask for a fountain, provided it be well made, they will acquire by it praise, and new and worthier orders, so long as their sole endeavour is to do their work well.

CHAPTER VI.

AN UNJUST LAW—THE "ABEL"—BRINA THE MODEL AND I IN DANGER OF BE-
ING ASPHYXIATED—MY FIRST REQUEST—BENVENUTI WISHES TO CHANGE
THE NAME OF MY ABEL FOR THAT OF ADONIS—I INVITE BARTOLINI TO
DECIDE ON THE NAME OF MY STATUE—BARTOLINI AT MY STUDIO—HIS
ADVICE AND CORRECTIONS ON THE ABEL—LORENZO BARTOLINI—GIUSEPPE
SABATELLI—EXHIBITION OF THE ABEL—IT IS SAID TO BE CAST FROM
LIFE—I ASK FOR A SMALL STUDIO, BUT DO NOT OBTAIN IT—MY SECOND
AND LAST REQUEST—THE PRESIDENT ANTONIO MONTALVO—I DON'T SUC-
CEED SOMEHOW IN DOING ANYTHING AS I SHOULD—I TALK OVER MAT-
TERS AT HOME—COUNT DEL BENINO A TRUE FRIEND AND TRUE BENE-
FACTOR—HIS GENEROUS ACTION.

HILE I was pondering a subject for a statue which should silence the idle and malevo-lent, it happened that a competition in sculpture was opened in Siena, in which no one could compete but those who were of that country and province. Naturally I determined to compete. The only other competitor was the young sculptor Enea Becheroni, a pupil of the Academy there. An-other wished to enter into the competition, and this was Giovanni Lusini, an accomplished sculptor who had lately returned from Rome, where he had been pensioned for four years, he having gained the prize at the quadrennial competition of our Academy at Flor-ence. But he was not allowed to come in; for although, like Becheroni and myself, he was a native of Siena, he

was inadmissible because he had passed the age decreed by the rules. This competition was called *Biringucci*, from the name of the worthy man who by his will had founded a prize and pension for sculpture, as well as others for painting, architecture, and various sciences that I do not remember. The studies and pensions established by him had been in existence for more than 300 years, and are still in existence, but, by one of those curious combinations that some would call a fatality, precisely in this very year, when it would have been most welcome to me, the prize for sculpture was struck out by one stroke of the pen.

I had 'already for some time prepared myself for this competition, which required that the artist should be shut up in a room by himself, and there should make, in the course of one day from morning till evening, a sketch in clay of some subject drawn by him by lot at the moment of entering the studio. For a considerable time I had made nothing but sketches; and within a space of time certainly not greater than that allowed by the competition, I had in fact made some dozen, and by practice I had become so rapid in composition, that whatever subject might be given me, I felt fully equipped, so as to be able to come out of the struggle with honour.

One day—it was Sunday—I was standing in my little studio in the Via del Palagio, and modelling one of these sketches, the subject of which was Elias carried away in the chariot. I was working with goodwill, and was happy and in the vein. My father had come to see me, and he was sitting and reading quietly the Bible. The bell rang, and a letter was given me bearing the post-mark of Siena, and I recognised the handwriting of the secretary of the competition, Signor Corsini. I

opened the letter, and read that the Government had
suppressed the pension for sculpture as being superfluous, and had disposed of the sum by appropriating
it to a chair at the University, and therefore the competition would not take place. I see, as if he were now
before me, my father start up suddenly and exclaim—
" Sagratino Moro Moraccio" (which is, literally, "Cursed
Moor of the Blackamoors "), "what have you done?"
With one blow of my fist I had smashed to pieces my
poor Elias, and he saw it on the ground between the legs
of the horse.
" Read," I said, giving him the letter.
Scarcely had he fixed his eyes on it, than he grew red,
stamped with his feet, and repeated his usual " Sagratino
Moro." I was at once aware that I had acted ill in giving way thus brutally to my irritation. This I have recounted out of love of the truth, and that those who
know me now may see how different I was then, and
how ludicrously that excitability of character which I
still feel, but which I have learned how to repress, was
exhibited in the tragic destruction of that poor sketch.
And this too was of advantage, just as the gossip and
incredulity about the first triennial was. The refusal to
give work was also of advantage, when I went seeking
about from studio to studio, and it was denied to me,
even in terms of scorn. It was all of advantage to me.
It obliged me to concentrate myself, and, seeing myself
rejected on all sides, to will and to know, and with God's
assistance to make my place with my own unassisted
powers. It was all right—thoroughly right; I repeat it.
Who can tell? The pension of Siena was for ten years.
May God pardon me, but I always feared that that pension might prove to me, as it had to others, a Capuan
idleness.

I began now to turn over in my mind a new subject which should be serious and sympathetic, and into which I could put my whole heart, strength, will, hopes, and all—and I found it. Among the pictures, bronzes, and *terre cotte* of Pacetti's shop, where I used often to wander about, I was struck by a group in *terra cotta* of a *pietà*. The figure of Christ specially seemed to me beautiful; and I had half a mind to make a dead Christ, and went about ruminating in my mind over the composition. Certainly a dead Christ would be, as it always is, a very sublime theme. But yet I was not satisfied. I wished to find a new subject; and as the Bible was familiar to me, the death of Abel suggested itself, and I seized upon it with settled purpose. I sought for a studio to shut myself up in with the model, and I found one in the Piazzetta of S. Simone, opposite the church. Then I put together a few *sous* to buy me two stands, one for the living model and one for the clay. Among the nude figures which I saw in the evenings when I went to draw, I selected the one that seemed to me best adapted to the subject, and I arranged with him to come to me every afternoon, as I was employed in wood-carving all the morning. I had already made several sketches, but I wished to make one from life, so as to be sure of a good movement and a true expression. It was on Shrove Thursday in 1842, and all the world who could and wished to do so, were walking about in the Corso. The model and I were shut up together in the studio, and it was nothing less than a miracle that that day was not the last of both of our lives. Poor Brina is still living, as old as I am, and he still stands as a model at our Academy.

And this is the way in which we ran the risk of losing our lives. In the studio which I had hired there

was no way of putting up a stove, except by carrying
the tube up through the upper floor, and so out through
the roof. The expense of doing this was large, and for
me very large; so I determined to make a sketch from
life, and from this to put up my clay, and I hoped
to be able to go on with the model without fire until
the warmer season came on. But these days were so
extremely cold that the model could not remain naked
even for a few minutes; and we determined to warm
the room with a pan of coals, in which apparently there
remained a residuum of the powdery dregs of charcoal.
The brazier having been lighted, and at intervals stirred
up, the room, which was small, was soon tolerably warm.
I was intent on modelling with my tool the outline and
planes of my sketch, and moving about the model to
assure myself of the movement and the *ensemble*, when
I felt an oppression on my head; but I attributed it to
the intensity of my labour, and on I went. Suddenly I
saw the model make a slight movement, and draw a
long deep sigh, and the eyes and the colour of his face
were like those of a dead man. I ran to help him, but
my legs would not hold me up. I half lost my senses,
my sight grew dim. I made an effort to open the door,
and fell to the ground. But I had strength enough
left to drag myself along to it, and kneeling, I laid hold
of the lock; but the handle would not move, and with
the left thumb I was obliged to raise the spring, and
with the right hand to draw the bolt, and to do it
quickly. I was wrestling with death, as I well knew,
and I redoubled my efforts with the determination not
to die. By good fortune, by my panting I drew in a
little breath of pure fresh air through the keyhole, and
at last I pulled back the bolt, and threw it wide open;
and there I sat drinking in full draughts of the outer

air. In the streets there was not a living soul, but I could hear the joyous shouts from the races in the Piazza or Santa Croce near by. Poor Brina gasped and rolled his eyes. The air which came blowing into the room revived him, but he could not rise. I had entirely recovered, except that I felt a tight band around my head. I ran to the nearest shop, got a little vinegar, mixed it with water, and dashed it over his face. We then extinguished the fire and went away.

I began to model the statue a few days after. My mornings up to one o'clock were employed in wood-carving, and all the afternoon I modelled. In this way I went on for some time, and the statue was fairly well advanced, but I required a little more money. The want of this made me rather doubtful whether I should be able to finish the model in time for the exhibition in September. I required thirty or forty *pauls* a-month for five months in order to go on until September. By the advice of Signor Antonio Sferra, a publisher of prints, I made a petition, to which Professor Cavaliere Pietro Benvenuti, Aristodemo Costoli, Giuseppe Sabatelli, and Emilio Santarelli were kind enough to append their names. This petition, which I now have under my eye, and which I copy literally, was as follows. It was not dictated or written by me. My friend Giuseppe Saltini, now Government Physician at Scrofiano, did me this favour :—

"ILLUSTRISSIMI SIGNORI, — The undersigned being desirous to submit to the judgment of the public a work of sculpture at the exhibition of the Academy of Fine Arts during the current year, has begun to model for his studio a figure, of life size, representing a Dying Abel. Family circumstances have, however, deprived him of the means which were required to bring this work to a conclusion. Regretting to find his money and labour spent thus far to no purpose, he refers himself to the philanthropy of his countrymen, in the hope that they will lend him their assistance. The sum required he has calculated at only forty francs a-month until the time of the said exhibition.

"He begs to inform all those persons who will kindly lend him their aid and honour him with a visit, that the statue which he has begun is at his studio, opposite the Church of S. Simone, where the undersigned will be glad to express to them his gratitude, and where the undersigned professors, in attestation of their goodwill, have not disdained to honour him with their approbation.—He subscribes himself as their most devoted and obliged servant,

"GIOVANNI DUPRÈ.

"STUDIO, 15th April 1842.

"CAV. PIETRO BENVENUTI.
ARISTODEMO COSTOLI.
GIUSEPPE SABATELLI.
EMILIO SANTARELLI."

The signatures of the subscribers were as follows :—

	Lire		
Maria Bargagli, widow of Rosselli del Turco	2	0	0
Antonio Sferra	4	0	0
N. N. will pay in all as above	4	0	0
E. Merlini	3	0	0
E. Ba.	3	6	8
M. M. will pay in all as above	2	6	8
G. C. pays at once	10	0	0
T. D. B. will pay up to September . . .	6	13	4

And thus I obtained 26 lire and 4 crazie a-month for five months, which were sufficient to enable me to finish the "Abel." From that time forward I have troubled nobody.

Thanks to the aid of those generous persons who assisted me, and whose names as I read them thrill me to the heart, I went on every day with my model, carefully copying him, and giving a proper expression. There was a moment when I hesitated as to the name I should give to my statue,—or I should rather say, that this hesitation was induced by the Cavaliere Pietro Benvenuti, who thought that, in consequence of the absence of any clear attributes to explain the subject, I should rather call it an Adonis. I had never been greatly impressed either by the name or story of Adonis, and I never had wished to join the devotees of Olympus; but my respect for this gentleman made me somewhat hesitate, and before going on further, as the difference of subject required a difference of character, expression, and style, I determined to ask the judgment of some one in whose decision I could in every way safely confide—and this person was Bartolini. With this view I went one morning to his house in Borgo Pinti, having already informed myself that the hour when he could receive me was between half-past five and six o'clock in the afternoon. I see him as if it were now. He was seated in his garden, with a cup of coffee, which he was slowly sipping when I approached him and said, "Signor Maestro, would you do me the favour to visit me at my studio, and give me your opinion on a statue that I am modelling?"

He answered: "You have called me *maestro*, and that is all right; but I do not know you: you are not one of my scholars at the Academy. Who is it, then, who supervises your statue, and who is your master?"

"I had some time ago some lessons from Magi and

Cambi, and I am not unknown to you, who had the kindness to praise a little statuette of mine in wood, the Santa Filomena. But I have asked neither Magi nor Cambi, nor any one else, to correct the statue that I am now making, and this for very good reasons."

Bartolini smiled at these words, and said to me, "To-morrow at six I will come to see you. Leave your name with the servants, and go in peace."

In the evening, when I went home, I said to my wife : "Listen. Call me early to-morrow morning, for before six I must be at my studio, as a Professor is coming to see my statue."

And she called me, poor dear—and called me in time. How it happened I know not, but I was late, and six o'clock was striking as I passed the Piazza di Sta Croce. When I arrived at my studio, I found in the hole of the door-lock the card of Bartolini, on which he had written in pencil—"Six o'clock in the morning." I ran immediately to his studio in the Porta San Frediano to make my excuses, and to inform him that I had been but a moment late. His carriage was still at his door. He had not taken off his coat, and he was correcting with his pencil a statue, so that the workman might see as soon as he arrived where he should work. As soon as he saw me, and before I had begun to exculpate myself, he said, "Never mind; there is no harm done. I will come again to-morrow. *Addio!*"

It is scarcely necessary for me to say that the next morning I was at my studio by five o'clock, and at six Bartolini knocked. He came in, looked at the statue, scowling, and pronouncing one of his oaths, which I will not repeat. I begged him to tell me where I was wrong, and how I could make it better. He asked me what was the subject, and I told him that I intended it for a

G

Dying Abel. I then showed him the sketch, upon which was the goat-skin that as yet I had not put on the large model, in order first to study carefully the nude underneath. And then I told him the objection that Benvenuti had made, and his proposal to change the subject. Bartolini answered, "You will do the best possible thing not to change it, for, as far as regards the clear indication of the theme, nothing more could be done. Besides, the goat-skin, which immediately denotes a shepherd, the wound on the head, and the expression of gentleness, explain that it is Abel. Now, I will give you a little counsel as to the unity of expression, to which you must carefully attend. The face, you see, is gentle, and is that of a just man who pardons as he dies. The limbs also correspond to this sentiment. There is only one discord, and that is in the left hand. Why have you closed it, while the right hand is open, and just as it should be?"

"I closed it," I answered, "in order to give variety."

"Variety," said the master, "is good when it does not contradict unity. You will do well to open it like the other,—and I have nothing else to say."

This comforted me, but wishing to draw from him something more, in an exacting tone I said, "And as to the imitation, the character, the form?"

"The imitation, the character, and the form of this statue show that you are not of the Academy."

Other words he also added, which it is not proper for me to report. As to the feet, he only made a movement with his thumb, and I said, "I understand."

He looked at me, and added, "All the better for you if you have understood."

This ended all the correction of my statue made by this singular man. It was the first and the last.

Bartolini was disdainful and unprejudiced, and called
things by their real name; and if any one seemed to
him an ass, he called him an ass, though he might be
senator or minister. He knew that he was a great sculptor, and liked to be so recognised by all. He was often
epigrammatic, and to his pungency he frequently added indecency,—liberal and charitable, jealous of the
decorum and education of his family, an admirer of the
code of Leopold, Frederic the Great, Napoleon the
Great, and the principles of Eighty-nine. He liked to
be called master, and detested to be called professor.
He ridiculed all decorations, but what he had he wore
constantly. As a sculptor he was very great. His example was better than his teaching. He restored the
school of sculpture by bringing it back to the sound
principles of truth. His enemies were numerous and
very provoking, but he took no pains to conciliate them.
When he was irritated, he struck about him right and
left, lashing out fiercely, and laughing.

I went on and finished my statue, shutting out everybody except my dearest friends, among whom was Professor Giuseppe Sabatelli, who, after seeing my work and
signing my petition for assistance, took a liking to me.
And every morning, with a knock which we had agreed
upon, he came to my studio to sit for a while, before
going, as usual, to paint the *cupoletta* of the Chapel of
the Madonna in the Church of San Firenze. He used
at once to sit down and say—"I am not ill, but I am
tired." He was thin and pale, and his black moustaches
made his gentle and quiet face look even paler. Only
few and kindly words came from his lips. As a companion, he was mild and pleasant. His memory comes
over me sadly, and seems like the remembrance of something dear which has been mislaid, but not lost.   ·

By the first days of September I finished the Abel;
and the caster Lelli, who was then also a beginner,
undertook the casting, and gave his service in the most
friendly way, so that the expense should be as small as
possible. All my friends, indeed, came forward to aid
me in making the mould and casting, and removing the
outer mould, with that brotherly love that I still recall
with emotion. They are still living : Ferdinand Folchi
the painter, who served me as model for the hands;
Ulisse Giusti, the carver; Bartolommeo Bianciardi,
Paolo Fanfani, and Michele Poggi, all carvers. They
came to help me to raise and turn over the mould, or to
give me any other assistance. Folchi and Sanesi assisted
me in taking off the waste mould; and, in a word, all
were eager to see my work finished and put on exhibition.
Bartolini told me to select the place at the Academy that
I thought best; and that if I found any opposition, as no
one but the professors had any right to make the choice
of place, to come to him there in the school, and he
would arrange it for me.   I had no occasion to avail
myself of this frank and kind offer, for no sooner had
Benvenuti seen me and the statue than he said, "Select
the place and the light that you prefer."

As soon as the exhibition was opened there was a
crowd about my statue. Its truth to nature, its appro-
priateness of expression, and the novelty and sympathetic
character of the subject, made a great impression, and
every day the crowd about the statue increased. But
little by little it began to be whispered about, first in undertones, and then more openly and authoritatively, that
the statue was worth nothing, because it was not really
a work of art, but merely a cast from life; that I had
wished to take in the Academy, masters, scholars, and
the public; and that such a living piece of work thus

introduced as if it were a work of art, while in point of fact it was a mere cast from life, ought at once to be expelled from the public exhibition. And this scandalous talk, which was as absurd as malign, originated among the artists, and especially among the sculptors. It was pushed to such a point, that in order to make the fraud clear, they obliged the model, Antonio Petrai, to undress, and laying him down in the same position as the statue, they proceeded with compasses and strips of paper to take all the measures of his body in length and breadth. Naturally they did not agree in a single measure; for, without intending·it or thinking about it, I had made my statue four fingers taller and two fingers narrower across the back. This beautiful experiment was made in the evening; and the President of the Academy, who by chance surprised them in the very act, reprimanded all severely, not heeding whether among them there were professors.

But none the less this malignant and ridiculous accusation was still kept up, and nothing was said of the failure of the attempted proof. The model himself, who persisted in affirming that the statue was modelled and not cast, was openly jeered; and one person went so far as to tell him, that for a bottle of wine he could be made to say anything. But the person who thus insulted Petrai had better have let him alone, for Tonino—who, poor man, though now old, would still hold his own perhaps—added certain arguments to his words which no one dared to resist.

Signor Presidente Montalvo was quite right in expressing his disapproval of this dirty and impertinent examination, which was made without giving notice to the President and Director of the Academy; but, besides this, he felt all the more inclined to assume my defence on account of a little debt of conscience that he had towards me, and that he wished to pay off.

One day, before resolving to take a studio on lease, I made up my mind to petition the Grand Duke to give me one gratis. The Government had then at its disposition several small studios, which were given away, without rent and for an indefinite time, to those young men who either in painting or sculpture gave good promise not only of aptitude, but also of goodwill and proper conduct. As I did not think myself wanting in all these qualities, and specially the last two, I determined to make an application, driven to it indeed by necessity. But before presenting my petition I wished to inform the President of it, and to beg that he would be so kind as to lend me his support, as I well knew that petitions of this nature were always passed on to him for due information.

Montalvo was a perfect gentleman, and of an ancient and wealthy family, instructed in the history of art, a great admirer of it, and a very good friend of all artists, especially of those who to their artistic skill added an outward practice of religious duties, to which he was a devotee—though, as far as sentiment, enthusiasm, and real taste for art go, he was not distinguished.

Accordingly, I went one morning to pay him a visit at his rooms in the gallery of the Uffizi—he being also a Director of the Royal Gallery. I must here premise that I was not much in his good graces, because I had not studied at the Academy, which he believed to be the true nursery of an artist. As soon as he saw me, suspecting perhaps what I had come to ask, he said to me—

"And what do you want?"

"I come, Signor President, to say to you that I have made a petition to his Royal Highness the Grand Duke in the hope of obtaining a studio to make a model of a statue that I wish to exhibit this year in the Academy. My means are narrow, because I have a family; and before presenting this petition to the Sovereign, I have thought it my duty to inform you, and at the same time to beg your aid, and to use your influence that it may be answered favourably."

He answered, "You are not a pupil of the Academy, and therefore you have no right to ask for a studio, which the grace of the Sovereign grants only to those who have completed their studies in our Academy of Fine Arts."

"If I have not studied," I answered, "at the Academy, I have competed there, and gained the triennial prize, which is the end of the studies at the Academy."

The good Signor replied with impatience, "Which, then, do you think that you are, Canova or Thorwaldsen?"

"God save us, Signor President, I never thought this! But it may be permitted to me to observe, that even Canova and Thorwaldsen began from small beginnings, and were not born at once great sculptors, as Minerva sprung from the head of Jove."

You see that I really had no luck this morning; for the Director, rising, said to me, "Ah, then, as you argue in this way, I will tell you that, if the petition is referred to me for information, you shall have nothing," and then reseated himself.

I made my bow, and went out. But when I was outside, and wished to put on my hat, I found it was completely crushed: without being aware of it, I had reduced it to this state. So much the better. You lose as far as your hat is concerned, but you gain in character; and I counsel all young men who find themselves in a similar situation to take the same course.

But for all this, I repeat, Cavaliere Ramirez di Montalvo was a good and excellent man; but everything irritated him which seemed to him in the least to run off the rails. In his view, a youth who had not come out of the wine-press of the Academy could have little good in him, and he looked upon him as being a schismatic or excommunicated person. The Academy was to him the baptism of an artist, and outside of it he saw neither health nor salvation. I fell under him, and he crushed me. *Parce sepulto.*

But he was soon obliged to go back on this academic puritanism. His friend Cavaliere Pietro Benvenuti spoke to him in praise of this germ which was budding forth outside the privileged garden; and he soon began to regret having treated me with a *nonchalance* more appropriate for a pasha than a Christian. I believe this—and more, I am sure of it; for having gone one day to invite him to come and see a statue which I was modelling, he received me with singular kindness. It was as if he had never seen me before, much less had spoken to me so severely only a few months before, when I urged him to look with favour on my petition for a studio. I was moved to invite him, not only because by nature I am not tenacious in my resentments, but because I knew that he desired to see me—perhaps because he regretted not having been able to further my request. In a word, I went to see him, and found him most kindly disposed, as I have said; and he accepted my invitation, and came to call upon me at my studio in San Simone, where I modelled my Abel.

I have said that Cavaliere Montalvo was rather deficient in his sentiment and taste for art, but he liked the contrary to be thought of him. He was not indeed entirely without a certain discernment, and he had enough to enable him to distinguish an absolutely bad thing from an absolutely good thing. He was, in a word, a connoisseur in a general way ; but his dignity as Director of the Royal Galleries, and even more as President of the Academy of Fine Arts, required him to conscientiously believe himself a connoisseur with refined taste. What I was then ignorant of in this respect I now clearly know, but I had a suspicion of this from the manner in which he looked at my statue, and by his expressions of praise, which were interlarded with commonplaces which he had learned from the stale formulas of the Academy. And in order that I should not imagine that he had found everything as it should be in the statue, he wished to point out some defect, and what he discovered was this, that the left ear seemed a little too far back, by which the jaw was enlarged beyond what it should be.

I have promised from the beginning to tell the truth, and I will tell it, with the help of God, even to the end. I must here confess that I acted like a hypocrite. Instead of answering, " It does not seem so to me, but I will measure it to assure myself," I told him that he was right, and I was much obliged to him ; and ·more, when he favoured me with a second visit, I said to him as soon as he came in—

" Look at the ear."

" Have you compared it with the model ? "

" Yes."

" Have you moved it a little more forward ? "

" Eh ? what do you think ? "

" Ah ! now it is right."

When I think of this, now that I am old, it seems to me a very bad thing, a most vile lie, under which (may God pardon me !) was· concealed perhaps a secret sentiment of vengeance ; and yet that lie made him a friend to me, and so he remained as long as he lived. But thenceforward I have always guarded myself from lying, and above all, from making game of any one who trusted me.

I return to the event of the exhibition. My name was on the lips of all; some praised me to the skies, some despised me as the most vulgar of impostors. Bartolini, Pampaloni, and Santarelli openly assumed my defence. The Grand Duke asked Giuseppe Sabatelli about it, and he assured him that the statue was really modelled, and not cast from life, and that he had been an eyewitness of my work, staying in my studio every morning, and had seen me working at it. I was exposed to a tempest of words and looks diametrically opposed to each other. The meaning of the two parties might be rendered by precisely these words, "great artist," "miserable impostor." My poor wife consoled me by saying—

"Do not be troubled, do not listen to them. They are irritated because you have done better than they. They will talk and talk, and at last they will hold their peace."

"Yes, my dear Marina, they will hold their peace; but in the meantime, what an injury they have done me! A certain person perhaps would have given me an order for the statue, as I know; but after all this absurd and evil-minded chattering, he mistrusts me, and will now do nothing, and I am crushed and overcome by the very thing which ought to have given me reputation and cleared my path for me. In the same way that I have made this statue, I know that I can make another. The will to do it is not wanting, but how can I bear the expense. My earnings, as I well see, are not sufficient to support the family, and to pay the model, the rent of the studio and the casting, and to buy what is necessary

for the studio. Besides, I tell you, dearest, that I cannot
allow you to fatigue yourself with so much work. You
labour all day and all the evening, you have a baby to
nurse, you get little repose at night, and do you think
that I can allow you thus to wear your strength out? I
hoped to enable you to get some rest, and to lead an
easier life, and I thought that I saw before us, after I
had breathed the last breath of life into Abel, the beginning of our intellectual and loving life ; and now I find
that these are and were only vain hopes."

"Do not be troubled, Nanni," said that blessed
woman, and she said nothing more, only her eyes were
swimming with tears.

. In the meantime, without knowing it, I had a friend,
in truth a real friend and benefactor, in Count F. del
Benino. Count Benino was an old man of noble and
ancient family, and a bachelor, who lived in his own
palace in the Borgognissanti, and in precisely that on
the Lung' Arno which was designed by the able architect
and engineer Professor Commendatore Giuseppe Poggi.
Count Benino had taken a liking to me when I was a
little boy in Sani's shop. He was a great and very intelligent lover of the Fine Arts, and everything relating to
them, and was extremely interested that his house should
be a model of good taste, from the modest furniture of
the entrance-hall up to his own private cabinet, which
was a wonder to behold. The walls were surrounded by
bookcases of solid mahogany, his study desk was also of
mahogany ; the chairs were covered with polished leather,
and the floors were of inlaid wood and polished with
wax. The books on the shelves were bound simply in
leather in the English style. Upon his desk, among
his books and papers, were various objects of great
value—as, for instance, an antique bronze inkstand orna-

mented with figures and arabesques, ivory paper-cutters with richly carved handles, portraits in miniature of persons dear to him, and little busts in bronze and figures in ivory set on the cases of the desk, which were divided into compartments to hold his papers.   In person he was tall and erect, thin, and with full colour, blue eyes, and perfectly white hair.   He spoke with invariable urbanity and facility, not infrequently with pungency, but always with proper restraint.   He dressed very carefully, and he liked the conversation and sought the friendship of artists.   From the time when I was a youth in Sani's shop and worked for him as a wood-carver, and afterwards while I was working by myself in the Borghese stable, up to the time when I was making the Abel, when he was one of the subscribers to my petition for assistance, and indeed the largest of them, he never lost sight of me, but often came to pay me a visit while I was modelling Abel, and showed himself delighted with it, and sure of my future ; and now, perceiving this scandalous plot to put me down, he was indignant.   He came to seek me out just at the moment when I was thoroughly discouraged and knew not to what saint to recommend myself, and after saluting me with his customary " Sor Giovanni, che fa ? " (" How are you, Mr Giovanni ? "), seated himself on the only seat I possessed, and seeing that I was oppressed with thought, though I endeavoured to put a gay face on it, said to me—

" Oh, don't give up !   Courage !   Don't you hear how these donkeys bray ?   What they want is a good cudgel and a hearty beating.   Don't think about it.   I know what I am talking about.   I frequent the studios, and I see and feel what a disloyal and foolish war they are waging.   But do not give them time.   You must ward off the blow and give them two back. In one studio I heard a fellow, whom I will not stop to name (but names are of little importance)—I heard a fellow, who, with a contemptuous laugh, said, 'The Abel he could cast, because the figure is lying down, but a standing figure he cannot cast. He will not make one this year, nor any other year.' And all the others laughed. This happened only a few moments ago, and I have come now to tell you that it is your duty to silence these snarling curs. So, deàr Sor Giovanni, you must make another statue, and this time a standing figure ; and . . . now be silent a moment. I imagine very well what you will say. I understand it all, and I say to you, Quit this studio, which is not fit to make a standing figure in, and go and look for another at once. Order the stands which you require, think out your statue, and I will pay whatever sum is necessary. You know where I live ; come there, and you will find a register on which you must write down the sum that you need, and put your signature to it ; and when you have orders and work to do, which will not fail to come, and have a surplus of money, you may pay me back the money that I advance. Say nothing. I do not wish to be thanked, —first of all, because I am not making you a present, and then because I have my own satisfaction out of the proposition I make to you. What I want is to laugh in the face of these rascals who are now deriding you, and me too, because I assert that I have seen you at your work. So you see that I, too, am an interested party. Without spending a penny, we have an advantage, which, with all my money, I could not otherwise get. And now, dear Sor Giovanni, *a rivederla*. I shall expect you, to give you the money you need. Lose no time, keep up your spirits, and think of me as your very sincere friend.

CHAPTER VII.

THE GRAND DUCHESS MARIA OF RUSSIA AND THE COMMISSION FOR THE CAIN
AND ABEL—THE PRINCE OF LEUCHTENBERG AND A PLATE OF CAVIALE AT
CAFFÈ DONEY—AN UNUSUAL AMUSEMENT THAT DID SOME GOOD—AGAIN
THE GENEROSITY OF COUNT DEL BENINO—BARTOLINI'S HUNCHBACK, AND
IN CONSEQUENCE A RETURN TO THE ABEL—BARTOLINI GETS ANGRY WITH
ME—EXAMINATION OF THE MATERIALISTIC OR REALISTIC IN ART—EFFECTS
OF THE REALISTIC—DO NOT HAVE GIRLS ALONE BY THEMSELVES FOR MODELS
—SUBSCRIPTION GOT UP BY THE SIENESE TO HAVE MY ABEL EXECUTED IN
MARBLE—A NEW WAY OF CURING A COUGH—SIGNORA LETIZIA'S RECEIPT,
WHO SENT IT AND PAID FOR IT HERSELF—ONE MUST NEVER OFFER WORKS
GRATIS, FOR THEY ARE NOT ACCEPTED—THE GRAND DUCHESS MARIE AN-
TOINETTA ORDERS THE "GIOTTO" FOR THE UFFIZI—HAS ABEL KILLED
CAIN?—STATUE OF PIUS II.—A FOOLISH OPINION AND IMPERTINENT ANSWER
—I DEFY THE LAW THAT PROHIBITS EATING.

 RAN home with all speed, elated and full of
enthusiasm, to tell my wife of the charming
proposal of Count Benino. My wife, poor
soul, could not understand all this delight,
this vehemence and excitement, in praise of that kind gentleman; and without saying it, she made me understand
that she should have greatly preferred my continuing as
a wood-carver, without troubling myself about an art
which hitherto had only given me disappointment and
worry. With her eyes she seemed to say to me, "Don't
bother yourself, Nanni, about it."

I looked about to find a studio, and took one in the
Niccolini buildings in Via Tedesca, now Via Nazionale.

I ordered two large modelling-stands—one for the living
model, the other for the statue in clay. "A standing
statue he will not make," they said; but I will make it,
and in movement too. The idea of Cain came at once
into my head. Cain, the first homicide, fratricide! A
fierce and tremendous subject, and one of great difficulty.
I made the sketch, and it seemed to me that I had
divined the movement and expression. Among the
artists, it was soon known that I had taken a new studio
to make another statue. Those who had laughed at first,
laughed no longer. My friends encouraged me, and
added fuel to the fire. I had also some offers for the Abel
—insufficient if you will, but enough to encourage me.
Among the others I accepted that of Signor Lorenzo Mariotti, an agent of the Russian Government, who lived in
his own house in the Piazza Pitti. He came to see me,
and said that he should like to order the statue of Abel,
whenever I would make it, for what it cost me, and when
it was done he would help me to sell it. The expenses
were calculated at 800 *scudi;* and he offered me this
price, with the understanding that whatever sum it was
sold for above the 800 *scudi,* should be divided between us.

The marble was procured, and I was already modelling with ardour the statue of Cain. Fortunately the
Grand Duchess Maria of Russia, daughter of the Emperor Nicholas, was passing through Florence. She had
already heard the discussion, *pro* and *con,* which this
statue had raised. She wished to see it, and was so well
pleased by it that she did not conceal her delight. She
was in company with her husband, the Prince of Leuchtenberg. They went into my private studio and saw the
Cain, only just begun. She exchanged some words with
the Prince, and he was much pleased, and embraced me.

Then the Grand Duchess, pressing my hand, said, "The Abel and the Cain are mine." Then they departed. When I went home and told the good news to my wife, it seemed as if she had a little more faith in what I was so convinced of—viz., my future career as an artist.

For the rest of the time that the august Prince and Princess were in Florence, he never omitted to pass some half-hours of the morning in my studio, because he liked so much to see me at work. He spoke Italian extremely well, and it amused him to talk with my model Antonio Petrai on various subjects ; and as he was such a strong and well-made fellow, one day he asked him if he would like to measure his strength at fisticuffs with any one ; and Petrai —who knew well enough who it was who asked the question, and was embarrassed about making a proper reply— after much hesitation could only say "Aho !" upon which the Prince laughed heartily and gave him something.

Who would have thought that such a handsome youth, so tall, squarely built, and so spirited, would have died only a few years later of an insidious disease? He was the son of Prince Beauharnais, Viceroy of Italy in the troublous times of Napoleon I. One day he came and carried me away from the studio, because he wished to see with me the statues which ornament our Piazza della Signoria and the Loggia of Orsanmichele ; but first he would go to Doney's to breakfast. As soon as we were seated, he ordered *caviale*. "*Caviale!*" answered the waiter, "we have none." "Bring *caviale*," said the Prince, sharply; but before the servant could reply he made a sign to the master, who was at the desk, and he knocked loudly on the marble to call the waiter back. After a little while a magnificent plate of *caviale* was served. I wish to note this anecdote, as it depicts the courteousness, affability, and popularity of this Prince,

who, though he had married the daughter of the Emperor
of Russia, had not forgotten that he was born and educated in Italy.

In the meantime, Mariotti, by order of the Grand
Duchess, made the contract for the two statues, Cain and
Abel, and the price fixed for the Abel was 1500 *scudi*, and
for the Cain 2000 *scudi*. The contract which I had made
with Mariotti was torn up, and I gave him out of my first
receipts the sum he had given me; but as to the remainder, the 700 *scudi*, which was to be divided between us, he
would not receive it, saying that the Grand Duchess
had already paid him enough. And this, for Mariotti,
whom they call *mangia-russi*, was a good action.

In the meantime the good Count del Benino lent me
a considerable sum of money to pay the rent of my studio,
for the modelling stands and tools, and for the models,
as also the daily sum I carried home for household expenses. This was all registered in a book, with the sums,
the dates, and my name signed in receipt. And all this
together came to the amount of about 100 *scudi*.

Now that I had two good commissions, and the relative
advances on them, I went to Palazzo del Benino, this time
to pay rather than receive, and therefore with lighter and
freer spirit. I was anxious to cancel this debt, which
weighed upon my mind like an incubus, which I had felt
was increased and renewed every time I was forced by
necessity to ask for more money; and poor Del Benino,
who perceived my reluctance, encouraged me, and made
me feel that it was indifferent to him whether he gave
more or less, trying to distract me while he counted out
the money. But this time, as I have said, I was gay and
light-hearted, and caused my name to be announced by
the servant in a loud voice: in short, I was in bearing
and in words slightly proud.

H

The Count was seated writing in his usual place. He put down his pen, and staring at me with his blue eyes, said, "Sor Giovanni, welcome! I am delighted to see you. What charming thing have you to tell me? Yes, what can you tell me that I do not already know? To begin, then, I congratulate you truly—truly. You see, this is for me a new satisfaction : you cannot imagine the pleasure I feel in now seeing certain faces cloudy and sad which a few months ago were bursting with laughter. And I divert myself very much playing the ignoramus with them, saying, ' Then it appears that this youth is going straight ahead, *per Bacco !* The Abel! that stands for what it is—I mean to say, that if the artist has cast it from life, as you say, the Grand Duchess Maria has caught a fine crab; but the Cain! that is scarcely begun, and they tell me that she has seen it only in the clay, and liked it, and given the order for it, and other like things ; for the desire to torment them does not fail me, and they were much teased and molested by my bitter words, which I pretended not to mean and ran on. So I have diverted myself, and so I will divert myself. Now, then, again I congratulate you. And now tell me if I can do anything for you. I am at your service."

"Signor Conte, I have come to repay the money which you have lent me, with so much generosity and kindness, to enable me to make my new model of Cain, which, God be thanked, has so much pleased the Grand Duchess. If I had not already begun this, she could not have seen it ; and who knows if she would have taken the risk to order even the Abel? I feel, but cannot express all the importance of your valuable aid. This aid, so timely, has been for me a second life, without which, who knows what would have become of me, discouraged, despised, and probably deserted by those who now cry out, ' Beautiful,

beautiful!' Here am I, then, to thank you cordially, and
to return the money I have borrowed." While I was speaking the Count gradually lost that gay and lively expression which was habitual to him, and at my last words
looked at me with an expression of seriousness and
regret that I knew not how to interpret. Then he
said—

"There is time enough for this; don't be in such a
hurry. This is only the beginning; a thousand things may
occur, and it will do you no harm to have a little money
in the house. On the contrary, it may be convenient.
Now think of study and your reputation; and to pay
your debt to me there is time enough."

"Listen, Signor Conte: I have come here on purpose,
and have brought the money. I do not need it for the
present. Let me pay this material debt; that other great
moral substantial debt, the infinite good you have done
me, I can never repay, and never should wish to." The
Count grew even more earnest and serious. He held the
paper of our accounts mechanically in his hand, and tried
to prove to me that there was time enough, and that I
should keep the money; but seeing that I insisted, and
held out my hand for the papers to see the sum due,
drew it back with vivacity, and with flashing eyes said
to me—

"Oh, leave me, dear Sor Giovanni, this satisfaction."

He tore up the paper and threw it in the basket. I
was mortified, and had half a mind to be offended, but
the kind expressions of this excellent man prevailed.
He took my hand and pressed it between his, saying—

"Don't take it amiss, but leave me the consolation
that I have been able to assist, even in the least degree,
in the sale of your work—as you say, opened for you a
future which I hope may prove full of honours. And

moreover, you must know that it has always been my
firm intention to assist you until the road was open and
easy before you.   I did not at once open my mind to
you, because then, perhaps, you would not have accepted the offer; therefore I said, you will sign the contract,—and in good time you will pay.   Now you have
really paid me, because that small sum of money has
secured your future and given me a great satisfaction."

It is necessary now for me to touch upon a question
vital to art, and which was being agitated just at the
time I was modelling the Abel.   This work served to
inflame it, and to encourage as much one side as the
other—that is, either the idealists or the academicians in
opposition to Bartolini, who, while he was not naturalistic in the strict sense of the word, proposed to in-
troduce this principle into his teaching by bold inno-
vations.   It is necessary for me to speak of this, inasmuch as this dispute and my statue served as the tar-
get for the shots of one as well as the other parties,
and had the effect of estranging Bartolini from me—
although, as we shall see later, it was another and less
justifiable cause that made the great sculptor indignant
with me.

When Stefano Ricci, Master of Sculpture in the Royal
Academy, died, it was wisely decided to call Lorenzo
Bartolini to his place (this was a little before I modelled
the Abel), and Bartolini took possession of the school
with the air of a conqueror.   Various were the causes
for his extremely overbearing conduct.   First, the opposition his demands encountered on the part of the President and others of the Academy; then his before-men-
tioned principles of reform, diametrically opposed to
those now taught in the school; also, finally, the heated
political and religious opinions, which were discussed

with little charity on either side. He altered everything, theories and systems. The position of his assistant, Professor Costoli, was unpleasant; but he was obliged to remain. He prohibited all study from statues, and restricted the whole system of teaching to an imitation only of nature; and he pushed this principle so far, that he introduced a hunchback into the school and made the young students copy him. This daring novelty raised a shout of indignation : they cried out against the profanation of the school, of the sacred principles of the beautiful, &c. ; said that he was ignorant of his duties as master, and that he misled the youths, extinguishing in them the love of the beautiful by the study of deformity; and many other accusations of this agreeable sort, in a freer and more pointed style than mine.

Neither was Bartolini the man to allow this deluge to fall upon his head, which, together with much that was true, carried with it a torrent of errors and unreasonable absurdities. As he understood well the clever use of the pen, he launched forth certain articles so stinging and cutting that they were delightful. The Abbé Chiari and the Abbé Vicini were treated by old Baretti with distinction as compared with the treatment Bartolini gave the Anonymous Society of the Via del Cocomero. I recollect one of the foolish arguments raised by his detractors against Bartolini, which was so ingenuous that it showed in its author more emptiness and smallness of mind than cleverness or bad faith. This is what he said : " The expert gardener, by means of his art, transforms a forest which is rough and horrid, as nature made it, into a beautiful grove, by rooting out plants, opening alleys, pruning into a straight line the projecting branches," &c. How much this comparison of the grove to the human figure diverted Bartolini is

not to be told.   I have not before me his sharp stinging
words, and I do not wish to spoil them by repeating
them from memory, but to me he appeared to be as
pleasant and brilliant a writer as he was admirable as
an artist.

This dispute was rekindled, as I have said, on the
appearance of my Abel.   I do not remember by which
side was first pronounced my name and my work, but
certain it is that Bartolini said that the most convincing
proof of the excellence of his method was "precisely the
Abel," which statue was made by a youth who knew
nothing of Phidias or Alcamenes, nor of the others—who
had not breathed the stifling air of the Academy—that he
had trusted himself to beautiful nature, and that he had
copied her with fidelity and love.   After this there was
fresh sarcasm against him and his system of copying
nature, even when deformed, &c.   Added to this, there
were long-winded eulogies on my work, and I could see
that these were advanced merely to put this man in bad
humour.

He had taken a dislike to me, and wished to tell
me so.   He sent his father-in-law, Dr Costantino Boni,
to summon me.   I went, and when I arrived he received
me in the great ante-room, and said to me, with his usual
striking bluntness, " I have sent for you to tell you that
I do not wish to see you again."   How astounded I was
by these words you can imagine who know the veneration
and affection I had always felt for this celebrated master;
and I could only reply—" Why ? "

" Why !   You have no more need of me, nor I of you ;
stay in your own studio, and don't come any more to
mine."

It appeared to me so strange, not to say unreasonable,
that he should send for me to tell me not to come to

him, that I could not do less than reply that I had come to his studio because he had sent for me, and that I was very sorry to be forbidden to return, as I always wished to learn.

" No matter," replied he ; "you understand—each one for himself," and this he said in French. Because you must know, that when he was excited he preferred that language either for speaking or writing.

Notwithstanding this, the next year, as I wished for a reconciliation,—having made the model in clay of the Giotto, which I wanted to try in the niche of the Uffizi, to hear the opinion of my friends about it, and to correct it where it was necessary, before its execution in marble, —I wrote to Bartolini begging him to come to see my statue in its place to give me his authoritative opinion. He replied in a manner specially his own—I might almost say with his own brutal sincerity,—that which distinguished him from his sugared and often hypo- critical contemporaries. He could not deceive; he held me in aversion, and he wished me to know it, not by his silence, but by a letter. Here it is : " Dearest, the thing which above all things I like in this world is to see the races in the Cascine; but as I have so much work which prevents me, just imagine if I shall come to see your statue ?"

Observe, I do not say that I expected precisely such a reply, and I was a little stung by it; but I understood him, and really liked it better than if he had made an excuse and told a lie. All men should be true to them- selves. Bartolini was still angry with me, as I found out afterwards, because, in the discussion about the hunch- back, my name being brought forward, I did not enter into its defence. In fact, if a similar discussion were now to arise on this subject, it would seem to me

cowardly to draw back and not clear up a point of
controversy of the greatest importance; but then, being
young and a beginner, how could I presume to offer my
support to Bartolini? Would it not appear pretentious
in me even to assume to be the defender of so great a
master? It seemed to me so then, and it seems so now.
Let it not be thought that I did not do this while arguing with my artist friends; it was quite otherwise, and
this was the way in which I drew upon myself their ill
feeling and dislike. And the defence of the Bartolini
system which I then made was in a much more absolute
sense than that which I now make; for while I see that
Bartolini was right in carrying back art to its first source
—that is (and we should thank him for that), to the imitation of nature—he went beyond bounds in proposing a deformed person as a model. It is very true that Bartolini
never affirmed, as his enemies assert, that a hunchback
was beautiful. He said that it was as difficult to copy
a hunchback well as a well-formed person, and that a
youth ought to copy as faithfully the one as the other;
and when the eye had been educated to discover the
most minute differences in the infinite variety of nature,
and the hand able to portray them, then, but only then,
was the time to speak, and select from nature the most
perfect, which others called the *bello ideale*, and he the
bello naturale. But that blessed hunchback still remains,
who, in the strict sense of the word, is not the real
truth; for in what is deformed there is something deficient, which removes it from the truth, however natural
it may be. It is a defect in nature, and therefore not
true to nature.

But it happened then as it happens always: the
reform of Bartolini and the dogmas of the academicians
never came to an end. They might have confined

themselves to the indisputable principle that one should imitate life in its infinite scale of variety, avoiding always deformity. But once they had begun with the meagre child, the adipose old man, the lean or flabby youth, they went on through thick and thin. It would not have been so bad had they really appreciated what Bartolini meant to say, and that is, that *copying* anything was very well as a mere exercise and *means* of learning one's art—or, to use his expression, of "holding the reins of art"; but the misfortune was, that some took the means for the end, and so went wrong.

But nevertheless, this Bartolinian reform was of great advantage. Let us remember how sculpture was then studied. The teaching of Ricci was only a long and tedious exercise of copying wholesale the antique statues, good and bad ; and what was worse, the criterion of Greek art was carried into the study of nude life—the characteristic forms of the antique statues supplanting those of the living model. The outlines were added to and cut away with a calm superiority, which was even comical. The abdominal muscles were widened, the base of the pelvis narrowed, in order to give strength and elegance to the figure. The model was never copied ; the head was kept smaller, and the neck fuller, so that, although the general effect was more slender and more robust, the character was falsified, and was always the same, and always conventional. This restriction of nature to a single type led directly to conventionality ; and once this direction was taken, and this habit of working from memory, following always a pre-established type, the artist gradually disregarded the beautiful variety of nature, and not only did not notice it, but held it in suspicion, believing that nature is always defective, and that it is absolutely necessary to correct it ; and in

this, they said, lies the secret of Art. And yet Bartolini cried aloud, and, so to speak, strained his voice to
make himself understood, and stood up on a table and
beat his drum for the hunchback. But as soon as a sufficient number of people is collected to make a respectable audience, one must lay aside the great drum and
begin to speak seriously. And this is just what the
maestro did: he gave up the hunchback, inculcated the
imitation of beautiful nature in all its varieties of sex,
age, and temperament. But, in the ears of the greater
number of persons the beat of the great drum still
sounded, and the words of Bartolini were not understood. From that time to this there have been no
more statues of Apollo, Jove, and Minerva. Chased
from this earth, they returned to their place on Olympus
—and there they still remain.

Still the seed of deformity had been sown, and struck
strong roots. There are some men who grub in filth
and dirt with pure delight, and have for the ugly and
evil a special predilection, because, as they say, these are
as true representatives of nature as what is beautiful
and good, and are in fact a particular phase of that
truth which, as a whole, constitutes the truly beautiful.
And reasoning thus, this school, or rather this coterie,
has given us, and still gives us, the most strange
and repulsive productions, improper and lascivious in
subject, and in form a servile copy of such offensively
ugly models as Mother Nature produces when she is
not well. What would you say, dear reader, if you
were ever to see a hideous little baby, crying with
his ugly mouth wide open, because his bowl of pap has
fallen out of his hand? or an infamous and bestial man,
with the gesticulations expressive of the lowest and most
vicious desires? or a woman vomiting under a cherry-

tree because she has eaten too much? or other similar
filthinesses of subject and imitation, which are disgusting even to describe? For myself, I am not a fan-
atic for ancient Art: on the contrary, I detest the academic and conventional; but I confess that, rather than
these horrors, I should prefer to welcome Cupid, and
Venus, and Minerva, and the Graces, and in a word all
Olympus. But, good heavens! is there no possibility of
confining one's self within limits? And if we abandon
Olympus and its deities, is it necessary to root and grub
in the filth of the Mercato Vecchio and in the brothel?

Now we will return to our story. At the time I was
modelling the Cain, and as it were for the purpose of
repose, I made a little figure of Beatrice Portinari,
which I afterwards repeated in marble, I know not how
many times. For this statue I had used as a model a
tolerably pretty young girl who was named likewise
Portinari. I tell this little story for the instruction of
young artists. There will even be two of these stories,
for I omitted one in speaking of the Cariatidi of the
Rossini Theatre; and these little matters show how one
should treat the model. One morning, when I had the
Portinari for a model, the curate Cecchi of the Santissima
Annunziata knocked at my door and told me that he
wished to come in to have a few words with me. I
replied that for the moment I could not attend to him,
as I had a model, but that if he would have the goodness
to come back a little later, we should then be alone, and
he could speak to me at his ease. After dinner he
returned, and said, "Have you a certain Portinari for
a model?"

"Yes," I said.

"Then you must know that this girl is engaged to my
nephew; and as I have learned that she comes to you as

a model, and as I absolutely will not allow my nephew
to marry a model, I have already so told the girl, and
she denies that she comes to you. Now I beg that you
will do me the favour to let me come in when she
is here. I will then surprise her, and blow into the air
this marriage arranged with my nephew."

"Listen," I said. "This sort of thing I do not like.
I cannot lend myself to do an injury of this kind to this
poor girl, who comes here to be my model. She has
confided to me that she is in want of money, having
larger demands than her daily earnings will supply.
She has said nothing about her being engaged, in which
case I would not have employed her unless her mother
or other near relation came with her. But, since it
seems to me reasonable that you should not wish your
future relation to go out as a model, I will promise you
not to so employ her any more; and the first time she
comes, I will tell her that I do not want her again, and I
will warn her not to go to others. Are you content?"

He seemed to be tolerably well satisfied, and I did
as I had promised.

Here is the other little story of the model of the
Cariatidi. Every morning there came to me as a model
a girl who lived in the Prato, and was a weaver. The
first morning, she came to the studio with a *subbio*.[1] I
took no notice of it; but the second and the third, as
well as the fourth time, she had always under her arm
this clumsy and heavy thing, so I asked her—

"Why do you carry about that *subbio?*"

She answered: "I have a lover. If I meet him in
the street, I tell him that I am going to my employers."

"What occupation has your lover?"

"He is a butcher."

[1] Weaver's beam.

Ah! thought I. "Look here, you must do me the favour to bring your mother with you when you come again."

"The mother cannot leave her work."

"Then bring some one else; one of your relations, or a lodger—at all events *some one*. I will not have you here alone."

I had scarcely spoken these words when I heard a knock at the door. "Hark! it is your lover who knocks," I said, as a joke.

I went and opened the door, and found there a sturdy youth as red as a lobster.

"Who do you want?" I asked.

"Are you the painter?"

"No, I am not a painter."

"Nonsense! let me come in. You have got Anina in there to paint. I want to have one word with her, and will go away at once."

"And I tell you that you don't know what you are talking about."

"If you take it so," he said, "let me come in;" and he pushed the door with all his force.

I, who had been warned, was ready with all my strength, and shut the door in his face. I went back into the studio, and found the girl, who, only as yet half dressed, was trembling like a leaf. I crossed the court of Palazzo Borghese, and opened carefully the door which gave upon the Via Pandolfini, and made signs to the girl to follow me. I looked out on the street to make sure that the youth was not there, and said to the girl hastily, "Go away, and don't come back to me, even if you are accompanied by some one."

The young man stayed in the Via del Palagio, and walked up and down for some hours before my door;

but I saw no more of him, and know nothing more.
The conclusion : girls as models—never *alone.*

I return to where I left off—to the Cain.   There was
in Florence at that time a certain English lady, Mrs
Letitia Macartney, who had been living for some time in
Siena.   She wished so much to see the Abel reproduced
in marble, that on her return to Siena she issued a paper
which invited the Sienese to make a subscription for this
purpose.   I have before me that paper, dated 12th
December 1842, a few days before the Grand Duchess of
Russia had given me her commission.   This invitation to
my townsmen had a great success, for in a few days sheets
were covered with signatures, among which all classes
figured—.beginning with the Governor Serristori, the Archbishop, the clergy, the university, the gentry, and the
people, and finally the religious corporations.   Certainly,
that excellent lady could not have had a better result from
her touching appeal, which ran as follows : " I beg the
Sienese not to reject my humble petition, and that the
poor as well as the rich, whoever reads these words, will
put his signature, and will contribute a half *paul* to assist
his townsman, who has so well proved that he deserves
encouragement.   Those who wish to give more than the
small proposed sum can privately satisfy their generous
impulses in the way they think best,—on this paper they
are begged not to exceed the sum named."   And by half
pauls only, the not small sum of 100 *scudi* was collected ;
and if this good lady had added that the half *paul* was to
be paid every month for a year or fourteen months, I am
sure that my townsmen would not have refused it, and that
the Abel would be to-day at Siena.

The sum of money and the list of subscribers were
sent to me, and I preserve the latter jealously; and after
these many years I read over the names with heartache,

thinking how all these have disappeared, together with the good Signora Letizia. And now I am speaking of her, I will mention something which will cause her to be appreciated and loved, even as I loved and admired her.

A short time after she had issued the appeal for my Abel, she came with a nephew and her two sisters to establish herself in Florence. She was about fifty years of age, enthusiastic for the beautiful wherever she found it. She had a small gallery of ancient pictures which she had collected with careful study in her wanderings through Italy. She had taken an apartment in the Piazza di Santa Maria Novella, and I often went there with my wife to pass the evening; and on her part the Signora Letizia often came to look me up in my studio. She liked to discuss with me artistic things, and when I could not attend to her, she said good-bye and went away.

Then it was, either from too hard work or on account of the dampness of the room in which I worked, or both together, I took so tiresome and obstinate a cough, that it gave me no peace night or day. I tried many things to get rid of it, and all in vain—decoctions, ass's milk, care, all were useless. La Signora Letizia having urged me a thousand times to take care of myself and to get rid of that cough, said to me so seriously that it made me laugh—

"It is absolutely necessary for you to get well."

"Bravo !" I said ; "that is what I have been thinking of for the past month, and I have done everything for that purpose—the advice and prescriptions of the physicians have not been neglected ; but now seriously I must get well—Go away, cough !"

"No, don't joke ; you must get well, and I mean to cure you. Listen," she said, " what you ought to do: you should buy a quantity of pine-wood, and with this line all the walls of your studio from top to bottom, leaving space between the wood and the wall; and you must do the same for the floor. Have the window open some hour of the day when you are not in the studio, that the current of air may not do you harm."

It seemed an odd thing to me. I could not understand what all this wood had to do with my cough; but to content her, I said that I would do as she advised. In the meantime I continued to cough in spite of the pot of lichen which I kept hot in my studio; and every day when this poor lady came to see me and saw that her advice was not followed, she appeared serious and disappointed, and finally said—

"Do you think, Signor Duprè, that my advice could do you harm?"

"Certainly not," I said.

"Then why don't you follow it?"

"I must wait a few days; just at present I cannot. But I will do it—of this you may be sure; and I am very grateful to you: it seems to me that it will be more comfortable and warmer."

She soon went away, and I seriously considered that I ought to try and content her, not that I thought the remedy effective. I said to myself—"My trouble is either a cold or something else; it is in the stomach, or the throat, or the bronchial tubes, and surely is not owing to the walls of my studio. But what shall I do? I must satisfy her. Certainly it will cost something to line all the studio with wood from top to bottom, and the floor; but what a strange idea has come into this lady's head, and with what seriousness and impressiveness she urges me to use pine-wood!"

Shortly after, I heard a knock at the door and saw three

or four loads of boards in the street. The head carter said to me—

"*Is this wood to come here?*"

I had ordered no wood, I replied. Then he showed me a card on which was written my name and the number of my studio, and added—

"This wood has been ordered and paid for, including the carriage, and—is it to come here?"

"Certainly," I said, "it is to come here." It was un-loaded, and I gave the men a little money, for although they had been paid, it would do them no harm. I sent immediately to call Petrai, who, besides being a model, was also a carpenter, and told him that I wished, in the quickest possible manner, to use this wood to line the studio walls and plank the floor; that he was to employ as many men as were necessary, and that they could not go to bed until this work was done.

The blacksmith was immediately set to work on the irons which were to support the boards, the mason to fasten them to the walls, and men to saw and nail. All the day and all the evening it appeared to be the devil's own house, and I was in the midst directing and overseeing the work.

The next morning, when I entered my studio, I felt revived by the odour of the pine and the air so sensibly dry, and I said, "If this work does no good to the cough, no matter; but it is certain that I find myself much better. Besides, I like the colour of the wood, which is gay. I like the smell of the pine. The floor is better to walk upon, and it is drier than any carpet. The air circulates everywhere. *Viva* Mrs Letitia! And now, how to repay her for this wood which she has bought for me? Ah! this is not so easy. To talk of giving back the money is useless, and it would also be in bad taste,

I

for I know how sensitive this lady is; but as a present I will not receive it." As it happened, I had a small bust of Beatrice in marble, which she had always admired. I sent this to her house, and she was so much pleased that she never ceased to speak of it to me. And the cough? The cough diminished day by day as if by enchantment, and in a week I was perfectly cured.

Whilst I am speaking of favours received and the manner in which I requited them, independent of the sentiment of gratitude which I always preserve for those who have rendered me a service, I must add that Mrs Macartney was pleased with the little bust of Beatrice; so also was Del Benino more than delighted with a bust in marble of the boy Raphael which I had copied from a painting by his father, Sanzio, who had painted the little boy when six years of age. At the bottom of this portrait was written in red, "Raphael Santii d' anni sei, Santii patre dipinse."

I saw this work of mine only a few years ago in the palace belonging to the heirs of Count del Benino.

As I have alluded to that excellent man—of whom, as you see, I retain such an affectionate remembrance—I will mention that I asked permission of his heirs by letter to be permitted at my own expense to make a little memorial of him in marble, and to place it in the chapel of the villa where Del Benino was buried; but I have never received any answer.

It appears that works either for love or money are not wanted. Here is another example of this. It must be now four or five years since the lamented Professor G. B. Donati, the astronomer, came to my studio with the engineer Del Sarto, to tell me that the commune of Florence intended to place a sun-dial on one side of the Ponte alla Carraja, exactly at the beginning or end of the

terrace, where there is at present a kiosk; and in order to
have an elegant and artistic thing, it came into the head
of Donati, or some one of the Municipal Council of Art,
to have a figure in bronze holding a disc on which should
be marked the meridian, and the hand of this figure
should be held gracefully in such a manner that its
shadow indicated the hour.   The idea pleased me.   I
made a sketch, and Del Sarto the engineer sent me the
exact dimensions of the terrace.   He liked the sketch,
and asked me what the cost of such a work would be,
adding that unless the price was small they would not be
able to order it.   I replied that nothing could cost less
than this, as I intended to present the model, and the
Municipality would only have to pay for the casting in
bronze.   I had an estimate made by Professor Clemente
Papi, who asked a very reasonable sum—seven or eight
thousand lire, I believe; and he signed a paper to this
effect, which, at the same time with a letter I had written
repeating the offer of my work gratis, I sent in an enve-
lope to the Municipality: and since then I have heard
nothing.   Poor Donati is dead; the sketch and the model
of the terrace are in my studio.   Count Cambray Digny
was then syndic.   On Ponte alla Carraja, in place of my
statue, there is a kiosk where papers, wax-matches, &c.,
are sold.   Even this is not the last of the statues I
have offered as a present which have not been accepted,
but I will not mention them here.

Meanwhile, as I was finishing the model of Cain, the
Grand Duchess Maria Antonietta ordered of me a statue
for the Uffizi.   I selected Giotto, and she presented this
statue to the Commission for erecting statues of illustrious
Tuscans, which, while they ornament the Loggia, serve
to recall past glory and to advise one to study more and
to chatter a little less.   In roughing out the statue I

found a flaw which split the marble in two. I was obliged to throw it away and to buy another block. When the good Grand Duchess heard of this, she insisted upon re-paying me the price of the new marble. I note this because so generous an act is uncommon.

The Cain was exhibited, and, as was natural, was less liked than the Abel,—first of all, because the enthusiasm raised by the former statue had too sensibly wounded the self-love of many ; and then, because some of my friends were too zealous, and their excessive praise of it before it was on exhibition created a public opinion in its favour which perhaps was not justified by its merits, for the difficulties of the subject were very great. With a phrase more witty than just, they said, " This time Abel has killed Cain ; " but Bartolini, who generally liked wit, said this was unjust and stupid, and declared that I had overcome a thousand times greater difficulties than in the Abel. But that witticism was prompted by sus-picion and passion, and it came from those same persons who said that the Abel had been cast from life.

Being proposed by Bartolini, I was elected Professor of the Academy. At that time, being invited by some of my townsmen, I went to Siena, where I was received with warmth and fraternal love. I was a guest of the Bianchis—of that charming Signora Laura who had always been so good to my poor mother and my family. That dear lady, and Carlo, who is still alive, and Luigi, who, alas ! was too soon snatched away from the love of his re-lations and of Siena, rejoiced in seeing me made the sub-ject of honour and ovation by all the citizens, who came to the palace to greet me.

I remember with emotion that crowd of people, and those deputations of the *contrade* and academies of the city, sent to bring me salutations and presents. These were the first flowers that I gathered and smelt in the garden of my youth; and their perfume I still smell, and it is now perhaps even more delightful, for it is associated in my memory with a time when I had no remorse.

A subscription was opened on the spot, promoted by the Cavaliere Alessandro Saracini, the Count Scipione Borghese, the Count Augusto dei Gori, and the Marquis Alessandro Bichi-Ruspoli. The statue which they ordered was of the Pontiff Pius II., Eneas Silvius Piccolomini.

These four gentlemen were good friends of mine; but I saw Saracini oftenest, as he came to Florence on business affairs. He had an intelligent love of Art, which he practised a little for his amusement, and he was President of the Institute of Fine Arts at Siena. One day he came to me quite breathless. He said that he had seen, in a shop or store-house near the Via Faenza, a wall all painted over, and that it was concealed by carriages, carts, wheels, and poles—in fact, it was at a carriage-maker's.

" But what painting is it ? " I asked.

" I do not know—I cannot say what it is; but it appears to me very beautiful," he replied. " It is like Perugino, or certainly of his school."

" Wait a moment," I said ; " here in the neighbourhood is some one who understands these things better than you or I ; " and we went to Count Carlo della Porta, and to Ignazio Zotti, painters who lived in the Niccolini building with me. They lost no time, and we all four went to the place. Carlo della Porta having placed a ladder against the wall, mounted, and stayed there only a few moments, then descended, and made Zotti go up. They then, after exchanging some words, expressed the opinion that it was by Raphael.

The clearing out of this place, and the arguments for and against the decision on the part of the Government, and the ultimate destination of the picture, are all well known, and I pass to other things. Having finished the Giotto, I went to Rome to make studies there for the statue of Pius II. I stayed there a month, and lived at the Hotel Cesari, Piazza di Pietra. It was the month of December 1844.

I must confess, whatever it costs me, that the Eternal City did not make the most favourable impression upon me; and except the ruins of ancient Rome, the Colosseum, the Pantheon, the Forum, with its triumphal arches and colonnades, all the rest excited in me no enthusiasm. But I must admit I had been spoiled by too much praise; and I was so vain, that while I accepted everything with apparent modesty, I was so puffed up internally with pride that at times it would show itself in spite of me. I remember once at the house of the Signora Clementina Carnevali, where every evening were to be seen all the most distinguished persons in Rome, either in letters or art, strangers as well as Italians,—I remember, I say, to have replied in a most impertinent manner to some one who asked me how I liked the monuments and the art of Rome, and what above all had most pleased me. I replied—and I blush to repeat it—" What I like best is the stewed broccoli "—a reply as outrageously stupid as insolent, and I wonder that those who heard it could have taken it in good part. For myself, as I feel to-day, if a young artist had replied to me in such a manner, he would have got little good out of it, and so much the better for him !

But I had better luck ; my foolish reply was repeated by every one, and so clouded by vanity and pride were my eyes, that I fancied it excited mirth and approbation, while it really deserved only compassion.

O Minardi ! O Tenerani ! O Massimo d'Azeglio ! you

who were present, but now dead, cannot see the *amende* which I make. However, you knew me later, and were aware of my repentance. But as for you, excellent Clementina—who are alive, and will read, I hope, these pages—if then you smiled with compassion, because you are so good you will to-day smile with approbation and praise.

And now, gentle reader, would you like to see how headstrong and proud I had become? One evening—Christmas Eve—I proposed to go to the midnight Mass at St Peter's. I set out at ten o'clock from the Via Condotti, where I had passed the evening with some of my English friends whom I had known in Florence. Mrs ——, to whom I had disclosed my purpose, said, " Take care ! you are not much acquainted with Roman streets; you had better take a carriage to go there. If you do not, you may easily lose your way in the streets of Rome. They are very confusing by day; imagine what they are at night ! " If this lady had not given me such a warning, it is probable that I should have done as she suggested; but because she had given it I despised it, and determined to go by myself to St Peter's.

I walked until two o'clock without even being able to find the bridge of St Angelo. I got bewildered in all those streets and lanes which are comprised between San Luigi dei Francesi, Piazza Navona, San Andrea della Valle, San Carlo a Catinari, Teatro Argentina, Il Gesu, and San Ignazio e la Minerva ; and after having walked for two hours, I found myself at the point I had started from. Then, more obstinate than ever, though overcome by weariness and mortified pride, I persisted in going up and down all sorts of streets unknown to me, and often very filthy, and again coming across the same *piazze*, the same fountains, until at last I found myself at the foot of the Campidoglio steps. The people whom I met in the streets here and there returning from the Mass could have shown me the way, not to go to St Peter's, but how to return to my hotel, had I been less headstrong, and had I inquired for the Piazza Colonna or Piazza di Pietra, where I lodged. But no; it appeared to me to be a humiliation. I wished to find the hotel by myself; and I did find it finally, but in what a condition I leave those to judge who know Rome, and the sharp pavements of its streets, but, above all, tired out, and more than this, humiliated and without supper. It was two o'clock. The Hotel Cesari was shut, and I had to wait until they opened it for me. I asked for supper; they replied that they had nothing, and that if they had it they could not give me anything, because they were prohibited by law from supplying any food on that night. I should have been glad of any little thing, but could get nothing. My pride was singularly punished that night, and I went to bed hungry. At first I strove in vain to go to sleep, then I dreamt all night of eating, and awoke in the morning rather late. I could not realise that I could get up and have a good breakfast. I went over again in thought the weariness of the night, the hunger, the annoyance, and I felt weak. But finally I said to myself, I will eat now, and another time I shall be wiser. Now to breakfast! After going out of the hotel, I turned to the right to go into the Osteria dell' Archetto. It was closed; the *caffè* next door was closed. I ran into the Piazza Colonna, and found all shut up—*caffès*, pastry-cooks, everything closed. I asked, angrily and with a bewilderment easy to comprehend, what was the reason of this, and was told that during the time of the religious ceremonies no one could sell anything to eat. I was stupefied, and walked along slowly, not knowing where to go. Until after twelve o'clock neither the *trattorie* nor the *caffès* would be opened. I would not go back to the hotel, as I feared a refusal such as I had the night before. I began to feel very faint; for nearly twenty hours I had eaten nothing. I saw the people gaily walking about, smiling, smoking, and looking well-fed and of good colour, and I felt angry and envious. They had eaten leisurely and at home, or in the *caffè* or *trattoria* before ten o'clock, the hour prescribed. I had slept until that hour, and dreamt of eating, and when I went out intending to get something to eat, it was too late. Fortunately, one of my friends, the engraver Travalloni, saw me, and coming to meet me, said, "What is the matter? Why do you look so scared?" I told him my story, and he laughed, and taking me by the arm, said—"Come with me." After a few turns he entered a doorway half closed, and pushed me up a dark staircase, where there were the savoury odours of cooking, all the more grateful to me because my appetite was so great. The staircase opened upon an ante-room, also dark. We closed the door and knocked at a smaller door. It was opened, and I found myself in a spacious hall, well ventilated and full of people, who were sitting eating and drinking cheerfully at table.

"What is this?" I asked. "Can I get anything to eat here?"

"Yes," he said; "give your orders."

The waiter, with a napkin over his shoulder, was standing before us. I was like a full flask which, being upturned, can with difficulty empty itself. There was such a variety of odours in the room, and such a quantity of things to eat, that I could not get out a word; and my friend, seeing my embarrassment, hastened to say to me—

" Will you have some soup and a cutlet?"

" Yes; two," I replied.

" Will you have Orvieto or good Roman wine?"

" Do me the favour to bring anything you please, so long as you bring me something to eat and drink. I can't stop to choose."

And the good Travalloni, turning to the servant, said—

" Bring at once a flask of Orvieto, such as I drink—you understand?—some bread, some soup, a cutlet, cheese, and fruit."

That day Travalloni appeared to me to be a man of genius.

CHAPTER VIII.

LITERATI AT MY STUDIO, AND THEIR INFLUENCE ON MY WORK—CALAMATTA'S
OPINION OF TENERANI, OF BARTOLINI, AND OF MYSELF—HIS DEFENCE OF
MY ABEL IN PARIS—PIUS II.—ACADEMICIANS AND "NATURALISTI"—LUIGI
VENTURI—PRINCE ANATOLIA DEMIDOFF AND THE PRINCESS MATILDE—
THE STATUETTE IN CLAY OF THE PRINCESS MATILDE IS DESTROYED—OUR
MINISTER NIGRA PRESENTS ME TO THE EMPEROR NAPOLEON III.—BEAUTY
DOES NOT EXIST OUTSIDE OF NATURE—PRAISE PUTS ONE TO SLEEP—THE
INCOHERENCE OF BARTOLINI.

Y studio, as I think I have already said, was
the resort of many of the literary men of the
time—Giusti, Thouar, Montazio, La Farina,
F. S. Orlandini, Enrico Mayer, Girolamo
Gargiolli, Giovanni Chiarini, Filippo Moisè, and sometimes, but rarely, G. B. Niccolini, Atto Vannucci, and
Giuseppe Arcangeli. These distinguished men, all talking with me, and bringing forward their theories of Art,
somewhat confused me in my ideas. I said, at the very
beginning of these memoirs—and the reader, I hope,
keeps it in mind—that I had received no education, and
my judgment was not trained to discern and distinguish
the laws of the beautiful, which, the more deeply one
studies them, the more they scatter, and seem, as it
were, to fly from us. I was attracted to Art by a purely
natural sentiment, which I sought to express by a simple
imitation of nature ; and so far, I think I was right, for
whatever other path we may take, supported however it

may be by philosophic and æsthetic reasons, it will prove
utterly fallacious unless it lead to this end, of imitating
the beautiful in nature, and will surely lead astray the
young artist, even though he has a good natural talent
and a lively fancy.

Yes, sir; my poor head was perplexed, and I began to
distrust nature, with its imperfections and its vulgarity.
The warm and imaginative utterances of La Farina made
all the words of Niccolini seem colourless to me, for
though given with antique beauty, they came from him
with difficulty. The pure and touching morality of
Thouar conflicted with the humoristic and cynical freedom of Montazio. Giusti, who might have set me right
in my opinions, kept at a distance without giving a
reason why; and in this he was wrong, for I should
have given heed to him. But he contented himself
with writing to the advocate Galeotti, telling him that
I was surrounded by a number of fops who spoiled me,
and that if I did not shut myself up in my studio, as
I did when I made the Abel, I should not succeed in
making anything good. This outburst of Giusti's I only
knew many years afterwards, on the publication of his
letters.

I remember one day, when Giusti was with me, I
recited from memory the canto in the 'Inferno' relating
to Francesca, but when I came to this passage—

> " Quali colombe dal desio chiamate
> Con l' ali aperte e ferme, al dolce nido
> Volan per l' aere dal voler portate ; "

he interrupted me, saying, "You recite well and intelli-
gently the verses of the divine poet; but you, too, fall
into the error into which so many have fallen—copyists,
printers, and commentators—that of placing the semi-
colon at the end of the line, after the word *portate*,

instead of putting it in the middle of the line, after the word *aere*. This punctuation makes Dante guilty of a blunder, he attributing to the doves, besides desire, which is most proper, also will, which belongs properly to man. Try and place the comma and the pause after the word *aere*, and you will see what a stupendous philosophical value it gives to the verses. Listen; I will repeat them to you :—

> ' Quali colombe dal desio chiamate
> Con l' ali aperte e ferme, al dolce nido
> Volan per l' aere; dal voler portate
> Cotali uscir dalla schiera, ov' è Dido,' " &c.

This correction, so clear, so easy, so just, satisfied me immediately, and from that day I have always recited these lines in this way. The unintelligent did not perceive the change of sense, but those who were more attentive and refined gave me praise for it; but I rejected it at once as belonging to me, saying that the correction was due to Giuseppe Giusti.[1]

In making my Giotto, I followed my inspiration by drawing upon nature for that type of rude good-nature which constituted the outward character of my statue; and although some of my literary friends, who were more

[1] The distinguished Signor Carlo Ara of Palermo informs me that this new punctuation did not originate with Giusti, but with Muzzi. And, in truth, Giusti did not tell me that it was his, but simply recommended me to try to say it and understand it in that sense; and I, supposing the correction to be his, recited and wrote it so. The distinguished Carlo Ara pointed out to me the way in which I could verify his assertion; and I am glad to be able to correct an error (involuntary on my part), and to take this occasion to thank the distinguished Signor Carlo Ara.

The distinguished Signor Angelo Cavalieri of Trieste writes to me that this new punctuation of this Dantesque simile does not convince him, and he gives his reasons; but upon this I am not competent to enter into a discussion.

attached to the antique and the so-called *bello ideale*, blamed me, and some artists of distinction opposed me openly, I firmly adhered to the sound principle of imitating nature. The Giotto was finished without a moment's indecision, although, as I have said, I had been revolving over and over again in my mind the conception of a beauty ideal and beyond nature, but which, without great judgment, becomes conventional.

About this time a controversy occurred between me and a great artist which it may be well to speak of here, because, although it will show how tenacious I was of this principle of imitating nature, yet it will also show how much I was affected by it, and how the acerbity of this artist produced a change in me, which certainly he did not desire. His fear was lest I should fall into a servile copying of life; and had his language been more measured, we should easily have understood each other. But he took a different course, and I now proceed to give the history of this controversy.

I had a short time previously completed my model of Giotto, and, as I have said, some among the artists most tenacious of the classic rules attacked me sharply, but Bartolini defended me. I was therefore somewhat irritated when Calamatta, accompanied by Signor Floridi, the draughtsman, came to my studio. He came in with a magisterial and rather arrogant air. I received him politely and with respectful words, such as became me towards the author of the famous mask of Napoleon I. He looked at "Abel" and "Cain" without opening his mouth, and as if he found in them nothing either to praise or to blame; but when he came to the "Giotto," he said, "I have heard a good deal of talk about you, in which you have been lauded to the skies, and I wished to come and ascertain with

my own eyes whether you were entitled to your fame ;
and I confess to you, though what I shall say may
seem bitter to you, that in the presence of your works
your fame disappears ; and if it be permitted to me to
make a comparison, I should say that you produce the
same effect upon me as if I saw a balloon inflated with
gas rising majestically in the air, and which, after arriving at a certain height, bursts, and afterwards leaves nothing to be seen." I answered that such things might
be thought, and even spoken, but a little more graciously, and I said no more. Calamatta rejoined, with
some irritation, that he was a person who could not
endure the ugly—that it was his instinct to denounce
it with the same vivacity and earnestness that one
does when there is a cry of fire, and some place is in
flames. I began then to lose my patience : still I only
contented myself with asking whether he was quite sure
that there was a conflagration, and whether he was absolutely called upon to extinguish it ; and finally, added
that Bartolini, Tenerani, and others had seen my works,
and had spoken of them in very different terms. This
only more irritated poor Calamatta, and he said that
he had just come from Paris, and had visited Tenerani
at Rome, and his insipid and hard mysticism had seemed
pitiable to him; and that, on coming to Florence, he had
found in Bartolini the most filthy and offensive realism,
carried to the point of proclaiming the beauty of deformity, and that in response to his just criticisms upon
the injury that he was thus doing to the true principles
of Art, Bartolini had advised him to come to my studio
and see the application of those principles which he
censured,—and now, after examining my works, he perceived that I was sliding down a steep declivity, which
would soon precipitate me into naturalism and deformity,

and though he recognised in me a certain talent, he warned me to avoid that false school and those insidious precepts, and more than all, to be on my guard against treacherous and lying praises. All this was very fine, if it were granted that I was on a false road. But as I did not think so then, and still less now,—and besides, as I was young, flattered, and praised, and those words of his, "that I should be on my guard against insidious precepts and treacherous praises," seemed to me a very unjust accusation against Bartolini,—I indicated to him that I should be glad if he would leave me in peace, and in fact, as he had declared my works to be ugly, and of an ugliness that he abhorred, he was not in his proper place here; and as to his counsel, not having asked for it, I should not take the trouble to consider it. Poor Calamatta was angry at this, and taking by the hand Floridi, who during the whole squabble was on thorns, he said, "Let us go away; let us go away; let us go away"—and away he went.

Poor Calamatta, my illustrious friend. If any one had said on that day, when we separated with such unpleasant feelings, and on my part with so little kindness, "The time will come, and soon, when he will be your most open defender and friend," I would not have believed him, and I should not have wished to believe him,—and yet it so turned out. In 1855, eleven years after our disagreement, he was in Paris, and on the Jury of the Fine Arts at the World's Exhibition. I had sent a model of the "Abel" in plaster, and among the jury the doubt arose whether it was not cast from life. As in Florence that opinion was originated out of evil-mindedness, so it was repeated in Paris from speciousness, and heedlessness of judgment. Calamatta, whom I had not seen since that famous day, although he frequently re-

turned to Florence, undertook to defend my work with
sound reasoning and friendly warmth, but he did not
succeed in convincing the entire body of the jury of their
error of judgment; and in assigning the prizes, out of
mere regard for Calamatta they gave to " Abel " one of
the last. Calamatta then rose and said, " Gentlemen,
our judgment of this work must not be given in this way.
I have endeavoured to show you by artistic reasoning
that this statue is really modelled in clay, in imitation
of beautiful nature. I have pointed out that certain imperfections which are always found in nature have been
wisely avoided by the artist. I have shown you clear
proofs of modelling in the mode of working the clay. I
thought that I had convinced you that so noble and
refined a whole is rather the creation of the mind,
through a studious and loving imitation of parts, than a
mechanical reproduction by casting ; and finally, I have
demonstrated, and you have conceded to me, that the
head is of equal merit with all the rest of the body, and
this could not have been cast from life. From these
considerations, which arise from the examination of the
work itself, and without regard to the artist, whom I
have only once met in Florence, and who is, I believe,
inimical to me, I am of opinion that your judgment of
this work should be reconsidered, and if it seems to you
to be proved that this statue is a cast from nature and
not modelled, and in consequence a falsification and
not a work of art, you ought not to adjudge to it even
the lowest prize, but to exclude it entirely from the
Exhibition, and in so doing you should give your reasons
for such a decision in writing, and under your signatures,
—and in such case I shall retire from the Jury of Fine
Arts, and shall publish in the journals of Paris my reasons for withdrawing." After this discourse there arose

K

an exceedingly animated discussion, and the President decided that a new examination of the model should be made ; and as many were convinced by the good reasons put forward by Calamatta, the second examination of " Abel " resulted in a complete success, and at the next voting the golden medal of the First Class was awarded to me.   The news of this, derived directly from Cala- matta himself, was sent to me at once by Rossini, who had conceived a strong affection for me, and honoured me with his friendship.

I now return to the point where I left off.   After Giotto I began Pius II. ; and filled as my head was by the criticism of the academicians, the eulogies of the *naturalisti*, the contempt of some to whom the subject was displeasing, and more than all by the exceptional character of the studies I had made for this work, I began it unwillingly, and strove (strangely enough) to conciliate the academicians, copying from the life with timidity, where boldness and fidelity were required— boldness, that is to say, in accepting frankly the stiff paper-like folds of the pontifical mantle, and fidelity in copying them.   In consequence I made a washed-out work, and I pleased neither one party nor the other, and much less myself.   I make this statement so that young men may be on their guard against allowing themselves to stray from the true path, which is this—viz., to em- body the subject in its appropriate form by the imitation of living nature, to strive for truth of character in the general action and in all the particulars, and in proportion as the subject is historical and natural, as in portraiture, to adhere all the more closely to nature.   In such a case as this statue of Pius II., it is necessary to be naturalistic —avoiding, of course, all minutiæ which add nothing to the beauty of general effect and the truth of character.

Has it ever happened to you, courteous reader, to meet a person with whom your personal relations brought you often in contact, and who, reserved and serious by nature as well as on account of his social position, differed from you, who are perhaps too vivacious and open ; and on the one side you feared to displease him by your vivacity, and on the other you were annoyed by his reserve ? In such a case, if certain allowance be made on both sides—as far as you are concerned by listening with attentive deference to his wise counsels, austere maxims, and high principles, and on his part by an indulgent consideration for your free and vivacious nature—has it not happened to you that insensibly and firmly a harmony of relation has established itself which it is difficult to break, —and this for the undeniable, however recondite reason, that there is a sympathy between entirely different natures which causes each to compensate for the other ?

In like manner as this may have happened to you, so it happened to me with Luigi Venturi, then private secretary of his Royal and Imperial Highness the Grand Duke Leopold II. He often came to my studio by order of the Grand Duke, for whom I was making a statuette of Dante and another of Beatrice. He took a liking to me, which I have returned sincerely, even till to-day ; and he is the oldest and most affectionate of my friends. After the revolution of '59, with the loss of his high position he lost also a great portion of such friends as come with Fortune and flee with her. But neither the ingratitude of some nor the fickleness of others ever drew from him a lament. He was contented with those who remained, and I was one of them. Our long and intimate connection has at last harmonised our characters,—he making me more temperate, and I (as I dare to hope) making him more open and vivacious. His friendship, as well as that of others of whom I shall speak in the proper place, has strengthened my judgment and tempered my fancies. Trustworthy, honest, and sincere friends are a great fortune—and I have had such, and have kept them. To distinguish the good from the bad requires study, and we must learn how to get rid of chatterers and adulators.

And this warning I feel it my duty to give to young artists, for whom these memoirs are specially written. I have already said, in speaking of models, " Girls unaccompanied as models, no ! " now I add, " Nor even married women without the express consent of their husbands." Here is a little incident which may serve as a lesson.

Prince Anatolio Demidoff often came to my studio. He gave vent to his annoyance at the delays and the infinite difficulties interposed by Bartolini in completing the groups and statues of the monument ordered by him in honour of the memory of his dead father. To listen to the Prince, he seemed to have a thousand good reasons; but the consequences he drew from them, and the bold, unjust measures which he proposed, I could not but think blameworthy, and I strove in every way to moderate him, and to dissuade him from carrying out his intentions. My frank and loyal defence of Bartolini, so far from exasperating him, as often happened when he was opposed, made him more kindly towards me, and he proposed to order of me a great work worthy, as he was pleased to say, of my genius. He had a thousand projects, and among them he spoke to me of a colossal statue of Napoleon I. He was at that time tenderly inclined toward the Bonaparte family. His pride in being connected with it, as well as the charms of the beautiful Princess, his wife, were in great measure the cause of this enthusiasm. He treated me with great kindness, invited me often to dinner and to his evening receptions, and talked very freely with me in regard to works that he wished me to make for him.

About this time the Princess came one day to my studio, and told me that she wished me to make her portrait—not merely a bust, but the whole figure, almost half the size of life. I answered that I should like much to make it, for I was persuaded that it would give the Prince pleasure; but she hastened to say that the Prince must know nothing about it. I had not sufficient presence of mind to reply that without his consent I could not undertake it—and I was wrong, I confess: but the Princess stood before me blandly insisting; and overcome by the beauty of the model, I agreed to make it and keep it a secret from the Prince. She gave me a number of sittings, and I was going on satisfactorily with the statuette, and had already a good likeness, when unexpectedly the Prince came one day to see me, and after exchanging a few words and taking a turn through the room, he stopped before the modelling-stand, on which was the clay of the statuette covered with wet cloths, and said—

" And what have you got here ? "

" Nothing, your Excellency—nothing."

" Let me see what there is under here."

" But there is nothing ; it is only a mass of infirm clay, and is not in a state to show."

" Let us see, my friend,—I am extremely curious." And so saying he lifted up the cloths, looked at it, and then said seriously, " Very good—very like ; " and then . in a sharp tone added, " And who has ordered this ? "

. " Listen, Signor Principe. The Princess has ordered this statuette of me, for I see that you recognise it as her portrait—and she ordered me to show it to no one, not even to you, Signor Principe; for I believe she wished to give you a surprise, and to present it to you when it should be finished in marble."

He answered, "The Princess has done wrong in ordering her portrait without my consent, and you have done wrong in complying with her request. I do not like these surprises, and when the Princess returns for a sitting you must request her to go about her business; and you may tell her that you do this by my order. And besides—and this I say particularly to you—destroy this work, and think no more about it."

I felt that the Prince was right, but to throw down this work was a bitter pain to me; and besides, I was unwilling to displease the Princess, who so earnestly desired to have this statuette, and who had already expressed her satisfaction with it. My face must have been very expressive at that moment, for the Prince, taking my hands in his, said—

"My dear Duprè, I understand your embarrassment and annoyance, but it is necessary that this should be done. I do not like, and I will not have this sort of thing, and I like still less this way of doing it. Do you understand? A portrait of the Princess, or even a statue of her, would be a charming possession, and I should particularly like one by you. I have already a beautiful statue of Madame Letizia by Canova, and this of my wife would make an admirable pendant; but I repeat that this way of doing it does not please me, and though I may seem harsh, I again say to you—Destroy this statuette, and let us say no more about it."

While he was speaking I thought to myself—This statuette and portrait of his wife he does not wish to have, but rather wishes to have a statue of her of life size; and so much the better. And then, considering that he had said he did not like the way in which it was done, I perceived, as I ought from the first to have perceived, that he objected to the Princess coming to my studio to sit, and I answered—

"You shall be obeyed. To-morrow the Princess is to return to give me a sitting, and I will tell her all, and this clay shall go back into the tank. But I hope that you will not forget that you have spoken of a life-size statue of the Princess; and as this work would require considerable time, and it might be more convenient to her that I should model it in your own palace, I could——"

He did not let me finish my sentence, but, embracing me warmly and kissing me, said—

"Thanks, dear Duprè, that is right. That is what pleases me, and that is the way it shall be done. And now, *addio*." And pressing my hand, he departed.

The day after, at one o'clock, the usual hour, the Princess arrived, gay and laughing, as usual; and after giving a glance at herself in the mirror, and arranging a little her hair, she seated herself and said—

"I am ready."

I had not as yet thrown down the statuette. There it stood uncovered, just as the Prince had left it the day before.

"I am very sorry, Signora Principessa," I began, "to give you some bad news. The Prince was here yesterday."

"I hope you did not allow him to see this portrait?"

"Yes, he has seen it—he has seen it, Signora Principessa. It was useless to try to conceal it from him, and I did wrong to endeavour to do so, for he was perfectly aware of its existence when he came here. He must have been exactly informed about it ; and so sure was he that I was making your portrait, that he planted himself here precisely before the modelling-stand, and seeing that I was unwilling to uncover it, he uncovered it himself without any ceremony.   He told me that I did wrong to begin the work, and that I must not go on with it, and, in fact, he has expressly ordered me to destroy it and throw it down."

While I was thus speaking she stood disquieted and frowning, and then said that it was unjust, absurd, and ridiculous, and that I must not give heed to him, but that she should stay, and I must go on with the portrait. After a while, however, she grew calmer, and decided to go away ; and this was well.   But she did not give up the matter, and the day after, she wrote to me to say that she should return to give me more sittings.   I had not yet thrown down the clay, not only on account of my natural unwillingness to do so, which is excusable, but also because of the advice of Prince Jerome, the brother of the Princess Matilde, who insisted that the Prince could not pretend to anything more than that the work should be suspended.   But of this I was a safer and better advised judge than he, and well knew that a husband is the legitimate master of his own wife, and of any portrait of her.   But I repeat, I allowed the statuette to remain because I disliked to destroy it. The Princess did not return as she had promised, and wrote again to me to expect her another day.   This went on for some time ; and finally, when I saw her again, she told me that she was going to Paris with the Prince, and that on her return we must go on, and if the Prince persisted in his ideas, she would recompense me for the work I had done on it.

In fact, she went to Paris with the Prince, and there

she remained; while he, recalled by the Emperor Nicholas
of Russia, went to St Petersburg, where he found that
a decree of divorce had been demanded by the Princess and signed by the Emperor. The Prince gave me
nothing further to do, except some slight things which
are scarcely worth mentioning, and the Princess entirely
forgot her promise. And as I am now on this matter,
and in order to make an end of it, let me leap over
eleven years, and say that, having exhibited in Paris at
the Exposition of 1855, besides the model in plaster
of the Abel (as I have before narrated), a reproduction
in small of this statue in marble, which I desired to
sell, I wrote to the Princess asking her to purchase
it. This I did to remind her indirectly of her promise to recompense me for the labour I had given to
her statuette, but she never answered. I now make
another leap over twelve years more. In the Exposition
Universelle at Paris in 1867, I was one of the Italian
Jury on Sculpture; and one evening, at a reception at the
Tuilleries, I was presented by our minister Nigra to the
Emperor, who had on his arm the Princess Matilde.
As soon as she saw me she said, " We have known each
other a long time;" but I, remembering how she had
treated me, pretended to have no remembrance of her.
And the Emperor looked at me through his sleepy eyes,
and must have thought me either remarkably forgetful or
a great fool. The Princess, naturally, never deigned to
give me another look.

And now again I return to my works. After Pius II.
I put up a figure of life-size representing Innocence.
This was ordered of me by Signor Tommasi of Leghorn;
but later, with my full consent, it remained on my hands,
and was bought by Prince Constantine of Russia. I
have determined not to judge my own works, though

here and there I may give a little hint; but in order that these memoirs may be of some use, it is well that I should indicate the spirit of the principles which guided me in my work. I have said that my faith in the pure imitation of nature was somewhat shaken by the criticisms of my Giotto as being too naturalistic. Some reasonings by my friends, and above all, certain articles by Giuseppe Arcangeli in the 'Rivista, Sul Bello Ideale,' as well as the compliments and eulogies of my statue of Innocence by Borghi, ·finally persuaded me that there does exist a *bello ideale* impossible to find in nature, and this beauty should be arrived at by an imitation of the antique, and by the aid of memory.

Nothing is more dangerous than this theory. Beauty is scattered over universal nature. The artist born to feel and perceive this beauty (which is the object of art) has his mind and heart always exercised in seeking it out and expressing it. He discerns in nature one or more living forms that in some degree approximate to the type he has in his mind, and the reality of these, by strengthening his ideals, enables him to work the latter properly out. The artist who is without his ideal, and forces himself to find it outside of nature, torturing his memory with what he has seen or studied in the works of others, makes but a cold and conventional work. The animating spark, the heat, the life, does not inform his work, for he is not the father, but only the stepfather of his children. To this school belong the imitators— that is, the timid friends of nature.

On the other side, but in much greater numbers and with much greater petulance, are the *naturalisti*, who despise every kind of ideality, and especially despise it because they have it not. Neither is their heart warmed by strong and sweet affections, nor do they

with their eyes or their mind seize, among the multiform
shapes of nature, a type, a movement, or an expression
which, assiduously pursued, awakens and fecundates the
idea within them.   The first ruffian or harlot of the streets
taken by evil chance suffices for them, and they delight
to drag this noble art of ours through filth and ugliness.

Each of these extremes I have sought to avoid.   But
it is none the less true that, at the period to which I have
arrived in my narrative, I was carried a little away, by
the discourses and writings of literary men and critics of
Art, on the road that leads to the conventional and
academic.   This bad influence weakened my faith in
nature and my courage in my work.   And the Pius
II., the Innocence, and the Purity are, so to speak,
the mirrors in which are reflected my want of faith,
uncertainty, and weakness of mind during these three
years of artistic irresolution.   In seeking after the perfect I lost the little good that my genius had produced
in my first years, uninfluenced by all these discussions,
and what is of more importance, by all eulogies both of
good and of bad alloy.   Yes, also of bad alloy.   The
young artist should take heed of all the praise that
he receives.   He should hold it in suspicion, and
weigh it, and make a large deduction.   Eulogy is like
a perfume, grateful to the sense, but it is better to in-
hale it but little, little, little, because it goes to the head,
lulls us to sleep, and sometimes intoxicates us and be-
wilders us so that we lose our compass.   One must be
prudent. Flowers of too strong an odour must be kept
outside the room.   Air is necessary—air.   I hope that
these words will fall into the ear of some to whom they
may do good—I mean, of those who not only sniff up
praise with eagerness, but are discontented because they
do not think it sufficient, and who re-read it and talk of

it with others so as to prolong their pleasure, and preserve all the papers and writings which speak of them,
without perceiving that this is all vanity and pettiness of
heart.

For the rest, it is very easy to see how one may vac-
cilate, and even fall; and on this account I deem it my
duty, for the love that I bear to young men, to put them
on their guard against the blandishments of praise.
Imagine, dear reader, an inexperienced youth of spirit
and lively fancy, who in his first essays in Art finds
it said and written of him that he has surpassed all
others, has begun where others ended, that he is born
perhaps to outdo the Greeks with his chisel, that Michael
Angelo must descend from the pedestal he has occupied
for centuries, and other similar stuff—more than this,
expose him to the envy of the Mæviis, and those light
and inconsiderate flatteries, which are all the more dangerous when made attractive by courtesy and refinement
of expression,—and you will have the secret of his vac-
cilations, even if with God's help he is not led utterly
astray.

At this most trying time of my life the peace of my
family was somewhat disturbed by these influences.
My wife was disquieted because I had prevented her
from carrying on her occupation. Our daily necessities
increased with the growth of our children. Then there
were requirements and troubles on account of my father,
thoughts about my sister, as well as my brother, who
wished to become a rougher-out in marble, and who
brought to my studio very little aptitude united with
great pretensions on the score of being my brother.
All these annoyances were partly confided to my friend
Venturi, to whom I poured out all my mind; and he
with wise and kindly words consoled me.

Not the least affliction to me was Bartolini's un-
concealed animosity, of which I had a new proof in
a fact which it is here the place to narrate. I hope
that the reader will remember that I made, while in
the studio of Sani, a little crucifix which the Signor
Emanuel Fenzi bought for the chamber of his son
Orazio, who married the noble Lady Emilia of the
Counts Della Gherardesca. About this time Signor
Emanuel desired to make my acquaintance, and having
become intimate with me, wished to have me often with
him. Thus he discovered that this crucifix he had
bought of Sani was my work, and I cannot say how
much this delighted him. To his dinners and *conver-
sazioni*, which were frequented by many foreigners as
well as Italians, Bartolini often came ; but he was never
willing to renew his relations with me, although my
bearing towards him was that of the most affectionate
consideration. As long as this unwillingness was concealed or perceived by few, I bore it quietly; but it
happened that it was soon openly exhibited. One
·evening after dinner the *salon* of Signor Fenzi was filled
with guests, and gay with all sorts of talk. Soon, as was
natural, the conversation fell upon Art ; and Bartolini,
who was an easy and clever talker, affirmed that the
arts were in *decadence*, for various reasons : first, because
of the want of enthusiasm and faith among the lower
and upper classes, both of whom were sleeping in
a *dolce far niente;* and second, because the artists had
abandoned the right road of imitation of beautiful
nature, and were pursuing with panting breath a chimer-
ical beauty, which they called a *bello ideale;* and last,
because the vices of both had usurped the place of
the virtues of our ancestors, and luxury, apathy, and
avarice had drawn out of our beautiful country activity,

temperance, modesty, and liberality,—and he illustrated this by various instances of ancient temperance and modesty. While Bartolini was speaking, Signor Fenzi went into the chamber of the Cavaliere Orazio and brought out the " Christ," which, by reason of the long time that it had been executed, and perhaps of the kisses of the pious Signora Emilia, had an antique look, and showing it to the *maestro*, said—

" Look at this work."

After examining it, he said, " The proof that our artists of old were as able as they were modest can be seen in this work. The artist who made it, and who probably was only an *intagliatore*, would have been able to make a statue such as perhaps no one to-day could."

At this Fenzi replied, with a smile, " Excuse me, but you are in error. This is a modern work, and there is the artist who made it," pointing me out, who was just coming in at that moment.

Bartolini laid down the " Christ," spoke not a word more, and did not deign even to look at me, although· he had praised the work. This did not seem just, either to Fenzi or to any of the persons there present.

CHAPTER IX.

HE elevation of Pius IX. to the Pontificate, the amnesty and reforms granted by that Pontiff, which initiated and awoke the liberal sentiments of all Italy, were perhaps felt more in Florence than elsewhere, almost all the political refugees from the different States having for some time past found a safe and peaceful home there, owing to the character and patriarchal laws of the Grand Duke. This drew me away from the serene quiet of my studio, and with the others I shouted, "Long live Ferruccio! Pius IX.! the press! the civic guard and Gioberti!" and all the rest. The principal leader of our peaceful demonstrations was the advocate Antonio Mordini, and after him came Giuseppe La Farina, and others. Not a petition was made to the Government or a deputation sent to the Prince in which I did not take part. Whether our honest demands were of use to the country, I will not discuss, but certainly my work suffered not a little from this state of things. Nor was I the only one to abandon the studio; all, young and old, were possessed and inflamed with a national aspiration for independence from foreign occupation. The consequence of all this excitement was, that I was taken away from my studies and work; and, in short, while there was a great deal of patriotic enthusiasm, there was but little study, very little profit, and much idle talk on questions more or less futile, by which family peace was destroyed, and friendship made a matter of caution and suspicion.

Although in these memoirs I do not propose to speak of politics (not feeling equal to it), I wish to touch on the great events that produced the revolution of '48, as they were one of the causes of interruption in my art; and even in politics, in consequence of the turn things were taking, I found myself set aside. Some of my friends whose views went far beyond mine left me, and the others that had remained stationary blamed me even for those temperate aspirations that were those also of the Government. I was disheartened, self-involved, and ill at ease. With the growth of the revolution, the departure of the Grand Duke, and the dread of a dangerous crisis, artistic life was not one of the most flourishing, and I had not work of any kind, except to retouch the wax of "Abel and Cain," that the Grand Duke had given an order to Papi to cast in bronze.

Seeing this, I concentrated all my life in my family affections. My studio had become deserted; my scholars —Tito Sarrocchi, Luigi Majoli, and Enrico Pazzi—had left me to go to the camp. They returned afterwards, but were always tossed about on the wave of the revolution. Only one of my workmen, Romualdo Bianchini, was left dead on the field, the 29th of May, at Curtatone.

I passed my days in great sadness. Antonio Ciseri, with whom I had contracted a friendship from my earliest steps in art, had his studio near mine, and we used to exchange visits. Although he was not a facile talker, his nature was open and ingenuous; and as his principles in art, his morals, and his habits agreed with mine, a strong friendship grew up between us, which has never diminished; and if years have whitened our beards, our hearts have not grown old, and we love each as in our early years. To-day he is one of our first painters, and has a number of able and devoted scholars.

Amongst my friends was also Dr Giuseppe Saltini, who for many years had been a physician in the employment of the Government, and now leads a hard life with restricted means, on account of having so many children. Now I will describe an evening passed most pleasantly in those times. One day some clever men came to see me —Prati, Aleardi, Fusinato, Coletti, doctor and poet, and others that I do not remember. They said to me, "Is it true that in Florence there are, as in the days gone by, *improvisatori* poets? We [it was Prati who spoke] are curious to hear one, and have not the pretension, as you can imagine, to expect high flights, but only free verses, and really improvised. Here is Aleardi (whom I present to you), who is a confounded sceptic on the subject of improvisation, and says that these people commit to memory a great quantity of verses of various measures, and when the occasion offers itself, have the art of patching them together in such a way that the mosaic resembles a real picture. You must know, however, that my friend is very slow in composition,—much slower than I am, although he is a far abler and more graceful poet."

"I believe," said I, "I know just the person you are looking for, and Aleardi will be disabused of such a notion. It is a certain Chiarini, called Baco, who keeps a little stall under the Uffizi, and I have heard him

L

many times, alone or in company of others. It was real improvisation; the flow of his ideas was not common or vulgar, and he invested them with a graceful and vigorous form. You shall hear him. I will take upon myself to invite him to come. Return here, and I will tell you when he is able to do so, for he is a man who has much to do. During the day, as I have said, he attends to his little shop under the Uffizi, and in the evening he is engaged to go here and there on purpose to show his skill as an extempore poet."

The poet having been engaged, and an appointment made for my friends at the studio, trial of his improvisation took place; and he did not know who his listeners were, which was perhaps as well, for who knows how much the poor poet might have felt embarrassed by the presence of such men? A table was constructed by laying a board on two trestles. I had invited, besides Prati and the rest, Ciseri the painter, Giulio Piatti, and some others whom I do not remember. The table was laid with great simplicity—some bread, sausages, and wine serving only as a sort of excuse for animating our poet with a little food and drink. Before anything else was done, Aleardi and Prati besieged the *improvisatore* with questions to ascertain how far his culture went; and although he showed that he was familiar and well acquainted with the poets, beginning with Homer and Virgil down to our times—so that he could repeat by memory some of the most beautiful fragments—as far as history, geography, and critical works went, he really knew very little, or at least so pretended. Then without further preamble Chiarini said, "Some one give me a theme. I feel in the mood for singing;" and seating himself whilst waiting, he began a prelude upon his guitar, which was sometimes soft and mournful, and then again loud and stirring. Seeing that we delayed giving him a subject, he began to sing off verse after verse in *ottava rima*, and stringing together a series of piquant and pointed re-marks against us, ridiculing our torpor and indifference. I cannot describe our hearty laughter in hearing the deluge of sarcasm and biting epigrams launched at each of us in turn by way of stirring us up. The verses were so flowing, fresh, and spirited, that they really did not seem like improvisations, so that Prati, a little irritated, after a brief consultation with the others, gave out the following theme : "The death of Buondelmonte of the Buondelmonti." Our poet began as if he had studied the subject before in all its parts, situations, colouring, names, dates, and particulars, the circumstances and sad consequences of that tragic death, and sang with inspired freedom, and with always increasing warmth and passion. The tender and pure love of the Amidei, the betrothal and pledges made between the two families, the insidious and malicious conduct of the mother of the Donati, the frivolities of Buondelmonte attracted by the saucy beauty of her daughter, the perjury and breaking away of the compact with the Amidei family, the marriage arranged with the Donati, the preparations for this marriage, the rage of the Amidei and their fol-lowers for such an atrocious insult and want of good faith, their schemes of vengeance, the conspiracy, the ambush and murder at the foot of the statue of Mars (where he interpolated in a masterly way the saying of Mosca—

"Lasso ! capo ha cosa fatta, che fu 'l mal seme della gente Tosca")

—it seemed as if the whole thing stood there before him, not as a picture, but a living and breathing reality ; while he, with his head and eyes uplifted, was heedless of our enthusiasm and shouts of applause. He sang for almost two hours ; and when he had finished, all bathed with perspiration, he put down his lute and drank. Prati and the others embraced him with effusion, only regretting that, owing to the rapidity and rush of the poet's inspiration, they had been able to retain but a few lines. Prati, however, repeated and perhaps somewhat refashioned a whole verse in *ottava rima*, and not content with expressing his admiration in words, wished to prove it to poor, tired, and excited Baco by dictating an improvised sonnet to him, of which I remember the first four and the last three lines.

In order, however, to understand Prati's verses, it is necessary to know that in those days the Capponi Ministry had fallen, and Guerrazzi come into power. Prati, who had suffered some persecution from him, owing to having in his harangues before the Circolo Politico Moderato fulminated Pindarically against this Titan from Leghorn, whilst praising the *improvisatore*, lashes out against the opposition. Here are the verses, and I regret I have only retained these in my memory:—

> " S' improvvisan ministri alla recisa ;
> S' inalzan nuovi altari a nuovi dèi ;
> Ma un improvvisator come tu sei,
> Per la croce di Dio ! non s' improvvisa."

> " One soon may improvise new ministers,|
> Unto new deities raise altars new ;
> But an improvisator like to you,
> By God's own cross ! one cannot improvise."

And the last three lines are :—

> " Felice,
> Che almen tu vivi alla febea fatica,
> Nè sei di quelli che una nuova Italia
> Tentando improvvisar, guastan l' antica."

" Happy you live in your Phœbean toils,
    Not one of those that our new Italy
    Striving to improvise, the antique spoils."

And, placing his signature at the bottom of it, he presented it to Chiarini, whose face, when he had read it
and seen by whom it was signed, assumed an expression
of admiration mingled with regret touching to behold.

The evening passed gaily. Prati also improvised,
encouraged (which is saying a great deal) and accompanied by Chiarini, and, despite his puffing and blowing,
said some very fine things. At last we separated, en-
gaging our *improvisatore* for another evening in another
place; but this I shall omit.

This symposium of artists was one of the few pleasures
of those days, when my interest and enthusiasm for Art
were relaxed, and I had no opportunity to work, as I
have before said, because, except retouching in wax
the Abel and Cain, and some few portraits, I had
absolutely nothing to do. In connection with these
statues that the Grand Duke had ordered in bronze,
let me say that, having finished in marble the Abel,
the Grand Duke saw it, regretted that he had not ordered
it himself, and that it was to go away from Florence.
I proposed, to satisfy his wishes, to make a replica; but
he was set upon having the original. It was in vain I
said that any replica made by him who had originally
made the model is always and substantially original, the
artist in finishing it always introducing modifications
and changes which make it an original and not a copy.
His Highness was not satisfied with this reasoning, and
preferred that it should be cast in bronze, making the
mould upon that which was already finished in marble.

I answered, " In order to do that, I must have the
permission of the owner."

"Right," he said to me; "and if, as you assure me, the marble is not injured by making the mould, I am certain that permission will be given."

I wrote to the Imperial household of Russia that his Highness the Grand Duke wished to have a cast in bronze of the Abel, taking the mould from the finished marble that I was making for his Imperial Majesty (the Grand Duchess Marie having presented both this statue and the Cain to her father the Emperor Nicholas). The answer was precisely this: "If the Abel is finished, have it boxed up and sent immediately."

I showed the answer to the Grand Duke, who smiled and said—

"One cannot deny that the answer is not very gracious; but now, as I really desire to have this statue in bronze, tell me, could not a mould be taken from the plaster-cast?"

"Your Highness, yes; and for this, only the consent of the artist is required."

"And do you give this consent?"

"I prefer to take the mould from the plaster-cast rather than from the marble, because the cast is the more accurate—in fact, is the true original."

And so it was settled. And at the same time, he ordered also the Cain, from which I removed the trunk that served as a support in the marble, bent a little more the arm and the hand, which was upon the forehead, and remodelled it almost entirely in the wax.

. About this time Giuseppe Verdi came to Florence to bring out his 'Macbeth.' If I mistake not, it was the first time he ever came among us; but his fame had preceded him. Enemies, it is natural, he had in great numbers. I was an admirer of all his works then known, 'Nabuco,' 'Ernani,' and 'Giovanna d'Arco.' His enemies said that as an artist he was very vulgar, and corrupted the Italian school of singing; and as a man, they said he was an absolute bear, full of pride and arrogance, and disdained to make the acquaintance of any one. Wishing to convince myself at once of the truth of this, I wrote a note in the following terms : "Giovanni Duprè begs the illustrious Maestro G. Verdi to do him the honour of paying him a visit at his studio whenever it is convenient for him to do so, as he desires to show him his Cain, that he is now finishing in marble, before he sends it away." But in order to see how much of a bear he really was, I carried the letter, and represented myself as a young man belonging to the Professor's studio. He received me with great urbanity, read the letter, and then, with a face which was neither serious nor smiling, he said—

" Tell the Professor that I thank him very much, and I will go to see him as soon as possible, for I had it in my mind to do so, wishing to know personally a young sculptor who," &c.

I answered, " If you, Signor Maestro, desire to make the acquaintance as soon as possible of that young sculptor, you can have that satisfaction at once, for I am he."

He smiled pleasantly, and shaking my hand, he said, " Oh, this is just like an artist."

We talked a long time together, and he showed me some letters of introduction that he had for Capponi, Giusti, and Niccolini. The one for Giusti was from Manzoni. All the time that he remained in Florence we saw each other every day. We made some excursions into the neighbourhood, such as to the Ginori porcelain manufactory, to Fiesole, and to ;Torre del Gallo. We were a company of four or five: Andrea Maffei, Manara, who afterwards died at Rome, Giulio

Piatti, Verdi, and myself. In the evenings he allowed
either the one or the other of us to go to hear the re-
hearsals of ' Macbeth ;' in the mornings he and Maffei
very often came to my studio. He had a great deal of
taste for painting and sculpture, and talked of them with
no ordinary acumen. He had a great preference for
Michael Angelo ; and I remember that, in the chapel of
Canon Sacchi, which is below Fiesole, on the old road,
where there is a fine collection of works of art, he remained on his knees for nearly a quarter of an hour in
admiration of an altar-piece said to be the work of Michael
Angelo. I wanted to make his bust ; but for reasons
independent of his will and mine, this plan could not be
carried into effect, and I contented myself with taking a
cast of his hand, which I afterwards cut in marble and
presented to the Siennese Philharmonic Society, to which
I have belonged since 1843, when, as I have before
said, I went to Siena. The hand of Verdi is in the
act of writing. In taking the cast the pen remained
embedded in it, and now serves as a little stick to my
sketch of Sant' Antonino.

Verdi seemed to be pleased with the Cain, the fierce
and savage nature of which he felt in his very blood ;
and I remember that my friend Maffei endeavoured to
persuade him that a fine drama, with effective situations
and contrasts of character, with which Verdi's genius
and inclination fitted him to cope, could be made out of
Byron's tragedy of ' Cain,' which he was then translating.
The gentleness of character and piety of Abel con-
trasted with that of Cain, excited by fierce anger and
envy because the offer of Abel was acceptable to God ;
Abel, who caresses his brother and talks to him about
God—and Cain, who scornfully rejects his gentle words,
uttering blasphemies even against God ; a chorus of

invisible angels in the air, a chorus of demons under ground ; Cain, who, blinded by anger, kills his brother; then the mother, who at the cry of Abel rushes in and finds him dead, then the father, then the young wife of Abel ; the grief of all for the death of that pure character, their horror of the murderer; the dark and profound remorse of Cain; and finally, the curse that fell upon him,—all formed a theme truly worthy of the dramatic and Biblical genius of Giuseppe Verdi. I remember that at the time he was much taken with it ; but he did nothing more about it, and I suppose he had his good reasons. Perhaps the nudity was an obstacle. Still, with the skins of wild beasts, tunics and eminently pictur-esque mantles can be made ; at all events he could have set the subject to music if it offered him situations and effects and really attracted him, for Verdi has shown in his many works that he possesses that sublime and fiery genius which is adapted to such a tremendous drama. He who had conceived the grand and serious melodies of 'Nabuco,' the pathetic songs of the 'Trovatore' and the ' Traviata,' and the local colour, character, and sublime harmonies of ' Aida,' might well set Cain to music. Should Verdi at any time read these pages, who knows what he may do ?

And here perhaps it is best for me to make a slight digression, in order to speak of the character and dis-position which specially belong to every artist indepen-dently of everything else—of his studies, of what he copies, and of the fashion of the day. Who would have thought that so sweet and strong a painter as Giotto would ever have risen out of the harsh and coarse mosaic-paintings of the Byzantines and the teachings of Cimabue? Variety of character, truth of movement and expression, broad and flowing draperies, colouring at once temperate, airy, and strong, were, it might be said, created by him, and took the place of the hardness, and I could almost say deformity, of the Byzantines and the dryness of the works of Cimabue. Nor did Fra Giovanni Angelico show less originality and individuality in his works. He lived in the full noon of the naturalistic school of Masaccio, Lippi, and Donatello, and his pure spirit drew its inspirations from the mystic and ideal sources of heaven, the Virgin, and the saints, not only in his subjects, but in their treatment. Michael Angelo, solitary in the midst of a corrupt, avaricious, and lascivious civilisation, by his temperament and will was conspicuous for his purity of morals, his large liberality, and his intellectual love; and despite of Raphael and Leonardo, those most splendid planets of Art, he maintained his originality, and his great figure towers like a giant among them.

The artist by nature, developed by study, becomes original and has a character distinct from all others, and in no way, not even in the slightest characteristic, can, despite any exterior influence, be different from what he is. For if Giotto had been born and educated in the sixteenth or seventeenth century, he would not have painted the vain pomps and the archaic frivolities of that period; nor would Fra Angelico at the school of Giulio Romano have given himself up to the lasciviousness of his master; nor would Michael Angelo have been warped, nor was he warped, by the strength of those giants Leonardo and Raphael. The artist, then, is what he is and such as he is born, and study will only fertilise his genius, his nature, and his propensities, nor can he with the utmost force of his will conceive and create a work contrary to his nature and to his genius. Michael Angelo would never have been able, even with a hundred years of the most powerful effort, to create a Paradise like that of Giovanni Angelico; and Fra Angelico would never have imagined even one of the figures of the Last Judgment in the Sistine Chapel. I remember—and this is my reason for this digression—that one day Rossini, speaking to me confidentially of Art in general, and upon this subject and all its bearings (and he was a competent judge), came by degrees to speak of music, and of the individual character of the composers he had known, and in regard to Verdi he spoke thus: "You see, Verdi is a·master whose character is serious and melancholy; his colouring is dark and sad, which springs abundantly and spontaneously from his genius, and precisely for this reason is most valuable. I have the highest esteem for it; but on the other hand, it is indubitable that he will never compose a semi-serious opera like the 'Linda,' and still less a comic opera like the ' Elixir d'Amore.' "

I added, " Nor like the ' Barbière.' "

He replied, " Leave me entirely out of the question."

This he said to me twenty-two years ago in my studio in the Candeli, and Verdi has not yet composed a comic or semi-serious opera, nor do I believe that he has ever thought of doing so ; and in this he has been quite right. The musical art and Italy wait for a ' Cain ' from him, and they wait for it because he himself felt the will and the power to create it.

I remember also another judgment and another expression of Rossini's in regard to Verdi. One evening after dinner I stayed on with him, because he liked to have a little talk. He was walking slowly up and down the dining-room, for he did not like to leave the room, the unpleasant odour which remains after dinner giving him apparently no annoyance. The Signora Olimpia, his wife, was playing a game of cards called *minchiate*

with one of the regular friends of the house—I mean
one of those inevitable sticks that old ladies make use
of to amuse them and help them to pass the time at
cards.

Some one always arrived late, but Rossini would not
see everybody. This evening, if I mistake not, came the
Signora Varese, Signor de Luigi, and others whom I
did not know; then two youths, who apparently were
music-masters, and they, after saluting the Signora,
turned to Rossini with these words: "Have you heard,
Signor Maestro, the criticism of Scudo on the new opera
of Verdi, 'I Vespri Siciliani,' which has just been given
in Paris?"

" No," answered Rossini, rather seriously.

"A regular criticism, you know; you should read it.
It is in the last number of the 'Revue des Deux Mondes.'
And then they began to repeat some of these opinions
of Scudo's, with adulation, which, if courteous, was little
praiseworthy. But Rossini interrupted them, saying—

"They make me laugh when they criticise Verdi in
this way, and with such a pen! To write an able and
true criticism of him, requires higher capacity and an
abler pen. In my opinion, this would require two Italian
composers of music who could write better than he does
himself; but as these Italian musical composers who are
superior to Verdi are yet to come, we must content ourselves with his music, applaud him when he does well," ·
and here he clapped his hands, "and warn him in a
fraternal way when we think he could have done better."
As he finished these words he seemed a little heated, and
almost offended, as if he thought that these people had
come to give him this news by way of flattering him, or
in order to have the violent criticism of Scudo confirmed.
The fact is, he must have already read the criticism itself,

as I had seen the number of the 'Revue' on his table before dinner. The conversation then changed, and nothing more was said.

About this time the Emperor of Russia, who was passing through Florence, honoured me with a visit. I should have passed over in silence this fact; but as it was the occasion of a false impression, by which I appeared to be the most stupid and ignorant man in the world, it is better that I should narrate exactly what occurred. Signor Mariotti, the agent for the Russian Imperial household, who, the reader may remember, had procured for me the commission for the marble of Abel, sent me word that during the day the Emperor would come to see the Cain, which was already finished in marble. I waited for him all day; but towards evening, an hour before nightfall, I dressed myself to go away, not believing that any one would come at that hour. Just as I was going out I heard a disturbance, a noise of carriages and horses, and saw the Emperor stopping at my studio. It was nearly dark, so, with a stout heart, before he descended I went to the door of the carriage and said—

"Your Majesty, I am highly honoured by your visit to my studio, but I fear that your Majesty cannot satisfy your desire to see the Cain, as it is nearly nightfall, and I should like to show this work of mine in a more favourable light."

The street was full of curious people; the studios of the artists my neighbours were all open, and they were in the doorway; the ministers of the Imperial house put their heads out of their carriage to see what was the reason the Emperor did not get out, and with whom he was talking. The Emperor, with a benign countenance, answered—

"You are quite right; one cannot see well at this hour. I will return to-morrow after mid-day."

I bowed, and the carriages drove on. This stopping of the carriage and its driving on again after a few words had passed between his Majesty and myself, led some ass to suppose that I had not been willing to receive the Emperor, and some malicious person repeated the little story; but not for long, as the next morning he returned with all his suite.

As soon as he descended, he said to me—

" *Vous parlez français ?*"

" *Très mal, Majesté.*"

"Well, I speak a little Italian ; we will make a mixture."

General Menzicoff, Count Orloff, and others whom I do not remember, accompanied the Emperor. As soon as he entered the studio he took off his hat, to the great astonishment of his suite, who all hastened to imitate him, and remained with his head uncovered all the time he was there. He was of colossal build, and perfectly proportioned. The Emperor Nicholas was then of mature years, but he looked as if he were in the flower of manhood. He talked and listened willingly, and tried to enter into the motives and conceptions of the artist.

Amongst others he saw a sketch of Adam and Eve that I had just made with the intention of representing the first family. He saw it, and it pleased him. He said it would go well with the Cain and Abel; and from these words, one might have taken for granted that he had ordered it. But I have always rather held back and been little eager for commissions, so that I did not feel myself empowered to execute it. Then, also, I had taken this subject for my simple satisfaction, and certainly with the intention of making it in the large, which I did not, however, carry into effect; for if I had done so, I should probably have offered it to him, as he had been so much pleased by the sketch. The Emperor was most affable with me, and showed a desire to know something about me besides my studies and works that he had before his eyes, so I satisfied his wishes. Nor is it to be wondered at that so important a person as he was should inquire into the particulars of simple home-life, for he was (so I afterwards heard) a good husband and father. He accompanied the Empress his wife to Palermo, as her ill health made it necessary for her to be in that mild climate, perfumed with life-giving odours. He married his daughter Maria Nicolaiewna to the Prince of Leuchtenberg, who was a simple officer in the army; but as he became aware that the young people loved each other, he wished to procure their happiness. A good husband and a good father; pity it is that one cannot say a good sovereign ! His persecutions and cruelty towards Poland, especially in regard to her religious liberty, and even her language, which is the principal inheritance of a nation, are not a small stain on that patriarchal figure.

If the young reader has the good habit of not skipping, he will remember perhaps the danger I ran of dying asphyxiated in my little studio near San Simone in company with the model, whilst I was making the sketch for the Abel. Now I must speak of another grave peril that I ran of certain death, had it not been that Divine Providence sent me help just in time. It was the 12th of April 1849 : for some days past a crowd of rough and violent Livornese had been going about our streets with jeering and menacing bearing ; and insults, violence, and provocations of every kind had not been wanting. That day a squad of these brutal fellows, after having eaten and taken a good deal to drink, would not pay their reckoning ; there were altercations and blows, to the damage of the poor man who kept the wine-shop ; and as if that were not enough, there were other gross im-

proprieties. This happened in the Camaldoli of San
Lorenzo, at a place called La Cella, where the population
was crowded and rude. The cup was overflowing, and
at a cry of, "Give it to them! give it to them!" they
fell upon these scoundrels; and although the latter were
armed with swords (being of the Livornese national
guard) and stilettoes, they were overwhelmed by the
rush of the populace, disarmed, and killed.

This was like a spark, and spread like lightning
throughout Florence. There was a great tumult and
angry cries for men from Leghorn. Everything served
as a weapon; every workman ran out with the implements of his trade, and even dishevelled ragged
women ran about like so many furies with cudgels,
shovels, and tongs, screaming, "Kill them! kill them!"
There were many victims. The soldiers who were in
the Belvedere fortress, as soon as they heard the reports
of the guns and the cause thereof, came down from there
like wild beasts, such was their hatred against these
people, from whom they had received every kind of
insult, even to finding two of their companions nailed to
the boards of their barracks one day—acts that were a
dishonour to the good reputation of the open-hearted
Livornese, with their free mode of speech and quick intelligence. Timid people retired and shut themselves
up in their houses, the shops were closed, the streets
deserted, and one saw some people running and others
pursuing them, as dogs hares; reports of guns were
heard, now close by and now in the distance, cries for
mercy, the drums beating the *generale*, and the mournful
tolling of the big bell,—all of which produced a fearful
and cruel effect.

I lived in a house over my studio, in Via Nazionale, a
short distance from the spot from which came the fatal

spark. At the sound of the beating of the *generale* I rushed up into my house to arm myself, to run to join our company. My colonel was the Marchese Gerini, and the captain Carlo Fenzi. My poor wife! I see her still crying and supplicating me not to leave her, saying, " What are you going to do?—to kill or to be killed? Stay here, and if they come to attack us in the house, as they said they would, then you will defend these poor little ones." I yielded; but Sarrocchi, who was in the house with me, in spite of his father's tears and prayers, would go, and our company went forward and protected these Livornese Guards from the fury of the populace as far as the station of Santa Maria Novella. The company was led by the second lieutenant, Engineer Renard. I went back down into the studio and tried to work, but could do nothing. That constant noise of running, questioning, firing of guns, the beating of the distant drums—a dull sound, strange and fearful—had so irritated my nerves that I walked up and down the studio, taking up a book and putting it down again. At last I resolved to go home again, all the more so that I had left my wife feeling anxious and every moment fearing that something might happen to me. I had my studio dress on, which consisted of a linen blouse and red skull-cap. Just as I was going out I heard some screams, lamentations, and a rush of people. I looked out, and saw a squad of furious men following and beating with sticks a poor Livornese, who, not being able to go any farther, fell at the corner of the street, by the Caffè degli Artisti. That bloody scene made me ill; and compelled by compassion for that poor young fellow, I ran and thrust myself into the midst of the crowd that surrounded the fallen man. He was wounded in the head, and bleeding freely; one eye was almost put out, and

M

he held one hand up in supplication, but his infuriated
assailants beat at him as if they had been threshing
corn. " Let him alone ! Stop ! Good heavens, don't
you see that the poor young fellow is dying ? " They
turned and looked at me. " What does he say ? Who
is he ? " asked these assassins. " He is a Livornese also,"
was the answer. The eagerness I had shown in favour
of that unfortunate man, the red skull-cap that I wore on
my head, and my accent not being that of a vulgar Florentine, gave strength to that assertion. From the dark
look in their eyes and their sardonic smiles I became
aware of my danger, and wished to speak; but these
infuriated beings screamed out, " Give it to him ! give
it to him, for he is also a Livornese !" I felt that
I was lost. A blow, aimed at my head, fell on my
shoulder, and some one spat in my face. A person,
whose name I do not recall, an ex-sergeant and drill-
master of our company, arrived in time to save me.

" Stop !" said he—" stop !" and with these words he
interposed and warded off the blows aimed at me. The
words and resolute action of this man in sergeant's uniform carried weight with them, and to put an end to all
this excitement he shouted out, " I bear witness, on my
honour, that this is the Professor Duprè, sculptor, corporal in our company, and not at all a Livornese."

The crowd had thickened more and more, and in it
there were some who knew me and echoed the words of
this courageous and spirited man, so that I was saved.
In the meantime my scholars, Enrico Pazzi and Luigi
Majoli, armed with long iron compasses, had rushed to my
succour ; and it was fortunate that they were no longer
needed, as, being young and brave-spirited, and Ro-
magnoli, with these weapons in their hands, who knows
what might have been the consequence ?

CHAPTER X.

MY WIFE, MY LITTLE GIRLS, AND MY WORK — DEATH OF MY BROTHER LO-
RENZO—DEATH OF LORENZO BARTOLINI—THE BASE FOR THE "TAZZA"—
EIGHT YEARS OF WORK, ONLY TO OBTAIN A LIVING — MUSSINI AND HIS
SCHOOL — POLLASTRINI — THE SCHOOL IN VIA SANT' APOLLINI — PRINCE
DEMIDOFF AND THE MONUMENT BY BARTOLINI — THE NYMPH OF THE
SCORPION AND THE NYMPH OF THE SERPENT, BY BARTOLINI — MARCHESE
ABA — COUNT ARESE — THE FOUR STATUETTES FOR DEMIDOFF — AMERIGO
OF THE PRINCE CORSINIS — HIS ROYAL HIGHNESS COUNT OF SYRACUSE, A
SCULPTOR—"SANT' ANTONINO" STATUE AT THE UFFIZI.

HE events of that day already belong to his-
tory, and it .is not for me to narrate them.
Those of the Livornese who could escape
from the fury of the populace were part of
them shut up in the Fortress da Basso, and part of them
packed like anchovies in the railway-carriages. Guerazzi
was imprisoned in the fortress of the Belvedere, and the
reins of the government were provisionally put into the
hands of the Municipality, Ubaldino Peruzzi being *gon-
faloniere*. That same evening the ensigns of liberty that
the republicans had hoisted in the *piazze* and the street-
crossings in Florence, were torn to the ground. Thus
ended the enormities of. these so-called democrats, who
were in fact only the scum and unrestrained rabble of the
flourishing and active city of Leghorn.

In the meantime affairs in my studio went from bad
to worse. The political vicissitudes, the uncertainty of
the present, and fears for the future, preoccupied every

one, and no thought was given to the Arts. I had no
work to do, and lived a secluded life of poverty with my
little family, fearing that the apprehensions of my poor
wife would be realised: often we were in need even of
the mere necessaries of life, and one thing after another
went to the *monte di pietà* in order to supply our most
pressing wants. Sorrows, disillusions, and mortifications
were not wanting: one of my children died, the only
boy that I ever had; the statue of Pope Pius II. that I
had made for Siena was despised and kept shut up in its
box for month after month, the aversion taken to it being,
they said, occasioned by the disaffection of Pius IX.
What Pius II. had to do with Pius IX. I do not know.

The Grand Duke returned; but the joy felt for his
return was embittered by the presence of foreigners, and
thence there were fears, suspicions, and ill-repressed rage,
so that Art suffered in consequence—Art, that lives and
breathes in the quiet and life-giving atmosphere of
peace.

The Grand Duke having returned, I went to make
my bow to him. He received me with his usual kindness, and asked me about my works and my family.
I spoke out sincerely to him, touching lightly, not to dis-
tress him, on my misfortunes. He remained thoughtful,
and dismissed me with benevolence. Some days after,
he sent his secretary Luigi Venturi for me, and talked at
length with me about works that he was thinking of
giving me. In the meanwhile, remembering that in times
gone by I had occupied myself with wood-carving, he
asked me if I could make or direct some work that he
was thinking of having executed for a present he wished
to make to his daughter Princess Isabella, who was to
be married to Prince Francesco of Naples. Already,
before Isabella, his eldest daughter, the Princess Augusta,

. to whom he had given my two little statuettes of Dante and Beatrice, had been married. The work for the Princess Isabella was, however, of an entirely different kind, being a casket for jewels. I accepted this commission with gratitude, although it was not a real work of sculpture ; but remembering that our old artists had executed works of the same kind, and that Baccio d'Agnolo, a famous architect, used to make the *cassone* that contained the trousseau of the young Florentine brides, and gloried in signing himself Baccio d'Agnolo, carpenter, I was contented. And besides, to speak my mind clearly, it is not the material or the thing itself that counts for anything. A little *terra cotta* of Luca della Robbia, or an *intaglio* of Barili, is worth more than a hundred thousand wretched statues in marble or bronze. I therefore made and showed him the design for the casket. In shape it was rectangular, and stood on two squares, ornamented on all sides ; the cover was slightly elevated, and on the top was a group of three figures representing maternal love ; in the six spaces were six subjects taken from the Bible representing holy marriages. These, I thought, were real jewels—family jewels. They came in order as follows : Adam and Eve in the terrestrial paradise before the Fall, Isaac and Rebecca, Boaz and Ruth, Esther and Ahasuerus, Tobit and Sarah, David and Abigail. The Grand Duke liked the idea and the design, and asked me in what wood I should carve it. I answered, in ivory, for two reasons : on account of the smallness of the figures, which would not admit of another material ; and then because ivory is in itself beautiful, rich, and most adapted for this kind of work. Fortunately, it was not necessary to look for the ivory, as in the Grand Duke's laboratory there was a most beautiful elephant's tusk. He gave it to

me ; and after having cut it up into as many pieces for
the *formelie, cornice,* and *lamine* as were required for this
work, there remained a large piece, which I still keep.
I set myself to the task, and worked with a will, as the
marriage of the Princess was soon to take place.   In
the construction of the square I employed a man from
the cabinetmaker's, Ciacchi; for the ornaments, Paolino
Fanfani, a clever wood-carver and my good friend, whom
I had known when a boy in Sani's shop, where I used to
work at wood-carving.   Two poems by Luigi Venturi,
" Lo sposo, la sposa e gli sposi," which form part of his
poem " L'Uomo," were placed inside of the box.

     And here I am at work.   Consider, friendly reader,
if you are an artist, and after long study and anxiety
have ever obtained the hoped-for compensations and
triumphs, the more deserved because so earnestly la-
boured for, that you now see an artist occupied, on a
work difficult indeed, but very far from being of that
ideal greatness that his hopes and the applause previously
given him have led him to anticipate and desire.   The
smallness of the work, the material, and even the
tools for working it, reminded me of the humbleness
of my origin.   I felt sick at heart, and then flashed
into my mind the fear that I might be obliged to return
to wood-carving.   Not that I despised that art—I have
already said the material is of no account; but I .
wanted to be a sculptor, and meantime I had nothing
to do, and my family looked to me for support.   This
thought gave me strength, drove away the golden dreams
of the future, even the memory of the smiling past, and
I worked all day long and part of the night.   My poor
wife, who was always so good and active, attending to
the household economy and to the education of our
little girls, comforted me with her simple and affectionate

words. Sometimes, returning home with the children,
she would stop to see me, and would look at and praise
my work, and perhaps, because it reminded her of our
early years, would say—

"Beautiful this work, is it not, Nanni?"

"Yes; do you like it?"

"Yes."

But in this exchange of loving words there was a
certain sadness, and although it did not appear on the
surface, yet the ear and eye of him who loves hears
and sees what is hidden below. We remained silent,
and she, taking the little girls by the hand, said good-bye
to me, and I was deeply moved, and resumed my work.

Added to all this, we were preoccupied about my
sister, who would not remain any longer in the Con-
servatorio of Monticelli, and could not return to my
house on account of incompatibility of temper between
her and my mother-in-law. At last I arranged that she
should be with my father; and this proved satisfactory,
as he thus had some one to look after his house, and
she some one to lean upon. As soon, however, as this
was settled, we had other troubles, and of a graver kind—
my brother's illness. Already for some time past, after
the work in the studio had fallen off, the maintenance of
this brother had been a serious thing to me; but with a
little sacrifice and a little goodwill, this difficulty had
been got over, and the hope of better days kept up
the courage in both of us. But he constantly grew
worse, and we had no hope of his recovery. In his wanderings he always spoke about me and my works, and it
seemed as if his mind at times was clearer and more
active. Perhaps this is so because the soul feels the day
of its freedom approaching, and is breaking the chains
which bind it to the body, and drawing nearer to its

immortal life. We say that it is wandering, because we do not understand it; the veil of the flesh obscures our spiritual vision, and we cannot comprehend the meaning of the strange and mysterious words we use. Having partaken of the blessed Sacrament, he expired, at peace with God, in the first days of January 1850. My poor brother! poor Lorenzo! strong and handsome of person; open and gay of nature, and generous-hearted; loving work and not minding fatigue, with a frank sincere smile that often came to soften the sharpness of his words. In those days a man of high intellect and great spirit, burning with a love for all that was truly beautiful, also left us. Lorenzo Bartolini died, after a few days' illness, of congestion of the brain, not young in years, but always very young in his affections and inspirations. Some moments before he was overtaken by illness, he was working on the marble with the energy and precision of a man in the prime of life. Whatever was the cause, he was taken ill, and neither the efforts of science, nor the love of his family, nor the interest and concern of every one, was able to save him. He was universally lamented, even by those who disliked him; for genius, though at first it may irritate the weak, in the long-run commands admiration and love.

His works remain as an example of the beautiful in nature, which is the mainspring of Art. In the foregoing pages I have already touched on his character as a man. I have also mentioned the reasons why he kept me at a distance; and now it is pleasant for me to remember that some time before his death he became reconciled to me, and the reconciliation took place in a most singular and casual way. One evening at Fenzi's house, after dinner, we were all assembled in the billiard-room playing pool: there were also some ladies, who were not kept away by the cigar-smoke. Bartolini came in ; and Carlino Fenzi, as soon as he saw him, went forward to meet him, and said—

"Good evening, Professor."

"*Accidenti* to all Professors ! "

"What kind of a speech is this? Have I offended you ? "

"Offence or no offence ! I have said *accidenti*, and . . . if you don't know anything, go and learn ;" and with this he passed into the other rooms. Carlino stood there as if he had been made of stucco, and turning to me said—

"But what stuff is this? Do you understand any-thing about it ? "

"Dear Carlino," I answered, " I understand it all, and will tell you at once. Bartolini does not wish to be called Professor."

"What ! but is he not Professor Bartolini? "

"That he is,—a Professor, and one of the most able, and perhaps the oldest of them all ; but he has a dislike to be called so, because he says all Professors are asses. "

"This may be, and may not be," replied Carlino, "but I knew nothing about it ; and besides, how does he wish to be called? A Cavaliere? It seems better to me to be an honourable Professor than a Cavaliere."

"No, my dear fellow, not even a Cavaliere, although he does not at all dislike being one, as you see he wears the ribbon of his order constantly in his button-hole."

"Well, what then ? "

"He wishes to be called master," I answered.

"Dear, dear ! oh, this is beautiful ! And I, who knew nothing about it, what fault is it of mine? Does it seem to you proper or well-bred to come out with that word before everybody, even before ladies? To me it seems not only not like a master, but not even like a schoolboy."

" Have patience, Carlino, and don't let us talk any more about it : bury it under a stone, and leave it alone. Listen ! they are calling out your number ; " and so the matter ended.

The day after, I had a model, Tonino Liverani, called Tria—a beautiful model, and Bartolini's favourite one, the same from whom he modelled when making his group of the Astyanax. Half an hour before mid-day he said to me—

"Signor Giovanni, would you be so kind as to send me away a quarter of an hour earlier to-day? I must be at the *maestro's* at twelve o'clock.

I replied, "Certainly—of course; dress yourself at once and go ; do not keep him waiting."

Whilst Tria was dressing, I thought over the *accidente* or the *accidenti* on the previous evening, and if that horrid word did not go down with Carlino because it was said at his house, neither did it please me, for in my quality of Professor it wounded me more than it did him. But, in fact, joking apart, I was really grieved to see such a great man descend without any cause to the use of such puerile and unbecoming expressions, the more so that he was made an object of ridicule because Carlino took the matter seriously. I said to myself, Shall I send him a message or let it go ? If I let it go, he will think that I am afraid to say what I feel, or that I am so weak-minded as to think that sally of his the most natural thing in the world : in the one case, as in the other, I shall cut a bad figure, and Bartolini despises men who are afraid or stupid. Then, too, who knows if a frank sincere word, spoken at any rate with respect and reason, such as I should say, would not do him good? All depends on Tonino's reporting it straight.

" Have you any orders, Sor Giovanni? When shall I return?" said Tonino.

" Listen, Tonino ; you must do me the kindness to say to the *maestro*, that last night he let fall from his mouth a word that displeased me, because those who heard it did not know why he used it, and having heard his reason did not appreciate it. Take care ! not a word more or less, and don't make a mistake."

And having gone over his lesson two or three times, he repeated it quite right.

" You will return to-morrow morning at nine o'clock if Bartolini will let you, and then you will give me his answer."

The day after, at nine, Tria appeared and said to me—

" I told the *maestro*, you know."

" Well, what did he answer?"

" He replied in these words : 'You must say to Duprè that I thank him. I also was aware that I had done wrong, but it was too late. Salute him.'"

Some evenings afterwards I saw him again at Fenzi's house : I was playing billiards. He shook my hand and said "Good evening," a thing he had not done for a long time.

After the little ivory casket that I have already spoken of, the Grand Duke ordered me to compose a base for the famous Table of the Muses in *pietra dura* that is in the Palazzo Pitti. This work made me happier, as I was free to imagine and execute it in the manner I thought best, and a rich and elaborate subject occurred to me at once. The Table of the Muses is round; in the centre is Apollo driving the chariot of the sun, and en-circling him are the attributes of the Muses. As the

artist who made the top of the table had taken for his
subject Apollo as the father of the Muses, I in my work
gave to him the attributes of the sun, as fertiliser of the
earth.   In the base immediately under the table, I preserved its circular form, throwing out at the top a sort of
capital supported by jutting brackets, and richly ornamented.   Beneath this is a cylinder covered with figures
of children (*putte*) engaged in the rural occupations and
pleasures of the various seasons.   In the spring they are
sporting, and playing on instruments, and dancing among
flowers ; in the summer they are cutting and bringing in
the corn; in the autumn they are harvesting and treading
grapes; in the winter they are digging, hoeing, and
sowing.   This cylinder thus storied over is set upon a
large disc with mouldings and bevelled slope, upon which
the Seasons are seated, in varied attitudes, and weaving a
garland of the flowers and fruits which the earth produces
during the year.   Spring is peacefully sitting, lightly
draped, crowned with daisies, and holding her head
somewhat elevated, to express the reawakening of Nature.
Summer has her *torso* nude, is crowned with ears of corn,
and is more robust of form than the others.   Autumn is
crowned with grapes and vine-leaves, entirely dressed,
but without a mantle.   Winter is crouching down, pressing her knees together, is entirely enveloped in her mantle,
has a cloth on her head, and is expressive of cold.   The
garland which unites the figures is hidden behind Winter,
is more slender, and composed solely of fruits.   Each of
these four figures seated upon the disc stretches forth
a foot upon a projecting ledge or bracket, which is
in plumb beneath the upper brackets, which support the
capital; and these four lower brackets, making part of the
disc and jutting forth from it, form the base and foot of
the entire column.   In the spaces between the figures

on the upper bevelled slope of the disc, ornaments with
the attributes of the elements are carved—for the earth
a growth of acanthus-leaves, for the water a dolphin, for
the air an eagle, for the fire a vase with flames. Full of
goodwill, I put my hand to the work with new hopefulness. I remember those days of a new awakening
within me of interest in my art, and trust in Providence
for the support of my little family, which had been increased by the birth of Luisina, dear little angel, whom
God took to Himself again, now some four years ago. In
going from us, she left behind her the memory of her rare
virtues, that softens the bitterness of our great loss. My
poor little angel, pray for us. My eyes are dim with
tears, but I feel how true it is that sorrow only rekindles
the light of faith.

I worked with true enthusiasm, getting up at an early
hour, and after a slight breakfast with my family, going
down into the studio, which was almost under my own
room. I kept note of all my expenses, to have some idea
of the price I should ask for my model, as it was his
Highness's intention to have it cast in bronze. I was
very light-hearted, as I have already said ; and the principal reason for my being so was, that I saw by means of
this work the bread for my family was provided for. I
had not put aside a *soldo*, and the various works I had
made during eight years—that is to say, from '42 to '50—
had yielded me barely enough to live upon, because the
inevitable expenses of housekeeping had absorbed all the
little I had beyond. I lived day by day, hoping always that
fortune would smile upon me as in my early years; and now
with this work of the pedestal for the table, I felt at ease.

I have thought it opportune to enter into these minute
particulars, that the young artist may learn two things
from them : first, not to give himself up with too much

assurance to the joys of early triumphs; and secondly, not to get discouraged in the bitter days of want and disillusions, when he feels himself forsaken. I know so many young men who become dejected at once, and inveigh against adverse fortune, against the injustice of men and their neglect, and other phrases equally idle, proud, and foolish.

My studio was no longer what it used to be at one time—no longer the place of rendezvous of applauding friends and admirers who followed the fashion of the moment; these all went about their own affairs, and had nothing more to do with me. Some of the most distinguished amongst them, after the Restoration, were refugees, some in one place, some in another. Venturi was the only one who remained, and he came often to see me, and we talked at length about Art. Ciseri also was a good and faithful friend, and used to come to take me for a long walk in the evening. Mussini, whom I had known a short time before, first left for Paris, and then returned to go to Siena as Director of the Institute of Fine Arts there, where he still teaches, and from his admirable school have come such famous artists as Cassioli, Franchi, Maccari, and Visconti, who died a miserable death from drowning at Rome.

I knew Mussini in 1844, when he had finished his four years of *pensionat*, and was on his return from Rome. Mussini was then a remarkable young artist, having gone through a varied and severe course of study. His compositions were serious and careful, and as a draughtsman he followed the style of our Florentine school of the *quattrocento*. Those qualities he showed in his first pictures, the Expulsion of the Profaners of the Temple, Sacred Music, and the Allegory of Almsgiving. In his last sketch, which he made in

Rome, Abelard and Heloïse, he changed a little from his first manner, or I should better say from his first method: in the "Abelard" he followed the modern German school—Overbeck perhaps. As soon as he had returned to Florence he set to work on his Triumph of Truth, abandoning his first views, enlarging his style, freshening his colouring, and taking his inspiration from Leonardo and Raphael. We became friends. He was rather a small thin young man, with black hair, black eyes, and olive complexion. In his conversation he was vivacious, sententious, and decided; an admirer of Phidias and Giotto above all others; also of Raphael, Michael Angelo, and, in modern times, of Ingres and Bartolini. His companionship and friendship were of great use to me on account of his frank and sound advice on Art. He went for some time to Paris, and returned, as I have already said, to occupy the place of Director of the Institute of Fine Arts at Siena—a post that he had begged me to ask for in his name; and in this way I lost the friendship of Enrico Pollastrini, who had asked for it for himself. As soon as I heard that the post was vacant by the death of Menci, I advised Mussini by letter to apply for it. He answered me at once, thanking me for my advice, but adding that at present he did not wish to leave Paris. Two days after, in another letter he told me he had changed his mind, and begged me, as I have said, to make an application in his name. Pollastrini, who knew neither of my advice and counsel to Mussini nor of my having asked for the post for him, came to see me, to get me to promise that I would support him in his demands for the place. Poor Enrico! he died but a few months ago. He was an excellent man, affectionate, and ready to serve a friend, but mis-

trustful and irascible. He would take offence at a mere
nothing, and once in that vein, he was capable of
not bowing to you for some time. I did not like
him the less for all this. He never did any harm
to anybody; and I believe he would not have killed
even a fly, much less have been of injury to any one.
May God give his soul peace! He came, therefore, to see me and get me to pledge myself in his
favour; and when he heard that I had recommended
the nomination of Mussini—for by my petition it was
to be understood that I supported him—he was annoyed,
and did not hide his resentment, saying that he should
not have expected me to show this preference, or to
put another before him. I answered that I knew nothing about his having asked for the nomination, and
that what I had done had been from a desire that a
clever artist, and one so able to teach, should not remain in a foreign land. These reasons, instead of bringing persuasion to him, only embittered him the more,
and he was angry with me for a long time. But below
the surface poor Enrico cared for me, and has shown
it in a thousand ways.

I have said that Mussini was a master of sound and
true principles in Art; and so he is still, for his school
at Siena has produced, and produces, excellent results.
Beyond these principles, he had the power of com-
municating and exemplifying them to others, and this
is a most important and invaluable faculty in a teacher.
Before he left for Paris, he kept a school in Via Sant'
Apollonia, where, amongst other scholars, I remember
a certain Pelosi di Lucca, Gordigiani, and Norfini, now
painters of repute. He begged me to take the direction
of his school, and I accepted, not without observing to
him that I had not the necessary qualities for that place;

but he insisted, and I yielded. Things, however, went as it was natural they should go; the school lingered on awhile, and after a few months was broken up.

As it seemed to me, from his drawing, that Gordigiani had talent for sculpture, I advised him to give himself up to that art, and he readily came to my studio and began to model with goodwill. But, either because the material he had to handle was difficult to manage on account of its novelty, or because impatience got the better of him, one fine day he threw his tools and work to the ground, and would have nothing more to say to them. He gave himself up to painting portraits, and succeeded so well that he has now become the portrait-painter most praised amongst us, and has made for himself a really enviable position. Nevertheless, I believe that if he had had a little constancy, he would have succeeded as well in sculpture as in painting, because few understand as well as he does the form and relation of planes.

At this time I had a commission to finish in marble two statues by Bartolini that he had left unfinished; the "Nymph and the Scorpion" for the Emperor of Russia, and the "Nymph and the Serpent" for the Marchese Ala-Ponzoni of Milan. With regard to this there were certain ill-natured reports against me that I think best to clear up. Some time before, Prince Demidoff had engaged and even begged of me to finish some of the figures of the great monument to his father that Bartolini had left incomplete. I would not accept this commission, because the master had worked on them a great deal himself, and it seemed to me irreverent, and not a thing to be done, to continue and finish his work. I endeavoured to make the Prince understand that as Bartolini had worked upon it himself, and

N

the work was so well advanced, it had more value left as it was than if it were finished by my hand, be it even with all the love of an artist. The Prince did not appear to be much persuaded by this reasoning, and insisted, saying that my principles in art were the same as those taught by Bartolini, and the veneration felt by me for him was a pledge of the love I would employ in finishing these figures. I thanked the Prince for the too great confidence he placed in me as an artist, but I begged of him not to insist in carrying out this idea of having the work finished, either by me or by any other —for he, in order to force me to accept, said that otherwise he should give it to some one else, and added (exaggerating out of kindness my worth in art) that it would be my fault if it chanced that the artist was not fully equal to the arduous enterprise. I answered that I thought other artists abler than myself, but was of opinion that the statues ought to be left as they were. In order to convince him, I reminded him, as an example to the purpose, of the Medici monuments in San Lorenzo, before which no one would dare to say, " What a pity these figures are not finished ! " if he did not say it with regard to Michael Angelo himself. And if, instead, they had been finished by other hands, with a good reason he would curse Clement, who, after having betrayed his country, had wished to offer this offence to art and Michael Angelo's fame. This, God be praised, cannot be said, because the statues of Day and Night are just as that divine master left them. These words, said with the conviction and the warmth of an artist, who was a poor one to boot, and wishing and longing for fame and fortune, so entirely convinced the Prince, that he was quite satisfied; and pressing my hand in silence, which was more eloquent than words, he left me.

If this conduct of mine was praised by some people in the hopes that it had not been quite liked by the Prince, my acceptance of the order for the two statues for the Emperor and the Marchese Ala afterwards, gave rise to a number of remarks : " See his consistency of principles and opinions ! " they said. " How is it that the same reasons that were held out for his refusing the figures in the Demidoff monument do not hold equally good for these ? Are these not also statues of Bartolini's, and to be finished in the same way as those ? "

And here I come to an explanation of this point, where it would seem as if I had been in contradiction with myself. On one of these statues, the " Nymph and the Scorpion," for the Emperor of Russia, Bartolini had never worked with his own hands—in fact, it was not finished, not even blocked out. On the other, for the Marchese Ala, he had worked, but how? The head, where he had wished to make a change in the arrange-ment of the hair, had been so cut away that there was a finger's-breadth of marble in the blocking-out points wanting on each side, so that it was ugly to see ; and in addition to this, he had bent the forefinger of the left hand that rests on the serpent under the palm of the hand, perhaps because in undercutting it the last joint of the finger had been broken. Now this finger, bent back and dislocated, looked very badly, when com- . pared with the model in plaster, where the fingers were all extended, and pressed upon the serpent's neck ad-mirably. I therefore accepted both these commissions, —the one because it had never been touched by Barto-lini's own hand, and the other because I was willing and able to put it straight. However, before touching the statue, I made the Marchese Ala acquainted with the serious defects there were in it, which Bartolini would

certainly have remedied had he had the time to finish it;
and I asked for his permission (and on this condition
alone accepted the work) to cut off all the top of the
head with the locks of hair where it had been injured,
in order to replace it exactly in the way that Bartolini
had first imagined and modelled it, and to add a piece
of marble to the hand to remake the forefinger. He
consented to these conditions. In order to make sure
myself that I was right, before cutting away the defective
parts, I had a mould and cast taken from them, that any
one might see how they stood before I touched them,
and how by taking the original model for my guide, I
had replaced them: and I then said (as I now write),
that all who were sensible and reasonable understood
and were satisfied; as to the others, I do not know what
they thought, nor did I care for them then, nor do now.
I finished the two statues, copying the original models
where these were carefully finished, and interpreting
them where they were barely indicated, selecting suitable
models from life; and so I satisfied those who trusted in
me, and my own conscience.

Some time previous to this the Marchese Ala had
given me an order for the "Sleep of Innocence"—a
statue of a child sleeping—which I had already executed
a long time before for my excellent friend the Marchese
Alessandro Bichi-Ruspoli of Siena. I therefore repeated
this child in marble by commission of the aforesaid
Marchese Ala; but being rather changeable, he afterwards declared to me that this work did not entirely
satisfy him, although it was conscientiously done, and
that he should take it only because he had engaged to
do so. I answered that I wished my works to be taken
because they were liked, not because they were ordered,
and begged that he would not speak of it again. He

thanked me, and promised to give me another order for portraits of his three pretty little children ; but subsequently I heard nothing more about it.   One day, being in Turin, and finding myself at Vela's studio, where I had gone to pay him a visit, I saw a very graceful little portrait-group, full length, such as that able artist knew how to make and is in the habit of making.   I asked, " Who are these pretty children ? "

" They are the children of Marchese Ala," replied Vela.   " It is already some time since he ordered this work, but he has not yet put in an appearance.   I have written him so many letters, to which I have received no answer, that I don't know what to think."

I then recounted to him what took place about my little Putto, and the promise he had made of giving me an order for the little group.   Vela answered that he was astonished and annoyed ; but as the commission had been given to him, and the model was in plaster, he begged me to speak to the Marchese in order that he might be able to finish the work.   I do not know whether Vela ever did put the group into marble.

As regards myself and compensation for the affair of the Putto, which had been left hanging for so many years, he took my Bacco della Crittogama ; but as the Marchese was subject to very long periods of melancholy that prevented his thinking about anything for a good while, I heard nothing more on the subject, until one day Count Arese, to whom I began to speak about this affair, said to me—

" Leave the matter to me.   Write me a letter giving me an account of this affair, and I will send you the money.   I have business relations with the Marchese Ala, and will send him your receipt, and there will be an end to it."

I did as he said, and was satisfied.   What a pity it is
that that most noble gentleman was so often afflicted by
such a malady !   He was and is one of the most intelligent and generous patrons of art.   The first Italian
and foreign painters and sculptors had co-operated to
make his house splendid and enviable for its works
of art.

As I have already said, Demidoff kept these statues
just as Bartolini had left them, and placed them in his
villa of San Donato.   One evening after dinner, as we
were walking together through its magnificent apartments, he stopped in one of the little sitting-rooms and
said to me—

" Your little statuettes of Dante and Beatrice would
look well here on small pedestals in the corners ; but
there ought to be four.   And you may complete the
number, by making a Petrarch and Madonna Laura, if
you like."

" I should like to do so."

And I made these other two statuettes.   At present I
do not know who has them ; they were sold at Paris a
few years ago, together with a great many other works
of art belonging to the Prince.

The dinners that the Prince gave in that magnificent
and enchanting house were most splendid.   I met there,
besides strangers that I do not speak of, Matas, the
Prince's architect, Baron Gariod, my good friend Professor Zannetti, Prince Andrea Corsini, and that dear
son of his, young Amerigo.   One evening we were playing billiards together, and having finished our game of
carolina, he said to me—

" Come away; let us take a turn through the rooms ;"
and looking at and talking about his statues of Pradier,
Bartolini, and Powers, the stupendous Fiamminghi, the

Canalettis, Titian, Greuze, the arrases in the large hall,
the columns of malachite, remarkable both for their size
and finish, and a thousand other objects of exquisite
taste and great cost, the young man's eyes sparkled with
joy and enthusiasm, and looking me steadily in the face,
he said—

"I am going away soon, you know, to Spain. On my
return, I want to do great things, and you must help
me. I want a house that shall not be inferior to this."

I replied, "If you desire, you can have one even
more beautiful. I know the suite of rooms in your
palace, and the masterpieces of art in your gallery.
With the riches you possess, and the will that is not
wanting, you might, as I have said, surpass even this
enchanting abode."

A short time after this, he came to my studio to say
good-bye to me. Dear young man! with a pure heart
and open mind, an enthusiast for the beautiful, and beloved by all, he went away, and not one of us saw him
again. He died in a foreign land, where he had gone
to bring away his bride.

Bartolini's statues being finished, I made a bas-relief
of Adam and Eve by commission of Cavaliere Giulio
Bianchi of Siena ; after which I retouched in wax the
pedestal of the Table for its casting in bronze, and in
the meantime prepared to model the statue of Sant'
Antonino for the Loggie of the Uffizi. From this time
forth things began to go more evenly and liberally with
me, and fears of falling back into poverty disappeared
by slow degrees. Already the rent of my studio, which
was not small, was no longer a weight to me, as by
sovereign decree the studio which had been left by
Professor Costoli on his promotion to the presidency of
the Academy after Bartolini's death was given to me.

The statuettes of Beatrice and Dante of themselves alone almost supplied enough for the daily wants of the family, as I always had one or two of them to make at a time. I think I have made about forty of them, and one of them deserves comment.

Before the Princess Matilde, who was married to Demidoff, left for Paris and was separated from her husband, the Grand Duchess of Tuscany ordered my Beatrice, with the intention of presenting it to that lady. The divorce having ensued, she did not give it to her, and the little statue remained for some time at her Highness's, and afterwards she gave it to her brother, the Count of Syracuse, who used to amuse himself by working in sculpture. This sculptor-Prince, without the slightest improper intention, but rather from a sort of good-natured, easy-going way, used to keep this statuette of mine alongside of his own, and it sometimes happened that persons praised him for it; and he must have felt not a little embarrassed to clear up this *quid pro quo.*

It appears that sometimes, perhaps because this annoyed him, he made matters so far from clear that the statuette passed off as his own work. One day a Neapolitan lady came to my studio, a Princess Caraffa or Coscia (I cannot say which with certainty, but it is a matter that can be verified, for she told me that she was a descendant of the family of Pope John XXIII., who is buried in our San Giovanni, where one sees his fine monument between the two columns on the right-hand side). This lady, when she saw the Beatrice among my other works, exclaimed—

"Oh! the graceful Portinari by the Count of Syracuse! Is it not true that it is charming?"

"Princess," I answered, "I do not know if that little

figure is pretty or not, but I am glad that you think so, for it is mine, one of my very first works. I modelled it in 1843, inspired by that sublime sonnet of Dante which begins—

'Tanto gentile e tanto onesta pare,' &c.

I made the first copy of this statuette for Signor Sansone Uzielli of Leghorn; the second for the Grand Duke, which, with the young Dante, he gave to the Princess Isabella his daughter, who married the Prince Luitpoldo of Bavaria; and the one that you saw was presented to the Count of Syracuse by the Grand Duchess."

The noble lady smiled, and said, "I must have been mistaken."

The Count of Syracuse was a great lover of sculpture, and occupied himself with it as much as was consistent with the position he occupied. Several of his works are most praiseworthy, and I keep some of the photographs of them that he was so kind as to send me.

To return to my Sant' Antonino that I left unfinished. This model cost me an immense deal of work. The subject required character, bearing, and attitude of an absolutely simple and natural treatment, such as I gave the Giotto; but fearing to meet with censure from the lovers of the classic, I kept doing and undoing my work in my sketches, as well as in my large model. It is useless! One must be decided, and sure of the side one wishes to take. This see-sawing between ideal beauty and truth to nature in portraiture will not do, just as it would be absurd and bad to adhere entirely to nature in other subjects, especially sacred ones.

And although imitation of beautiful nature is the foundation and substance of any work, yet the mode of seeing it and reproducing it constitutes the style that every artist, who is elevated, great, and pure, draws from within himself, according to his subject and the measure meted out to him by nature and education.   In portrait statues one must abandon the ideal, even as regards the ordinary rules of the just proportions of the body.   Sant' Antonino was named thus because he was small of stature.   I was tempted several times to make him faithfully just as he was, small and crooked; and I made a sketch of him thus, which I still preserve, and it is precious on account of the little stick on which he leans, for this stick was no other than Giuseppe Verdi's pen. But I did nothing more with it, as I was vacillating between the rules of art and the close imitation of nature; and it is just this close imitation of the details of nature that constitutes the character of a portrait statue — a sound canon put wisely in practice by the ancients, as can easily be seen from their statues of the philosophers in the Vatican, such as the Zeno, and more particularly in that of Diogenes; and in the bas-relief of Æsop, where one sees even the absolute hump on his back. But the copying in detail from nature does not mean a too close imitation of every little thing, of every wrinkle; these are the mechanical nothings that are, as it were, the battle-horse to those who make a trade of art, and should be left to them.

CHAPTER XI.

CLOSE IMITATION FROM LIFE—MY ILLNESS—I AM IN DANGER OF LOSING MY LIFE
—LUIGI DEL PUNTA, HEAD PHYSICIAN AT COURT—THE GRAND DUKE FUR-
NISHES ME WITH THE MEANS FOR GOING TO NAPLES—I LEAVE FOR NAPLES
—A BEGGAR IMPOSTOR—ANOTHER AND MY BOOTS—SORRENTO—MY NEAPOLI-
TAN FRIENDS—PROFESSOR TARTAGLIA AND THE HYDROPATHIC CURE—THE
MUSEUM AT NAPLES—LET US STUDY THE GOOD WHEREVER IT IS TO BE
FOUND—A STRANGE PRESENTATION.

 HAT my words may not be obscure, and that one may see with sufficient clearness the difference that exists between the details that constitute different types and the minu-tiæ that must be left out, I will mention where this sound principle of art is to be found. For greater brevity and clearness I will speak of busts. The bust in bronze of Seneca in the museum at Naples, the bust of Scipio Africanus in the statue-gallery at Florence, the Vitellius, Julia and Lucius Verus, the Cicero of the British Museum, and another Seneca at the Capitol, each has a distinct character of its own. So firm and decided are the details of those different faces, the planes are so clear and certain, the life so shines in the eyes, the breath so seems to come from the lips, that they have been for centuries the study and stumbling-block of all artists; for after that period you do not find anything, unless it be some *terre cotte* of Luca della Robbia, and a bust of a bishop by Mino da Fiesole, in

which you do not find every hair, and, in fact, every possible minutia.

The error into which these two schools run—that is to say, the Academic and Naturalistic—is this, that the one, exaggerating its general rules, neglects detail, and so becomes hard and cold; whilst the other, multiplying them *ad infinitum*, falls into minutiæ which make art vulgar. These are both errors, both ugly, both false.

Does this brief tirade, half dictatorial and half careless, bore you, gentle reader? If so, skip it, for I cannot let go the opportunity, from time to time, of making a good critical observation when it occurs to me, and I think it well not to omit doing so. Young artists will, I am sure, be grateful to me; and besides, though these few words may have bored you, they serve as a warning to them on the importance of different characteristics, and are also of use to me, I do not say as an excuse, but as a frank statement of opinion, for in my Sant' Antonino this rule is not clearly carried into practice. The importance of speaking the truth and loving it is clearly given by Dante when he says :—

> " Che s' io al vero son timido amico
> Temo di perder vita tra coloro,
> Che questo tempo chiameranno antico." [1]

As I am an ardent lover of truth, I wish to speak it now. With regard to this statue, if I had not the strength of mind to reproduce the saint just as he was, with all his peculiarities, in other statues it has been my study to do so, and I believe not without success.

But in the meanwhile—I do not know for what reason

[1] " And if I am a timid friend to truth,
  I fear that I may lose my life with those
  Who will hereafter call this time the olden."
                    —DANTE : *Paradiso*, Canto xvii.

—a general feeling of uneasiness took possession of me, and a prostration of strength, that prevented me from thinking or working. Added to this, I had attacks of giddiness, and was obliged to spend entire days sitting down without being able to do anything, and feeling sad and melancholy. My medical friends—Alberti and Barzellotti—recommended exercise, meat diet, and a little good wine, which in those days (1852) could scarcely be found genuine. They ordered me to take preparations of iron and zinc, but my health grew worse every day. It was now three months since I had gone to the studio. I went out sometimes in the carriage with my poor wife, and we used to go into the country, or on the hills of San Domenico, Settignano, or Pian di Giullari. Sometimes I went out on foot, but accompanied by and leaning on the arm of Enrico Pazzi, Luigi Majoli, or Ciseri, who one day took me by the railway to Prato, where we remained until evening. After that I began to feel a want of appetite, nausea, and sleeplessness, and then my friends really became alarmed about my health.

The Grand Duke Leopold, that excellent sovereign, who was called the *babbo*—I know not if from affection or derision—was for me (and for many others who do not think proper to admit it) really paternal in his care and timely help. Almost every day he wished to have news of my health; and constantly sent Luigi Venturi, his secretary and a friend of mine, to make inquiries. When he heard that matters had come to this bad pass, he charged his private medical attendant, Luigi del Punta, to come and examine me, study my disease, and suggest a remedy. Del Punta, before coming to see me, acquainted my medical advisers with the order he had received, and a consultation was fixed for the following day, which was the 8th of September, 1852—the Feast of the Virgin. On that morning Alberti and Barzellotti arrived

first, paid me a little visit, and then retired into the sitting-room to wait for Del Punta. The sitting-room was
next to my room. Del Punta came in, and they talked
for a long time, but in an undertone, so that I heard
nothing, except one word pronounced by Del Punta,
which put me in a great state of apprehension, and that
was "tape-worm." The idea that I could have that ugly
malicious beast inside me frightened me, and when they
came into my room they found me in a much worse condition than when they had left me a little time before.
I always remember the piercing look of Del Punta,
anxious and penetrating. Then he began to question
me, and examine me all over, by auscultation, thump-
ing, and squeezing me. His inspection was a long one;
but as he proceeded little by little, his expression became more *open*, his beaming frank eyes met mine, and
I could almost say that a mocking smile played about
his lips. Seeing me still staring at him, he gave me a
little tap with his hand on my shoulder, and said, "Well,
be of good cheer; there is nothing serious the matter."
And seeing that I did not believe him, he added, "I
tell you you haven't a cabbage-worth the matter with
you!" and he said this with emphasis.

Well, my dear reader, that foolish expression did me
good. If he had assured me in the usual way, and with
select phraseology, that I had nothing serious the matter
with me, it would not have had the eloquence or efficacy
of that slang word blurted out with such force in the
face of the sick man, before the other medical men, with
my poor wife listening sadly and anxiously, my little ones
about me, not understanding, but full of vague fears on
account of their mother's sadness and the novelty of the
thing. It brought with it, I say, such a sense of conviction, that it was for me a true and positive affirmation.

Poor Luigi! as learned in medicine as you were genial as a friend, on that day you gave new life to me when I seemed to see it fleeting from me. You so vivacious, so full of health—I so weak and ill; who would have then said that so soon you would be gone?

After having assured me and my wife that there was no serious disease, that I should certainly recover, he added that I required a special method of treatment that had more to do with a regimen of life than with medicine, and that he would refer the result of the consultation and his examination to the Grand Duke. In fact, he reported to the Grand Duke (as I afterwards learned), that in the condition in which I was, I could not have lived; my nerves were so shattered that I had become very weak, and that I suffered from vertigo and could hardly stand, and at last had lost my appetite and power of sleeping. It was urgent that I should have rest; and this would consist in taking me away from home, away from my studio, from Florence, from all—in one word, sending me off on a journey, not a long one, but far enough to distract me from cares and thoughts that oppressed; this was the only remedy, he said, and could be freely adopted, as I had no internal disease. It was necessary that I should have a companion that I liked with me, and he suggested that my wife should accompany me.

A few days after, the Grand Duke informed me by means of his secretary, Venturi, that it was necessary for me to have a change of air, and that Professor del Punta had advised Naples, as it was a bright cheerful place to stay in—where the air was mild, and where there were many pleasant things to distract one: that I must therefore make my arrangements to go there; that my wife and one little girl must accompany me; and that I was not

to give a thought to anything, as he provided for everything during the time that was necessary for my recovery, and he recommended me to his minister Cavaliere Luigi Bargagli.

Every day that preceded my departure, Professor del
Punta came to see me, and encouraged me to be of good
cheer also, on the part of the Grand Duke. The preparations for our departure were many, and by no means
trifling. It was necessary to make arrangements so
that the work in the studio should not be without direction, and should be carried on carefully. Tito Sarrocchi,
then my scholar and workman, was intrusted with the
direction of it. The works in hand, besides the statue of
Sant' Antonino, were, " Innocence and the Fisherman,"
for Lord Crawford of London, and some busts. As to
models in clay, I left a Bacco dell' uva Malata, that Sarrocchi had charge of until my return. My friends,
artists and not artists, came during those days to say
good-bye to me, some of them consoling themselves
with hopes of my recovery, and others fearing that they
should never see me again, so emaciated and sad was I;
and Antonio Ciseri wept in saying good-bye.

Good gracious! how long and tedious is this narrative
of your illness!

Long! yes or no. Long for you perhaps, who, as it
would seem, have never been ill, and who do not know
what a consolation it is for one who is suffering from
the same malady as yourself to hear about such illness
from one who is at present quite well. If it annoys
you, have patience—some one may benefit by it; and
at any rate, for the present I have done.

The night that preceded my departure, that dear
saintly woman my wife remained up all night to put
everything in the house in order, and to prepare what

was needed for us—that is, myself, my wife, and Beppina,
our second daughter. I had at that time four daughters :
Amalia, who is the eldest; Beppina, who went with
me ; and Luisina and Emilia, who remained at home with
their grandmother and Amalia. I lost Emilia quite
young, dear little angel. Her little body rests in the
cemetery of San Leonardo. Gigina I lost when she was
grown up, and will speak of this in its place.

The journey had to be made by short stages in a *vettura*,
so that it was necessary to hire a carriage and keep it
at one's own expense as far as Naples. We left on the
morning of the 20th of October 1852, arrived on the
28th, and lodged at the Hotel de Rome, Santa Lucia.
That eight days' journey in the sweet company of my
wife, the pretty, innocent questionings of Beppina about
the fields, the rivers, and the villages that we passed
by one after the other, the novelty of the life, the pure
country air, and the hope of regaining my health, had
softened the asperity of my suffering. Apathy and sadness gradually gave way to a desire to see new things ;
my wife's questions and those of my little one obliged me
to answer, and sometimes to smile. I felt my appetite for
food return, and I slept peacefully some hours every night.

In this way I arrived in Naples—in that immense
city, so crowded with people, so noisy and deafening on
account of the numbers of carriages, shouts of the coach-
men, of the people offering things for sale, of jugglers,
beggars, all speaking in a strange difficult dialect most
unpleasant to a Tuscan. In this city the first impression made upon me was a mixture of wonder and anger.
It seemed to me as if one could do all that those good
people were doing without being obliged to scream and
throw one's self about so much. Here a coachman
smacked his whip within four fingers of your ears, to ask

o

you if you wanted his carriage; there a man, selling iced
water and lemonade, screamed out at the height of his
voice I don't know what, and, to give it more force, beat
with his lemon-squeezers against his metallic bench, like
Norma or Villeda on Irminsul's shield; a little farther
on a half-naked beggar, with his ragged wife and children,
shouted out, "I am dying with hunger," with lungs that
a commander of a battalion in the battle-field might
envy. These beggars, however, are for the most part
impostors.   One day—it was a *festa*—I was returning
from San Gennaro, where I had been to Mass with my
wife and little girl.   I saw a man extended on the
ground with his body and legs inside a doorway, his
head and his arms out into the street; his mouth was
green with grass that he had been chewing, and some
of which was hanging out of his mouth. The people
passing by looked, and then went on their way talking and laughing as if it was nothing.   I was stunned,
indignant, and full of pity, and turning to my wife
(and even I flinging about my arms in the Neapolitan fashion), said, with all the Christian and human
resentment that I was capable of, "How is it possible
that, in such a flourishing and civil city as this, a poor
Christian is left to die of hunger in the street for want
of a little bread which is denied him by his unnatural
brethren, and is obliged to feed upon the food for
beasts?" And I ran at once to a pastrycook's near
by for some cakes, because I thought bread would be
too hard food for a man reduced to such a state; and
with a light heart on account of the good action, I took
them to him that I might see him eat them, and as
soon as he was a little restored give him some *soldi.*
Clever indeed!   You little thought that the man was
an impostor! I bent over him, called him; he did not

answer. I put a cake to his mouth, and he looked at
me, took the cakes, and hid them in his bosom between
his shirt and his skin, and this kind of a bag was crammed
full of bread and other things. Some inquisitive people
had stopped to look on, and seeing this, it seemed to me
as if they laughed at my simplicity.

And as I am on this question, and my memory serves
me well, I will tell you of another beggar. In front of
the Hotel de France, Largo Castello, where I was
staying, is the Church of San Giacomo. At the door
of this church a poor man stood from morning until
night trembling, half naked, and barefoot. It made me
feel badly, comfortably lodged as I was, and sitting smoking my cigar on the terrace, to see that poor creature
out in the cold with his feet in the mud. More than
once my poor wife had given him some *soldi;* but one
day when it was raining heavily, and the poor man was
out in it all, with his feet nearly covered by water, a
happy thought struck me, inspired by Christian charity,
and I said, "I am here under cover, and have boots on
my feet, while that poor wretch is there outside with no
shoes on; I will give him my boots." I rang the bell;
the servant came, and I said to him, "Raffael, take
this pair of boots to that poor man over there by the
door of San Giacomo."

"Yes, sir," said Raffael, and away he went.

I went back on to the balcony to enjoy the effect of
my good deed, imagining that I should see an expression
of amazement and joy on the man's face. Nothing of
the sort ; he remained there with the boots in hand as if
he did not know exactly what sort of things they were,
and when Raffael told him that I gave them to him, and
pointed me out to him on the terrace, the man turned,
looked up, and, always holding them in his hand, made

signs of thanking me; then he put them down on the ground near his feet, and continued to stretch out his hands to the people entering the church ! "Ah, poor man," I said, "he wished to put them on to-morrow morning; he must wash himself, of course, and dry his feet before putting them on. How stupid of me! The people are just going in for the *novena* (it was Christmas-time), and he does not want to lose a chance *grano* to buy him some bread." But the next morning he was still barefooted, and it was raining. I said to my wife—

"Look, I sent that poor man my boots yesterday, so that he should not wet his feet, but he has not put them on. What do you think is the reason? What should you say?"

"He probably wishes to keep them for Sundays," was the serious answer of that dear simple woman.

"You are joking, my dear; that man is old, and if he keeps them for Sundays he will not see the end of them. I say that he has sold them."

"And I say, that if he had two or three *lire* to spare, he would have wished to buy a pair, poor man!"

We each remained of our own opinion. Late in the day we went out, and, approaching the poor man, I said to him—

"Why have you not put on the boots that I gave you? Are they tight?"

"Your Excellency," he replied, "if I put the boots on, no one will give me another penny. I have sold them, your Excellency; and may the Virgin bless you."

A few days after my arrival at Naples I went to Sorrento. The discordant noise of the town annoyed me, and I wished to try that little place, so much praised for

its climate and for its quietness, and so full of association
with that illustrious and unhappy man, Torquato Tasso.
I went there with my friend Venturi, who had come to
Naples for a few days with the Grand Duke.

Sorrento is a charming little town seated on the crest
of a hill called the Deserto. . It is surrounded on the
left by woods of orange, citron, and lemon trees, and on
the right by the sea with the island of Capri, that seems
to rise up majestically from the deep blue waters.   On
the far horizon one catches a glimpse of Nisida and
Baia. This small town is inhabited by fishermen, orange-
packers employed on the large landed possessions in the
neighbourhood, and by most clever workers of inlaid
wood, who have made their art so much in request by
the thousand little trifles, so pretty in design and so carefully executed, that they make. Garguillo's manufactory
is much renowned, and justly so.   Not only do you find
on the pieces of furniture cornices, fillets, meanders,
and other graceful ornaments, but also. extremely pretty
figures inlaid on the boxes, little tables, and other nick-
nacks with which well-to-do people embellish their rooms.
Here the air is mild, and the sun is tempered by the
shade of laurels and orange-trees.   The character of the
inhabitants is gentle and laborious, and through their
acts and their words there breathes a quiet, ineffable
melancholy, like the memory of a sweet pure dream.
Their complexion is dark, and also their hair; their eyes
have long lashes, and are cut in almond shape.   It seems
as if they looked with infinite sweetness at something im-
measurably far off; their smile is sad, as if it recalled to
them a lost existence that hope induced them to think
not irretrievably lost.   This favoured, I should almost say
ideal, bit of nature, at a few miles' distance from the
thoughtless vulgar noise of the inhabitants of Naples, is

a thing commented on by all, but by no one reasonably explained. The climate so temperate, the air perfumed with the scent of orange-flowers, and the sweet melancholy on those faces, instead of rendering the place agreeable to me, made me profoundly sad. Why did my heart not open itself to the enjoyments of that pure, serene, and most beautiful nature? Why was it that that bright sky, that tranquil sea, that quiet industrious life, rendered me more sad and thoughtful? Perhaps it was because being so very weak I did not feel the strength within me to reproduce in art any of those many impressions that the mind took in and fancy clothed in most varied forms. One day I visited Tasso's house; and whilst, as usual, the cicerone explained in his way the singularity of that abode, I dwelt in imagination on the life and vicissitudes of that unhappy poet, and recalled the secret joys of that passionate soul after he had finished his Christian epic: I saw the courteous, handsome cavalier, the inspired poet, envied and conspired against by the favourites of the Duke and the *literati*, his rivals; the looks of the ladies, whose frank admiration was veiled in the shadow of profligacy; then the disorder, confusion, first in the heart, and then in the brain of poor Torquato, the suspicions of the Duke, his imprisonment, his lawsuit, his resignation and death; and I wept.

I decided to return to Naples—for this quiet full of fancies drove me back into myself, and made me more sad. I took up my abode in the centre of the great city, in Piazza Castello, at the Hotel de France, on the angle of the Strada dei Guantai Vecchi. In this hotel strangers were continually coming and going, and changing every day. The windows of my little apartment opened on the Piazza, and the mid-day and westerly sun

bathed them in heat and light. Some artists, in compassion for my condition, came to give me courage; and
among them I remember with profound sadness, for almost
all of them are now dead, Cammillo Guerra, Giuseppe
Mancinelli, Gigante, and Tommaso Aloysio Juvara, who
had such a tragic end in Rome. The warmth of your
heart turned your brain, my poor friend! but in your last
moments you acknowledged your sin, and God will have
been merciful to you. The other younger artists who
are still alive are the sculptors Solari and Balzico, the
miniature - painter Di Crescenzio, and Postiglione the
painter. But my health was always the same. Professor Vulpes, to whom I had brought a letter of recommendation from Professor del Punta, continued to follow the same treatment as that indicated by the other
Florentine doctors,—that is to say, prescribing preparations of iron, meat diet, rest, and tranquillity of mind.
And in the meanwhile I had no desire to eat; my sleep
was restless and of short duration; my legs would ill support me, and my mind was so depressed that I could not
endure to read more than a few pages. As to writing, I
was obliged to stop every moment or so; ideas got confused, and I could not separate them from each other
or give them any proper shape. It was a great fatigue
to me to give my news to Venturi when he desired to
hear from me.

At last the longed-for day came which was to decide
the question of my health. It was already two months
since I had left my home; and although the journey to
Naples and the air there had been somewhat beneficial
to me, yet I was very far from entertaining the slightest
hope of recovery—or rather this recovery was so slow
as to make me lose all patience. At this stage good
Professor Smargiassi, seeing me always so weak and

melancholy, said to me, "Why do you not try the water-cure?"

"What do you mean by water-cure?" I replied; and he explained it to me, adding, "Here in Naples there is Professor Tartaglia, who has effected some wonderful cures." He told me of some, and he added that he himself had tried this cure and had got well. As Smargiassi was a serious man, with a temperate habit of speech on all matters, his words carried weight with them, and I consented willingly to consult this hydropathic professor, and so sent for him.

Professor Tartaglia was an exceptional Neapolitan— that is to say, he had nothing of the vivacity of speech and manners that is peculiar to this warm-hearted, exuberant, and imaginative people; he spoke little and quietly, listened a great deal, and observed attentively. When he had heard of my complaints, he examined me, and after that said : "You have no disease, although you may not feel well ; you will recover quietly and easily—of that you may be sure. In the meanwhile I will tell you that I shall not come again to see you ; but instead, you must come to see me every morning at twelve o'clock to give me an account of how you feel. To-morrow you must take your first bath. Don't be alarmed—it is not a bath by immersion ; you are not to go into the water," and he gave me the directions to be followed ; and as he was going away he said, "Let alone the medicines that you have taken thus far."

The first morning this hydropathic cure seemed very arduous. To get out of one's bed and put on a sheet drenched with cold water is not the pleasantest thing in the world, especially at that season of the year (it was the last of December); but after the first impression, I can assure you that the external warmth finally produces a pleasant effect, and gives strength and elasticity to the body. After the bath, walking exercise should be taken for at least an hour. To my objection that I could not walk, the Professor answered, "Walk as much as you can, rest a little, and then continue to walk, and so on; you will see day by day that your strength will return, and with your strength, courage and happiness." In short, after a month of this treatment I was so well that I could walk easily eight miles during the day. When I wrote to Florence of the new cure that I had begun, Del Punta was frightened, and said that he would not be responsible for the result of this resolution of mine, which, to say the least, was hazardous; and that I ought not to have undertaken it without the advice of an ordinary practitioner—that is to say, of an allopathic doctor. His making this a condition tranquillised me, as Professor Tartaglia was really an allopathic doctor; but in some cases that were rebellious to that system of treatment he adopted hydropathy. Then, too, the result was so satisfactory, so decided, that all objections fell to the ground, and nothing more was said about it.

By degrees I felt my strength returning, and my heart expanded with hope. Delightful artistic thoughts, that had so long lain dormant, sprang into life within me, one by one, like the first leaves in April; and Will, precious gift, mysterious, immortal power, again took and held its empire over me, and pronounced itself. During the days just passed, the smiling country, the glorious sun, the terrible beauty of the sea, the joys of men, the creations of art, and (sad to say) even the affectionate care of my dear ones, were irksome to me; and now, with pleasure, slowly and by degrees I began to feel a desire and thirst to enjoy these good things, thinking about them and loving them with more intensity of understanding and hearty sincerity. Every day there was a new excursion to be made: Capodimonte, with its immense park and rich gallery; that beautiful walk, the Strada Maria Teresa, now Vittorio Emanuele; the Certosa of San Martino, where one enjoys a view of the whole city, of the sea and all the Campagna-Felice, of Vesuvius, of Monte Somma, of Portici, Resina, Capri, and Nisida. Then I felt a desire to see the Royal Museum, unique in the world for its great riches in ancient bronzes; the Flora, Venus Victrix, Callipige, Aristides, the equestrian statues of the Balbi, father and son; the seated Mercury; the Sleeping Faun, and a thousand other statues, big and little; busts, in marble and in bronze, of exquisite beauty, all or almost all of them having been dug out of the ashes of Herculaneum and Pompeii. On certain days, or I should rather say at certain moments, a sight of these works of sculpture sets one on fire, and fills one with courage and a strong desire to do something; but at other times it gives one a feeling of dismay, discouragement, and fear that cannot be described. This difference of impression deserves to be examined a little, and he who is bored must here skip; the young artist, however, I am certain, will follow me attentively. I have made a promise to myself not to leave these papers as food for mere curiosity, for, seriously speaking, there should be no satisfaction in that; whereas a little value and profit will be found by every one who has the patience to follow me.

Yes, dear friends, sometimes, in seeing certain works of art, one burns with enthusiasm, with a fire, a desire to do, that is really marvellous, and we ease our minds with the conviction that this is a sign of our strength. Illusions, dear sirs—illusions! To the eyes of the artist all works of art ought to be the occasion of examination and serious hesitating thought; and when these outbursts of immoderate confidence in ourselves occur, they are a sign that our sight is obscured by pride, or that we are not able to comprehend the degree of beauty in such works, and consequently the difficulties that have been overcome to produce them. We must correct ourselves of both these defects, and learn to respect even mediocre things, as by this method we arrive at the discovery of something good even in these, if not as a whole, at least in their intention and germ, and this will always be something gained. As a young man, I have found myself laughing compassionately at some of the most beautiful works of art, both ancient and modern, and this merely because my natural pride had been excited by light or false praise. The complacency that we feel in ourselves and our works comes in part from a species of exclusiveness and belief in the infallibility of the principles we profess. Not that I would counsel any disloyalty to the principles that are our guides in art—no, indeed, for we must keep entirely true to them; but it is a very different thing to despise all other schools that are removed from ours. For instance, why despise the Academicians, who are tenacious of the study of antique statues, in order to keep within bounds the turbid torrent of the *veristi*, who in their turn, through their coarse adherence to nature, lose the idea of the beautiful? Let us, on the contrary, respect them for their intentions and motives, at the same time that we make certain reservations as to the final consequences that would result from this distrust and refashioning of nature. The fault of the Academic school lies in this, that instead of saying, "Study the antique; look how well they knew how to choose from life and how to interpret it," they say, "Here, copy these casts; apart

from them there is no health or safety for you.   Nature
is imperfect; you must improve on it, and, imitating the
Grecian and Roman statues, you will learn to purge
nature from all her imperfections." So saying, the intention, which is good, is spoiled by its application of exaggerated rules.   But, I repeat, the intention is good;
therefore let us look to that whilst we reject its application.   On the other hand, why should we despise the
naturalisti in all that they have that is good—I mean, in
their axioms and rules—which, in short, putting aside
amplification and exaggeration, means the imitation
always in everything of nature?   We have always accepted and insisted upon the imitation of nature, that is
of beautiful nature, putting aside that exaggeration which
leads to folly, absurdity, and licence of conception, and
to ugliness of form, detail, and minutiæ.

The same may be said of the mystics, the purists,
colourists, lovers of effect and *barocco*, &c.   Let us take
the good where we can find it : not, indeed, make a
mixture, a medley, as some have been fantastic enough
to imagine, by which we should arrive directly at eclec-
ticism, which is the most foolish thing in this world; but
putting our minds into the study of all these schools, we
shall be able to find good reasons for their teachings.
Separating them from excess and exaggeration, we shall
find ourselves in a wider, clearer, higher atmosphere,
and the impressions that we receive from works of art
will not produce despondency or rejoicing, our judgments will be more temperate and just, and our own
work will be done quicker and better.   This does not
mean, indeed, that we are to remain indifferent before
works of art.   Alas for the man who is indifferent ! for
the artist who before some work of art stands cold and
without feeling !   A young man who is ardent, boasting,

and proud, can correct himself, can be trained by difficulties and instances, by emulation or jeering. The
timid will become animated, and take courage, moving
with measured and cautious steps on his arduous journey, and, by reason of his timid, gentle character, conciliate the goodwill of his masters and fellow-students; but
the indifferent and cold of nature has too much the air
of a simpleton or an arrogant person, and he is fled
from and left in his stupid ignorance.

And here, gentle reader, is one of these happy mortals
who live their little day in dreamland. A person came
to see me one day bringing with him a young man who
might have borne a quarter of a century weight on his
shoulders. He was of medium height, with broad shoulders, bent slightly, owing, perhaps, to his being twenty-
five years of age; he had a black beard, bronzed complexion, and wandering eyes. He looked all about him
and saw nothing. I say that he saw nothing, for he paid
the same attention to my cat as he did to the head of the
Colossus of Monte Cavallo, which stood on a stand in
the room, and to my "Abel" as he did to me or my stool.
He spoke no Italian, not even French; but the person
who accompanied him, and who was competent in all
respects, spoke for him, or rather of him, for the young
man himself never opened his mouth to utter a word,
although he kept it half open even when he was looking
at the cat. This very polite person said—

"You will forgive me, Signor Professor, if I take you
away from your occupations for a few brief moments;
but I could not forego the pleasure of regaling you with
a visit from, and making you acquainted with, this young
sculptor, who is on his way to Rome, where he goes,
not, indeed, to perfect himself as an artist, but to prac-
tise the profession which he has so nobly and splendidly

illustrated by his genius.   As he is undoubtedly born to
fame, and the whole world will talk of him, I wished to
bring him to you, and make you really acquainted, that
you might some day be able to say, 'I have seen him
and spoken with him.' "

I stood there like a bit of stucco, looking at the young
man, and then at the person who had spoken to me
thus.   Then I answered—

"Tell me, does this gentleman speak, or at least
understand, Italian?   Has he understood what you have
just said of him?"

"Oh no! he only speaks English; he is an Ameri-
can."

"The Lord be thanked," muttered I to myself, "that
the poor young man understood nothing!"   But this
polite person, misunderstanding my question, began—

"Now I will tell him what I have said to you."

And he began in English to repeat the little tirade
that he had given me, and this genius of a young man
nodded his head at every phrase, looking at me, at the
stool, and at the cat!

CHAPTER XII.

POMPEII—A CAMEO—SKETCH FOR THE BACCO DELLA CRITTOGAMA—PROFESSOR
ANGELINI THE SCULPTOR—ONE MUST NOT OFFER ONE'S HAND WITH TOO
MUCH FREEDOM TO LADIES—A HARD-HEARTED WOMAN WITH SMALL IN-
TELLIGENCE—THE SAN CARLO, THE SAN CARLINO, THE FENICE, AND THE
SEBETO—MONUMENT BY DONATELLO AT NAPLES—THE BAROCCO AND MIS-
TAKEN OPINIONS—DILETTANTI IN THE FINE ARTS—PRINCE DON SEBAS-
TIAN OF BOURBON—IS THE BEARD A SIGN OF BEING LEGITIMIST OR
LIBERAL ?—I AM TAKEN FOR A PRINCE OR SOMETHING LIKE ONE—"THE
BOTTLE" FOR DOORKEEPERS AND CUSTODI OF THE PUBLIC MUSEUMS
OF NAPLES — PHIDIAS, DEMOSTHENES, AND CICERO ALL AGAINST RUG-
GERO BONGHI.

 SUMMONED up all my little stock of pa-
tience, and moved slowly towards the door,
they following me. Thanking the gentlemen, I shut them out, and returned in silence
to my work. This happened some thirty years ago, nor
as yet does it seem as if the prophecy about that young
man were realised.

To return to ourselves. "Appetite comes with eating," as the proverb has it; and in fact, by degrees, as
I visited the museums, the churches, and the studios of
the Neapolitan artists, I felt an increasing desire to do
something, to try again to draw or to model, were it but
a mere trifle. One day, after having gone over the
whole breadth and length of the excavations at Pompeii,
I was examining a mosaic pavement made out of a great
many pretty little coloured stones, some of them broken

away from their place; and bending down to examine it closer, I touched one of the stones. The *custode* hastened to say to me, "Don't touch, signor—the regulations prohibit it." It cannot be denied that I have always been disposed to respect all regulations; but since I had seen them broken, even by those who ought to have been the first to respect them, I had taken them in dudgeon. I looked at the *custode*, and he at me, and we understood each other at once. I took a turn, went to the door, looked to the right and to the left of me, and coming back, as I was taking something out of my pocket I dropped some money on the ground.

My friend picked it up for me, and I gave him a *carlino*. We returned to the room where the mosaic pavement was. It represented a race of animals, hares and dogs, on a yellow ground. Some of the little stones were loose, and already many were missing; they were small squares about as large as my little-finger nail. I bent down again, and stretched out my hand, looking at the guard, who for decency's sake turned in the other direction; and I took the little stone, on which, with a great deal of patience and increasing gusto, I drew and engraved a small head after the fashion of a cameo, roughing it out at first with the point of a penknife, and finishing it off with sharpened needles fastened into little handles, which I used in the place of small chisels and burins. I always keep this little head, which was set in gold as a pin, and sometimes wear it in my necktie. When I look at this small piece of workmanship, I am astonished at my patience and my eyesight at that time.

To tell the truth, when I picked up that little stone I had no idea of working on it, but merely took it as a remembrance of the day and the place. In touching it,

I thought that it had been shaped and put there by a man like myself, two thousand years ago. In holding that little square stone between my fingers, it seemed to me as if my hand touched the hand of that man, who then was full of life. I thought of his scant dust, now dispersed, transformed but not lost! Where is this dust now? I, where was I then? While I was thinking on this, my good Marina approached, and said—

"Do you find any beauty in that little stone?"

"No. I was thinking that it is very old. I was thinking that it is a fusion of fire, and in substance lava. But was not Vesuvius unknown at the time that this city was constructed? Could you imagine that they would have been so insane as to have built on the outskirts of a mountain vomiting fire? Have you not observed that in all the many paintings on these houses, where you find over and over again landscapes, sea views, animals, figures, in fact everything, that there is never the slightest trace of a view of Vesuvius? If it had been there, surely they would not have failed to reproduce in painting such a marvellous phenomenon. Therefore it could not have been there; and yet all these mosaics are made of lava, and all the surrounding country at a certain distance below the surface of the ground is covered with it. It was not there, I say, in their memory; but when was it there?"

"Do you know?" said my wife.

"I?—no, indeed."

"Then you can imagine if I do."

After this small cameo, I wished to model a little figure in bas-relief, which it was my intention to have executed on a shell cameo, and I gave the order for it; but the workmen employed for this kind of work are so unintelligent that if you take them away from the work

P

they are accustomed to do almost mechanically, they are
not able to succeed in doing anything. The little figure
represented Medicine. She was seated on a stool, and
with a little stick was pushing aside the bushes to
look for some medicinal plants ; but in doing so a serpent had wound itself around her stick, as it is said to
have happened to Æsculapius. Behind the stone on
which she is seated flows a little stream of water, to
denote the salutary action of water by which I was
cured, and to which she turns her back.

I also made a new sketch for the Bacchino della
Crittogama, which was the one that I afterwards made
of life-size on my return from Naples. The one I had
left behind me in clay was very different, and I destroyed
it. I had this new sketch baked, and I remember
one day when I went to get it from the man who sells
terre cotte, near Santa Lucia, to whom I had given it to
bake, that I found him arguing with a stranger who had
taken it absolutely into his head to buy it. It was useless for the man to say that the statuette did not belong to
him ; that he could not sell it ; that it was not finished ;
and that his little figures of Apollo, the Idolino, Venus,
and Flora were far better and more finished than this
sketch : he only kept repeating, " I like this, and want
to buy it ;" and all persuasion was useless. I put an
end to the discussion in two words, saying to the man—

" Sell it to him."

" How much must I ask ? "

" A thousand *lire.*"

At which the good *touriste* immediately put down the
Bacchino, and went away in peace. Some two months
after this I presented this little sketch to a priest from
Verona, whose name I do not remember, but who
came to preach the Lenten sermons at our cathedral

in Florence. I regret to have given it to him, for it is always well that a man's sketches should remain in his family, and also because, for all his eloquence, he has never since reported himself to me. Can he really be dead? *Requiem æternam.*

In this manner the time passed by, alternating the long walks in the neighbourhood of Naples with a little work and some artistic visits to Mancinelli, to Balzico (then but a young student), to Smargiassi the landscape-painter, and to Gigante, the famous water-colourist. I did not fail to try to find the sculptor Cavaliere Angelini, whom I had already known in Florence; but for some inexplicable reason I could not see him, and this was what happened. I went to his studio, and his men told me that he had gone to the Academy to lecture to the young men. I went to the Academy, and was told that he desired me to wait, because he was giving his lessons. I waited a good long time, and when he came out he said that he was in such a hurry he could not pay any attention to me then, but that I must come to his studio on a certain day at a certain hour. I went there and knocked; no one answered, and the soldier who was mounting guard at the Serraglio dei Poveri close by said that every one had gone away more than two hours before. It seemed to me a little strange, after having named the day and hour; but more or less forgetfulness in an artist means nothing—in fact it is a sort of sauce or dressing to an artist's character, be he young or full-grown, on horseback or on foot. Dear me! such things are easily understood; and if I had not been a little tired, I should not even have thought of it, and would have returned another day. But when, and at what time? Should I have ever found the door open?

My hotel was very far from the poorhouse, but the

two places were not very dissimilar; for although all my
expenses were paid by the Grand Duke, it had not yet
become the fashion to squander and waste after the
ways of to-day; and be it from education, temperament,
or other motives, I felt it my duty to economise for that
good gentleman's purse even more than for my own,
and therefore my inn could really be called a poorhouse
in spite of its pompous name, for it was a third-class
hotel; but the distance was great, and, to mortify the
Professor a little, I wrote on his studio door—" *G.
Duprè at home on such a day and such an hour.*"

He will come, he will certainly come, to see me at
my inn to make his excuses. Poor Angelini! he is
certainly absent-minded, and am I not also absent-
minded? He will come to find me out. Yes; I
stayed in Naples six months, and never saw him.
Something beyond absent-mindedness, I think; but so
it was. I told all this for amusement to his colleagues,
but they took it seriously to heart,—so much so, that
at one of their academic meetings they proposed me as
an Associate-Professor : and Angelini seemed delighted,
and warmly supported my nomination, so that naturally
it was passed; but I never went into his studio. Oh
no.

Yes; I repeat it ten, twenty times over. My dear
colleague, this happened in the month of January
1853; see what a good memory I have. You, it is
quite natural, have forgotten it, because he who is
guilty of such things does not take heed of them, neither
should the person to whom they are done, unless he be
as black as Loredan, who wrote down the death of the
two Foscari in his book of Debit and Credit. Therefore let it be understood, that I did not take note of it,
and don't remember it; but if you ever take it into your

head to return to Florence, and, passing casually through
the Via della Sapienza, you would like to rest a little in
my studio, you can do so; and the best of it is, that I
do not name the day or the hour, only take this journey
and make this visit soon, for we are now both old, and
I shall not return to you, for I am afraid of finding the
door shut!

Here I come to the moral. I speak of artists. The
desire to see the works and also become acquainted
personally with contemporary artists is a good sign; it
indicates a spirit of emulation, a wish to learn, and
form bonds of friendship, so to discuss and bring to
light errors and doubts on questions of art. But if
the artist with whom you desire to speak names a
certain day and hour, then answer at once, " Thank you
very much, but I cannot come." Tell him this untruth—
it will be but a small sin; whereas he who imposes upon
you a day and hour gives himself so much importance
that he resembles that ugly and haughty signor called
Pride.

There are some medicines so proper and efficacious,
that once you have taken them, you are radically cured,
and for good. Angelini cured me of the wish to
knock at studio doors; and the Signora Marchesini
cured me of another habit, formed either by custom or
stupidity, of shaking hands with everybody, especially
with women. The Signora Marchesini was at that time
(I am speaking of about thirty years ago) an aristocratic
lady of a certain age—one of those persons who, without
even taking the trouble to turn to look at any one who
came to see her, would answer the salutation and bow
prescribed by good breeding with an *addio* and a "good
evening" when one took leave, were it even at midnight. Such was the Signora Marchesini.

One night I went into her box at the Pergola, and
going up to her I bowed and put out my hand. Ass
that I was! I did not know that this act of familiarity
was not allowed to *inferiors;* and putting aside nobility
of birth, I was her junior by thirty years, and perhaps
this offended the austere lady more than anything else.
The lesson, however, was a good one; and from that
day, in fact from that evening, I have never since
been the first to offer my hand to any woman, old or
young. All this nonsense reminds me of a much rougher
and more vulgar instance of haughtiness, from which
my beloved wife was the sufferer. She was as simple
and good, poor darling, as the woman who offended
her was hard and proud.

I had gone to pay a visit to a friend of mine, a
gentleman of noble birth, education, and tact, with
whom I had friendly relations. My wife was with me,
and he was in the drawing-room with his, who was
French by birth, much younger than himself, and whom
he had lately married. As soon as my friend saw me
he spread out his arms, and we embraced each other;
my wife, with a feeling of spontaneous tenderness,
pressed forward to embrace the young lady, but she
drew back, perhaps not thinking it beseeming or according to etiquette to embrace a woman the first time she
saw her, even although she was much older than herself. My poor Marina, with her purity of soul, did not
feel offended, but turning to me she timidly asked,
" Have I done wrong?"

" You! no, my dear; but another time stand on your
own ground. That woman did not deserve to be embraced by you."

My friend took no notice of anything, and shortly
after we left the house. I do not know why, but this

remembrance goads me more and more every day; it stimulates my love for her who now smiles at all these miseries—she who was so worthy of all honours, who desired and was able to keep herself always good, mild, and compassionate—a good wife, a good mother, truly a lady by her virtues, and not by reason of her birth and riches. More I should like to say, but cannot ; I look with anxious love for the words that fail me, and I think that the innermost lineaments of that temperate, strong, patient soul can be felt but cannot be portrayed.

I continued to get better and better in Naples. The medical man insisted that I should walk a great deal and take simple and abundant food—a little soup, roast-beef, and a plate of vegetables, and nothing else, for dinner; for breakfast, after my bath and walk, a glass of cold milk and some bread. As a distraction for my mind, he recommended my seeing and talking with people I liked, and going to the theatre of an evening. At first the theatre bored me ; I did not understand those little *bouffe* comedies in dialect at the Fenice and San Carlino, and all those repartees of Punchinello irri-tated me. It was bad for me to go to the San Carlo, where they were giving the 'Trovatore' with the Penco, Fraschini, and the Borghi-mamo, and 'Othello' with the Pancani, for they made me weep, not on account of the dramas themselves, which I already knew, but on account of the music, which had such a strong effect on my nerves. For these reasons I was obliged to give up the music at San Carlo, and 'Punch' at San Carlino and the Fenice, and took refuge in the Sebeto, a very small theatre, where for the most part were represented dramas in bad taste, artistically speaking, but not as far as morals are concerned—exaggerated characters, forced situations to create immoderate effects, &c.,—in fact,

dramas of the Federici stamp, to touch the hearts of
the populace, but not calculated to influence them with
voluptuousness, the more dangerous when veiled in the
attractive, graceful, and polished forms of cunning so-
phistry. Then these dramas were not in dialect, and
' Punch' only came in at the farce, and for such a very
small part that I could bear him, and little by little
began to understand and appreciate him. As I have
already said, the theatre was a necessity for me, and it
entered into my *sage's* system of treatment; but he added
that I was not to take the recreation by myself, but in
the company of my wife and child, and with as much
ease as possible, so that it was necessary to take a small
box, which, as the theatre was so small and unpretend-
ing, was not a very great expense. Perhaps the idea
of economy never once occurred to the generous sovereign who came to my aid, but I used to think of it, as I
have before said.

Thus, with so much to divert my mind, during the
day going to see the public monuments and the churches
in which this immense city is so rich, and at evening
to the theatre, my recovery was completed. Nor were
there wanting splendid works of art, besides the collection of ancient bronzes, unique in the world, and
wonderfully useful to the students of sculpture. The
Church of San Gennaro, with its monuments, amongst
which are those of Carlo d'Angio, Carlo Martello, and
Clemenza his wife ; San Paolo, built on the ruins of
the Roman theatre where Nero used to appear in public and declaim his verses, and where Metronate gave
his lessons in philosophy, which were attended by
Seneca as his pupil (what a lesson to young men !) ;
Santa Chiara, with its monuments to the ancient kings
of Naples, which once was all frescoed over by Giotto,

and has been most barbarously whitewashed by Berio Nuovo; Sant' Angelo a Nilo, with that splendid monument to Cardinal Brancaccio, one of Donatello's finest works; and San Domenico Maggiore,—all these monuments, as much for their beauty as for the historical records they contain, are worthy of the greatest attention and study, and are calculated to inspire ideas and a desire to work.

But often it happens that the most valuable things one has, so to speak, at one's very door, are not thought anything of—not even noticed; and such was the case then with some artists in Naples, who either did not remember or were not acquainted with their own artistic treasures. I remember a young sculptor who often lamented that Naples was wanting in art of the middle ages. I reminded him of the monuments above mentioned, dwelling especially on that by Donatello, to which he answered that he did not know it. "Go to see it," I said; "it is unpardonable in you not to know it."

After some time I saw the youth, and said to him—

" Well, did you see the monument by Donatello, and what did you think of it?" to which he answered, " I found that I had already seen it once before, but did not remember it."

" Then," thought I to myself, " there is an end of all hope for you."

It is certainly a most painful fact that some of the finest works of our elders are either entirely ignored or not cared for, but it is most sad when this indifference comes from young men who have dedicated themselves to art. That the usual ignorant *ciceroni* who show strangers the sepulchral chapel of the Princes of Sangro take no notice of the monument by Donatello is natural enough, but it is none the less disgusting to hear them pouring forth their opinions after the following fashion : "See, gentlemen, these statues are the stupendous work of the famous Venetian Antonio Corradini. Observe the two statues that stand in the arch by the columns of the high altar; they are miracles of sculpture ; one is by Corradini, and one by Quieroli. The first represents the mother of the Prince Don Raimondo, who restored and enriched this chapel—which was founded by the Prince Don Francesco in 1590—with precious marble. The statue represents Modesty—one of the principal virtues that distinguished the Princess. See, gentlemen, she is enveloped in a transparent veil, beneath which is revealed the whole of her figure : this is a method of sculpture unknown even to the Greeks, for the ancients only painted their draperies, but did not cut them in marble. The other prodigy of art is a statue representing the father of the Prince himself as ' Disinganno.' In this statue behold a man caught in a net; you see all the meshes of the net, and inside it the body itself." The stranger, meantime, stands there open-mouthed, admiring these statues, in which, to tell the truth, one could not too deeply deplore the time and patience that have been wasted on work whose only object is to arrest the attention of vulgar people, who take all these material and mechanical difficulties for the essential and only aim in art. All this, I repeat, is disgusting if you like, and rather ridiculous ; but the people of the country, and most particularly artists, ought to laugh at such works as these, as well as their admirers. This mania for the difficult and surprising, to the detriment of beauty itself, which is so simple, has carried corruption into art itself as well as to its amateurs — so much so, that dresses of rich stuffs, embroideries, laces,

and like trifles, which need but a little patience and
practice to produce, have to-day become so much in
vogue as to really make one fear that art is in danger,
and that research and study to reproduce the beautiful
will be replaced by work of a sort of asinine patience,
which surprises and impresses only simple-minded, vulgar
people, and dilettanti. And àpropos of dilettanti, I wish
to express my opinion that although they may take pleasure in painting and sculpture they are not of the slightest use to these arts. Dilettanti are generally gentlemen—fine gentlemen, sometimes even princes—and in
consequence of their station and wealth, are surrounded
by a cloud of small-minded people, who, owing to the
respect and deference they feel for them, are induced to
praise them. This cheap praise, which is taken so unceremoniously, engenders in those who give it a false and
sophistical tone, with which they quiet their consciences,
ever muttering, "You ought not to have said this; it is
not just—it is not true." As this internal grumbling is
irksome, the mind builds up a sort of reasoning that
holds out as long as it can, and then falls for want of
that solid foundation, Truth, that alone can uphold any
structure, be it scientific, artistic, or literary. With him
who receives the praise, matters go far more easily; he
does not give it another thought, or if he does, it is from
excess of vanity that he sniffs the remaining odour from
that small cloud of incense.

In Naples there were two of these dilettanti princes,
—one a painter, the other a sculptor. His Royal Highness Don Sebastian, Prince of Bourbon, brother-in-law
of the King of Naples, was the painter, and His Royal
Highness Count of Syracuse, brother of the same king,
was the sculptor. The last named died a little after the
revolution in 1860, and of his artistic merits I have

already spoken. I shall therefore now say two words about his Highness Don Sebastian. I had the honour of being presented to him by the Grand Duke Leopold, who was at that time in Naples with his daughter the Princess Isabella, married to Count Trapani, who was expecting to be confined. Having been some time in Naples myself, I went to pay my homage to him, and he then made me acquainted with his Highness Don Sebastian, who was without pretensions, a simple, modest man. He asked for advice, and he asked for it with such eagerness and persistency that it showed a desire to know the absolute truth, that he might correct him- self—and not truth disguised under a veil of complimen- tary praise, which only misleads. And I, with the mildest words that I could find in the vocabulary of truth, gave him briefly and generally some advice; for his wish to do something really good was above his school and the studies he had followed. Although, as I have said, he had a sincere desire to hear the truth, yet I became aware that the language I used was quite new to him. I can add, however, that he did not feel hurt by it, as he often wished to see me and hear me, and corrected himself or tried to do so in many things, thus indicating confidence and goodwill. At this time he was painting a large picture for an altar, which he pre- sented to the church of San Giacomo degli Spagnuoli, above Toledo, and I remember that he gave me a draw- ing of it. He had taken refuge in Naples with the king his brother-in-law, owing to the part he had taken as a Legitimist against the government of Queen Isabella, who had confiscated all his revenues; and he mitigated the bitterness of exile and poverty by his devoted love for art. After some time he was restored to his country, and reinstated in his property, so that at last he must

have comforted himself with his own bread, having
known how salt was that of exile. He returned to his
country, and who knows if he did not cut off his beard,
which he used to wear full and long, after the fashion of
Spanish Legitimists? Strange to say, in Italy at that
time, especially in Naples, a beard was the sign of just
the contrary—that is to say, of a Liberal; and the
annoyances caused by the police on this account were
so ridiculous as to be quite disgusting. One was
obliged, however, to conform to all this, for if a young
man desired not to be exposed to worse annoyances, he
was obliged to shave his chin. He might keep his
moustache and whiskers after the German fashion, or
wear his whiskers alone like the English—he was quite
free to do that; but a beard on his chin, be it long or
short, indicated Liberalism : and as I have said, he was
immediately marked by the agents of Del Carretto,
Minister of Police, and, willing or no, was obliged to
shave to avoid something worse. At that time, therefore, the manliness of a Neapolitan showed itself everywhere but on his chin. In all Naples—with the rare
exception of some foreigner, the Prince Don Sebastian,
who was anything but a Liberal, the Count of Syracuse,
and Count of Aquila, brothers of the king, whom the
police hounds could growl at but not bite—not for a
million of money could a beard be seen, unless it were
mine, which, although not so luxuriant as it is now, was
still more than enough for the police.

During the days that the Grand Duke remained in
Naples, he desired to see the museums and other monuments of this great city, and wished me to accompany
him, out of simple kindness, for his Highness acted
as my guide, being much better acquainted with them
than I was. This driving up and down the streets of

Naples in a Court carriage, with a full beard on my face, upset all the ideas of those poor *sbirri*. Some people took me for a Spanish Legitimist; and others—especially the sentinels at the palace—christened me at once a relation of the royal family,—so much so, that they presented arms to me every time I passed by. Must I admit that I took pleasure in this, returning their salute and passing before them as if I had been a true prince? " *Viva* my beard !" said I to myself; " but see how things are going in this country! Some people are sent almost to the gallows for wearing a beard, and to me they are presenting arms. One evening, however, even I came very near being sent to prison. I was walking in the Strada Toledo, and about to return home. Near the turning of the *Orefici* by the Palazzo dei Minis-teri, there was a print-shop lighted by a reflected lamp, that threw a light upon it as brilliant as day. There were some French engravings, such as the Death of Richelieu, the Death of the Duke de Guise, and I know not what else. I felt a hand on my shoulder; turning round I saw some one gazing attentively at me, and before I had time to ask him what he wanted, some one else took the man by the arm and said, " Don't occupy yourself with him ; he is one of the royal house-hold;" and away they went in the crowd, and I saw them no more.

I hurried home, for, fear of finding others who might not share the same opinion. My wife and little one were waiting for me to go to the theatre, and I re-member that they were then giving ' Edmondo Dante, Count of Monte Cristo,' a monstrous production which lasted twelve hours—divided, however, into three even-ings. My little box was on the first tier near the or-chestra, — and such an orchestra ! Two violins, one double-bass, a clarionet, and a flute, the music being pieces adapted from the 'Trovatore'; and such an adaptation! Good heavens! All this cost me—that is to say, cost the Grand Duke—four *carlini*, including "the bottle," for in Naples one must always pay for "the bottle" to every one. Really in that fortunate country one required to have a *carlino* always in hand. I don't know how it is now, but then every one was constantly drinking. Ushers, inspectors, *custodi*—all asked for "this bottle" with the utmost frankness and in perfect seriousness. I, who went often to the museum, wished to have my cane to lean on, as there were no chairs to sit down on; but "No, sir,"—the porter, with his great cocked-hat, came and took it away, having the right to do so, as it was against the regulations. When I left he gave it back to me, always saying, "Your Excellency, the bottle," pronouncing these words with such dignity that you would have thought they were part of the royal regulations; and I used to give it—that is to say, a half-*carlino* at every section. Pompeian paintings, statues and bronzes, Etruscan vases, Renaissance paintings and drawings—each had a *custode*, and all wanted a drink. Perhaps now they are no longer thirsty, which will be all the better for the poor visitor. I paid these half-bottles, or rather half-*carlini*, most unwillingly, for to be always paying out is in itself most tiresome; and I was more out of temper than really tired, not being able to find a seat anywhere. One day a painter who was copying there was moved to pity, and offered me his stool. It is not unnatural that a man who was both poor and unwell, should be unwilling to pay out money in gratuities, and should look upon that given to the porter as the hardest part of all, as it was to pay him merely for taking away the stick he had to lean on. The consequence was, that not being able to bear this *lucro cessante* and *danno emergente*, as they say in law, I made bold to say to this high personage (he was at least a palm taller than I), "Listen, signor; I will no longer give you the bottle."

"Why not, Excellency?"

"Because you take away my stick, which would be a comfort for me to lean on."

"Well, well," he answered, "keep your stick, Excellency; but remember the bottle."

"I understand, I quite understand—and add a little more to it."

And the eyes of that Argus brightened, although he was by way of shutting them as far as the regulations were concerned. The necessity for drinking, it seems, belongs to this people, and it must be on account of the hot air they breathe, all impregnated with the salt from the sea. Therefore I fancy this desire of theirs has not yet been allayed, for even I drank a great deal when I was there, only it was water, which is so good, so fresh, so light, that it is a pleasure to drink; but alas! so many prefer "the bottle." If, however, even against the natural order of the country, this has been suppressed amongst the subalterns, it has been adopted by the heads themselves, as the Minister of Public Instruction has decreed an entrance-tax for every one who wishes to see in our galleries the works of Raphael, Michael Angelo, or our other glorious fathers, who in their simplicity certainly never thought of being obliged to show themselves at so much a head like some wild beasts.

It is a curious thing (which induces me to think that thirst must be in the air of Naples) that this bottle-tax was instituted by a Neapolitan, the Honourable Ruggero Bonghi, who, be it said with all due respect, seems to be

less anxious for the decorum of art and the advantage of
artists than for an economy which, to say the truth, is
but a shabby one. I know quite well that artists are free
from this tax, but they must be provided with a certifi-
cate, which is always a restriction; and it is also true that
artists, and those who are not artists, can enjoy free entrance, but only on *festa* days. It comes to the same as
if to one who said, "I am hungry," you answered, "You
shall eat next week." Is it believed that only those
students who are provided with certificates are to become
artists? Art learns more from example than from pre-
cept, as it is with every other thing. I should be curious
to know if Demosthenes and Cicero lived before or after
the Treatise on Eloquence, or if Phidias studied at the
Academy, and paid a tax for admission. Then, also, this
is the common property of all, and therefore its advan-
tages should not be restricted. The answer is, that the
entrance-tax is used for the maintenance and decorum
of the galleries themselves. The decorum and support
of the public galleries never suffered from the want of
this in bygone days ; why should they feel the need of it
to-day?

Q

CHAPTER XIII.

NEVER MAKE A PRESENT OF YOUR WORKS—POPE REZZONICO BV CANOVA—
TENERANI—OVERBECK'S THEORIES—MINARDI AND HIS SCHOOL—A WOMAN
FROM THE TRASTEVERE WHO LOOKED LIKE THE VENUS OF MILO—CONVEN-
TIONALISTS AND REALISTS—AN AMBITIOUS QUESTION AND BITTER ANSWER
—FILIPPO GUALTERIO.

HE church of Gesu Nuovo was at that time under the ordinance of the Jesuit Fathers, and one of these fathers, who was devoted to the church, set on foot a work which did him much honour. Though the church was beautiful in its design and decorations and rich in marbles, the high altar was of wood, and this was quite out of keeping with the general effect. Padre Grossi, who was as learned as he was zealous in his religion and a lover of art, made the resolve that this altar should be entirely renewed and reconstructed of precious marble, and he succeeded in carrying this into effect. Everybody contributed—the Court, the nobility, the people, owners of marble, and artists. It was not, however, yet finished; some ornaments were still wanting, and among these the panels of the pyx. I was asked by Padre Grossi to make a model for this to be cast in silver, and I cheerfully accepted the commission. The subject, which was singular and unusual, but extremely pleasing, was suggested to me by the Padre himself. It represented a

youthful female figure, accompanied by an angel, at the foot of the altar, who came to partake of the mystic bread. As soon as I had finished the model, I sent it to Padre Grossi, who expressed his satisfaction with it. Not so the superior and the other fathers, to whom the subject seemed to be too unusual. The superior wrote me a very courteous letter of thanks, the substance of which, stripped of all its sweet and useless phrases, was that he could not give his approval to the work. I then took back my model and presented it to Professor Tommaso Aloysio Juvara, who kept it as a pleasant memorial of me; and thus this work also, which was intended as a present, fell through.

The time for my return to Florence now drew near, for my health could now be considered as quite restored, save that a slight melancholy still hung about me, induced by an importunate and persistent feeling that made me doubt my own powers to overcome the difficulties of art, and of that art upon which I had at first entered, as it were, in triumph. I was oppressed by a torpor or indecision, a sense of something vague and undefined, resembling that state of moral weakness which shows itself in sudden impulses and as sudden prostrations—all indications of lively fancy and active sensibility, together with a great weakness of judgment and will. In a word, I had become a coward. In my excited imagination I felt the beauty of art, but I could not bring myself to lay hold of it, and express it, and reproduce it. I desired to go back to my first steps, and so felt my vanity offended. The *bello ideale*, ill defined and ill understood, smiled upon me with all its flattering and illusory charms. At slight intervals I seemed to feel these allurements, and then again I suddenly fell into uncertainty.

" E quale è quei, che disvuol ciò che volle
E per novi pensier cangia proposta ; "[1]

this was my state, and it afflicted me.

The decision which was to overcome all my uncertainty came to me from an idealist, or rather from an imitator of Greek art, Canova, and from one of his works not drawn from the ideal, but from life. I was about to return from Rome to Florence, when, as I stood looking vaguely about one morning in St Peter's, a prey to fleeting and changeable thoughts, my eyes were arrested by the statue of Pope Rezzonico. How often I had looked at that grandiose monument and passed on ! This time the movement and expression of concentrated feeling in this statue, united with a sentiment of imitation so strong, and yet so free from minute and servile detail, made a great impression on me ; and this was all the more vivid, because I could confront it with the other statues of the same monument, all of which are characterised by mannerism and imitation of the antique. This comparison stood me in stead of the most powerful of reasonings and criticism, and I seemed to hear a voice issue from those marbles which said, "See the great affection and study that Canova has given to these statues, and still they do not speak to your heart like that praying figure of the Pope. Why is this? Reflect !" And, in fact, I know no subject more worthy of consideration than to seek among the statues of Canova for the reasons of his oscillation between the imitation of nature and the imitation of the antique ; for exactly here is the knot of that grave question which even to-day keeps artists divided into two schools—that of the Academicians and that of the *veristi*.

[1] " And like to one who unwills what he wills,
And changes for new thoughts his purposes."
—DANTE : *Inferno*, Canto ii.

Doubtless nature is the foundation of art, as beauty is its object; and to forget either one or the other is to fall into error. If we kept these two cardinal points in our mind, and made them both subjects of study in our works, all our discussions and disputes would cease. But it too often happens that the Academicians, holding too strongly to the beautiful as the end to be attained, forget that its foundation is in the truth or nature; while the Realists, blindly trusting to nature, which when it is not subjected to selection is a bad foundation, lose sight of the true end, which is beauty. Now in the works of Canova we see a constant endeavour to harmonise the beautiful with nature; but as the cry of *bello ideale* (a magic phrase invented at that time) was then loved, with the painter David leading the chorus, and the imperial cannon sounding the accompaniment, the interior voices and protests of the Christian artificers were either drowned or lifted to the hundred pagan deities whom the epicurean philosophy of the time demanded, and to whom they burned their incense. But the genius which nature had given to this great artist triumphed over the tendencies of his time, over the cry of pedants and the imperial favours; and the Pope Rezzonico, and Pius VI., and the Magdalen, are there to demonstrate the singular force of that genius which alone battled against the torrent of the schools and the tyranny and customs of his age. These works of his are rays of that light which first illuminated the mind of this great artist, when, still young and free in his inspirations, and unbiassed by rules, counsel, and praise, he conceived and executed that wonderful group of Icarus.

In this careful spirit of examination and reasoning I again reviewed and studied the masterpieces of ancient and modern art, and many of the judgments which had been distorted by my poor brain during my first visit were afterwards rectified. I became attached with reverent friendship to Minardi, Tenerani, and Overbeck; and although all three followed the school of the mystical ideal, which was far from conformable to the rich and inexhaustible variety of nature, I admired in them their profound conviction in the excellence of their school; and although Tenerani united to his mysticism the graces of antique form, still it seemed to me that precisely on this account he was often a timid friend to nature. When, however, he was not dominated by a preconceived idea—I mean in his portraits—he was really and incontestably true to nature. His Count Orloff, though inspired by the statues of the philosophers in the Vatican, is not inconsistent with this opinion; and his Pellegrino Rossi and his Maria of Russia are perfectly original, and show no preoccupation of his mind except with nature. And it then seemed to me strange, as it still seems, that an artist, in portraying a fact or a personage, however ideal, should attempt to draw it purely from an idea, and not from living nature; for his idea is for the most part only a remembrance of what he has seen. The two processes are quite different; for the idea reaches out for the source of truth or nature, which is infinitely varied, while the memory retains types and figures of other works of so small a scale in variety that its extreme ends soon meet each other.

Overbeck was more ideal and mystical than Tenerani. He placed all the charm of art in the conception alone, and rarely or never used a model. One day he said to me, in a tone of the most absolute conviction, that models (or nature) destroyed the idea. This theory, which is eminently false as a general proposition, has a

certain truth when applied to sacred subjects and repre-
sentations of divinity, and specially in regard to those
artists who in painting a Madonna make a portrait of a
model. The imitation of life is certainly necessary even
in sacred subjects; but it is difficult so to select and
portray them that the religious idea does not become
obscured, as well on account of the vulgarity as of the
excessive realism and expression of the model. The
expression it is absolutely necessary that the artist
should create, if he has it in him,—and only so far as
this Overbeck was right. Then, indeed, is the opportunity for the *bello ideale*, which is so ill understood
and ill treated; for the ideal is in substance nothing
else but the idea of the truth in nature, and diffused
over all creation, as well in the material as in the intellectual world. And every artist of heart and just perceptions feels it and sees it, and recomposes its scattered
parts by means of long study and great love.

Minardi, the father, so to speak, of all the artistic
youths of his day, strove to reform them in taste and
composition, founding himself on the works and the
canons of the *Cinquecentisti*. This recognition is all the
more due to him when we remember that precisely at
this time, when he was endeavouring to carry out this
reform, he had before him Camuccini and all his school
in full vigour, and that now Minardi's school is flourishing and strengthened as much by the conquests he has
made in variety of imitation from nature as in mastery of
colour. I have said that Minardi was like a father; and
so he was. He treated his young pupils as if they were
his children, kept them in his own studio, and I have seen
three—Consoni, Mariani, Marianecci—and many others
around him gaily jesting with their venerable master. His
portfolios and albums were always open to all, and he

delighted to show them, and, while looking over their
studies and compositions, to add those words of explanation, counsel, and warning which are so useful to young
artists. I seem to see him now in that great studio of his,
which was somewhat in disorder, and encumbered with
easels, drawings, cartoons, books, prints, and antique
furniture—the air filled with clouds of tobacco-smoke
which issued from the pipe he had always in his mouth,
and he himself always working or talking, reading or
writing. He was affable, gracious, and eloquent, and,
with those little eyes looking through his spectacles,
he seemed to read into your soul ; and if he found it
sad, he threw out a word, and awakened it again to life
and courage. One day, seeing me more than ordinarily
melancholy, he rose from his work, took me by the
hands, and puffing from his pipe a larger volume of
smoke than usual, asked what was troubling me ; and
when I had made a clean breast of it to him, he laid his
pipe down, and embracing me, said, " Cheer up, my son !
drive away from your head all those whims : go back to
Florence, take up your work again with courage, and
have more faith in yourself and in your powers. It is
an old man who is speaking to you, who neither can nor
will deceive you." The words of the excellent master
went straight to my heart, and filled it with courage,
hope, and peace.

In this way, with studying the ancient monuments,
and going about among the living artists, I passed
several days in Rome. The models, and particularly
those of the artists I have named, I found more robust
and rounded than our Florentine models, which are for
the most part slender and lymphatic. Among our girls
you will not find, though you should pay a million, such
necks, so firm and robust, and at the same time so soft

and flexible, and like the examples which Greek and
Roman art has left us. So it seems that, without seeking for the cause of the contradiction between the living
nature I had found in Florence, and that which was
represented in antique art, I had come to the conclusion
that the Greeks and Romans worked purely from ideas,
and corrected nature according to that established rule
which we call convention. Nothing is more erroneous
than this notion, and the proof of it I found in Rome
itself, as I shall now tell.

Whoever is familiar with the Roman people will have
observed a notable difference between the figures of the
common people, and especially those of the Trasteverini
and the Monti, and those of the higher classes who are
in better circumstances. The latter are more slender,
with a fine and white skin, and often with chestnut hair;
while the former have dark eyes, skin, and hair, are
harsh and short in their ways and voices, and for a mere
nothing throw up their barricades, and blood runs without
much lamentation over it. You can easily see in these
people their uninterrupted derivation from those fierce
legions who planted their eagles over all the then known
earth. Nor is the blood in the women different from that
in the men; and if the men carry their knives in their
pockets (they certainly did then), the women carried,
thrust across their massive knots of ebon hair with much
taste, a sharp dagger with a silver handle, which was in every
way capable of sending any poor unfortunate devil into
the other world. One day (it was Sunday towards evening) I was, as usual, dreaming about those busts or necks
of Minerva and Polymnia, and the Venus of Milo, and
I know not how many other antique statues, which
seemed to me to give a solemn contradiction to all my
little models of pastry that I had left in Florence, and I

fixed my eyes on the neck of every woman that I passed. This examination induced me to modify in measure my opinion as to the conventionalism of the necks of the antique statues; and I should have been satisfied, and have changed my mind entirely, even had I not purely by chance gone on into the Trastevere. Here there was a great number of young persons, both male and female,—the men either in the pot-houses, or gathered around the doors, or standing in groups, and the girls in companies of three or four walking up and down the street of the Longaretta. Among these I saw one who, if she had been made on purpose to prove that the necks of the antique statues were not conventional, could not have here offered a more absolute proof. There were three girls, two small, and one large who was between them. She walked along with a slow and majestic step, talking with her companions. A sportsman who spies a hare, a creditor who meets a debtor, a friend who finds another friend whom he thought to be far away or dead, these give a weak notion of my surprise in beholding this girl. My dear reader, I do not in the least exaggerate when I say that I seemed to look on the Venus of Milo. Her head and neck, which alone were exposed to view, were as like that statue as two drops of water. I was astounded. I turned back to look at her again, and it would have been well for me had I contented myself with this; but I wished to see her yet once more. The girl, who had not an idea within a thousand miles of what I was pondering, nor of the corrections that I was formulating on an æsthetical opinion of such great importance, suddenly stopped, and taking the dagger from her hair, advanced towards me, and with a strong and almost masculine voice, said to me, "Well, Mr Dandy, does your life stink in your nostrils?" I shot off home directly, looking neither to the right nor left; and when I arrived I told my wife what had happened, and she reproved me gently for making my studies so out of time and place. Now I ask, why this disdain? Had I been guilty of anything improper in looking at the girl? Is it possible that she could have really been offended? I do not believe it. I know something about women, and I know that it is their weakness to try to attract attention. It is more probable that there was some one near her to whom the girl wished to show that in respect to anything touching her honour she was too fierce to allow any other person even to look at her. Leonardo none the less counsels us to study from nature, in the open air, not only by looking, but also by taking notes; and he makes no exception as to the Trasteverini. For the benefit of young artists, I propose to add a note on this subject to all new editions of Leonardo.

The discovery of this beautiful head and neck of the antique style and character set upon a living girl (and what a complexion!) led me to consider how many other parts of incontestable beauty which we find in the antique statues, and so readily believe to be born of the imagination of the Greek sculptors, are really to be found in nature; and the Greeks only selected them for imitation. But if this be so, how can the absolute deficiency of such models in our day be explained? Then I considered the different education of this people, their warlike lives, their games, and prizes at throwing the disc, racing, boxing, and the esteem in which physical beauty was held. If, indeed, for these reasons there is in our day a deficiency of fine models, we are not absolutely without them, as this spirited and beautiful girl clearly proves; and I firmly believe she must have been in respect to all the rest of her body an excellent model. Hence the necessity of carefully selecting our models. In this re-spect, however, we find ourselves in a much more difficult position than the ancients. First, because, as I have said, their education lent itself more efficaciously to the development of the body; and then, because the public games afforded far greater opportunities to see and select among them.

The first thing which assures a good result to a work is the selection of good models; and after taking great heed of this, good imitation is of absolute necessity. I have observed that he who exercises little or no selection, and contents himself with the first model he sees, belongs to that class of conventional artists who allow themselves such an infinity of additions and subtractions, and cor-rections of the model, that generally only the remnants of nature are to be found in their works; while those who follow the opposite school copy the model min-utely just as it is, and even with all its imperfections. If the former remain cold and false, the latter are vulgar and tasteless; for they carry their love for truth to such an excess, that they do not distinguish the beautiful from the ugly. Nay, they prefer the ugly, because to them it seems more true because it is more common. It hap-pened to me once to be in the studio of one of these young artists, who was engaged on I do not remember what work. When the model was stripped he was beau-tiful to see: a small head, squared breast, an elegant pelvis, delicate knees and ankles, and, in a word, seemed the "Idolino" itself, living and speaking. Will you be-lieve it?—he was set aside.

"But what are you doing?" said I. "Don't you see how beautiful this boy is? Copy him fearlessly. He is beautiful as Idolino himself."

"That is exactly why I do not want him as a model.

I am afraid it will be said that I have copied my Idolino."

To such a point did their aberration arrive. But at the same time, I am sure that if this model had fallen into the hands of one of the idealistic reformers of nature, he would have been corrected (that is, ruined) in every part, according to the suggestions of his stupid conventionalism. This mania of correcting nature is in itself extremely injurious, and the young artist must be constantly on his guard against it. A finished artist may sometimes do this, because in his skill and experience he finds the limits and the measure of the liberty which are permissible. Indeed he is not aware of the corrections that he is making, and believes that he sees it so; but this depends on the habit of seeing and portraying beautiful nature. But a youth who once is set going on this incline never stops; for he finds it far easier to draw freely on his memory than to keep within the proper bounds of imitation.

I repeat, then, that he who does not select from beautiful nature with studious love shows little faith in her beauty, and thence come carelessness and unwillingness to portray her, and then a headlong fall into the conventional. He, however, who finds the beautiful in everything, or rather, he who despises antique art and calls it conventional, even though it be by Phidias, is quite as conventional himself in his realism. His wish is to be considered naturalistic and realistic at all hazards, even to denying nature itself, in case it reminds him of anything classic (as we have already seen), and at last he goes so far as to puzzle his brains and struggle to arrange the model and draperies so as to make them appear naturalistic.

I have seen an artist get into a rage because his draperies would not come upon the natural model just as he wished, and who kept tossing them about and disarranging them so that they should not seem to be artificially disposed. I observed to him that he was really arranging them artificially, so that they should not appear to be so arranged. He was making a seated figure in a cloak. After the model had seated himself, and thrown the cloak about him in folds which were perfectly natural, and fell beautifully about his body and knees, the artist kept foolishly changing them, putting them out of their proper place, because, he said, that as they came naturally, they looked as if they had been artificially disposed.

"But that is not so," said I. "They arrange themselves naturally, and you keep disarranging them exactly like those artists whom you blame for being imitators of the antique and conventionalists,.and you are in this neither more nor less than a conventionalist like them, and even worse, for they always strive to put the folds in their proper place, in a certain number and a certain disposition; and though this is detestable and tiresome pedantry, because it destroys that variety which is the first attribute of nature, still they are not renegades to it as you are, when you thus obstinately insist on placing the folds where they cannot possibly be, with the pretence that otherwise they would seem adjusted. You, even more than they, are an illogical conventionalist."

But to be just, I must say that at this time the neophytes of the new school were few and scattered. The school, indeed, is new only in so far as it has carried us into the excessive, the negative, and the illogical; for the school of the *veristi* is as old as art itself, and its principles are correct. Indeed, strictly speaking, it has one single principle, the imitation of nature; but what the ancients meant was imitation of life in its perfection, while the moderns (at least some of them) mean all life, all nature, even though it be ugly. More than this, they prefer the ugly and deformed, not perceiving that the deformity of nature is outside of true nature, since any defect alters the essential character of nature, which con-sists of a harmony of parts answering to beauty. In a word, the deformed, which is the same thing as the ugly, is nature debased, and thus ceases to be nature. I am well aware that the *veristi* deny that they prefer vulgar and ugly nature; and if their denial were justified by their works, I should entirely agree with them, and my discourse on this subject would be entirely futile. But saying is not the same as doing.

I returned to Florence quite restored in health, strengthened by the example of the works of art in Rome, and inspirited by the brotherly words of those old and venerated artists, who, alas! now sleep the eternal sleep, or rather, who have waked from the brief sleep of life to one eternal day. The discovery of the famous head and neck of that Trasteverina had cured me of my prejudiced belief that the ancients corrected nature according to their completely ideal mode of look-ing at it—a belief which induces in the mind of the art-ist a weak faith, slight esteem of nature, and thence an unwillingness to imitate it, and an effrontery in cor-recting it.

Before going to work in my studio I wished again to see and study, in view of my new convictions, our own monuments. I made the tour of the churches, palaces, and public and private galleries, just as if I was a stranger. To many things indeed I might call myself really a stranger, for I had either never seen them, or but slightly and superficially. From this examination I came to the conclusion that the artists of all times studied their predecessors, and only imitated nature after having studiously selected what was conformable to the idea which first rose in their minds. Henceforth the way was clear, the light shone upon it, and the objects of art which I examined came out distinctly and really in their true aspect. Never to my intellect had the veil which covers the subtle and recondite reasons of the beautiful seemed so clear and transparent; and I felt tranquil, satisfied, strong, and ready to devote myself to my new works in the studio. One incident, however, did momentarily disturb this peace and security of mine.

One day I was in the Pitti Gallery, and passing through the room where the two statues of Cain and Abel are placed, I saw a youth who was drawing from the latter. He seemed from his aspect to be a foreigner. I spoke to him not only to assure myself of this fact, but also (I confess) because it gave me pleasure to see him copying my statue, and I wished by exchanging a few words with him to taste still more strongly this pleasure, which, for the rest, is excusable in a young author. Approaching him I said—

" Do you like this statue ? "

" Yes, very much ; and that is the reason I am copying it."

" It seems," I said, as I saw he did not recognise me, " to be a modern work, does it not ? "

" Certainly ; so modern that the author is still living— though one might say that he is dead."

" What ! I do not understand you. How can one say that he is dead when he is living ? " and I could scarcely restrain the wonder and emotion that these singular words created in me.

" It is indeed a very sad fact, and is very much talked

about; but it seems that the poor artist, so young and full
of talent——"

"Well?" I interrupted him suddenly.

"It seems that he is going mad."

I was silent. These last words wounded me to the
quick, and I remembered that during my past sufferings
I too had a fear lest I should lose my head, but I never
suspected that this idea had entered into the minds of
others. I went out of the room without even saluting
the young foreigner, and walked up and down in the open
air, going over in my memory my past suffering, my
voyage to Naples, the cure I had undergone, and my
re-establishment in health both in body and spirit, and
at last I became tranquil, and almost smiled in recalling
this strange conversation with the young foreigner.

I set myself to work with good will, and threw down
the first model of the Bacchino dell' Uva Malata,
which I had left without casting in order to remake it
according to a new conception that had come to me in
Naples. Secure of the road I meant now to take, convinced in my principles, which in substance did not differ
from those that had guided me in my first statues, I
modelled with great rapidity the small Bacchus, the
Bacchante, and a figure of the daughter of the Marchese
Filippo Gualterio, lying dead.

I first made the acquaintance of Filippo Gualterio
at Siena, in the house of my friend Count dei Gori, in
the first revolutionary movement of 1847. He was a
thorough gentleman, of careful education, a lover of art,
an enthusiast for beauty, a facile writer of the moderate
party, not then in favour of the unity of Italy, but attached heart and soul to the theories of Gioberti as set
forth in the 'Primato.' Out of pique, on account of
some annoyance he had received from the Pontifical

R

Government, of which he was a subject, he exiled himself from his native country, Orvieto, and joined the revolutionary movement of Turin, Florence, and Genoa. Later he took a prominent part in the revolution of 1859, embraced the cause of unity, became Minister, and shortly after died of paralysis of the brain.

The statuette of the Bacchino so much pleased my friend Pietro Selvatico, who happened to be in Florence precisely at the time when I finished it, that he made a drawing of it as a *souvenir* in his album. This able writer and distinguished critic and historian of art was also an artist and accomplished draughtsman, or rather he was so until an obstinate disease in his eyes deprived them of that clearness of vision which is necessary to mastery as a draughtsman.

CHAPTER XIV.

THE NUDE—THE STATUE OF DAVID—RAUCH—THE BASE OF THE TAZZA—
THE CHAPEL OF THE MADONNA DEL SOCCORSO—SEPULCHRAL MONUMENTS
FOR SAN LORENZO—THE 27TH OF APRIL 1859—COUNT SCIPIONE BORGHESI
—A GROUP OF THE DELUGE—COMPETITION FOR WELLINGTON'S MONU-
MENT, AND A GREAT HELP.

 BEGAN to work, as I have said, upon the
figure of the Dead Girl, and upon the Bac-
chante, two subjects diametrically opposed
to each other,—the Bacchante representing
the festivity, the dance, the libations, and the weariness
resulting from them; the Dead Girl, the innocence of a
few short days of life, the repose and the joy of an eternal
peace. This is a good method whereby to temper the
expression and form of one's works, and I recommend it
to young artists, since continually playing on the same
string finally begets an annoyance and weariness, which
exhibit themselves in the work. If the Bacchante had
not been modified by this dead figure, which recorded
an innocent life and a serene death, it might have degen-
erated and lost that beauty which is only to be found
in what is good.

One other piece of advice. In conceiving and working out subjects which, in their intention as well as in
the manner required to express them, tend towards sensuality, one should inspire one's self with a purely intel-

lectual love. To this kind of love one should adhere tenaciously, for it is easy to go astray. Such love seizes, and desires, and prefers to attain what is good, in which is included all that is true and all that is beautiful; but the seductions of the senses veil the eyes of reason and light the fires of voluptuousness. Therefore we should be careful, in order that art, which is the mistress and mother of civilisation, should not lower itself to be the corrupter of taste and habits. It is not in the least in regard to nudity that we should be circumspect, but in regard to the conception, the expression, and the movement of the statue; in a word, to the state of mind, the idea, the interior condition of the artist. Thus, for instance, one may look at a figure entirely nude, like the Venus of the Capitol, and be impressed merely by a reverent admiration, or by quite the opposite sentiment. The purest and most sacred subjects, the most completely clothed figures,—as, for instance, a nun, or the Santa Teresa of Bernini,—may be impressed by an unequivocal sensuality. No! nudity does not offend modesty. If it did, all the works of Michael Angelo deserve condemnation; while on the contrary, as every one knows (I appeal for the truth of this to the most prudish; to the priests, to the popes, who ordered and placed in the churches the works of this divine man— and in so doing did well, though these figures, both male and female, are as naked as God made them), far from offending against decency in the least, they elevate the mind into regions so high and so ideal that their bodies are transfigured, so to speak, and clothed with a supersensual light in which there is nothing earthly.

About this period the question began to be agitated in respect to the David of Michael Angelo. Already for some time artists and lovers of works of art had

expressed a fear that this masterpiece should remain exposed to injury in the open air, and thus be subjected to
constant deterioration. A commission was nominated
to examine into the matter and prepare some manner of
placing under shelter this celebrated work. Professor
Pasquale Poccianti, president of the commission, proposed that it should be removed and placed in the Loggia dell' Orgagna close by, under the great central arch.
This proposition was supported strongly by Lorenzo
Bartolini, who had expressed his opinion several years
before in a letter addressed to Signor Giovanni Beneri-
cetti-Talenti, then Inspector of the Academy of Fine
Arts, and which I have seen. The Grand Duke, assured
by the opinion of such competent artists, ordered the
statue to be removed and placed under the Loggia, in
conformity with the advice of the commission, and with
the plans presented for this end by Professor Poccianti.
It was the intention of the Grand Duke to substitute for
the colossus that he removed a copy of it in bronze, to
be cast by Papi, and the order was given for making a
mould and casting it. I was not on the commission for
the removal; on the contrary, I was among those who
did not believe in the injuries which the statue was supposed to be suffering. I did not think that there was
any grave danger in allowing it to remain where it was,
or that the cause that had produced the very apparent
injury occasioned to the head and the left arm was constant dropping of water from the roof above; and as this
had already been guarded against, it seemed to me in-
advisable to remove it and withdraw it from public view.
I remembered also to have read that Michael Angelo
himself had strongly urged that it should be allowed to
remain where he had placed it, and where he, in working
at it, had harmonised it with its surroundings; for even

then doubts were raised lest it might suffer injury in that position. And besides, I did not consider it prudent to remove such a colossal statue, both on account of the danger of the operation, and because I thought it impossible to find another place so favourable for artistic effect and historical significance. Therefore, when I learned that its removal had been decreed, I regretted it extremely. Information of this intention was given me by my friend Luigi Venturi, from whom I did not conceal my regret; and as the Grand Duke was well disposed towards me, I decided to go that very evening to the Pitti Palace and humbly submit all the arguments which induced me to oppose this removal of the David. He received me with his customary kindness, and imagining perhaps that I desired to speak with him about some work which I was doing for him on commission (of which I shall speak in its proper place), he said—

"Sit down, and tell me what you have to say."

"Your Imperial Highness, I have heard with great surprise that you intend to remove the David from where it now stands, and to place it under the Loggia dell' Orgagna."

"Yes; that statue is, as you know, the masterpiece of Michael Angelo. It is suffering injury every day, and it is dangerous to leave it there exposed to the sun and the rain. It ought to be placed under cover, and the Loggia is not only so near as to render the operation of removal easy and safe, but it also is a most beautiful place, and with its great central arch will fitly frame this magnificent statue."

I answered—"I also always have thought that this statue suffers from its exposure to the frost and sun— although the marble is from Fantiscritti, and is of most durable quality; and naturally the idea suggests itself to one that it would be better to remove it where it would not be subjected to this slow but certain deterioration. But the grave question which has always preoccupied my mind has been the difficulty of handling this colossus, so weak in its supports ; and what renders this all the more difficult is the crack which is said to have been discovered in the leg upon which it stands, which is the weakest. I therefore think that if this crack exists, it constitutes another and principal reason why the statue should not be touched. But independent of this difficulty, which practised and scientific persons might possibly overcome, there is the question as to where it should be placed. This colossus is made for the open air, and to be seen at great distances; and the place to which it is now proposed to assign it is not in the open air, and has not the light of the sky, but on the contrary, a light reflected from the earth, so that only the lower part would be illuminated, and in a negative sense—that is, from below upward, and not from above downward, as from the light of the sky. The upper part would in consequence remain in a half light, so as to divide the statue into two zones : the one which would be in the half light ought to be illuminated, and that which would be illuminated ought to be in graduated shadow. And again, there is no distance : from the sides it is not sufficient, and in front the statue would seem too high in consequence of the steps of the Loggia. Nor only this : if for the reasons I have stated the statue itself would suffer, the Loggia would suffer still more, and would be enormously sacrificed, and in consequence of the colossal proportions of the statue, its beautiful arches would be dwarfed; and still more——"

"Enough!" the Grand Duke with vexation interrupted me. "These are considerations which might have been discussed, but now the thing has been decreed." And rising, he added, "Good evening,"—which being interpreted into common language, was as much as to say, "Go away; you bore me."

I bowed and went away. On the stairs I said to myself, "You have done a pretty business. You see how you were dismissed, and with what irritation. You had better have minded your business. What had you to do with this? Did he ask you to give your advice? No; you have your deserts, and will learn better another time." And slowly, slowly I returned home. But none the less I was not dissatisfied with myself for having spoken frankly to the Grand Duke on this matter. I had expressed my true opinion, and I should have felt more regret if I had been silent, inasmuch as I was thoroughly convinced of the utility and propriety of what I had said. Besides, I knew how good the Grand Duke was, and with what attention he had listened to me on other occasions when he interrogated me on questions relating to art in general, or to my own works in particular. But the phrase "decreed" still hammered in my head, and I said to myself, "Very well,—it is decreed; but his decree is not a decree of heaven. We shall see. After all, I have said what it seemed to me just to say, and there is nothing improper in that; and if there was any impropriety, it was on his part in not allowing me to finish. And there is this also," I said—"that colossus in the middle of the Loggia will dwarf all the other statues, and make them of little consequence; so that by an accursed necessity they will have to remove the group of the Rape of the Sabines, and the Perseus, which stand very well there, as well as the Centaur and the Ajax, and all the others along the wall, which are not placed well, whether the David is there or not."

But in the meantime, a fortunate incident gave a new direction to the affair of the removal of the David, and a great weight to my words.

One morning a gentleman came to my studio, who said he wished to see me. I, who then was accustomed to permit no one to pass into my private studio, went out to see him. He was tall of person, dignified, and benevolent of aspect; his eyes were blue, and over his handsome forehead his white hair was parted and carried behind the ears in two masses, which fell over the collar of his coat. He extended his hand to me, and said—

"For some time I have heard you much spoken of; but as Fame is frequently mendacious, in coming to Florence I wished, first of all, to verify by an examination of your works the truth of all I have heard of you ; and as I find them not inferior to your high reputation, I wished to have the pleasure of shaking your hand;" and he then took both my hands in his.

"You are an artist?" I asked.

"Yes," he replied,—"a sculptor."

I wondered who he could be. He spoke Italian admirably, but with a foreign accent.

"Excuse me,—are you living in Rome?"

"Oh no," he answered; "I lived there for thirty years, but now for some time I have been in Berlin. I am Rauch."

I bowed to him, and he embraced me and kissed me, and accompanying me into my private room, we sat down. I shall never forget his quiet conversation, which was calm and full of benevolence. While he was speaking, I went over in my memory the beautiful works of this great German artist,—his fine monument to Frederick the Great, his remarkable statue of Victory, and many others. I recalled the sharp passages between

him and Bartolini, and without knowing why, I could
not help contrasting his gentleness with the caustic
vivacity of our master. Their disagreements have long
been over; the peace of the tomb has united them; and
now the busts of both stand opposite to each other in the
drawing-room of my villa of Lappeggi.

Among other things, we discussed the question of the
removal of the David, and its proposed collocation under
the Loggia dell' Orgagna. He strongly disapproved of it,
and exhorted me to use all my influence (to use his own
words) to induce the Grand Duke to alter this decision.
I then narrated to him my conversation with the Grand
Duke, and the issue of it. He was surprised, and after
thinking awhile, said that perhaps there was no ground
to despair, and that I ought to speak of it again and to
insist. I answered—

"I really cannot do so. You, however, might. Your
name, and the friendship of the Grand Duke for you,
might perform miracles; and nothing else is needed, as
there is already a decree in the way."

"Leave it to me. To-morrow I am invited to dine
at Court, and I will manage so that they will speak to
me of this; and unless they ask me, I will not let it
be known that we have met."

A few days afterwards he returned and told me that
he had spoken at length on the subject with the Grand
Duke, who did not seem to be annoyed, but on the contrary, listened to him to the end; and then smiling, said
that I had advanced the same doubts and objections.
He then thought it best to openly confess that we had
talked together on the subject. Rauch went away
shortly after; but he so well managed the affair, that
the Grand Duke thought no more of the removal of
the statue to the Loggia, considering the means proper

to shield it from the injuries of the weather.   He also
sent for me to tell me that Rauch had advised him not
to place it under the Loggia, and I remember used these
words : "Rauch is entirely of your opinion in regard to
the ¡David, and he is a man who, on such a ground,
deserves entire confidence; and I wish to say this to
you, because it ought to give you pleasure, and because
it proves that you were right."

I thanked the Grand Duke for the attention and consideration he had paid to the reasoning of Rauch in
regard to the David, as well as for his kindness towards
me ; and this procured me a dismissal more benignant
than the previous one.   A short time after, I received a
letter from Rauch from Berlin, in which he spoke to me
of the David.   I showed it to the Grand Duke, who
ordered me to leave it with him.   But he returned it
a few days later, and I have transcribed the passage
relating to the David :—

"I learn with great pleasure that his Highness the
Grand Duke has resolved to leave the statue of David
in its place in consequence of the trial made with the
plaster cast.   But I should like to recommend to his
Highness to remove the group of Ajax and Patroclus
from its present position, and to arrange a proper place
of just proportion and with a good light, to receive
worthily this work of sculpture divinely composed and
executed by Greek hands.

"BERLIN, 17*th December* 1854."

This is the reason why the statue of David was allowed
to remain in its place for some twenty years more, and
until the fear of the danger which this masterpiece undoubtedly incurred induced the Municipality and the

Government to order its removal to the Academy of
Fine Arts, where it now stands, but where it is not seen;
for if the Government is liberal in spending many millions upon a Palace of Finance in Rome, it feels itself
so restricted that it obstinately refuses to spend a few
thousands to complete the building which is to harbour
the most beautiful sculpture in the world.

It was at this time that the Royal Manufactory of
Pietre Dure finished the restoration of the famous
Tazza of porphyry—a most precious and rare object,
which, from the time of Cosimo I., to whom Pope
Clement VII. presented it, had remained hidden in the
store-rooms, and in great part mutilated. Now, as I
have said, owing to the great care and intelligence of
the directors, united to the goodwill and money of the
Prince, it had been restored to its pristine beauty and
perfection. In order that this work, which is also an
historical record, should be properly exhibited by itself
in the Royal Gallery, the Grand Duke desired that it
should be placed on a base with a new and rich design,
which should at once be a completion and adornment of
the Tazza itself, and also offer an occasion for a work
of sculpture. In matters of this kind this excellent
Prince was intelligent, earnestly entered into them, and
gave full liberty to the artist who wrought for him; and
this work he would have carried out had not the revolution interrupted it. But let us not be in a hurry.

I imagined a base of a form naturally cylindrical, with
ovolo mouldings. That from below the base of the
Tazza descended in a vertical line to the base, which
stood upon a quadrate plinth. Between the base and the
Tazza—that is to say, on the first cylinder—was a complete history of the Tazza, by means of symbolical figures
which represented its origin, fortunes, and final destina-

tion.   Perhaps this Tazza once embellished the immense
gardens of the ancient Pharaohs; and when their empire
was overthrown by the power of Rome, all things great
and precious which the genius and power of the nation
had produced were either destroyed or carried off. This
Tazza, as well as the famous obelisks, were brought to
Rome.   On the fall of the Roman Empire, the Tazza
and obelisks remained, and the former was presented
by Clement VII., together with other precious objects
(among which was the Venus—so called—de' Medici), to
Cosimo I.   After the Medician domination was over, the
Tazza remained forgotten, until it was restored, as I have
said, and placed in the Pitti Gallery, where it now stands.

To express artistically this history, I imagined four
groups, representing Thebes with the genius of me-
chanics, Imperial Rome with the genius of conquest,
Papal Rome with the genius of religion, and Tuscany
with the genius of art.   *Thebes* is in a sad and thoughtful attitude, with a simple vest without mantle, and has
on his head the Egyptian fillet.   He holds by the hand
his genius, who frowning and unwillingly follows after
him and looks backward, recalling "il tempo felice nella
miseria."   In his hand he carries a pair of broken compasses, to denote his lost empire over science and
art; and at his feet is a truncated palm, around which
is coiled and sleeping the sacred serpent.   *Imperial
Rome* stands in a proud attitude, resting her right hand
on the consular fasces, and the left hand gathering up
her mantle, which falls to her feet.   She is crowned
with oak-leaves, and above her head is a lion-skin in
the shape of a helmet.   Her genius, with a bold step
and fierce aspect, grasps a lance and a torch, implements of destruction and emblems of iron and fire.
Papal Rome stands still, with three crowns on her head,

from which the fillets descend upon her breast. She is dressed in the pontifical robes, and holds closed upon her breast the Bible. Her genius, dressed in a Levite tunic, and with one hand holding a cross and the other placed upon his breast, in sign of faith and humility, treads on a serpent, the symbol of error, which even from the earliest time insinuated itself into the Church. *Tuscany* is in the act of walking. On the diadem which crowns her head are engraved the Tiber and the Magra, the rivers which bounded ancient Etruria. She holds the royal sceptre in her right hand, and in her left the palladium of the arts. Her genius is crowned with laurels, and leans upon a *cippus*, on which are disposed the implements which are used in the arts of poetry, music, sculpture, painting, and architecture, bound together by a branch of olive, to denote that the arts are only developed during peace.

This conception, which was clearly expressed in a sketch, met with the approbation of the sovereign, and he ordered me to model it on a large scale, to be cast in bronze. Afterwards, it seeming to me that the dark hue of bronze, added to the shadow cast by the Tazza itself, would injure the effect of my work, I sought and obtained permission to execute it in marble; and I was at once paid for my model. In the meantime, in consequence of rich work of great delicacy, it became necessary to seek for some marble which should be hard, white, and beautiful; for this work differed from others in having no back view, in which ordinarily the imperfections of the marble can be hidden, but was exposed on all sides, in consequence of its round form, every point of view being a principal one. Hence there was a difficulty in finding a block entirely free from blemish, and having no spots to injure the view of any important part. The search for this consumed much time; and when at last I had a clear hope that I had found it, the revolution first suspended, and afterwards ended, everything. I shall return to this subject later, and at present I shall go on.

At the same time the Grand Duke ordered me to decorate a chapel of the Madonna del Soccorso at Leghorn. Of this, which is the first on the left on entering the church, he had become the patron. The chapel was to represent the entire life of the Madonna. I made a large sketch, in relief, of the chapel and the ornaments of the altar, with statues and pictures on the side walls. In the great lunette over the altar, I designed and coloured the Annunciation of the Virgin. In the empty spaces between the arc of the lunette and the side walls, which are trapezic like half pedestals, were angels painted upon a mosaic ground of gold, and holding spread out rolls of papyrus, on which were written the prophecies of the Virgin and of Christ. The altars I made with columns and round arches, with a straight base, after the style of the *Quattrocentisti*. The table of the altar represented the return from Calvary of the Virgin with St John. Behind, in the distance, were seen the crosses, and the angels of the Passion weeping and flying from the sorrowful scene. This also I designed and coloured in my sketch. Under the table, and through a perforated screen, was seen the dead body of Christ, illuminated by hidden lights. The statues in the niches of the lateral walls were to be St John and St Luke, as those who had specially written about the Virgin. In the two lateral walls above the niches, there were to be two pictures representing the Nativity and the Death; and these compositions, as well as the sketches of the two statues of John and Luke, I did not carry out, relying upon the intelligence of the Grand Duke, which would enable him to judge from what I did do.

Besides this complex and important work—the Scriptural portion of which I was to execute, while in regard to the paintings and architecture, I was assigned the post of director, with an authority to select the artists, —besides this, I say, he ordered of me the monuments to the Grand Duke Ferdinand III. his father, to his brother, his sister, and various of his children, all to be erected in the chapel called the " Vergine Ben Tornata," which is in San Lorenzo, where at present is to be seen the monument of the Grand Duchess Maria Carolina. And all these monuments I designed, and made sketches of them, which were approved by his Highness ; and a royal rescript was made to me, signed by the President of the Ministry, Prince Andrea Corsini, ordering me to execute these works. But the 27th of April 1859, foreseen by all, unexpected by few, arrived and overthrew everything.

From all these statements, two facts are clear; the first, that the Grand Duke esteemed me—and the second, that I knew absolutely nothing of the revolutionary movement of these days : and this increased the not small number of persons, who held me in dislike, owing to the favour. which I enjoyed at Court, and owing to the works which were intrusted to me. These persons, whom I must not call artists, showed themselves, both then and after, to be sorely deficient in intellect and heart, in blaming me for my affection and gratitude towards the Prince, who treated me so beneficently.

I have said that the events of the 27th of April were quite unexpected by me. But how was it possible for me to know anything, when those who, above all, were so intimately acquainted with what was going on,

kept me at a distance, and some, as for instance the
Marquis Gualterio, who usually frequented my studio,
withdrew entirely from me? Besides, how many there
were who were as much in the dark as I, though they
were in a position that almost obliged them not to be
ignorant! I remember that the Sardinian Minister,
Buoncompagni, who lived in the Pennetti Palace in
Borgo Pinti, gave every week (I do not remember on
what day) a reception or party at which I met and
conversed, with the utmost frankness, with the Advocate Vincenzo Salvagnoli, Giovanni Baldasseroni, then
Minister, the Marquis Lajatico, the Marchioness Ginori,
as well as the Princess Conti and others, and all of us
were ignorant.

It was only on Easter morning (I believe it was the
antivigilia of the revolution) that I heard that something
was to occur, but vaguely; there was nothing positive
or precise. There was to be some sort of demonstration
or manifestation to induce the Grand Duke to enter into
a league with Piedmont for the war of independence. But
afterwards, reassured by one who ought to have known
more than I, that it was really nothing, but mere idle
talk, and childish vague reports, I believed him. And
then? The day after, I met Count Scipione Borghesi, my
excellent friend, who, as soon as he saw me, said—

" Well, I have just arrived from Siena ; and to what
point have we come?"

"About what?" I answered.

" About our request—about our demonstration, which
is already organised. It should take place to-day. What!
you know nothing about it?"

" I know nothing—and there is nothing to know ;
trust me, for I ought to know something about it," I
answered, assuming rather an air of authority.

S

My friend was a little disturbed at first; and then
smiling, he added—

"It may be as you say. Have you any commands
for Siena?"

"No, thank you. Are you going back to Siena
soon?"

"Eh? Who knows?—to-morrow—the day after to-
morrow—as may be."

"Good-bye, then," I said, and we shook hands.

The next morning, from my little villa which I had
rented at the Pian di Giullari, I went down to Florence,
taking my usual route, at about half-past eight, when I
saw a gathering of people, and groups here and there
crowded together and talking excitedly. I then began
to suspect something. I went to my studio, uncovered
my clay, and waited for the model, who should have
been there. She kept me waiting for an hour; and
before I could reprove her for her unpunctuality, she
told me that she had been detained by the great crowd
of the demonstration which blocked up all the streets
around Barbano, and that the Piazza was thronged with
people carrying banners and emblems. "Bravo!" I
said to myself, "I did know a good deal!" At the same
time, an under-officer and instructor of the Lyceum
Ferdinando, who lived over me, came to the window
and cried out "Viva Italia!" and his pupils repeated
his cry with enthusiasm. "Do you know what this
means?" I asked of my model, who was already undressed. "I cannot work now; dress yourself, and go."
She at once obeyed, and I remained thinking over the
fact. I desired that the Grand Duke should yield, as
in fact he did yield, to the League with Piedmont for
the war against the foreigner; and I was grieved when
I heard of his departure. On returning to the country,

I met my friend the advocate Mantellini with Duchoqué, and we were all very sorry for what had occurred, although I had nothing to do with the events which took place either before or on that day.

The desire to give an account of this day has kept me for some time from the regular order of my records, and I must now return upon my steps. When I had completed the model for the base of the Tazza, a desire came over me to model a group of colossal dimensions. I had selected as subject the universal Deluge, and with youthful ardour I had sketched out the whole, and had fairly well modelled some of the parts. But as at that time the English Parliament had decided to erect an imposing monument to the Duke of Wellington, and to that end had opened a world-competition, I stopped working on my group, and set myself to think out the monument to Wellington. I had, however, little wish to compete, because it seemed to me that the work would finally be intrusted to an English sculptor, and that love of country would naturally overcome that rectitude of judgment which is so deeply seated in the spirit of that great nation. And so it happened that I had, as I have said, little desire to compete ; and besides, I have always been opposed to competitions, and I shall explain my reasons for this elsewhere. But my friends at first began by proposing it to me, then said so much, and urged the matter with such insistence, that finally I yielded and competed. This work of mine I cannot exactly describe, because, not having seen it for many years, I scarcely remember it. Let me try, however. In the angles of the great embasements were groups representing Military Science, Political Science, Temperance, and Fortitude, each with his Genius. The four faces of the base were ornamented with *alti-rilievi*.

Above this rose upon another base the principal group of Wellington with Victory and Peace. There was a large contribution of Florentine sculpture sent to London, for Fedi, Cambi, and Cartei competed as well, and their models were exhibited before going to England. The sending of these models was not without risk, owing to their fragility—being in plaster—the minuteness of the work upon them, and the length of the journey. All these difficulties did not escape the attention of our benevolent sovereign, who had seen my model; and as soon as I had sent it off, he told me he thought it both prudent and even necessary for me to go to London to attend to my work and see it taken out of its box. I answered that I had no fear of its being injured, having had it so well packed, and depending on the Government officials who were intrusted to receive and see to the placing of these competitive works. These were the reasons I gave; but there were others of a more intimate and delicate nature, for out of respect for the other competitors I did not wish to appear as if I went to push forward my own work. On his Highness urging me more and more, I told him all my thoughts, and he replied, with a smile, "If it is on account of this, you can go at once, for Fedi came to take leave of me yesterday; and to facilitate your journey, I shall give you a hundred *zecchini*. I could give you a letter for King Leopold of the Belgians, my good friend, but that would be like a recommendation, so I shall abstain from doing so. Go and make haste, for if your work should be damaged on its arrival, who is there who could mend it? Therefore go; and good-bye."

CHAPTER XV.

PATIENCE A MOST ESSENTIAL VIRTUE—TRUST WAS A GOOD MAN, BUT TRUST-
NO-ONE A BETTER—A COMPETITION EITHER ATTRACTS OR DRIVES AWAY
MEN OF TALENT—A STUDY FROM LIFE OF A LION BY MARROCCHETTI—
ASSISTANT MODELLERS—SYDENHAM AND ITS WONDERS—ONE OF "ABEL'S"
FINGERS—NEW JUDGMENT OF SOLOMON—AN IMPORTANT QUESTION—AN
INDIAN WHO SPEAKS ABOUT THINGS AS THEY ARE—PROFESSOR PAPI AND
THE FAILURE OF THE FIRST CAST IN BRONZE OF THE "ABEL"—A MEDI-
CINE NOT SOLD BY THE CHEMIST.

 STARTED at once, and it was well that I did
so, for the vessel which had the case contain-
ing my model sprang a leak on account of
the bad weather, had to stop at Malta, and
arrived in London too late, as the term had expired for the
presentation of these models. If it had not been for my
having the bill of lading,—from which it was made clear
that I had not only sent it in time, but a long time before
I was required, and that this delay had occurred from
circumstances entirely independent of my will,—my work
would have been undoubtedly rejected. For this reason,
and through the good offices of William Spence, it was
accepted; and he made me acquainted with the royal
commissioner of the exhibition as the person intrusted
by the author of the work. When they proceeded to
open the case the commissioner wished me to be present,
that I might see in what state it had arrived—and it was
a truly lamentable state! The ship, as I have already

said, sprang a leak, and the water had entered the case
and softened the plaster figures, so that they were dis-
lodged from their places, and rolled about in the box in
all directions. Heads were detached from their bodies,
hands mutilated and broken, aquiline noses flattened
out, the helmets had lost their plumes and front pieces.
In fact, it was all a perfect hash! Besides this, as I had
wrapped them up in cotton-wool and paper, and the salt
water had penetrated and remained there for many days,
they had gone through a sort of special chemical process,
by which my sketch was coloured in the most varied
and capricious way. Blue, red, and yellow were mixed
up together with the most lively pleasantry; and if it
had been done on purpose, one could not have reduced
the poor work to a more wretched condition. I saw at
once that I needed all the *sang froid* possible, so I did
not utter a word, and ostentatiously showed a calm exterior that I did not really feel,—all the more because
already the greater part of the models had been put in
their places, and the exhibition and judgment on them
were imminent. Fedi, who was present at this disaster,
seeing me so cold, said to me, almost in a rage, " Why
don't you get angry ? "

" Why should I get angry ? " I answered. " Shall I
mend the matter by getting angry ? On the contrary,
see how well I shall manage, in a slow and orderly way.
I remember to have read somewhere—I don't recollect
where—that he who has to go up a steep ascent must
take it slowly ; and so shall I."

He was of the contrary opinion, and advised me
rather to leave everything alone for the moment, to
take a pleasant walk, and to set myself to work the next
day with a fresh mind ; and he himself, with praiseworthy thoughtfulness, offered to help me. But I held to

my purpose, thanking him for his advice and offer to
help me, as I felt confident that I should be able to do
it all by myself. I then at once informed the commissioner for the exhibition that, as I was empowered by the
author of the sketch, and was in his entire confidence, I
intended immediately to set to work and restore it. As
this gentleman commissioner understood not a word of
French or Italian, William Spence, then a young man,
was my interpreter. When he understood what it was I
wanted, he called a gentleman who was looking at the
models for competition, and spoke to him in a low voice
in his own language; but my young mentor, who, besides
his intelligence, had a fine sense of hearing, taking me
aside, told me what orders the commissioner had given
this gentleman.

It should be known that the English Government,
among the articles regulating this competition, had made
one which was most wise, as it partially guaranteed the
artist who had not been able to accompany his sketch in
person, and had no correspondents or friends who could
act for him, to repair any chance damages to his work.
For this they had appointed an able artist capable of
making the required restorations. This, then, was what
Spence told me: "The commissioner, as you see, called
that gentleman to tell him to pay attention to what you
are doing to this model, for although you have asserted
yourself to be the person intrusted by the author of the
work, yet he has not felt sure of it; and as you might
also be a person who, with bad intentions, propose to
damage it under pretence of restoring it, it was his duty
to prevent this,—so he gave orders to that gentleman, in
case he saw that your hand was guided by bad faith or
incompetency, to make you leave off at once, and to set
himself instead to work on it."

I understand I must give all my attention and mind
to the manner in which I do my work, though I should
have acted more freely had I not been exposed to a
supervision as reasonable as it was conscientious. The
consequence of a mistake or an oversight might be to see
myself set aside as an ass, or even worse, as an impostor,
and the heads and hands of my little figure mended by
another, Heaven knows how !

In the meantime, the sculptor or modeller who was to
watch me never lost sight of me, and being sure that I
knew nothing of his charge, observed every movement
of mine ; but after I had been at work about ten minutes
he was completely convinced, and declared that I could
be allowed to continue the restorations—*meno male !*
Plaster brushes, small knives, sharp tools, and all other
implements, had been largely furnished to me by Signor
Brucciani, a most able caster, and the proprietor of a large
shop, or rather a gallery of plaster statues, able to supply
any school of design, and what my friend Giambattista
Giuliani would have called a perfect *gipsoteca*.

And with regard to good Signor Brucciani, I must say
some words in his praise, not only because he provided
me liberally with plaster and tools, and help in my work,
but because he, a stranger in a foreign land, has known
how, with his activity, to acquire for himself the esteem
of a people who are as tardy in conceding it as they are
tenacious in keeping to it when once given.   From this
he derives his good fortune and enviable position.

When Signor Brucciani fell in with an active and open-
hearted compatriot, it brightened him up soul and body,
and he often wished to have me with him.   His wife and
daughter united a certain English stiffness with Italian
brio and frankness that they took from their husband
and father.   One day Brucciani and his family desired to

spend the day in the country and dine in Richmond Park. Everything Brucciani did he did well; and I hope he is alive and able to do so still. He brought with him several carriages, with everything that was required for the *cuisine* and table—furniture, servants, food, and exquisite wines, even ice in which to keep the ices, &c. A *viva* to him! for as the Marchese Colombi said, "Things can be done or not done." After dinner a caravan of gipsies, perfect witches, who live in that forest, made their appearance, and asked if we wanted our fortunes told. The request was odd enough; but being made in such a serious manner, it became really amusing. Naturally, as we had to give something to these poor gipsies not to humiliate them, we had our fortunes told; and as for the old woman that examined my hand, she guessed so much that was true that I was almost frightened, and drew away my hand. The old witch continued to point with her bony finger, and say, "There is still more, still more."

My work was rather long, and would have been tiresome; but as it was a necessity, I did it willingly, and succeeded very well. It is true, however, that both the architecture and the figures were strangely spotted with stains made by the salt water, and bits of paper and cotton-wool in which it had been packed. Some one advised me to give it all a uniform tint to hide this; but I insisted on leaving it in that way, trusting to the good sense of the judges, who were called upon to consider much worse defects than those produced by a chance accident. I remember that Mr Stirling Crawford, of London, on receiving some years before the two statues of "Innocence and the Fisherman," and a stain having made its appearance on the leg of one of these, wrote to me manifesting his entire satisfaction with these works, and

adding : " It is true that here and there there are some
stains in the marble ; but as I know that you do not make
the marble yourself, it would be absurd to reprove you
for this." There are but few gentlemen like him, however—so few, that I have never found another ; but on
the contrary, I have seen more than one who would even
buy a mediocre statue, to use no harsher expression,
provided it were made out of beautiful marble.

I remained in London about two months, and left the
day before the opening of the competitive exhibition.
The judgment was to be pronounced after the public
exhibition was over ; and there were a great many competing—nearly a hundred—and some of the models were
very beautiful. There were to be nine prizes given—
three first class. and six second. The Government reserved to itself the power of giving the final commission
without regard to the models that had received prizes,
as it might so happen that when the name of the sculptor
who drew the first prize was known, he might not be
able to offer sufficient warrant as to the final execution of
the work as to tranquillise the consciences of the judges
and satisfy public opinion. .This argument is a just one
when not vitiated by preconceived opinions or self-love,
which sometimes happens, as we shall see hereafter.

This was in itself a thing easily understood, but was
not understood by us, who went in for this competition.
Not so Marrocchetti, who, clever artist that he was, was
none the less wide awake and wise. With those who
instigated him to compete he reasoned in this way, saying : " They know that I am capable of doing this work.
Why, therefore, enter into competition with others, if not
to find out that there is some one else cleverer than
I am ? Very well ; but I choose to retire, and you can
take the other fellow—take him and leave me in peace.

So far this would seem prompted by nothing but the
fear of losing, which in itself is no small thing for a
man who has a name and has gone through his long
career applauded by all. But there is another and a
much more piercing and almost insufferable dread. Do
you know what it is? That of winning. Yes, that of
coming in victor before a poor young fellow, perhaps one
of your own scholars!" Thus he gave vent to his feelings one day to me, with the sort of intimacy that springs
to life quickly and vigorously between artists who are
neither hypocrites nor asses; and his words depict in
a lifelike manner the frank, and, I might say, bold
character of this original artist, who was most dashing,
and who, with a thorough knowledge of dramatic effects
in art, from the very exuberance of his strength, not
seldom had the defects produced by these qualities—
defects which were perhaps magnified by his assistant
modellers, who worked with too much rapidity and carelessness.

When he saw the photograph of my model he desired
to have it, and I was delighted to give it to him. He
wished me to choose something of his as a remembrance, and I did not need to be urged. I had set my
eyes on a most beautiful study of a lion from life in dry
clay, and so I asked him for that; but as that was a
thing precious to him, he asked me if I would not content myself with a cast of it in bronze instead of the
clay. On my answering that I would, he called his
caster, who worked for him in his own great foundry,
and ordered it to be cast at once. Two days after this I
received it, and keep it as the dear remembrance of an
excellent friend, and as a valuable work of art.

At that time Marrocchetti had finished his great equestrian statue of Richard the Lion-hearted. It is a singular

thing that Marrocchetti, in his long and glorious life,
made four equestrian statues—Emanuele Filiberto, the
Duke of Orleans, Carlo Alberto, and Richard the Lion-
hearted.   Each one of these statues bears a different
stamp, both as regards composition, feeling, and mode of
treatment ; one would say that they were the work of four
different artists.   This difference of work can be reasonably explained by the diversity of the subjects and the
distance of time that occurred between each work, neces-
sarily producing notable changes in the mind and style
of the artist; and also because Marrocchetti, on account
of the multiplicity of serious work he had in hand,
thought it advisable to have help, not only in the marble
work, but also on his clay models; and as those who
helped him were not always of his school, so every one
brought just so much of their own individuality to bear
upon the work as to alter the master's character and
style.   These are the sad but inevitable results for him
who has the bad habit of getting assistance with his clay
models.

While I was there in 1856 he had under his directions
a very able modeller—I think he was a Roman, by name
Bezzi.   Bezzi went on modelling, and Marrocchetti
directed his work, whilst he sat smoking and talking with
me and others.   Sometimes he would make him pull
down a piece he had been at work on and begin afresh.
This method seemed to me then, as it does now, a most
strange and dangerous one ; and it has not resulted happily, even amongst us, with those who have been induced
to follow it.

Marrocchetti was distinguished from other sculptors
by another originality—I was almost going to say oddity
—and this was, that he coloured his statues often to such
a degree that you could no longer distinguish the material

of which they were made. I remember to have seen an imposing monument composed of several figures that had been put up in honour of Madame de la Riboisière in the chapel belonging to the hospital which bears that name in Paris. It is completely coloured—I should better say painted all over—with body colour,—the heads, hair, eyes, draperies, all coloured so that it is impossible to distinguish the material in which it was sculptured. You could distinguish absolutely nothing; and if it had not been for the *custode*, who affirmed that the work was in marble, you might have thought it was coloured plaster or *terra cotta*. And this worthy man was so sure of having thus added beauty to his statues that he was much astonished that others did not imitate him.

Marrocchetti, there is no doubt, was wrong in loading on colour as he did; but it is a question not yet solved or to be lightly put aside as to whether a delicate veil of colour may not be tried on the fleshy parts. Grecian sculptors used colour, and ours also in the middle ages, although only on particular parts of the figure and on the ornamental portions of their monuments. The only one that I know of, amongst modern artists, who used colour with discretion, was Pradier. The English sculptor Gibson was more audacious. I have seen a Cupid by Gibson entirely coloured—the hair golden, the eyes blue, his quiver chiselled and gilt, and, incredible as it may seem, the wings painted in various colours with tufts or masses of red, green, blue, and orange feathers, like those of an Arara parrot.

Having seen the Kensington Museum, and the other sculpture and picture galleries in which London is so rich, I take pleasure in recounting a little occurrence that happened to me at Sydenham. Sydenham is a place some fifteen miles from London, in an open country, healthy, and rich in green vegetation. There is the famous Crystal Palace, where one can see a permanent exhibition of all the most beautiful things that are scattered about in different parts of the world, beginning with antediluvian animals reconstructed scientifically from some fossil bones found in the excavations of mines in Scotland and elsewhere. There are gigantic trees from Australia, one of which, having been cut in pieces, bored, and the centre extracted, to enable it to be transported, had been put together again and planted inside this palace. It is as high as a veritable campanile; at its base a door has been made, so that one can enter inside it; and it holds comfortably some thirty persons. All the tropical plants are there in fine vegetation, in conservatories heated by stoves, where the heat is so oppressive that one longs to go out and breathe the fresh outside air. There also can be seen that famous plant that grows in the water, with its flower floating on the surface. This gigantic flower, when I then saw it, measured not less than two metres in diameter, and the leaves flattened out on the water looked like open umbrellas. It seems really as if one were dreaming, to see such gigantic vegetation. Besides plants and animals from all parts of the earth—from the polar as well as from the tropical regions—there are the full-sized models of men taken from life, and coloured according to nature—Cretins, Esquimaux, savages, Tartars, Mongols, and anthropophagi, all in most natural attitudes, and in their various costumes. There are also full-size reproductions of pieces of Egyptian, Indian, Assyrian, Mongolian, and Moorish architecture; parts of the Alhambra Palace; some rooms from Pompeii; minarets and Chinese temples; sculpture (I mean, be it understood, reproductions in plaster) of the best Egyptian, Indian, Greek, and Roman works, as

well as those of the middle ages; Ghiberti's doors; the
equestrian statues of Colleoni, of Gattamelata, of Marcus
Aurelius; and even some modern works, amongst which
is my "Abel."

I knew that this statue of mine must be there, for
I had it cast by Papi, who had the mould ever since
he cast it in bronze; and when I saw it amongst
these masterpieces as a specimen of modern art, I felt
a certain feeling of complacency that I hope will be
forgiven me. But this complacency of mine was disturbed when I saw that one of the fingers of the left
hand had been badly restored, not merely formed in-
elegantly, but actually distorted, as the last phalange
was much too short. That little stump of a finger so
irritated me, that I gave it a blow with the stick I
had in my hand, and it fell on the ground. Ill-luck
would have it that one of the guards saw me, and
seizing hold of me, he carried me off to the commissary
of the exhibition. I was asked why I had damaged that
statue; and I answered that the finger was badly made,
and that I had broken it off by an involuntary movement. They replied that I could not judge whether
that finger or anything else was well done or badly done,
and in any case it was not permitted for persons to
damage the objects exhibited there; that therefore, for
this violation of the rules, I had incurred the penalty
decreed in such and such an article, and that they intended to keep me in custody. To tell the truth, this
Signor Commissary spoke French rather badly; but I
understood him very well, and with the best grace possible
begged to be forgiven, saying that the wish to damage
the statue had never entered into my thoughts, that
the finger I had broken was positively ugly, that it
must be remade as it ought to be, and that, as to having

it restored, I would myself bear the expense. But the commissioner was firm, and was about to consign me to a guard, who was to conduct me not exactly to prison, but to something of that kind. I then felt obliged to make my name known. At first he had no intention of yielding to my explanation, and there was an expression on his face that might be translated thus : " It seems to me strange ; it cannot be ; I don't believe it." Then he went on to say, " Your position as author did not give you the right to do what you have done, even admitting that what you affirm is true—and we shall soon see if it be really true (*tout de suite*). You are the author of that statue ; then remake the finger that you have broken." I was completely taken aback by this new judgment of Solomon, so simple and just. Calling to my aid a young modeller who was employed there, working a little and directing a little, the finger was soon remade. And so this odd adventure came to an end, proving the justice of the proverb, " Who breaks, pays."

I returned to Sydenham several times, because the quantity and importance of the things to be seen required time and attention ; but when I found myself near my own statue, I gave it a wide berth.

One day I found myself, or rather I should say I was taken by William Spence, to a great dinner given by the Artistic and Industrial Society in the dining-hall of the great Palace of the Exhibition. We were no less than four hundred, and Lord Derby presided. About the end of the dinner the toasts began, with speeches of which naturally I understood not a word ; but fortunately " Mino " translated them to me in a few brief words. At last an Indian officer of the English army arose with a face the colour of copper, and began to speak ; but after the first words, here and there in that immense hall, first in undertones, and then louder and louder, there arose a confused noise of voices of disapprobation. I understood nothing, and begged "Mino" to explain; and he replied that I must keep quiet, and he would afterwards explain everything. In the meantime the noise of disapprobation increased, and some loud words were repeated. The orator's voice could hardly be heard any more, but he was not disturbed, and waited until the tempest was a little calmed down before continuing. Then I heard a word repeated louder and louder, which "Mino" explained to me was "Enough." The only one who remained cold, passive, and silent was the president; and when the speaker saw that it was an impossibility to make himself heard, he bowed and sat down. After a little while every one rose from table.

"Now, then, relieve my curiosity. What has that officer said of so extraordinary a nature as to compel him to silence in a country like this, where really such entire liberty prevails?"

"What he has said," replied "Mino," "he could have said and repeated most freely; but he was badly inspired, and had the imprudence to name the Queen. Now amongst us the Queen, whatever may be the question, is never mentioned. The law—and more than the law, respect for her person—prohibits us from naming her. The officer who spoke is a colonel in our Indian army, and is, as you can see by the colour of his face, an Indian. He only arrived a few days ago on a mission, they say, of some importance. Now this is what he has said: The Indians, subjugated by the force and cunning of the English Government, having borne as much as is humanly possible to bear—the loss of their liberty, of their wealth, and of their religious faith; aggravated by the odious sight of their oppressors; every modest

T

demand of theirs rejected; weighed down every day
more and more by additional taxation,—for some time
past have burned with impatience to shake off their yoke
and regain their lost liberty. The English Government,
being aware in part of this movement, and in part ignoring it, he felt himself in duty bound to proclaim it
loudly, as much for the good of his own people as for the
English themselves. After having in vain attempted all
ways of adjustment with the Government of the Queen
(first time of mention), he hoped at least by these means
to open the eyes and move the heart of the Queen
(second time) in favour of those poor pariahs, assassinated
by a Government who, in the name of her Majesty the
Queen (third time), add to insult the derision of a people
whom it has enervated with the pretext of civilising it.
Revolution and war being imminent if their just demands
are this time again rejected, the Government being responsible for this disaster, and the Queen . . . and the
Queen—— Here the orator, as you saw, was unable to
continue, and already they had allowed him to say too
much. Neither the gravity of his revelations nor his
injurious assertions against the Government had been
able in the least to excite our delicate organisation, but
it was only and entirely on account of the sacred name
of the Queen being mixed up in his speech so impru-
dently and with so little judgment."

The fact is, however, that in less than five weeks from
the day that this poor Indian attempted to make the truth
known—explaining what was wrong, and revealing the
consequences that would follow, and counselling a remedy
—the telegraph, with its flashing words, announced the
Mutiny, the peril the English were in, and their calls for
help. It is true that the Queen was not then mentioned,
but for all that, men did not the less die. Methinks I can

hear it said, "What has this to do with your memoirs? In our opinion, it has nothing to do either with your life or with any artistic reflection that can be of interest to us."

But this objection bears only the appearance of reason. With this scene I wished to depict the temper and character of the English in general, and in particular of the two most prominent persons of that assemblage—namely, the Indian colonel and the president of the banquet. And who is there who does not see how useful and good these studies of character, taken from the life, are to the artist? The essential thing required to make a work of art beautiful and valuable is, that it should be a just expression of the passions and feelings of the various characters the artist wishes to represent. It is vain to look for the right expression amongst the mercenary models that one ordinarily makes use of. The model is used for all that is on the outside—movement, proportions, physical characteristics, beauty of form,—for all, in fact, except, however, just that turn of the head and look of the eye, that movement of the lips, dilation of the nostrils, and a thousand other signs and indications on the face which reveal the inner struggles of the soul. These passions and feelings are more or less intense according to the temperament, habit, and education of different individuals; and in the mysterious sea of the soul, tempests gather, and become the more dreadful in proportion as they are not kept in check by reason. Not to give a false expression to the subject we wish to treat, we must study all these differences. Love in Francesca does not manifest itself as in Ophelia, the madness of Orestes is not that of Hamlet, Ugolino's grief is not the grief of Prometheus, and Penelope's sadness is different from that of Ariadne's. There are natures in whom the soul is of such delicate fibre, and who revolt so haughtily against an insult, that, oblivious of physical weakness, they flash into anger, and rush blindly against the offender, whoever he may be. There are others, strong and robust in body, who take things comfortably and easily, and let alone the calumnies launched against them; which, in fact, have rather the effect of mosquitoes upon them,—they are disturbed for a little while, and then go quietly to sleep again. The acute thrusts of love wound but the external epidermis of these well-wadded souls. Giuseppe Giusti created a couple of these curious beings—man and woman—and he called them Taddeo and Veneranda. For them the sea that I spoke of is always becalmed, and their tranquil souls float peacefully about therein. There is, however, a calm very different from this, brought by reason into these fierce struggles of the soul. The first, instead of being a calm, is indolence, and all the fibres that make our whole being move and throb, are, as it were, dormant. But this calm I speak of is caused by the force of reason, and strengthened by the sentiment of temperance and charity.

How much self-control that Indian officer must have exercised over himself, knowing that he was proclaiming a great truth, which, had it been listened to and reparation made in time, would have prevented that most unfortunate war that he knew to be imminent, certain, and homicidal ! To hear the shouts crying silence to him, and not to be disturbed by them, continuing with a firm voice not any louder (which would indicate anger), nor lower (which would be a sign of fear), only stopping a little when the other voices grew louder and prevented him from being heard, and then again taking up his discourse without turning to the right or to the left, and repeating over again the last word that had been drowned by the noise,—I say that this produced on me the impression of a profound admiration for the man. Even now, after twenty years have elapsed, I seem to see that grand figure before me, and I feel all his manly tranquillity.

One of the peaceful natures, always content, so well described by Giusti in his 'Amor Pacifico,' and whom I knew well, was Professor Clemente Papi, an excellent caster in bronze. When I knew him he was between fifty and sixty years of age, of moderate height, stout build, and high colour, always laughing, always full of bright stories and little jokes. The muscles expressive of indignation had, as it would seem, been left out of his composition by mother nature. His brow was always smooth—there was never a frown on his face when speaking or listening, whatever might be the subject of discussion; and this constant habit of laughing made him laugh, or shape his mouth into a smile, even in the most serious moments of life. This man, who was in many respects most excellent, in his art, in his family, and as a master, appeared as if he had no heart, or as if it were made of sugar-candy; and yet he died suddenly of heart-disease. As I have said, he had a heart, but it was sugar-sweet; the bitterness of sorrow and the harshness of anger never in the least disturbed his state of calm, careless joviality. The following occurrence depicts Professor Papi's nature to the life: The Grand Duke having ordered a cast in bronze of my "Abel," and all the preliminary work for the fusion of it having been accomplished,—that is to say, the mould made on the original plaster, the earth pressed into that mould to form the kernel, or *nocciolo*, so as both to obtain lightness and to strengthen the cast—the wax cast having been made and the necessary touches given to it by myself—the whole cased in its heavy covering, armed and bound about by irons that it might bear the stream of liquid metal, and placed in the pit and heated to allow the wax to escape from the fissures, then baked that it might become of the consistency required for the operation,—the composition of the metal was prepared, placed in the furnace, and set on fire. After fifteen or twenty hours, the melting was accomplished—an operation easily related, but which was the result of many months of labour and great expense. The valve was then opened, that it might descend into the mould below. The strangeness of the enterprise, the time and sacrifices of those employed in it, the strange and almost mysterious spot where the operation took place, the heat from the furnace-fire, the gases that came from it, the anxiety of the workmen, their extreme fatigue in that decisive moment, the lamp that burned before the crucifix, and prayer that preceded the opening of the valve—all filled me with an undefined sense of the marvellous and unknown, of the fearful and sacred. The valve was opened, the metal flowed down the pipe into the main channel clear and liquid, as all metal is during this process. Joy was depicted on all the faces of those anxious persons who had toiled so long on the work. The metal had been already poured into the greater part; the mould, which had resisted well, cased as it was in its thick covering, and bound with hoops of iron, gave no signs of cracking, nor was any noise heard, as not unseldom happens when, as the metal flows in, the air inside has not an easy escape. Papi stood upright and beaming, ready to embrace his scholars, when all at once some little violet flames from the mouth of the furnace announced the cooling off of the metal, which gradually slackened its flow and lost its splendour. Stupor and depression were depicted on all faces—a mortal pallor, rendered stranger still by the light reflected from the furnace, making them look like spectres. The metal no longer flowed along, but began to drop in flakes like polenta, then became coagulated, and then stopped still. The statue was little more than half cast, and all was lost! At this sight the poor workmen, tired out, and torn with grief, threw themselves on the ground with violent contortions and weeping. I, between stupor and regret for the failure of the work, the seeming despair of those poor people, and the grief —although not visible, but still great—that Papi must feel, did not know what to say; it seemed as if my tongue were tied. I wanted to get away from that place of misery: it seemed to me as if those people, master and workmen, must be left alone to give vent to their sorrow. Papi came to my rescue. He came up to me, and said that he had promised the Grand Duke to give him the news of the casting, and that he had hoped to do so himself; but as it had failed, he did not feel courage enough to carry him the bad news, and begged me to do so. He shook hands with me, and turned to take leave of others that he had invited or allowed to be present at the casting.

The evening was well on when I went to the Pitti. I spoke to Paglianti, the royal valet of the Grand Duke, and asked if I could be permitted to have an audience. Paglianti knew me, and also knew that the Duke liked to see me. In a few moments I was shown into his study, and briefly told him what had happened. According to his wont, he listened thoughtfully and attentively, but did not seem disturbed by it. One would have thought that he was listening to a thing that might be anticipated as possible or probable. Then he began to speak—

"Poor Papi! poor man! Who knows how disappointed he must have felt, and how miserable he is now? And your work, too, which gave you so much trouble—all is lost! I feel deeply for your misfortune and that poor man's unhappiness. Let us think about consoling him. Return to him, and tell him in my name to be of good cheer, for there is a remedy for everything, and that I am certain he has nothing to reproach himself with; for, when one has taken every possible precaution to secure success in the execution of anything, and notwithstanding all, the work does not turn out well, no one can blame him for it, and I least of any one. Tell him that battles are won and lost in the same way. Sometimes even a mistake makes one win, and one can lose in spite of every forecast. Tell him this and more, all that comes into your head, to comfort him, and speak in my name. Go at once to him, console him, and your words will bring him a little calm. I am certain that you will do him a great deal of good, and that he may afterwards be able to rest to-night; but I am sure that if you do not speak to him, the poor man will not sleep."

I went almost at a run, and from Palazzo Pitti to the Via Cavour is a good bit of way. I was all in a perspiration. I knocked at his door, and after a time his maidservant appeared.

" Who is it ? " says she.

" It is I; open the door."

" Oh, is it you, Signor Professor? "

" Yes, it is I; open the door, I have a word to say to your master."

" The master is in bed ; you could speak to him to-morrow."

" No ; I must do so now. If he is in bed, no matter; he will be glad all the same."

" But if he is asleep, do you want to wake him ? "

"Asleep!" said I; "is he asleep?"

"Yes; he is asleep, I assure you. He has been asleep more than two hours, he was so tired when he came home."

"Well, then, since you assure me that he is asleep, my commission is at an end; and when he wakes up, which will probably be to-morrow morning, you may tell him that I had come in a great hurry to say two words to him that contained the power of making him sleep, but having found him in his first sleep, I shall tell him another time, although they may then seem quite stale."

To speak sincerely, such an extraordinary feat I have never been able to explain. To sleep after a similar misfortune—to go to sleep at once, immediately, two hours after, at his usual hour, the hour when those who have nothing on their minds sleep! And yet, now that I think of it, Napoleon slept on the night that preceded one of his greatest battles. So at least he wrote in his biography, and because it is printed, a great number of simple-hearted people believe in it as they do in the Gospel; and you, gentle reader, do you believe it? "*Mi, no !*" as Sior Tonin Bonagrazia would say.

It has been necessary to make this digression on character,—that is to say, on the difference between those who acquire calmness by virtue of their reason, and those whose senses are obtuse to all passions—differences which are visible to any one who observes with care, and that escape many, indeed most people who do not think. Let the young artist be persuaded that the study and observation of the true nature of love and human passions are most essential. Let them give up all thoughts of seeing these expressions in their models. One's studio models are common people, who certainly have their feelings and passions, but they are generally vulgar; and in any case, during the time that they are posing as models, they are thinking of everything except the moral condition of mind of the person they are representing.   One may answer, "We know this; the artist should himself give the expression required by his subject."   Quite right; but how can the artist seize hold of the right expression if first he has not seen it in life, and studied with attention beyond words?   Then it is evident to me, and other works show it without my words, that not a few artists expect and insist on finding expression in their models.   I remember an artist who flew into a passion because his model did not assume an expression of grief.   The model naturally laughed louder and louder, every time this simpleton said, "Don't laugh; be serious and sad; I want you to express grief."

It is true that this kind of study may occasion some little inconvenience—as, for instance, one may pass for being very stupid, because absorbed in observing and committing to memory, and hearing nothing that has been talked about.   One may answer at random, and be extremely ridiculous.   One may appear as a. somewhat offensive admirer, and give umbrage to some jealous husband.   One may even pass for a scatter-brain and imbecile.   But have patience!   With time and practice the artist will gain his point, and be able to study as much as he wishes, while assuming an air of indifference that will shelter him from the above-mentioned misconceptions.

He may, however, fall into other mistakes; and I here take note of them that he may avoid so doing. One evening I was at a ball at the Palazzo Torlonia at Rome.   I have no fancy for balls, but I like to see a great many people,—beautiful ladies, elegant dresses, and

naked arms,—and more than all, the expression of eyes
now languid, now animated—smiles now ingenuous, now
coquettish,—the weariness of the fathers, and the eager
concern of the mammas,—the reckless joy of the Don
Giovanni *in erba*, and the deceitful, washed-out look of
the Don Giovanni *in ritiro*. It is a pleasant as well as
useful study, as long as one does not change parts, and
instead of a spectator become an actor in the scene. The
"lime-twigs are spread out, the little owls are at their
places; so beware, ye blackbirds, not to be caught." There
I stood; the painter Podesti, with whom I had come to the
ball, had left me, carried away by the attractions of the
card-table. In one of the many rooms open for the cir-
culation of the company, and for the repose of dancers
and those not dancing, seated on one of the divans I
saw a young woman of singular beauty. She was about
thirty : several gentlemen surrounded her like a garland,
and she had now for one, now for another, some trivial
gay word; but in strange contrast with her careless words
and smiles was her austere brow, and the haughty looks
that came from her eyes. The turn of her head was
stately and attractive ; and a clasp of diamonds that was
fastened in her dark shining hair flashed every time she
moved. I never saw a more assassinating beauty than
hers ! Leaning against the wall on the opposite side of
the room, studying that face with its strangely variable
expression, all the women of history and fable with
which this singular beauty had affinity rose before my
mind. Less full of passion than Norma, less ferocious
than Medea, almost Helen, and, without an *almost*, a
Circe,—in fact, one of those women who promise one
paradise and prepare one an *inferno*—capable of killing
the body, the soul, and the memory of a man. When
I had got so far in my reflections, the young lady rose,

and coming straight towards me, she said these simple words—"*Monsieur, tandis que vous pensiez, je ne sais pas à quoi, la cire a coulé tout à son aise sur votre habit*"—and she passed on slowly, demolishing in two words my castles in the air. I found, in fact, that the shoulder and sleeve of my dress-coat were covered with wax, to say nothing of the suppressed laughter of the beautiful Circe. Of two things one must therefore be warned —to put one's self out of the dangerous proximity of lights, and to be careful to look at people with some reserve.

CHAPTER XVI.

UT it is time to return to the point I started
from, and to speak of the study of character
and spontaneous expression from life. In
fact it was in London that I had occasion
to see a picture of extraordinary beauty for strength and
truth of expression, in which the result of that study
was clearly demonstrated. This picture, on exhibition
at the School or Academy of Fine Arts, was of small
dimensions; the subject, a familiar one, or, as it is usually called, *genre*, was as follows: To the right of the
person facing the picture is a gentleman's country-house,
and outside by the garden-gate a mother is seated near
her little girl, who is ill, and reclines in an arm-chair,
supported by pillows. The mother has left off working,
and looks anxiously at the pale exhausted girl, whose
eyes are sunk deep in their sockets, and who smiles and
looks languidly at two little children, a boy and girl,

little peasants, strong, healthy, and robust, who are
dancing, and have evidently been invited to do so by
the parents of the little invalid.   It is autumn, the hour
a sad one.   The last rays of the sun are gilding the
dead leaves on the trees and on the bushes.   On the
left you see the father in close conversation with the
doctor, questioning him with anxious eyes, whilst he,
very serious and sad, hardly dares look at the unhappy
father.   To speak the truth, when *genre* pictures are
so full of interest and life as this, I prefer them to all
the gods of Olympus.   But, generally, they are entirely
wanting in this first quality, and abound in the second,
which becomes vulgarity; and so the foundation of art,
which is the beauty of truth, is wanting, and only the
"business" remains, with its puerile attractions.

I saw many other works of art, both in painting and
sculpture, at this exhibition of living English artists, but
none of them compared with that marvellous work.   I do
not remember the name of its author, and much I regret
it; but I have given a minute and exact description
of it.

In the National Gallery, rich in pictures of the Italian
school, I admired a marvellous cartoon of Raphael's,
slightly coloured, of the " Massacre of the Innocents."   It
is jealously guarded under glass.   Of the beauty of this
work as to form, I do not speak—it is Raphael's, and
that is enough ; but what most struck me was the brutal
movement of murdering soldiers, the desperate convul-
sive resistance of the mothers, pressing to their breasts
the little babes, whilst they scratch and tear at the
faces of the executioners ; and it would seem as if one
heard their sharp screams mingled with the cries of the
murdered infants.   The calm and flowing grace that are
the characteristic notes of that divine genius, do not appear

in this; but instead one sees and hears *parole di dolore*, *accenti d' ira, voci alte e fioche*, of the desperate mothers. Those who have not seen this cartoon and the others at Hampton Court, of which I will soon speak, cannot entirely appreciate Raphael.

I advise young artists who want to go to London to learn a little of the language of the country; they will find themselves the better for it. It happened to me, who knew nothing of it, one day to lose myself in that interminable city, and another day, very little to my taste, to find myself carried off in the train to Scotland. If, therefore, they learn a little English, they will under- stand that Leicester Square is pronounced *Lester Squere*. As I said, I lost myself in London, and this was how. I lodged at the Hotel Granara. Granara is an honest Genoese, who knows how to attend to his own affairs, as all the Genoese do, and more than that, knows how to secure the goodwill of his customers, almost all of whom are Italians. His hotel was at that time, in 1856, in Leicester Square. It was my habit then, as always, to go out very early in the morning and take a little turn before breakfast. I made it a study to observe well all the turnings, the names of the streets and their peculi- arities, so as to be able to return home, but did not succeed. I tried again and again for about two hours, before asking my way, to see if it were possible for me to find a street, a name, or a sign that I had seen before, but all was in vain. I was tired, had had no food, and had not a *soldo* in my pocket; and although I had with me the key of the place where I kept my money, this was of no avail in getting me a breakfast. Driven by hunger I put aside my pride, or rather my pretence, of finding my way to the inn, and asked a policeman. I asked him both in Italian and in French, but he did not

understand me, and presented me to another, but with
the same result. There I beheld myself lost in that
immense city, without a penny, and very hungry. It
must be admitted that my position was a rather serious
one—not that those excellent policemen did not perfectly understand that I had lost the way to my hotel, and
were most desirous of putting me on the right road to it,
but they did not know how, as they were not acquainted
with the name of the square that I inquired for. At
last, and it was quite time, one of them took out of his
pocket his note-book and pencil and gave it to me,
saying in good French, " *Écrivez le lieu où vous êtes logé.*"
I had hardly written the first word when the policeman
quickly said, " Lester Squere?"   " It may be so," said
I; but to make sure I finished writing out the address,
adding even the name of the hotel, and showed it to
him, to which the policeman said, "Yes, very well."   He
took the paper and begged me to follow him to another
policeman at the end of the street, to whom he consigned
me and the paper, and having exchanged a word or two
with him, returned to his post.   The new guard, without
uttering a word, took me to another and consigned me
to him, and so on, until in about half an hour I was
reconducted home.

You understand me, therefore, in England the knowledge of a little of the English language will do no harm,
and not be *de trop*, and by it you may avoid another inconvenience, that of finding a teacher at the wrong time and
place. Let me explain myself. The maid-servant who
had the care of my room got it into her head that she
would teach me to speak English, and she set herself to
work to teach me with a method entirely her own. She
seized hold of a chair and called it by name, then the
chest of drawers, then the bed, then the looking-glass, &c.,

and she insisted that I should repeat these names after
her in her language. The thing in itself was innocent
enough, but foolish, as both she and I lost our time by
it. For me it was not so much matter, but for her the
neglect of her duties might have lost her her situation ;
and therefore, with the language common to all—that is,
by gesticulations—I made her understand that she must
stop her lessons. Let the reader not think, however,
that I refused that good, and, let me add, beautiful
teacher in a rough way; no indeed, I am not a satrap.
I said to her—(beg pardon !) I gesticulated all this to her
nicely, and with a good grace. One must always have
every care to treat women in a gentle and respectful
manner.

Here is another story, always *àpropos* of the necessity
there is of knowing at least a little of the English language. Hampton Court is a palace of the Queen's, about
an hour's distance from London by rail. It is open
to the public on holidays. The palace is beautiful, and
contains many precious things; the country about is
green, fresh, and pleasant : therefore, as can easily be
imagined, there is always a large concourse of people.
I wished also to procure myself this outing; so, betak-
ing myself to the northern station, I took my ticket for
Hampton Court, and got into the train. In that country one goes along at the pace of twenty kilometres an
hour. Enchanted by the sight of the beautiful country
clothed in its deep-green mantle,—so new to us who are
accustomed to ours, so much more pallid, and burnt in
streaks by the greater fierceness of the sun,—I forgot
the pace we were going at, paid no attention when we
stopped, and did not hear them call out the name Hampton Court. I suppose similar things must happen to the
touristes who visit our Italy. Let us imagine one of them

U

to have taken a ticket for Certaldo, desiring to visit
Boccaccio's house ; the train stops, and the guard, with a
stentorian voice, more calculated to slur over than pro-
nounce the name, calls out, "Who is for Certaldo?"
(*chi è peccettardo*). Naturally the *touriste* does not understand, and allows himself to be carried on maybe even
as far as Siena. But this is not so bad as my case, for I
ran the risk of being taken on to Edinburgh. Fortunately I began to suspect that I had passed by the station
where I ought to have got out, and asked. The answer
was, that we had passed Hampton Court some time
since.

"What must I do?" I asked.

"Stop at the first station ; and this evening, by the
Edinburgh train, you can return to London."

"Are there no other trains before this one, that I may
return to London during the day to dine?"

"No."

"Many thanks!"

I got down at the first station, paid the difference in
my ticket, and, in the very worst of humours, took a
turn in the little village or hamlet,—I did not even care
to ask its name. I had some wretched food, and everything seemed to me bad and ugly.

Yes, yes; a little of the language of the country is
even more necessary than bread or than money, for the
English—and I think they are right—speak no other
language than their own. But they go so far as to pretend, when they come amongst us, that we should speak
English like them ; and here they are in the wrong.

When I got home to the hotel in the evening, Avvo-
cato Fornetti and Caraffa, my friends and companions
at the hotel, came to me smiling, and said, "Have you
amused yourself?"

I said, "Yes;" I did not tell them what had happened, for they were the kind of men who would have ridiculed me for a long time.

Beyond these few little mishaps, my time passed most pleasantly in London. My fellow-citizen Marietta Piccolomini was singing at the Queen's Opera House with Giulini and Belletti. Ristori was acting at the Ateneo Italiano. There were very often concerts of music, instrumental and vocal, where Bottesini, Giovacchino Bimboni, and the violinist Favilli played. I knew De Vincenzi, who was afterwards in the Ministry; and I again met Count Piero Guicciardini, Count Arrivabene, the *maestro* Fiori, that scatter-brain of a Fabio Uccelli; Monti, the Milanese sculptor; our Fedi; Bulletti, a carver in wood; Romoli, the painter and sculptor; and others,—in fact, a perfect colony of Italians.

Among the tragedies which Ristori acted in at that time, and which I already knew, I saw one that I liked extremely. It was the 'Camma,' by Professor Giuseppe Montanelli,—in my belief, a very fine work, and superlatively well interpreted, in its proud and passionate character, by the first actress, Signora Ristori. I heard the Signora Piccolomini, with her usual grace and intelligence, sing in the 'Traviata' and the 'Figlia del Reggimento.' Although these entertainments, be they prose or music, were deserving of all praise, yet the price of the entrance-ticket, according to us Italians, was enormously dear, being one pound sterling, which is equal to twenty-five *lire* and twenty *centimes* of our money. May I be forgiven if that is little? One must also take note that at that time, A.D. 1856, everything was done in a small way,—reasonable incomes, few requirements, small expenditures, and, smallest of all, taxation. The ciphers of millions in the great book of 'Debit and Credit' had not

yet been invented; the floating debt did not even exist
in dreams.   So that thirty *lire codine* at that time represented nearly a hundred francs of to-day.   Who is there
(I mean amongst us) who would wish to spend a hundred *lire* for a 'Traviata'?   Not I, indeed; for I remember, when I was an *abonné* at the Cocomero (now Niccolini), to have heard Ristori for four *soldi* a-night, and
she acted equally well, without taking into account her
youth and beauty, that inexorable Time will not respect,
even in celebrities.

"Then you went to a foolish expense; and you contradict yourself without even turning your page, for you
say that you would not spend the money, and at the
same time you inform us that you heard Ristori act in
'Camma'!"

I answer, "'Camma' cost me absolutely nothing, as the
Signora Ristori, who is as amiable as she is eminent as
an *artiste*, favoured me with an entrance-ticket;" and so
I clear up the apparent contradiction that the critical
reader was in such haste to bring forward.   Go on, however, and look sharply through these papers, where you will
find something of everything.   Moreover, you will be often
bored, but I hope you will never find any contradictions.
I have also a very good habit—that is, of re-reading
what I have written: and then, with a little art, one
succeeds in putting everything nicely in its place.   You
understand?   Then we will push on.

In order not to fail a second time in my intention of
seeing the royal villa of Hampton Court, I wrote that
name on a card and showed it to the guard every time
we stopped.   I got there at last.   The place all about is
very pleasant, with a wide, clear horizon, for the fogs
only have their home in London.   The palace, as may
be imagined, is large and majestic.   I don't remember

the style of its architecture, and don't want to refer to the
easy expedient of consulting a guide-book. I promised
myself that I would write my life, the thoughts that
came to me one after another, without help, trusting
only to memory. So I have done thus far, and intend
doing so to the end. The villa, as I have said, is majestic,
enclosed on all sides by gardens and orchards. The
interior consists of innumerable halls richly decorated
with paintings, somewhat out of repair, as they are no
longer used, it would appear, as a royal residence.
People crowd more particularly to the Queen's own
private apartments, to see her sitting-room, and even
her bedroom with its bed-furniture, and the thousand
rich, pretty, and curious things with which these rooms
are filled. The rest of the place, or the greater part of
it, such as the gallery of pictures and cartoons, is generally deserted. Yet the English are great lovers of art;
we see them with great interest frequent our galleries in
Rome, Florence, Venice, and Naples. But perhaps the
people brought by curiosity to Hampton Court belong
to the lower class, which has not in London the feeling
for art that the people even of the lowest class have in
Italy. In a great long hall, like a gallery, I saw the
eight cartoons of Raphael that were made for the arrases
in the Vatican. They consist of "St Paul preaching to
the Athenians;" "St Peter and the miracle of the fish;"
"St Peter and Ananias;" "St Peter receiving from Christ
the charge of guarding His sheep;" "Peter and John
healing the lame man at the gates of the Temple;" "Ely-
mas the Sorcerer punished by losing his sight;" and others
that I do not remember. He who has never seen these
cartoons, and the "Massacre of the Innocents" above
mentioned, can form no idea of the strength of Raphael
in that grandly fierce style initiated by Michael Angelo,

who spread therein so broad a sail as to make him
terrible to the beholder, and to occasion the shipwreck
of many in a smaller craft, who perished miserably,
desirous of following him on that fearful ocean.

There are other cartoons in the same gallery by Man-
tegna representing the "Triumph of Cæsar." Mantegua,
as all know, as an artist is an imitator of the antique :
the execution of the work which is merely the material
part alone is his own, for he took the conception,
character, and style, in generalities and detail, from the
antique.

Besides the treasures of art contained in the London
museums—and one may also call Hampton Court a
museum—there are the beautiful public walks called
parks. The largest, richest in avenues, fields, and lakes
peopled by innumerable ducks and fish, is called Hyde
Park. This is the promenade where all the fashion-
able world meet. Ladies and gentlemen on horseback
dash down the interminable avenues of this park, giving
loose rein to their fiery steeds. It is a fine sight to see
these animals, so elegant in form, and at the same time
full of fire, pawing the ground, neighing, and fretting at
the bit, from their desire to be off: but still more beautiful to look at are those gentle ladies on their backs ;
and when they are going at full pace, bending slightly
forward on their fiery steeds, their flowing skirts, in ample
undulating lines, giving a slender, flexible look to their
figures, you feel carried away, and as if you would
like to follow them in that rapid, anxious race, where
peril changes into pleasure, and where the inebriation of
the senses becomes ideality. Such is the fascination
youth, beauty, and strength produce on the mind and
senses of all natures susceptible of feeling. It is a
pungent pleasure ; the soul struggles in these meshes of

flowers, and their perfume inebriates and captivates it. I beg pardon of the reader, if, for an instant attracted by this race of beautiful ladies, my head galloped away with them. Another time I will hold the reins tighter; and it ought not to be difficult to stop this little horse of mine, sixty years old.

Hyde Park, as I have said, is larger than the two others, St James's Park and Regent's Park, and is about five miles in circumference, which seems a good deal; but so it is. These country spaces in the middle of London are, as have been justly said, the lungs of the great city. By means of these green oases, impregnated with oxygen, the air of that gigantic body of London, where millions of men swarm like ants, is constantly renovated. These parks are rich in timber, and flowers are there cultivated with every art. There are very few guards, for great respect is shown for the laws prohibiting the damaging of the plants. A curious but very just penalty is inflicted by them, and this is it: If Signor Tizio has damaged a plant, or only picked a flower, Signor Tizio, according to the gravity of the mischief he has done, is prohibited from entering those precincts for fifteen or twenty days. And this is not enough—it would be too little; his name is posted up to view at all the park entrances, specifying the damage he has done and the penalty inflicted on him, that everybody who goes there may read and laugh!

I was present in Hyde Park at the distribution of medals to the troops on their return from the Crimea. That great national *fête* was a splendid success—the whole army in arms and full uniform, every part of it in its proper place, cavalry, artillery, marines, and infantry. At the end of a large camp a throne was erected for the Queen, her children, and her husband, Prince Albert.

The Ministers, Court dignitaries, and Lords surrounded her. The ceremony was a long one. The troops had been on foot since early morning, and many were the numbers who received medals. The sun beat down with great force on our heads, for it was in the month of June. It is a fine sight to see the youth of England, tall, square-shouldered young fellows, with upright bearing and brilliant colouring; but notwithstanding all this, it would seem that for all their strength of nature they cannot endure hunger. I was present at some little occurrences that astonished me extremely: two or three of those young men fainted as if they had been delicate girls, although they had herculean chests and arms. But so it is: the Englishman, when the hour has come, requires absolutely to have his tea; if this fails, he can no longer stand on his feet.

That this must really be the case, was demonstrated to me by the affectionate solicitude shown by their comrades and the people carefully conveying these fainting youths to the ambulances. Instead of this with us Italians, we see young men of twenty bear long marches, discomfort, and hunger with a bright face. It is the difference of nature and habits in the two nations. I do not mean, indeed, to say that we do not feel hunger—in fact, I can say for myself that I feel it most ferociously; and if this expression seems exaggerated, I will correct myself and add, brutally and insolently, and will recount a little anecdote in proof of my appetite, especially after fasting. It is a trifling matter, that goes as far back as thirty years. At that time of juvenile effervescence one wishes for much and feels much, and is not very fastidious about ways and means. The fact is a curious one, and, to say the truth, would not be very pleasant for me to narrate were it not that it is peculiar, and with

the touch of a brush paints to the life the character of
my early youth. I had quite forgotten it, and it really
would have been a mistake to do so. Those fasting
English soldiers reminded me of it, and I am very glad
of it.

The benevolent reader must betake himself back to
the time when I was twenty-six years of age, which, in a
young artist, sometimes means being possessed of twenty-
six devils. True it is that with time and increase of
years these devils, alas! diminish. Therefore, at my
present stand-point, I feel myself absolutely free of
them, and could bear fasting and hunger without dreaming of committing the impertinence that, without other
preamble, I am about to narrate.

Lorenzo Mariotti, an agent of the Russian Government, as I have before mentioned, brought me a paper,
on which were written the following words :—

"Professor Duprè is requested to come at an early
hour to-morrow morning to Quarto. A. DEMIDOFF."

Quarto is an enchanting villa that was afterwards in
the possession of the Grand Duchess Maria of Russia;
at that time, it was the property of Prince Anatolio
Demidoff, who had bought it from Prince Girolamo
Buonaparte, the father of Princess Matilde. It is four
miles distant from Florence, on the skirts of the steep
hill of Monte Morello, enclosed by beautiful gardens and
a fine park. I therefore betook myself there at an early
hour; and in the hopes of quickly despatching my business, I had not thought of breakfasting before starting,
but merely took a cup of coffee. I got into the carriage,
and arrived there at about eight o'clock. It was a good
season of the year, being May, and the day was a

splendid one ; in its quietness and fragrance it reminded
me of those most sweet verses of the divine poet :—

> " "E quale, annunziatrice degli albori,
> L' aura di maggio movesi ed olezza,
> Tutta impregnata dall' erbe e da fiori." [1]

So I tasted the voluptuousness of these first warm
days in the pure quietness of our hills, and I looked
forward to a short conversation with the Prince (as I
imagined the motive of his summons), and a speedy return to Florence.   I dismounted, and told the coachman to wait ; he lighted his cigar, took a turn round the
villa, and then placed himself in the shade.   I asked
for the Prince, and was answered that he was not up.
Then I feared that I should be obliged to wait ; but the
message was, "at an early hour."   Who knows, however, what is an early hour to a gentleman?   I found
out afterwards, as the reader will soon hear.

I walked about in the apartment, in the court, in the
garden, and in the park, and from time to time I came
back to see if the Prince had asked for me ; but the
Prince had not yet called.   Two good hours were
already past.   The pure air of the beautiful country, the
pleasant shade in the park, the odour of the violets and
roses, all had served to sharpen my appetite.   I risked
asking a servant if he could give me some breakfast, but
he answered that no one could have anything to eat
before his Excellency had ordered his breakfast.

"And is it late before his Excellency orders his
breakfast?"

"Ah ! that is as it happens,— at mid-day, at one

---

[1] " And as the harbinger of early dawn,
The air of May doth move and breathe out fragrance,
Impregnate all with herbage and with flowers."
> —DANTE : *Purgatorio*, Canto xxiv.

o'clock—when he thinks best." So saying he left me,
and I began my walks again. The beautiful country
seemed to me less beautiful, the shady avenues of the
park had assumed a certain sadness and obnoxious
freshness, the odour from the flowers made my head
giddy! What was I to do? Return to Florence? It
was far. And what then of the Prince's message? I did
not wish to fail to meet his invitation. I reflected a
little, and then resolved to make a somewhat rash attempt, but which succeeded admirably. I had caught
sight 'of the breakfast-room, with its table all set out with
cups, plates, glasses, cakes, confectionery—in fact with
everything, even with flowers in crystal vases that were
a wonder to look at. I went into the room and rang
the bell with violence; in an instant a servant appeared
dressed in black, to whom I turned, and with my head
well in the air pronounced in a harsh firm voice the
one word—

"Breakfast!"

The servant disappeared, and returned almost on the
instant with a silver soup-tureen, which he placed on the
table before me, and then stationed himself behind me.
Two other servants brought me ham, tongue, *caviale*,
veal cutlets, cold galantine, and then asked if I wanted
Madeira, Bordeaux, or Marsala. I was satisfied with
the Bordeaux, and also partook of a plate of strawberries;
and as a last sacrifice, I sipped a cup of Mocha coffee
—really inebriating—lighted my cigar, and lost myself
in the thickest part of the park. I was really beaming.
I felt restored in body, and in a state of perfect wellbeing, feeling a certain sort of complacency with my
spirit, my genius, my quickness—my impertinence, let
us say—which, *au fond*, was of good service to me and
did nobody any harm. Carlo Bini assures us that the

prison so sharpened his brains that it was as much use
to him in expressing his ideas as style was :—

> " La prigione è una lima sì sottile,
> Che aguzzando il cervel ne fa uno stile ; "

and does not hunger, I say, sharpen the brain ?   I could
cite a thousand examples of well-known geniuses who
have grown up in the midst of privations and hunger,
but I do not wish to be pedantic.   This I know full
well, that I should never have been capable of such an
escapade had I not had that formidable appetite, nor
should I have had the idea of satisfying it in that way.
Necessity sharpens the intellect to invent and to act ;
health and physical wellbeing kindle and spur on the
fancy through flowering pathways of flattering hopes.
Who knows with how many beautiful *grilli* and beautiful
bright-coloured butterflies, swift of flight, a little glass of
Bordeaux, or better still, a glass of our good Chianti wine,
has brightened the life of poets and artists ?   I found
myself in one of those beautiful dreams.   My mind
wandered from one thing to another ; the past and the
future were mixed up together.   History and fable, religion and romance, light and serious love, the fantastic
and the positive, fine statues, fine commissions, friends
distinguished for rectitude and genius,—all passed before me.   The flowers in the garden seemed to me more
beautiful and more odorous than ever, the sky brighter
and purer ; and never did the hills of Artimino, Careggi,
or Fiesole, populous with villas, seem to me so fair.   I
never gave a thought to the Prince or to his having sent
for me, any more than if it had been all a dream.   And
all *was* a dream ; for I fell asleep seated on one of the
sofa-chairs made of reeds, and in my sleep my thoughts
went back to those beautiful legends of history and fable
—beautiful women, fine statues, sweet friends—and to

the delightful country, when a slight touch on my shoulder woke me from my placid sleep. It was one of the Prince's servants, who was in quest of me to take me to him. To judge from their dress, the Prince and Princess must have only been up a short time. The Prince was standing; he had a cup in his hand, and dipped some pieces of toasted bread into it. From the odour, I became aware that it was *consommé*. The Princess was seated, turning over the leaves of a book of prints. She was of rare beauty, and the time, the place, and mild season of the year made her seem even more beautiful. She ought therefore to have seemed and to have been an object of love and profound admiration to her happy husband ; and if you add to the attractions of youth and beauty, grace of education, culture of mind, and *prestige* of birth, the affection of the man who possessed her should have verged on idolatry. But, alas ! in life such perfect happiness never lasts ; and the reader remembers what I told of the end of this union.

"My dear Duprè, you have arrived a little late, have you not? I sent for you, but you had not yet come."

"Your Excellency, let me tell you. I arrived betimes —in fact, very early, as your Excellency indicated I should do in your note ; but——" And here I told him the whole story already known to my reader; and I cannot describe how delighted he and the Princess were with it. Now and again the Prince held out his hand to me, saying, "Bravo ! In faith, I like this. Bravo !"

Then he told me what was the object of his sending for me. It was to give me an order for a life-size statue of Napoleon I., in the very dress which he possessed, and would furnish me with. He would procure me a good mask and some authentic portraits ; but he begged me to make it in the shortest possible time. It was very evident that he wanted to please the Princess, because whilst he was speaking to me he looked with loving intensity at her, and from time to time caressed her with a gentleness almost childlike.

It has been said that this man was extravagant and almost brutal; but when I remember the expression of radiant joy he had on his face when he was looking at his wife while proposing to give her a statue, as if it had been only a flower or a fan—when I recall that I have seen him shed warm tears for the death of Bartolini, and when I remember his great charity in founding and maintaining the Asylum of Saint Niccolo,—I cannot but deplore the bad feeling and injustice of those who take pleasure in blackening his character, in misinterpreting facts, and maligning his intentions.

The order for the statue of Napoleon proved a failure, as also for that of the Princess, owing to the separation of husband and wife.   And now let me go back to my place, for oh, how I have wandered away from the fainting young soldiers in Hyde Park!

The exhibition of the models competing for the Duke of Wellington's monument was about to be opened, so I thought it better to return home—all the more, because I wished to stop in Paris on my way back, as I had been in too great a hurry to see it when I came through.   By this time, nothing that there was to be seen in London had escaped me, and I could describe with great precision the Docks, the Tunnel, Westminster, St Paul's, the Tower of London, the Houses of Parliament, &c., &c.; but to what use?   Are there not guide-books?   And my impressions are many, it is true, and not of the common run; but they would require no little space, and this would change the simple design and form of these papers.

.Two or three days before the opening of the exhibition of these models, the Minister of Public Instruction, accompanied by the royal commissioner and other officials, visited the great hall at Westminster, where the models were exhibited. Some English and a few foreign artists thought proper to accompany the Minister when he went to inspect these works. As for me, I felt no such wish; and not wanting to be thought rude, and as neither the commissioner nor any of the people with the Minister knew who I was, I reclined in my shirt-sleeves on one of the cases belonging to these monuments, and so passed for a common workman in the hall. The commissioner, in fact, only knew me as a person of trust, who had some ability in restoring a work in plaster. I hope the reader has not forgotten that little affair. I was consoled, however, by seeing that the Minister stopped some time to look at my work, although he passed by others in too much haste, excusable in many instances, but not in some, where attention and praise were merited. Be it as it may, I was well pleased that he stopped before mine—and all the more so, that I did not form a part of his Excellency's suite. In fact I have been always very slow in putting myself forward with Ministers of Public Works, and I don't know to what saint I owe this feeling of respect for the Ministry. With certain members I have had frank cordial relations, before they became Excellencies; afterwards, when once they were in the Ministry, as if by a sort of magic they became for me such respectable personages that I retired into myself, and kept most willingly to my own place. Then those poor gentlemen have so much to do that, without a doubt, if you wanted to see them, you would be told that they could not receive you. So the fact of it is, that I have so much respect for them, and just so much for myself, as not to be willing to annoy them, and there is not a Minister of Public Works who can say, "This fellow has bored me about this or that thing." True it is, that by the grace of God I have never felt the necessity of doing so. Once only, and that not on my own account, but from a sentiment of dignity and justice, negotiations were entered into with the Ministers Natoli, Correnti, and Bonghi, as to the completion of a base for my Tazza, which I mentioned some time back; and as it just fits in here, I shall now bring this story to a close. The subject is a delicate, and for me a trying one, but I shall discuss it with calmness, and in as few short words as truth and reason can be clothed.

The base of the Tazza that I had modelled was either to be cast in bronze or cut in marble, and the last was decided on. Whilst they were looking for a pure piece of close-grained marble, the revolution took place, and the Grand Duke left. My model had already been paid for, and I hoped that the present Government, sooner or later, would have confirmed the commission; but I hoped in vain. After several years had passed, I asked my friend Commendatore Gotti, Director of the Royal Galleries, to make known my claim to the Ministry, which was done; but I obtained nothing. Later, Professor Dall' Ongaro spoke about it to Correnti, the Minister, and also obtained nothing. At last Commendatore D'Ancona was most pressing in speaking to Bonghi the Minister, and Betti the Secretary; but then came the fall of the Minister with his Cabinet, and I was really tired out by the whole thing, with its long, wearisome, and useless negotiations. I must add, that as the model had already been paid for, the expense for executing it was all that was required ; and yet, notwithstanding all these recommendations, this little sum was not granted, and I was not given a hearing. And here it is to the purpose to remind the Ministers of our Government that I for more than fifteen years have occupied the gratuitous post of Master of Finishing; and as in the statute creating this office it is declared that the Royal Government is not wanting in funds to pay the professors who shall have done the most for the good of their young pupils, it is to the purpose, I repeat, to remind them of the office that I have filled, and to declare to them that the pupils I have taught are now for the most part young living artists—some of them already professors, *cavalieri*, and masters in the schools —and that meanwhile I not only have not obtained a recompense, but even my demand, which to my belief was but a matter of pure justice, was not even listened to. But enough of this. I return to London, or rather let me say I leave it, as my work was finished and in place, only waiting for the judges. I therefore packed my trunk, paid my landlord, said good-bye to my friends, and got into the train, thinking of that blessed Channel where I had suffered so much in crossing.

x

CHAPTER XVII.

MY FATHER'S DEATH—A TURN IN THE OMNIBUS—THE FERRARI MONUMENT
—I KEEP THE "SAPPHO" FOR MYSELF—THE "TIRED BACCHANTE" AND THE
LITTLE MODEL—RAPHAEL AND THE FORNARINA—THE MADONNA AND
BAS-RELIEFS AT SANTA CROCE AND CAVALIERE SLOANE—MY DAUGHTER
AMALIA AND HER WORKS—MY DAUGHTER BEPPINA—DESCRIPTION OF
THE BAS-RELIEF ON THE FAÇADE OF SANTA CROCE—I AM TAKEN FOR
THE WRONG PERSON BY THE HOLY FATHER PIUS IX.—MARSHAL HAYNAU
—PROFESSOR BEZZUOLI AND HAYNAU'S PORTRAIT.

Y stay in London had been rather a long one,
but it was necessary for the restorations (and
what restorations !) of my work, and also to
see the wonders of art collected by that
powerful nation, by force of will, money, and time. I
stayed there about two months ; and notwithstanding the
many and novel distractions which that vast city offered,
and the good health I enjoyed at that time under a
climate so different from ours, I felt every day more
and more keenly the ardent desire to see my family, so
that when I arrived in Paris I delayed very little. The
letters which I received from home breathed the same
affectionate longing that I felt myself; and the gay,
thoughtless life of Paris, instead of attracting me, disgusted me. My daughters by their mother's side in our
little parlour were always present to me; and knowing
their dispositions, and the loving wisdom of the mother,
I felt that tender, holy joy which is difficult to describe,

but such as a loving and beloved father feels for his dear ones. I had lost two years ago my poor father from cholera. The poor old man had at first resisted the fury of that tremendous disease. He lived at the Carra, beyond Porta al Prato. All around death reaped its victims,—young and old, poor and rich; it spared no one. Almost every evening, at dusk, I went to him to assure myself of his health. One evening I found him unwell and in bed; but he had no fever, and his servant-maid, a good girl, served him with affectionate zeal. I left him quiet. On going away I urged her to be attentive to my father through fear of the epidemic then raging. The girl assured me that I need not doubt of her being so, and that I might be tranquil. The next evening I went back to see him: he was still in bed, and was better; but he told me that he stayed there as a precaution, and that he was to get up the following day, having the physician's permission to do so. The door had been opened for me by a little boy, to whom he gave lessons in drawing and ornamentation—Gabriello Maranghi—who to-day is one of our ornamental marble-workers.

"Oh, Rosa," I said to my father; "where is she?"

"Rosa, poor thing, died this morning. She came back from marketing, put down her things, went into her room, and I have not seen her since. They carried her away a short time ago!"—and the poor old man was much moved.

This sudden news of a death so instantaneous upset me and frightened me for my poor father. It was the same whether he stayed there or was carried elsewhere, for in every district they died in the same way. I went away sad at heart. The next day he got up, and was pretty well, even gay—in fact, for several days continued

well, and went on with his work as usual. One morning
—it was Sunday—my wife, who had got up before me,
came into the bedroom, waked me up, and said—

"Nanni, get up ; father is ill."

I looked in my wife's face, and read there the nature
and gravity of my poor father's illness. I ran to him ;
he recognised me, and said—

"My good Giannino, you have done well to come
quickly to your father; I am so glad to see you before
I die."

He lived all day, but had spasms of pain and wandered in mind. Then he died, and his face became
serene, as if he were sleeping peacefully. Whoever has
lost a father knows the kind of grief it is !

As I have said, I stayed but a few days in Paris. I
saw, on the wing as it were, and without being able to
study them, the monuments of art in which that great
capital is rich. I repeat, I felt an irresistible desire to
return home. Of the artists, I saw only Gendron, whom
I had known in Florence; Anieni, a Roman ; and Prince
Joseph Poniatowsky, then in his prime. What was most
to my taste was to ride up and down the streets of Paris
in an omnibus to get an idea of the movement and
grandeur of that city; but an incident occurred to me
that prevented my having that desire any longer, and I
should have put an end to this going up and down even
if I had not already determined upon my departure.
This was what happened. I had just come from a walk
in the Champs Elysées, when I saw the omnibus which
goes from the Barrière du Trône to the Madeleine standing still. I said to myself : "Very good; I will get in here,
go through all the Boulevards as far as the Barrière, and
without even descending, turn about again, and when I
get back to the Rue du Helder (where I lodged), I will

get out and go home. The omnibus started, drove
through all the Boulevards des Italiens, des Capucines,
Poissonnière, &c., and arrived at the Barrière. The
passengers got out, the omnibus stopped, and the conductor said to me—

" *Monsieur, descendez, s'il vous plaît.*" .

I answered, "*Je ne descends pas moi.*"

" *Pourquoi donc ?* "

" *Parce que je retourne sur mon chemin.*"

The ill-concealed laughter made me aware of my mistake, and the conductor, with good manners, gave me to
understand that the drive ended there, and on account
of the lateness of the hour there was no return trip. I
got out, and was at least four miles from home. To find
a carriage, I was obliged to take a long walk towards the
centre of Paris, and finally found one, and had myself
conveyed home, muttering against my own stupidity.
The next day, without turning either to the right or to
the left, I returned to Italy,—to dear, beautiful Florence ; to the bosom of my family ; to my studies ; to
my works ; to my good pupils ; to my faithful workmen ; and to my dear friends. Fortune had favoured
me in London : my work had gained one of the first
prizes in the competition. Another prize was obtained
also by Professor Cambi.

I had scarcely got back from London when Count
Ferrari Corbelli ordered from me the monument for his
wife, the Countess Berta, whom he had lost a few days
before. This work, which he wished to see finished as
soon as possible, was the cause of my abandoning the
group of the " Deluge," which I had already sketched, as
I have before stated. The monument was composed
of a base, on which was placed the urn containing
the body of the deceased. Modesty and Charity, the

principal virtues of the departed Countess, stand leaning on the angles of the sarcophagus, and above these
the Angel of the Resurrection points the way to heaven
for the soul of the Countess, snatched from the love
of her husband and children. The monument stands
under an arch, on which are three *putti* who hold up
some folds as if they were opening the curtain of
heaven. The background is encrusted with lapis-lazuli.
This monument is placed in the Church of San Lorenzo,
in the chapel next to the sacristy. My friend Augusto
Conti liked the conception of this monument, but objected to the nudity of the child of Charity. I have a
sincere respect for his criticism, as I respect also the
one he made on the monument to Cavour. He is a
profound and conscientious critic of art ; and besides
this, he has had, and has, for me and my family, a truly
fraternal love, and I remember with emotion the part
which he took during the illness and death of my
daughter and my wife.

Contemporaneously with this work I modelled a
" Sappho," and put it at once into marble, by order
of Signor Angiolo Gatti, a dealer in statues ; but it
happened that when he should have received the statue
he had no funds, and so I sent it to our Italian Exhibition. The Government, which had set apart a sum of
money for the acquisition of the best works of art,
decided not to take my statue, so I have it by me
now. It seems to me (I confess the weakness) as if
I had been wronged, so to speak, and as if my poor
" Sappho" resented this wrong from the new Phaons: so I
have wished to keep my faith with her, since the deser-
tion of her lover had caused her death ; and although I
have several times had offers not to be despised, yet I
have never been willing to sell her. Who can tell where

this poor "Sappho" will be, and how situated, after my death?

At this same time — that is, in 1857 — I made the model of ·the "Tired Bacchante"; and the idea of this figure was suggested to me by a little model who was brought to me by her mother, and who had never before been seen naked by any one. The freshness of this young girl, her unspoiled figure, the delicate beauty, somewhat sensual, of her face, suggested as a subject the "Tired Dancer," which afterwards was converted to a "Bacchante"; and as some time before I had made a little statue, representing Gratitude, for the Signora Maria Nerli of Siena, the general lines of that statuette served me as a sketch for this. But were I to say that it was only the beauty of the model, the subject suggested so spontaneously to me, and the composition already made, that persuaded me to keep the girl and make the statue, I should not be telling the exact truth. The mother of this girl was one of those women who not only throw aside all a mother's duty and responsibility, but despising all decency, show that they are capable of worse things. I tried at first to dissuade her from taking the young girl about to studios, and so forcing her to lose all that a maiden has most precious—modesty; nor was I silent about the perils that she was exposing her to. But my words were thrown away, for she smiled at them as if they were childish: so I kept the young girl and made the statue. I can assure you that she was a good young creature, and when I had finished the model I dismissed her with paternal words. I saw her many years after, so changed and sad, that one could hardly recognise her. She told me her sad story, — a name was on her lips, but a daughter's love made her. conceal it. I repeat, she was good, and suffered, but not by any fault of hers. I have never seen her again: perhaps she is dead—the only good thing that can befall any of those unhappy creatures.

To some it may seem as if I have been rather tedious about this poor Traviata; but most people, I hope, have found my indignation reasonable, for the condition of such a girl as this is most sad and humiliating,—forced by her mother, who ought to be the jealous guardian of the modesty and innocence of her child, to strip herself naked before a man. Even though her mother remain there present, it is always a hard thing, and most disagreeable to a young woman jealous of her good name, and dreading the looks and thoughts of the man there before her. It is not even impossible that it may be thought I have studiously and affectedly deplored such cases as these, as if I wished to show myself better than I am. I have no answer to give to any one who thinks thus, for in these papers he will find nothing to justify such an opinion. I only desire to remind the profane in art, that when we have a model before us, our mind and all our strength is so absorbed in our work, and the difficulties are so great in taking from nature just so much as is required for the character, expression, and form of our subject, that nothing else affects us. He who does not credit this is not an artist, and does not feel art.

I see a little smile of incredulity, almost of triumph, come over the face of my unbelieving reader, and the old story, so often sung and perhaps exaggerated, of Raphael and the Fornarina placed before me, to belie my words. This case of Raphael and the Fornarina was a unique one, and quite different from the ordinary relations that exist between the artist and his models.

A model is for us like an instrument or a tool, necessary for our work: If good and beautiful, we prize her and respect her as we would a good tool; if neither beautiful nor good, we bid her be off. The Fornarina was beautiful, and perhaps she may have been even good; but unfortunately she was of a sanguine temperament, imaginative, and ardent, as she appears from the portraits Raphael has left of her. The graceful nature, the delicate figure of the young artist, and the prestige of his fame, roused the love and ambition of the beautiful Trasteverina.

> "Amor che a nullo amato amar perdona," [1]

> " Love, that exempts no one beloved from loving,"

seized hold of that angel and smothered him in its embrace. What has this most fatal story to do with our usual artistic life? To-day there are no more Fornarinas, and, above all, there are no Raphaels; and if by chance an artist falls in love with his model, why, he marries her, and there is an end of it. In conclusion, a good and beautiful model that willingly and honestly (I use this word for want of a better) does her business, I like and employ; but a simple, good-natured, ignorant young girl forced to this shame by her own mother, irritates me and makes me sad.

At this time they were making the façade of the Church of Santa Croce, with the most valuable aid of Cavaliere Sloane, to whom we are chiefly indebted that it was possible to complete this work. In the design of the façade there were bas-reliefs in the arches over the three doors : over the middle door the " Triumph of the Cross "; over that of the right nave the " Vision of Constantine "; and over the other, on the left, the " Refinding of the Cross."

[1] Dante, Inferno, canto v.

I had already made for the façade the Madonna, who stands high up over the *cuspide* of the middle door ; and because the subject was dear to me, as also the idea which it should convey, I was content with a price which would barely cover the cost of making it, without counting my work on the model. But these three bas-reliefs were much more arduous work ; and as I could not make them at the same rate as I had made the Madonna, I refused. Cavaliere Sloane, however, who much desired that these bas-reliefs should be made, came to me and begged me to accept them. As to the price, he assured me that we should agree, and that he would himself pay it, because he wished that the façade should be made by me. I took time to reply, and reflecting that the three bas-reliefs would take much more time than I had to dispose of, and desiring to help my two clever and affectionate pupils, I proposed to Cavaliere Sloane to divide this labour into three parts. The larger bas-relief, that over the central door, I would make ; the other two, over the lateral doors, should be made, one by Sarrocchi of Siena, and the other by Emilio Zocchi of Florence. Sloane was satisfied with my proposition, but with the understanding that I should be answerable for the excellence of these works, and while I should leave these artists freedom in their conceptions, I should direct them in such conceptions as well as in the execution. This I formally promised to do, and the work was decided upon.

These bas-reliefs, which I relinquished to my scholars, recall to my mind other works also given up to scholars, but not mine. Among these is Professor Costa of Florence. In the beginning of my artistic career, when I was making the "Cain" and "Abel," "Giotto," and " Pius II.," I had also a commission to make a statue representing

Summer, for one of the four seasons which ornament the palace once called Batelli. This commission, though a poor one, I should have executed, because I had engaged to do so, and poor Batelli had urged it in a friendly way; but Pietro Costa, then very young, studious, and needy, begged it of me, and I, with the consent of the person who had given the commission, gave it up to him, and it was a great success.

Now that I am speaking of my scholars, it is but just that I should mention my daughter Amalia. She used at that time to come and see me in my studio with her mother and sisters; and while the little Beppina and Gigina stayed out in the little square playing together and gathering flowers, Amalia remained in my studio silently watching me at work. When her mother was getting ready to take her home, she was so unwilling to tear herself away from gazing at my work, that I asked her one day—

" Would you like to do this work ? "

" Yes, papa," the child quickly replied.

" Well, then," I said, " stay with me."

Then I turned to my wife and said, " Leave Amalia with me for company ; she can return home with me." I arranged a slate on a little easel in form of a reading-desk for her, prepared some bits of clay, and showed her how to spread the clay to a certain thickness on the slate as a foundation ; then I placed before her a small figure of one of the bas-reliefs from the doors of San Giovanni, by Andrea Pisano, and I said to her,—" With this little pointed stick you must draw in the figure, then you must put on clay to get the relief; but first I must see if your drawing is like the original. Only the outline is necessary, and this line should only reproduce the movement and proportion of the little figure you have before

you.   Do you understand?"   The child understood so
well, that, at the first trial, she traced all the outline of
the figure correctly.   It must, however, be remembered
that Amalia and her sisters had taken lessons in drawing
from me, and had always kept them up.

From that day to this Amalia has never left the studio,
and art has become so dear a thing to her that she can
now no longer do without it.   Her works are well known.
Besides portraits, of which she has many, the greater
number of them in marble, she has modelled and executed in marble various statues and bas-reliefs.   The
statues are: the "Child Giotto," Dante's "Matelda," "St
Peter in Chains," the Monument of the Signora Adele
Stracchi, and that of our dearest Luisina—statues all life-
size, and except the "Matelda" and "St Peter," all cut
in marble; also two small statues, a "St John," and an
Angel throwing water, for the baptismal font in a rich
chapel of one of Marchese Nerli's villas; also a little
Angel, still in plaster, and a group of the Madonna and
Child with a lamb, for the Church of Badia in Florence.
The bas-reliefs are: the Madonna, accompanied by an
angel, taking to her arms the youthful soul of the daughter
of the Duchess Ravaschieri of Naples.   For Arezzo: the
Sisters of Charity conducting the asylum children to the
tomb of Cavaliere Aleotti, in act of prayer and gratitude;
eight saints in bas-relief for the pulpit of the Cathedral
of San Miniato; four bas-reliefs for monuments in that
same cathedral to the following persons—"Religion"
for Bishop Poggi, "History" for Bernardo Buonaparte,
"Physics" for Professor Taddei, and "Poesy" for the
poet Bagnoli; a font, with a small statue of Sant' Eduvige,
for the Countess Talon of Paris; a bas-relief for the lunette over the door of my new studio at Pinti; a little
bronze copy of the "Pietà"; a copy of the "Justice," also

in bronze ; a statuette of St Joseph, and a statue of St
Catherine of Siena, in *terra cotta*, for the chapel of a pious
refuge for poor children at Siena ; a little group in marble
of the *Virtù teologali* for Signor Raffaello Agostini of
Florence ; and a large statue, life-size, of the Madonna
Addolorata, in *terra cotta*, for the Church of St Emidio at
Agnone. All these works, you understand, were done
by her as a pleasant way of exercising herself in her art,
gratuitously, as is most natural ; but it did not so appear
to the tax-agent, who, however, was obliged to correct
himself by cancelling her name from the roll of tax-
payers, where it had been put. Poor Amalia, working
from pure love of art, doing good by giving your work
away, and often the worse for it in your pocket ; and
then to behold yourself taxed in the exercise and sale of
your work ! A pretty thing indeed !

As I am now on a subject that attracts me, I cannot
tear myself from it in such a hurry. It is not permitted me to speak of the artistic merit of my daughter.
My opinion would be a prejudiced one, both as father
and as master, and therefore I have restricted myself
only to note down the works that she has done so far ;
but I cannot refrain from making known the internal
satisfaction I feel in seeing my teaching productive of
such good fruit. It fell on ground so well prepared that
it sprouted out abundantly and spontaneously. The
consolation a master feels when he sees his pupil understand and almost divine his thought, is very great ; and
when this pupil is his own daughter, one may imagine
how much the greater it is. And when I think of her
modest nature, shrinking from praise, desirous of good,
tender and compassionate with the poor in their sorrow,
grieving as I do for the many irreparable family misfortunes, I still thank the Lord that He has let me keep this

angel, and also my other daughter Beppina, who is not less loving to us and to her husband, by whom her love is returned in a Christian spirit. She also is endowed by nature with sentiment for art, and her drawings and certain little models in clay are the indications of wide-awake, ready aptitude. I treasure a bust of Dante that she modelled, and that was cut in marble, and deplore that the new life she has entered upon, and perhaps a delicate feeling of consideration for her sister, have made her desist from the continuation of a career well begun. Now she is a mother; and the duties of a mother are so noble and so arduous as to repress any other tendencies even more natural to her and more attractive.

Now let us return to the façade of Santa Croce. I ordered the "Refinding of the Cross" from Sarrocchi, and the "Vision of Constantine" from Zocchi; and both Zocchi and Sarrocchi set themselves at once to work. Here is the explanation of the conception of my bas-relief: It seemed to me that the "Triumph or Exaltation of the Cross" ought to be explained by means of persons or personifications that the Cross, with its divine love, had won or conquered. The sign of the Cross stands on high resplendent with light, and around it are angels in the act of adoration. Under the Cross, and in the centre of the bas-relief on the summit of a mountain, there is an angel in the act of prayer, expressive of the attraction of the human soul towards Divinity. By means of prayer descends the grace that warms and illuminates the intellect and affections of man. The affections and intellect, divided from the Cross, again return to the Cross, and are expressed by the following figures that stand below: A liberated slave, half seated, half reclining, with his face and eyes turned upward, expressive of gratitude for his liberation,—for from the

Cross descended and spread over all the earth that
divine word of human brotherhood; and near the slave
a savage on his knees, leaning on his club; the stupidity
and fierceness of whose look are subdued and illuminated
by the splendour of the Cross. These two impersona-
tions are in the centre below, leaving the space to the
right and left for the following personages : On the right
of the person looking at the bas-relief is Constantine
unsheathing his sword when he beheld the sign and
heard the words, "*In hoc signo vinces*"; near Constantine is the Countess Matilda, whose pious attitude revealed her strong love for the Church of Christ, and
enabled it to put up a barrier against foreign arrogance,
and to defend the liberty of the Italian Communes; behind her, nearly hidden, owing to her holy timidity, the
Magdalen, to indicate that the ardours of lust were
conquered by the fire of divine love. On his knees,
bent to the ground, with his face in his hands, is
St Paul the elect, who from an enemy had become
the strenuous defender of the Gospel and apostle
of the Gentiles. St Thomas, with one knee on the
ground, a book in his hand, in a modest pensive attitude, recalls the words of Jesus, who said, "*Bene
scriptisti de me, Thoma.*" A little in the background,
near Constantine, is the Emperor Heraclius, dressed in
sad raiment, commemorative of the wars against the
Christians; and a Roman soldier bearing the standard
inscribed with "S.P.Q.R." closes the composition on
this part of the bas-relief. On the left side the principal
figure is Charlemagne; an unsheathed sword is in one
hand, and in the other a globe with a cross, emblems
of his vast dominions and his mission of propagating the
true faith ; he also represents the greatest material power
conquered for the glory of the Cross. Dante is near

him—the greatest Christian intellectual power—and he
holds in his hand the three 'Canticles,' called by him
'Poema Sacro.' Near Dante the poor monk of Assisi,
with his hands pressed to his breast, looking lovingly
and with fixed attention at the Cross. In these three
figures are represented the dominator of the world, the
dominator of the spirit, and the dominator of poverty
and humility attracted by love of the Cross. To complete this group you see St Augustine in his episcopal
robes, holding in his hand a volume of 'The City of
God'; and behind them a martyr with a palm, as pendant to the Roman soldier on the opposite side.

Such is the composition of the "Triumph of the Cross,"
which is above the middle door of that temple where the
ashes of Michael Angelo and Galileo rest, and where it
has been my desire for so many years that a memorial
monument to Leonardo da Vinci should be placed.
And, vain though it be, I shall always call for it louder
and louder, the more that I see the mediocrity that a
want of taste continues to erect there.

As it is not permissible for me to speak of the praise
I had for this work, I will not pass over in silence a
criticism that was made to me about my having selected
the Countess Matilda to put into my composition. It was
objected that the Countess Matilda served the Pope, served
the Church of Rome, but did not do homage especially to
the Cross. I have given the reason of her serving the
Pope. I have already given a few words in explanation
of that personage; and as for the distinction that there
is between the Church of Christ and Christ Himself, I
must frankly say that I do not understand it. Let not
the reader believe, however, that I am one of those
Christians desirous of being more Christian than the Pope
himself, and excessively intolerant and passionate. No;

I am with the teaching of the apostles, and that seems to me enough, for it includes all, even comprising the beautiful exhortation of Father Dante, when he says—

" Avete il vecchio e il nuovo Testamento,
   E il pastor della Chiesa che vi guida,"[1] &c.

" Ye have the Old and the New Testament,
   And the pastor of the Church who guideth you."

In fact—not now, but soon—I will let you know, and touch with your hand, so to speak, the fact that I am not in the good graces of some of those people who depicted me to the eyes of the Holy Father after the manner of a bad *barocco* painter—falsifying proportions, character, and expression. But, as I have said, I will return to this later on; and meanwhile, I must say that the Holy Father did not know me at all, as the only time that I had the honour of bending before him and kissing his foot he took me for another person. And it occurred when the Pontiff Pius IX. passed through Florence after his tour through the Romagna. The Grand Duke did all the honours of Florence to him. During the few days that he re-mained in Florence the Grand Duke accompanied him wherever he thought it would give him pleasure to go, and, amongst other places, he took him to visit the manufactory of *pietre dure*, and the Academy of Fine Arts; and on this occasion our president invited the College of Professors to be present, that we might see the Holy Father near, and perform an act of reverence to the Supreme Hierarch. The Pope was seated on an elevated place like a throne; on his left was the Grand Duke; the Ministers, dignitaries, and our president were standing near him. We were called, one by one, and pre-

---

[1] Dante, Paradiso, canto 5.

Y

sented by our president, Marchese Luca Bourbon del
Monte, to the Holy Father; and those who were presented prostrated themselves before him, kissed his foot,
and then returned to their places.   When it came to my
turn, the Grand Duke turned to the Pope and said—

"Here, Blessed Father, is the artist who made the
"Cain" and "Abel" that your Holiness seemed well
satisfied with."

And the Holy Father, turning to me, answered—

"I congratulate you.   They are two most beautiful
statues.   You have nothing to envy in the Berlin or
Munich casting."

"Most Blessed Father," I hastened to reply, "I am
not the caster of those statues, but——"

"Go," continued the Holy Father—"go, and may God
bless you;" and making one of those great crosses in
the air that Pius IX. knew so well how to make, he sent
me away in peace, in the midst of the silent but visible
hilarity of all those who had witnessed my embarrassment.   It is more than probable that the Grand Duke
rectified the mistake incurred by his Holiness; and I
should regret if I had remained in his mind as the caster,
when that merit belonged personally and legitimately to
Professor Clemente Papi.   But if it is easy to imagine
that that mistake was then cleared up, it is difficult to
say the same of the one at the present day, because it
is harder to rectify.   I heed very little the censure of
certain extreme Catholics, believing that I share it with
many whom I should wish to resemble in every respect :
but the censure of the Pope was indeed painful to me ;
and I managed in such a way, by showing myself just as
I am, that I obtained his goodwill.   But of this, as I
have already said, I will speak further on, and now I
return to my works.

The reader may have observed that I have made no mention of portraits, although I have made many. As, however, amongst these portraits there is one that made some noise, and as the things that were said, being magnified by passion and by the inexact information of the person who spread these reports, might lead those who are in the dark to form a wrong impression, I have thought best to narrate the facts as they were.

One day a gentleman asked to speak to me. He was a man of about sixty, tall, thin, with deep-set, changeable, and vivacious eyes, thick-marked eyebrows, long moustaches, lofty bearing, and with such a singular and expressive face, that when an artist sees it, he is at once possessed with a desire to make it a study. This gentleman said—

" Would you make my portrait? "

I answered, " Yes."

" How many sittings do you require to make the model? "

" Six or eight, or more, according to the length of the sittings."

" When could you begin? "

" The first days of next week."

" Very well: Monday I will be with you. At what hour? "

" At nine in the morning, if not inconvenient to you."

" Good-bye, then, until Monday. Do you know who I am? "

" I have not the honour."

" I am Marshal Haynau." And he went away.

Now, to say that, after having heard the name, I had pleasure in making his portrait, would be a falsehood; and yet the singularity of that face, the curiosity I had to become acquainted through conversation with a man of

such haughtiness and fierceness of character, the engagement I had entered into, and my pledged word, all took
from me the courage to renounce the work.   It is useless
to say how all my friends, and naturally even more, those
who were no friends of mine, declaimed against me.
The newspapers were full of attacks, the story of the
brewery in London, with all its details, was told, magnified and praised; in fact, to tell the truth, it was in the
days when I was taking his portrait, and then alone, that
I was made acquainted with the fierce nature of this
great person, as my only idea of him until then had been
a very indistinct and sketchy one.   The beauty of it
is, that in the conversation he held with me he showed
himself a quiet man, opposed to all cruelty, although a
severe military disciplinarian, and inexorable in punish-
ing refractory soldiers.   He made no mystery of this, and
he named to me the Hungarian generals and officers
that he had had shot, as the most natural thing in the
world; and because I blamed him for this, he answered :
With rebels one could not do otherwise, and that he
would have become guilty himself had he not punished
them.   But I, who had read of his cruelty to women,
children — to all, in fact — censured him for this, and
he denied it in a most decided manner, adding a story
which, if true, I don't know what to say.   Here is the
anecdote : When he had gained the victory at Pesth,
and had all the heads of the revolution in his hands,
they were all condemned to death by a council of war.
Amongst these were the Archbishop of Pesth and a
Count Karoli.   He had the *alter ego* in his hands, and
in consequence his orders had no need of the Imperial
sanction; but both the Archbishop and Count Karoli
had powerful friends and adherents at Vienna, and these
did so much, and exerted themselves to such a degree,

that, an hour before the execution of the sentence, the Imperial reprieve arrived. As he, however, thought both of these men more guilty than the others, owing to their high position, and as it seemed to him unjust that they should be saved and the others sacrificed, he called them all into his presence, and after having informed the two fortunate ones of the Imperial pardon, he added these words : " It is my conviction, in virtue of the proofs which I have in my hands, and which have been examined by the council of war, that the Archbishop and Count Karoli are the most guilty of any of you; but as our most gracious sovereign has saved them from the penalty that they deserved, it is not just that those who are less guilty should suffer from it ; therefore, availing myself of the power I have of *alter ego*, I spare the life of all." I can attest the truth of this story, not only in its general sense, but even to its wording. The truth of the story, I say, for as to the facts I know nothing. And I have made a note of it ; for if by chance it was not true, to the stain of cruelty one can add that of having told a lie to appear merciful. The fact was that he discussed all his affairs with facile prolixity. He spoke of art and the artists that he had known at Milan, Venice, and Bologna, in the days of our servitude to Austria, and through all his stories there was always something or other of the bombastic. He urged me to make his statue, but I decidedly refused to do so. He spoke to me about it several times, and at last I was obliged to speak openly to him, and he thought my reasons just ones. Then he manifested to me his wish to have his portrait painted on horseback, and asked me if I knew a clever artist with a name that would undertake the work. This question embarrassed me, being myself already compromised. I took some time to think about it, and fate was propitious, and gave me a companion with whom to bear the censure and abuse that only too certainly rained down upon us.

Early the next morning Professor Bezzuoli came to my studio, and said—" Let me see the portrait of Marshal Haynau."

"Certainly; here it is."

" Do you know," says Bezzuoli to me, " that yesterday I had to take up your defence? There were certain chatterboxes, that don't know even how to draw an eye, who, talking of you on account of the portrait you are making, said you ought never to have accepted it, and that they could never have abased themselves to do so. I answered that an artist when he makes a portrait is not occupied with politics. If the person whose portrait is taken is a scamp, he will always be a scamp, with or without his portrait, precisely like Nero, Tiberius, or other such beasts, of whom such beautiful portraits have been taken, that it is a pleasure to see them; but it never comes into the mind of anybody for an instant to say, Look what a *canaille* the artist must have been who made this portrait! So true does this seem to me, that if Haynau had come to me and given me an order to paint his portrait, I would have accepted his commission most willingly."

" Ah, very well!" thought I to myself, " I shall no longer be alone;" then I said to Bezzuoli,—" Thank you for the part you have taken in my defence. I still think if my colleagues only had an idea how I have been taken by surprise when I engaged to do this work, and how the originality of the head excited a desire in me, and if they felt how imperious the impulse born of that little capricious demon Art is—they would, I think, be more indulgent with me; and not only indulgent, but

they would even praise me when they knew that I had
refused to make a statue of Haynau for himself. And
àpropos of this statue, which I shall not make, I will tell
you about it presently; but first permit me to ask a question. I understood you to say that if this gentleman
had gone to you and asked you to paint his portrait,
you would have accepted the commission—did I understand right?"

"You understood perfectly."

"I then add that he will come. He wants a full-
sized portrait of himself on horseback. A large picture,
an attack in battle, or something of that kind; and later,
after mid-day, he will go to you for this purpose. Should
you like it?"

"I should like it very much; but how can you speak
to me with so much assurance about this?"

Then I told him what the reader already knows.
That morning the Marshal went with a note from me
to Professor Bezzuoli. In a few words all was arranged;
the picture was finished in a short time, and had a great
deal of deserved praise as far as work went, and bitter
censure for the rest, which he divided and bore in company with me—with less resignation, however, than could
have been desired from so old an artist who had thought
over and discussed the importance of the engagement
he had taken. This was the character of Bezzuoli, who
preserved even as an old man all the vivacity and impetuosity of open, gay-hearted youth; but at the same time,
he was mistrustful and touchy in the extreme. When I remember him, full of vivacity and *bonhomie*, the friend of
young men, with his frank, open-hearted, sincere advice,
and at the same time full of sensitiveness about the
merest nothings, and with childish and ridiculous am-
bitions, such as not to be willing to be beaten at billiards,

it makes me smile to think of the weakness of our poor human nature. He liked to invite a certain number of friends every Sunday to his villa near Fiesole, and after dinner to play at billiards. He who was unfortunate enough to beat Bezzuoli, was sure to find him cold and set against him for some time; and those who knew this, either for pastime and amusement, or for fear and interestedness, bravely lost, and the poor professor was full of joy, more even than if he had found some new striking effect in art.

Here ends the anecdote of that famous portrait. Further on I will speak of others that I had the order for and could not make, and why I could not make them.

CHAPTER XVIII.

UT if some of my very dear colleagues set themselves against me on account of the great Haynau portrait, not knowing that I had refused to make his statue, others were alienated from me, I do not know for what reason. I will speak of one of them, to show how a most respectable artist and colleague of mine, having been led into error, chose strenuously to abide by it, and thus broke up a relation that one might call friendship; for esteem is the first bond that draws one together and creates love, and I esteemed this colleague of mine, and pitied him for the error into which he had fallen.

When Augusto Rivalta came from the school at Genoa (his birthplace) to complete his studies in sculpture in Florence, his masters, and he himself, had great faith in my school, and I was, with him as with all my scholars, an open and free expounder of those principles that I believe to be good, and to lead directly towards the beautiful, under the guidance of truth. Rivalta was always confiding and studious with me; and as by nature he is endowed with no common genius, he is to-day a professor and active master at our Academy of Fine Arts. Now it happened one day, during the early days that he was under my direction, that I saw hanging on his studio walls a bas-relief of a Madonna by that above-mentioned colleague of mine, and the head of Bartolini's "Fiducia in Dio." I thought it wise to warn my pupil of the error into which too often even tried artists have fallen, which is that of looking at and reproducing in their own works reminiscences of such originals hanging in their studios to attract poor artists. Therefore that morning my lesson consisted of the following words :—

"When the idea comes to you to make a statue, it forms itself naturally in your mind, and takes a movement and character all its own, be it ever so undecided and vague, as an idea always is, until it has been fixed materially into shape ; but the idea is there (for him who has it), and is original. Then begins attentive study, and sometimes a long research to be able to find a live model who approaches nearest the idea that you have formed to yourself, and that you have already in your mind in embryo, or have indicated in your sketch. From the moment, however, that you have found the model or models, you must remain alone with them and your idea ; no extraneous images must come between you and your work. I am afraid that those casts there facing me, will in some way take from the originality of the character and expression that you wish to give to your statue, and you will do well not to look at them. Let us understand, however, that I say not to look at them whilst you are at work on your statue : afterwards you may look at them and study them as much as you wish."

Rivalta assured me that he did not look at them, for he understood very well, that instead of being of help to him they would have confused him, and that he found himself more free and unhampered when trusting himself only to working from the live model. Having established this most essential point in art, I left him, well pleased with both myself and him. But in the meantime, this obvious, clear, and easy lesson of mine created at first an angry feeling, and afterwards a rupture, between me and my colleague, the author of the bas-relief; and this happened because a youth in Rivalta's studio reported that I had said to my scholar, "Do not look at those casts, for they are rubbish." I heard this from Professor de Fabris, to whom our friend made a clean breast of it. It was not enough for him that this friend of ours took up my defence, saying that he knew me thoroughly well, and that I was incapable of saying such things, adding, that he ought himself to know well enough that I was averse to giving offence to any one, and so might feel sure there was some misunderstanding. But all this was useless, so that our friend De Fabris, for the sake of peace, thought best to speak to me of it. It can be imagined how astonished and how pained I was. I at once told him how the matter really stood, and begged that he would assure the professor of my affection and esteem for him as a friend and as an artist. It was all in vain, and he insisted in believing in a boy who had listened badly and reported still worse, rather than in me, or even Rivalta's testimony that I offered to bring forward.

I should not have mentioned this small matter had it not been to explain the sort of sensitiveness and obstinacy that one observes generally in the artist class, and most specially amongst us sculptors, although, to speak the truth, those defects showed themselves oftener, and to a greater degree, amongst artists of the past, or

who are now old. The young men of to-day are more
frank, more tolerant, and more friendly amongst each
other, and sometimes they even go to the excess of these
virtues by being frank even unto insolence, tolerant
even to scepticism, and careless, thoughtless, frivolous,
and even worse, in their friendship. Who ignores the
little bursts of temper and cutting words bandied between Pampaloni and Bartolini, between Benvenuti and
Sabatelli, and between Bezzuoli and Gazzarrini ? I shall
not write a record of them, out of respect for their names,
and for Death, who, under his broad mantle, has en-
shrouded them in solemn silence. Sleep in peace, pilgrim souls,—within a short time even we shall join you ;
and when we are awakened at the *dies iræ*, we shall smile
at our little outbursts of temper in this most foolish life,
and become for ever really brothers. We shall be happy
if we have nothing besides the remembrance of these little
sins, already forgiven us by God, if we have forgiven
others ! If by chance there be any one who thinks that
I have offended him by excess of vivacity of temperament or otherwise, even though it be involuntary, as
might happen easily, I beg his pardon.

    This little war of words, sarcasms, and what is worse,
reticences, I have always deplored ; and to succeed in
being less tiresome to my colleagues, and for want of
occasion to induce them to temperance, I have always
kept myself aloof, and have spoken of them as I could
wish them to speak of me. To be just, however, I
must declare that I have seldom been (openly, I mean)
exposed to the sting of their words ; and if, as it happened, I was once attacked with certain insistence in
the newspapers on the occasion when my three scholars,
Pazzi, Sarrocchi, and Majoli, exhibited their works in
the Academy, my friend Luigi Mussini, who handles the

pen in the same masterly way as he does the brush,
reduced to silence with one single article the poor
writer who had been put up to say evil of the works of
my scholars in order to do injury to the master. These
injurious words have been forgotten and amply pardoned,
but the beautiful and generous defence of my friend
I have never forgotten. I repeat, however, that these
little annoyances are much less nowadays than they were,
or at least they have changed form. To-day, instead of
suggesting in undertones and mellifluous words the defects of a work to some poor writer, adding many that
do not exist, and being silent as to its merits, it is rather
the custom to come out frankly and openly before your
face with a criticism which, if it has not the merit of
temperance, does at least not bear that ugly stain of
hypocrisy as a mask to truth. To this school, although
he be numbered amongst the old and the dead, Bartolini did not belong ; and although one of the elect in
spirit and strength, yet he sometimes allowed himself
to give way to passion. While he was a young man
in Paris, Canova was there making the portrait of the
Emperor Napoleon I. Bartolini demanded and obtained help from that great and beneficent artist ; but
being asked if he would return with him to his studio
in Rome, he refused : but to say, as he did openly to
me and to others, that Canova wished to take him with
him to put an end to his studies, was not in conformity
with the truth, or with Canova's well-known and benevolent character. To the sculptor Wolf, who one day
brought him a note from Rauch, he said, without even
opening it—

"How is Rauch?"

"He is very well, and sends you his greetings, as you
will see from the letter I have given you."

"Rauch," began Bartolini, . . . but I have said above that the dead sleep in peace, and the portraits of Bartolini and Rauch are also at peace with each other, for in my house, at the villa of Lampeggi, they look each other in the face, and smile good-naturedly. *Evviva!* So, perhaps, they smile in the true life eternal at the littlenesses of our brief life here.

It was at this time (1860) that I was obliged to leave my studio in the Liceo di Candeli, and with me all the other artists who were in that place had to go, as the present Government decided to place the militia there. This change made me feel very sad, for I had an affection for the place. I had improved it and enlarged it, renting a ground-floor in the next house, and putting it into communication with the studio. I had embellished the court with plants, fruit, and flowers. There my dear little girls used to amuse themselves at play, and gathered flowers to take home and arrange in a little vase to put before the image of the Madonna. One of them is no longer here, Luisina, of whom in time I will speak; but the other two—Amalia, who is with me, and Beppina, who is married to Cavaliere Antonio Ciardi—follow, even now, that pious custom, which others may make fun of, but which I love so much when I see these children of mine, in all the simplicity and pureness of their heart, make this act of homage to the Virgin.

My good Marina, who has also now joined our daughter and the other little ones and the boy (seven angels in all)—my good Marina tried to console me with her mild words. In her speech there was no excitement or speciousness, but a persuasive sweetness and serenity, learnt from duty and temperance. She had had no education—was a poor woman of the people, as I have said in the

beginning; but I never felt bored by her, never desired a more cultured woman to teach me lessons. It is
sweet to me to return in memory to the time that I lived
with my good companion; and I owe her so much! I
think that, if fate had given me another woman, who had
not had the patience to bear my crotchets and the quick
words that sometimes escaped me, who had doubted my
faith, who had bored me with tittle-tattle, with sermons
or other things, I think (God save me!) that I should
have been a bad husband and a worse artist. So that,
with a slight variation, I can repeat the words of the
divine poet :—

> " E la *mia* vita e tutto il *mio* valore,
> Mosse dagli occhi di quella pietosa." [1]

I had therefore to resign myself to leaving the studio
that I had an affection for; and the one I have now at
the Academy of Fine Arts was assigned to me, with the
charge of *Maestro di Perfezionamento*, without stipend, but
with a promise of compensations, which I have never
had, perhaps because I have never asked for them.

A fact that I ought to have narrated long before this
—quite domestic and intimate in its wondrous strangeness—I have kept silent about, owing to a certain sentiment that I cannot well define; but now, in recalling my
good wife and my dead children, I feel as if a voice within
me said, " Tell it !—write the fact as it is, without taking
anything from it or passing judgment on it." So here
it is. My second daughter, Carolina, was put out to
nurse. She was the only one that the good mother did
not bring up herself; but, from motives of health, she
could not do so. The wet-nurse of this little child lived
at Londa, above the Rufina. The baby was thriving,

[1] Vita Nuova, 39.

when all of a sudden a very bad eruption came out all over her and her life was in danger. The nurse wrote to us to come and see her. Without delay I hired a *calesse*,[1] and left with my wife : the grandmother stayed behind to mind the little eldest one, who afterwards died at seven years of age, as I have written in its place. Arriving at Pontassieve, we bent our way to the Rufina, and from there continued on to Londa ; on up a mountain, in part wooded with chestnut-trees, in part bare and stony, until we arrived at the small cottage of the nurse of my little one. The road circles around the hill, and in several places is very narrow, so much so that a *calesse* has great difficulty in passing,—as is most natural, for what has a *calesse* to do up on that hill and amongst those hovels? But we arrived, as God willed it. The baby was very ill, and there was now no hope that she could recover. We remained there a night and a day; and having given all the orders in case of the now certain death of the little angel, I took the mother, who could not tear herself from the place, away crying. As I have said, the road was narrow; and in our descent, the hill rose above us on our right, and on the left we were on the edge of a very deep torrent : I don't know whether it was the Rincine, Moscia, or some other. The horse went at a gentle trot on account of the easy descent, and we felt perfectly safe, as I had put the drag on the wheel. My wife, with her eyes bathed in tears, was repeating some words, I know not what, dictated by a hope that the child would recover. The sky was clear, and the sun had only just risen,—we saw no one on the hill, nor anywhere else,—when suddenly a voice was heard to say " *Stop!* " (*Fermate!*) The voice seemed as if it came from the hillside. My wife and I turned in

---

[1] Old-fashioned one-horse carriage.

that direction, and I half stopped the horse; but we saw no one. I touched up the horse again to push on, and at the same instant the voice made itself heard a second time, and still louder, saying, "*Stop! stop!*" I pulled in the reins, and this time my wife, after having looked all around with me without seeing a living soul, was frightened.

"Come, have courage," said I; "what are you afraid of? See, there is no one; and so no one can do us any harm." And, to put an end to the kind of fear even I felt, I gave my horse a good smack of the whip; but hardly had he started when we heard most distinctly, and still louder, the same voice calling out, three times, "*Stop! stop! stop!*" I stopped, and without knowing what to do or think, I got out, and helped my wife out, who was all trembling; and what was our surprise, our alarm, and our gratitude for the warning that had been given us to stop! The linch-pin had come out of the left wheel, which was all bent over and about to fall off its axle-tree, and this almost at the very edge of the precipice. With all my strength I propped up the trap on that side, pushed the wheel back into its place, and ran back to see if I could find the linch-pin, but I could not find it. I called again and again for the person who had come to my help with timely warning, to thank him, but I saw no one! In the meanwhile, it was impossible to go on in that condition. The little town of La Rufina was at some distance, and although we could walk to it on foot, how could the *calesse* be taken there with a wheel without a linch-pin? I set myself to hunt about on the hill for a little stick of wood, and having found it, I sharpened it, and with the aid of a stone, fastened it in the hole in place of the linch-pin. But as for getting back into the *calesse*, that was not to

z

be thought of; so leading the horse by hand, we slowly
descended to Rufina, neither my wife nor myself speaking a word, but every now and again our looks bespoke
the danger we had run and the wonderful warning we
had had. At the Rufina I got a cartwright to put in
another linch-pin, and we returned safely home. If the
reader laughs, let him do so; I do not. In fact, the
seriousness and truth of this occurrence, which happened
about forty years ago, filled me then, as it does now,
with a feeling of wonder and surprise.

In the first part of the year 1862, Marchese Bichi-Ruspoli of Siena gave me the order for a monument to be
placed in the cemetery of the Misericordia in that city,
where he had bought a mortuary chapel for himself and
family. He left me free in the choice of the subject, and
I decided on a "Pietà," a subject that has been frequently
treated by many artists at different times, as lending itself
to the expression of the most unspeakable sorrow, even if
looked upon from a purely human point of view; and if
one adds thought and religious sentiment, then its interest
gains tenfold, as it contains in itself, besides the beauty
of form in the nude figure, and the touching sorrow of
the mother, the mystery of the incarnation, of the death
and of the resurrection of our Saviour. The subject,
therefore, was highly artistic, exquisitely touching, and
particularly well adapted to a Christian sepulchre. But
with all these admirable qualities, the rendering of the
subject was extremely difficult, because so many great
artists of every epoch had done all they could, in painting as well as in sculpture, to express this sublime idea.
Wishing to keep myself from doing what others had done
before me, I thought a long time on this difficult theme;
but cudgel my brains as much as I would, my conceits
always bore the impress of one or other of those many

groups that one sees everywhere. As the gentleman who had given me the commission pressed me—in a polite way, it is true, but with some insistence—to let him see at least the sketch, I set to work with much ardour, but with little hope of succeeding. After a great deal of study, I made a small sketch, with which the gentleman pronounced himself content, and ordered me to set to work on it as soon as possible. When the stand was ready, the irons put up, the clay prepared, and the models had been found, one of my friends, who had come to look in on me, exclaimed on seeing the sketch—

"Oh, what a fine sketch! It is Michael Angelo's 'Pietà.'"

"What?" said I.

"Oh, I see I have made a mistake," said my friend; "it is quite a different thing."

But none the less, this was the impression he had received and proclaimed, and, if not absolutely correct, was yet a sincere, true, spontaneous, and disinterested one; for my friend, although far from being an artist, or even a *dilettante*, was very intelligent, and a lover of art. So from that moment my mind was made up, and I said to myself—"Either I will find some new idea, even though it be a less beautiful one, or I will abandon the commission." I put by all the things that had been prepared, went to work on other work, and thought no more of it. I ought rather to say that I thought of it constantly, perhaps even too much; for it was an irritated, futile kind of thinking, that did harm, giving me no rest even during my sleep, and not leaving my mind sufficiently free or my inspirations calm enough to seize hold of a new idea and make another attempt.

The gentleman who had given me the commission still pressed me, and could not understand why I had

set aside the work after having, as he said, so well conceived it, and after it had met with his own approval. To
which I only answered these words, "Have patience!"
And so he had, the poor Marchese, for I must do him
the justice to say, that seeing that this was a painful subject to me, he never spoke to me any more about it; and
only when affairs called him sometimes to Florence,
after having talked to me about many other things, he
would say, when leaving me, with his usual kind and
genial manner, "Good-bye, Nannino, *memento mei!*"
This blessed Latin in its brevity worked upon me more
than a long sermon would have done ; but it was useless
to try to set myself to make another sketch, for think
about it as much as I would, although in my brain there
were any number of mediocre groups of the "Pietà,"
there was still wanting the one of my own creation,
for the others belonged to me as some cantos of the
'Divina Commedia' do by force of memory. *Àpropos* of
this, here is a curious little story. It happened one day
when I was speaking with a man excellent in every
respect, that, being to the point, I quoted the following
well-known verses :—

> " O voi che siete in piccioletta barca,
>   Desiderosi d' ascoltar, seguìti
>   Dietro al mio legno che cantando varca," &c.

> " O ye who in some pretty little boat,
>   Eager to listen, have been following
>   Behind my ship, that singing sails along; "[1]

at which that excellent gentleman showed himself surprised, and asked if those verses were mine. I looked
at him attentively, and saw in his face that he was perfectly frank, serious, and ingenuous ; and so I had the

---

[1] Dante, Paradiso, Canto ii.

impudence to say *Yes*. I regretted it afterwards, and still do so. That gentleman died some time ago, and I should not have told this joke if he had been still living, for even withholding his name, he might have recognised himself and taken it in ill part; but for all this, I repeat, he was an excellent man, stood high in his art, was professor, *cavaliere*, and *commendatore* of more than one order, but as ignorant, as it would seem, of our classics as I am of the propositions of Euclid.

The reader, therefore, understands perfectly that I did not want to make my "Pietà" a work from memory or of imitation, and give out with a bold face another man's conception for my own. Therefore *pazienza*, — and months passed, and it seemed to me as if I no longer thought of it; but one fine day, when I was at home lying on the sofa reading a newspaper, and waiting to be called to dinner, I fell asleep (newspapers have always put me to sleep, especially when they take things seriously),—I fell asleep, and I dreamed of the group of the "Pietà" just as I afterwards made it, but much more beautiful, more expressive, and more noble. In fact it was a wonderful vision, but only like a flash—a vision only of an instant—for an impression as of a blow awoke me, and I found myself lying over the arm of the sofa, with my arms hanging loosely, my legs stiffened out straight, and my head bent on my breast, just as in my dream I had seen Christ on the Virgin's knees. I jumped up and ran to my studio to fix the idea in clay. My wife seeing me go out almost running, called to me to say that the soup was on the table.

"Have patience," I answered; "I have forgotten something at the studio; perhaps I shall stop there a bit. You eat, and I will eat afterwards."

The poor woman, I could see, did not understand

what was the matter, all the more because I had been hurrying them to send up the dinner; but she made no more inquiries. It was her nature not to enter too much into the affairs of my studio. In two hours I had made the sketch of that subject which had cost me so much thought, so many waking hours, and loss of sleep, and I returned home. I do not know whether I was more hungry, tired, or contented. My wife, to whom I explained the reason of my running away, smiled and said, " You might have waited until after dinner;" and perhaps, who knows that she was not right? but I was so astonished and out of myself on account of that strange dream, that I was afraid every instant to lose the remembrance of it. It is really a strange thing, that after having thought of, studied, and sketched this subject for many months, when I was least thinking of it (for then I was certainly not thinking of it)—all at once, when asleep, I should see so clearly stand out before me, without even an uncertain line, the composition of that group. I have often thought of it, and being obliged in some way to explain it, I should say that the position I took when asleep might have acted on my over-excited imagination, always fixed on that same idea.

If the reader has followed me so far, he may truly be called courteous; but who knows how many times he has looked with avidity in these pages, full of minute details of my doings, for some little facts, some little escapades which really define and give the impress of the moral character of a man, and not having found it, has closed the book with irritation, and has muttered between his teeth, " This man is really very stupid, or he imagines us to be such simpletons as to believe that his life has always run on in a smooth, pleasant path, where there are no stones to stumble over, or brambles to be caught by"? I will not judge if the reader be right or wrong in his reasoning, but it would be as wrong to think that my life had been perfectly exempt from the little wretchednesses that are as inherent to it as smoke to a fire, especially if the wood be green, as it would be to require for his own satisfaction that I should ostentatiously insist on this smoke at the risk of offending the tender and chaste eyes of those who, albeit not ignoring these things, love the light and abhor smoke. Then, also, in speaking of these little wretchednesses, one always errs, however faithful to the truth, in saying either too much or too little; and it is believed to be either exaggerated or underrated, according to the simplicity or malice of the reader: so it is better not to speak of them at all. These little details, these little moral wrinkles, ought to be cast aside, as they do not add an atom to the likeness of the person. The reader can imagine them, or, to speak plainer, he learns them from the voice of common report, which accompanies through life the acts of any man not absolutely obscure. But if in life there are brambles and pebbles that can momentarily molest the poor pilgrim, there are also errors and deviations which lead us astray. Grave misfortunes such as these, by God's mercy, I have not met with, although the danger has not been wanting. The least thought of the gentle nature of my good wife, so full of simplicity and truth, her deep and serious affection, her loving care of her children, and her total abnegation of self for them and for me,—this thought, I repeat, was enough, with God's help, to enable me to escape once or twice from danger; and I wish to say this, that the reader fond of suchlike particulars need not tire himself with looking for them here, where he will not find them.

In the moral character of a man, deviation from and

forgetfulness of his duties is an ugly stain, even uglier than deformity in art. In fact, deformity, which by itself alone is contrary to art, when introduced into composition, especially when historical or critical reasons require it, can be of use as a contrast, and be—not beautiful in itself, for that would be a contradiction of terms—but of use to the *ensemble*, and to the beautiful,—as, for example, the dissonances in harmony used sparingly, if they suspend momentarily the flow of that broad sweet wave, they make one hear it again more vividly, more unexpectedly, and transformed into other colour and form. If all this concerns and is of use to Art, which is the manifestation of the beautiful, it does not apply to morals, which are the manifestation and practice of Good. The one is relative, but this is absolute. The well-known aphorism, Truth before all things, lands one nowhere ; and I have shown that in being silent on some matters, one need not be false to her. But she is only cast into a slight shadow by these veils of decency and modesty ; and so Truth should show her matronly bearing.

I have spoken somewhat at length about this, because to some this exposition of my opinion may have appeared unseemly. Let them accept, then, with a kindly feeling, the reasons, which I think excellent ones, that have led me to this wise decision of representing the truth to each and every one's eyes in the most appropriate way, so that, while it attracts by the largeness and uprightness of its form, it leaves the spirit undisturbed and tranquil.

I set to work on the model of the " Pietà " with a feeling of assurance devoid of any of those outlooks of fallacious hope that so often preside over and accompany a work badly conceived and not sufficiently studied or thought out, with which the unsatisfied mind seeks to quiet itself, while the artist goes on persuading himself that he will better his idea as his work goes on, instead of which he finds out every day more and more the existence of those difficulties and doubts which increase in intensity as the strength to overcome them diminishes. And *àpropos* of this, I remember one day when I was making an excursion from Florence to Sant' Andrea, with Bartolini (it was on a Saturday, to stay over until Sunday evening at Villa Fenzi), as we travelled along Bartolini seemed to me gayer and more expansive than usual, and having asked him what was the reason, he would not tell me, but answered, " You will know why at Sant' Andrea ; I am going to tell at dinner when every one is present, for it is a thing of great importance, as you will be able to judge perhaps better than any one else." With these words he so roused my curiosity that it made that very short expedition seem a long one. Arrived at the Villa, *Sor* Emanuele, seeing the master so gay and almost beaming, turned to him and jokingly said these words, " I'll be bound you have found a new and beautiful little model."

" No ; and even those I have—and they are beauties —I sent off this very morning. But I am contented, because I had a thorn in my side—a thought that had been tormenting me for more than a year. There was one side of my group—the " Astyanax "—that I did not like. I have tried various ways of correcting it, but in vain ; for the evil was fundamental. I have formed a resolution, and ordered my work to be pulled to pieces. I have sacrificed more than a year's time, but I am certain that I shall be the gainer, because the work will come better both as to lines and the quickness of execution. I feel sure that the change is a good one."

Whoever is an artist understands the importance of

such an act, and the courage of a man who destroys a
work that has cost him more than a year's labour, and
admonishes those who are too quick in putting an un-
digested thought into execution.

As for me, I felt an admiration as much for that
heroic resolution as for his gaiety and indifference,
and was persuaded that only men of such a temperament know how to act and comport themselves in that
fashion.

I set to work, as I have said, on the group of the
" Pietà "; and although the novelty of the idea and harmony of lines gave me every reason to hope for success
in my work, yet the impetuosity with which I had gone
to work, the difficulty of giving the expression to the
Virgin's face in contrast with the divine stillness of the
dead Jesus, impossible to find in models—for the most
part the negation of all that is sublime in expression,—
all this acted so upon my poor brain that I began to
hear noises, which gradually increased to such an intensity that they deafened me, and I had to stop working,
not being able to go on.   The thought of my weakness
worked upon me so violently that it produced melancholy, insomnia, and aversion to food.   My good friend
Dr Alberti, who treated me, advised rest from work and
distraction,—but of what kind, as everything bored me?
Night and day I continually felt stunned by a buzzing
noise in my head, which was most annoying ; and what
is worse, sounds, noises, and voices, even of the most
moderate kind, became insufferable to me.   A coachman smacking his whip put me in a tremor, and I ran
at the sight of him.   At home my poor wife and my little
girls were obliged to speak in the lowest voice, and
oftentimes by signs.   As I have said, sleep had left me,
and all taste for food, and I grew thinner before one's

very eyes. I could not read two consecutive pages, and could not dream of writing. I used to go out of the house to escape melancholy, and walk for a long distance at a time without knowing where I was going. The buzzing in my head and the noise in the street tortured me. If I saw any one I knew, I avoided him, not to be obliged to answer the same tiresome question as to how I felt. If I went to the studio, my melancholy turned into acute pain on looking at my works which I could not begin to touch, and I felt my heart throb so hard that I cried most bitterly.

I could not continue on in this condition, and by advice of the doctor I resolved to go with my family to Naples. I hoped to recover my health in that great gay city, under that splendid sky, in that mild atmosphere pure and impregnated with life, and my hope was strengthened by the remembrance that I had once recovered my health there ten years before. I left on the morning of the Epiphany, the 6th of January 1863, and that night I spent at Rome at the Hotel Cesari. I did not stop in Rome, and saw no one. I saw mechanically —more than anything else, to amuse my poor family— the finest monuments of the Eternal City; and the day after took the road to Naples—a true *via crucis*, by which I hoped to regain my health. We arrived in Naples between eight and ten o'clock. I ordered the coachman to take us to the Hotel de France. There was no room to be had, so we were conducted to a poor, dirty little inn, with which, being late, we were obliged to content ourselves. The day following, my friend Giuseppe Mancinelli insisted (in spite of my opposition, not wishing to inconvenience him) that we should lodge in his house, Rampa San Potito, near the Museum degli Studii.

Mancinelli was an excellent man, an artist of merit, a

good husband and father, and a conscientious and amiable master at the Academy of Fine Arts there. I remember with emotion the fraternal care that he took of us. Poor friend! you too have left us, but the memory of your virtues and love still lives with us, and is a consolation to us in the midst of the coldness of so many who have never known the religion of friendship, or who, if they appeared devoted, only sought to steal the candles offered by the faithful to her altar.

The first days after my arrival at Naples were very sad. The noises and voices in that immense city nearly drove me out of my mind, added to which the weather was wretched—for we had nearly a month of rain—so there were no walks to be taken, and nothing to distract me. Fortunately I had all my family with me, and my thoughts were not in Florence, as they had been during my former visit. I gave no thought to my studio, and only, as if in a vision, the head of my Madonna appeared to me in the sad pose in which I had left her, fearing that I should never see her again. In vain Mancinelli and his family, and my friends Morelli, Aloysio, Maldarelli, Palizzi, and others, tried to rouse me out of my despondency. How well I remember with what pains poor Celentano, whom I then knew for the first time, tried to cheer me up! Poor Celentano! brightest light of that fine school that searches for and finds material in the universe of nature to embody the fantasies of the brain, how soon, and in what a manner, your light was extinguished!

Enough—enough of the dead, otherwise I shall fall into the elegiac, which would be ridiculous in these simple memoirs! But if it be true that every thought must be clothed in its own special garb, how sad is that of death, although through her veils shines the hope of heaven!

CHAPTER XIX.

ND yet I do not feel in the vein to stop talk-
ing of the dead. It is so sweet to go back in
memory to those dear persons that we have
loved and esteemed, and who have returned
our love. One day in Rome—it was in the summer of
1864—a young painter of the brightest promise had received a letter from his betrothed, who was a long way
off. In it she expressed the great anxiety she had
been suffering on account of a dream she had had, in
which she had seen her dear one drowning; and she be-
seeched him in the warmest manner to pay attention and
not expose himself to danger. The ingenuousness and
affection in this letter made the young painter smile, and
in his answer he jokingly expressed himself as follows:
" With regard to your dream, set your mind at rest, because if I don't drown myself in wine, I shall certainly

not drown in water." A few days after this some of his friends proposed to him to go and bathe, but he refused decidedly, and said, " Go, the rest of you ; I don't want to bathe, and shall go home," and he left them. Shortly after this his friends went, as they had decided, to bathe, and they saw a young fellow struggling in the water ; recognising him, they at once undressed and ran to his rescue, as it was evident that he did not know how to swim. Their attempt, as well as that of others, was vain, for the poor young man went down and was carried away by the current of the Tiber to a great distance from the spot where he had thrown himself in. This young man was universally and sincerely regretted. Painting lost in him one of her brightest geniuses, and Siena, his birthplace, a son that would have been a very great honour to her. Some studies sent by him to Siena, and a picture of San Luigi in the Church of the Madonna del Soccorso at Leghorn, bear witness to Visconti's talent, a name dear and revered amongst all artists. He studied at the Sienese Academy, under Luigi Mussini, who, besides his sound principles in art, had the power of being able to communicate them, and carried persuasion and conviction through the weight of example. Visconti was buried in Rome in the Church of San Bartolommeo all' Isola,[1] a short distance from the place where

---

[1] Poor Visconti is not buried in the Church of San Bartolommeo all' Isola. My friend Majoli tells me that I have made a mistake. His body was taken there, as it was found near there, and the funeral took place in that church ; but the body was taken afterwards to the Campo Verano, and buried in the lower part of that cemetery. A modest little monument called a *Pincietto* was erected over it by the subscription of several sorrowing and affectionate friends, and amongst these the good Majoli, who most particularly exerted himself in modelling and cutting a portrait of him in marble, and offering his work as a tribute of friendship.

his body was found, and Siena honoured him by having
a modest but touching monument made by his friend
Tito Sarrocchi and placed for him in the Church of
San Domenico. Visconti was a handsome young man,
healthy and strong, of olive çomplexion, black hair and
beard, endowed with an open, frank, loyal, and at the
same time modest, nature.

I return to the living, I return to Naples. About
this time the competition for the statue of Victory, as
a monument for the martyrs of the four revolutions,
1821, 1831, 1848, and 1860, was to be decided on.
Many were those competing for it, and all Neapolitans—
amongst these Pasquarelli and Caggiano, pupils of mine ;
and for this reason, as well as on account of my ill
health, I could not accept the position of judge. Giovanni Strazza was therefore invited to come from Milan ;
and he too died a few months ago, my poor friend !
He had a very cultivated mind, and was as amiable and
polished in manner as he could be. I knew him first
in Rome in 1844, when he was very young, and when
artists, amateurs, and all people crowded round his first
statue of Ishmael. To all, as well as to' me, he was open-
hearted, loyal, and sincere, and his words were always
urbane and pleasant. I saw him again at Vienna in
1873, when he was my companion in the jury for our
section of sculpture at the great exhibition. But let us
really return to the living, if that be possible.

The prize for the statue of Victory was adjudicated to
Emanuele Caggiano, and justly so. I think this statue is
one of his finest works. I have heard nothing of him
now for a long time, and am afraid that he does not
occupy himself with the same fervour that he displayed
when he began to work under my direction.

I revisited all the things that I had seen the first

time I was in Naples, with a feeling of *ennui*, and only
gave some attention to Pompeii, because there I had
the good fortune to meet the Commendatore Fiorelli,
director of the excavations, and some artists that I have
forgotten.   I remember, however, the brotherly solicitude shown me by my friends Morelli and Palizzi, and
this time even by Angelini, and the particular courtesy
of Signor Vonwiller, a most cultivated man, and so
great a lover of art that he has converted his house
into a real modern and most select gallery.   Here one
finds in perfect harmony all the best products of Italian
art.   At that time (and many years have since passed)
the pictures of Morelli, Celentano, Altamura, Palizzi, and
other clever painters of that beautiful school, were admirably exhibited ; there too, Vela, Magni, Angelini, and
Fedi had works ; and in the midst of these I felt honoured
also to find myself represented by my two statues of
Bacchini, the "Festante" and the "Dolente."   If every
city in Italy had a gentleman like Vonwiller, it may easily
be believed that art would derive great benefit from
it ; for taste backed by great fortunes has more direct
and potent efficacy than all the societies for promoting
art, where, with small sips and small prizes, the genius
of poor artists is frittered away.   Until the day when
these societies make the heroic resolution of only con-
ferring two or three prizes (be it for pictures or statues
of small dimensions ; the size does not matter, as long
as they are really beautiful), art will not advance one
step.   But in the meanwhile, let us take things as they
are and push on.

The repose and the balmy airs of beautiful hospi-
table Naples worked a wonderful change for the better
in my health.   Sleep, that beneficent restorer of the
forces, which for some time past had gone from me,

verily without my having murdered it, as Macbeth had,
or even in the least offended it, returned with its blandishments and its calm smiling visions full of pleasant
happy memories. It was the season of the year when
nature dons again her green mantle. In that happy
country, her awakening is more precocious, and one
could say that nature was there a very early riser; and
whilst the mountains were still all covered with snow,
on those sweet slopes, on those enchanted shores, the
little green new-born leaflets mix with the blossoms of
the apple, almond, and peach trees. The light morning breeze makes these leaflets and blossoms tremble,
and wafts to the air a sweet delicate perfume, that
revives the body and rejoices the spirit.

This reawakening of nature has in it I know not
what of harmony that is difficult to describe. It seems
as if the chest expanded to drink in the air with unusual
longing; the eyes are never weary of looking again at the
budding flowerets, whose odour one inhales with a chaste
voluptuousness, as of the breath of our children in their
mother's arms. The mysterious wave of life, that in-
sinuates itself in the earth, penetrating even into its
most infinitesimal parts, that prepares the nuptial bed,
and makes the budding vegetation fruitful; the wave,
that in the profound depths of the sea gladdens the life
of its mute inhabitants, gives joy and swiftness to the flight
of the birds in the air, makes the animals of the earth
walk with more erect, ready, and joyful step,—the wave
of life, more than all, operates wonderfully on man.
And I—I felt myself born unto a new life; nature
seemed to me more beautiful, her bounty more desir-
able; the wish to observe and to work returned to me,
the enjoyment of conversation, attention in listening,
temperance in discussions, and courtesy in contro-

versies, all impulses of the mind, wherein, it seems to me, lies the mysterious harmony of body and soul in perfect union—*mens sana in corpore sano.*

Having therefore recovered my health, and taken leave of my friend Mancinelli and his good family, I again left for Rome, with the intention of passing the approaching Holy Week there; but it so happened that my poor Luisina, the youngest of my daughters, fell ill. Some symptoms of her illness had already manifested themselves in the first days after our arrival; then she had to take to her bed, and became so much worse, that we were all in the greatest anxiety—two months of such anxiety as only a father can understand; and she was so sweet a creature, and so intelligent! Then she improved a little, but did not recover. We left hurriedly, because the bitterness of losing her away from home was unbearable to us. The affectionate solicitude of our friends at this juncture was really brotherly. Majoli, Marchetti, Mantovani, Wolf, and Tenerani came forward and showed us indescribable kindness, and I remember it with gratitude, that no time can ever efface or weaken.

After our return to Florence, under treatment the disease seemed to have been got under; she recovered her health, and we thought no more about it.

I took up my studio life again. As I stood before my work that I had left when in a state of such utter prostration, it seemed to me that I had almost a new spirit within me. The head of the Madonna, who, when I left, looked as if she was sorrowing for me, now seemed to me so full of sadness that I did not touch it again, and it remains just as it was when I left, tormented by the insupportable, atrocious, and stunning noise in my head. Tears of emotion, of gratitude, and of feeling ran down my cheeks as I stood before the clay, and, full of confidence, I set myself again to work. In thought I returned to the days of my sufferings, when the fear of losing my mind frightened me, and I dared not look at my children or at my good wife. These remembrances quickened the pleasure I felt in my new state of health, and I thanked the Lord from the bottom of my heart.

I had taken Tonino Liverani (nick-named Tria) as a model for my "Christ." He was rather too old for a "Christ," but I was not able to find another who united such majesty and grace of movement and of parts. Hardly had I put the whole masses together and begun to define some of the outlines, when he fell ill and died in a few days. I went to see him when he was at his worst, and the poor man was glad to see me, and was pained (as he said) not to be able to finish the "Dead Christ." With his deep sunk eyes, mouth half opened, and with the pallor of death upon him, he looked marvellously beautiful, and strangely like that type of Christ that good artists of the fourteenth and fifteenth centuries have handed down to us. Poor Tria, I still remember the long, piteous look you gave me when we bade each other good-bye !

Scarcely had I finished the model for the "Pietà," when I modelled the statue of Astronomy for the Mossotti monument, which is in the Campo Santo at Pisa, a work that I had pledged myself to make for its mere cost; and I did so most willingly on account of the reverent friendship that I had had for Mossotti. But even the expenses were not covered, and to all my pressing inquiries I never got a word of answer from the treasurer of the committee, in consequence of which the committee itself was never able to publish a report of its administration. But, that the word expenses may be clearly understood, I wish it to be known that that statue, with its sarcophagus, base, and ornamentation, I had pledged myself to make, and did make, for six thousand *lire*.   I have received *five thousand eight hundred and fifty;* there remain the *hundred and fifty,* which I am obliged to make a present of, after having given gratuitously my work on the models and the finishing of it in marble.   I don't know if it is so with other artists, but with me it has always happened that the works I have been desirous of making for their mere cost—which is like saying, as a present—have not been accepted, or, besides giving my own work, I have been obliged to add something from my pocket! Before these memoirs are finished the reader will find something else of the same kind which will serve as a lesson and warning to young artists, even if they ever feel within them the " softness " to work for nothing.

In another place I have said that, in the enumeration of my works, I should not make mention of the portraits. I was obliged, however, to deviate from that promise to speak of one that had occasioned a great deal of talk and false reports about me.   I must now speak of another that I was to have made, and did not—that is to say, the portrait of his Majesty King Victor Emmanuel. Why I never made it I cannot say myself, and perhaps the reader himself will not know after he has read the following account, unless he is satisfied with the explanation that I shall presently give.

The Superintendent of the Archives, Commendatore Francesco Bonaini, after having put in order and nearly reconstructed the archives of Pisa, wished to put in the main hall a marble bust, of almost colossal size, of Victor Emmanuel; and in order to determine the size and study the light, I went with him to Pisa to see the place

itself where the bust of the King was to stand. Having
seen it and fixed upon the size of the bust, I made
one condition, agreeing to all arrangements as to price
and time for making it. The condition that I made—a
most natural one—was that his Majesty should concede
to me the sittings required, that I might model him from
life and not from photograph. The syndic of the day
(Cavaliere Senatore Ruschi, if my memory serves me)
went to Florence, accompanied by some of the *assessori*,
to ask the King, first for the permission of placing his
portrait in the Great Hall of the Pisan Archives, and
then to grant the necessary sittings to the artist, and
settle the place, the time, and the length of the sittings,
according to his Majesty's pleasure. Both the one request and the other were granted most graciously by the
King with his usual affability, and he added that he knew
the artist and was well satisfied, and that, in the meanwhile, they were to wait for notice to communicate to me
that I might begin my work. Months passed, and this
notice never came ; Bonaini was pressing me, being in a
hurry to have the archives inaugurated, and I appealed
to his Excellency Marchese di Breme, Minister of the
Royal House, to beg the King to let me have the required
sittings, but my request met with no good result. Later,
after the death of Di Breme, I made the same appeal
to the Marchese Filippo Gualterio, who succeeded him
in that office ; but this appeal not only had no good
result, but did not even receive an answer. As the
affair of the inauguration of the Pisan Archives had
boiled over, Bonaini did not speak of it again, and
naturally neither did I. Here there would be some
observations to be made on this favour having been
asked for and granted, and then given up. As for me,
I resolve the question in a few simple words and say,

that as it is a most boring thing to all to stand as model, for a king it must be excessively so and insufferable, and therefore the notice to begin this boring business never came from the person who was to undergo it; and it is reasonable enough, and even satisfies me, who have posed as model two or three times.

About this time the Syndic of Turin invited me to form part of a commission of artists to pass judgment on the models sent up for Cavour's monument. I was then at Leghorn with my family, as my little girls were in need of sea-bathing. I had no need for it myself, and, in fact, I think that the damp salt air was not good for me, and I stayed there most unwillingly, so that when the invitation to go to Turin came I instantly accepted it with pleasure as a fortunate opportunity to change the air and have something to occupy my mind; and leaving my wife with the two youngest little girls, I took Amalia with me.

This competition, of which we were to judge, was a second trial, as the first had failed; the competitors were many, and some of them praiseworthy. My colleagues in the jury were, if I remember right, the Professors Santo Varni of Genoa, Innocenzo Fraccaroli of Milan, Ceppi of Turin, and another whose name I cannot recall. The examination was a long one, and the discussion, although opinions differed, was a quiet one : the majority pronounced itself favourable to a project of the architect Cipolla, which was in drawing; my vote had been for one of the two designs in relief by Vela. The reporter of our decision was Professor Ceppi. I returned to Leghorn to my family, and from there to Florence, where I again took up my work.

Signor Ferdinando Filippi di Buti, whom I had met at Leghorn, showed himself desirous of having a statue of mine to put in the mortuary chapel that he had built from its very foundation close to one of his villas on the pleasant hill that rises above the town. The subject was a beautiful one, and, after the " Dead Christ," I could not have desired anything better to make than " Christ after the Resurrection," and this was the very subject that Signor Filippi wanted of me.

The " Triumph of the Cross," the " Madonna Addolorata " that I spoke of further back, the " Pietà," and this "Christ after the Resurrection," are the strictly religious subjects that I have made—rather, that I have had the good fortune to make, because I believe that such subjects, always beautiful in themselves, when they find the soul of the artist disposed to feel them and comprehend them, are also capable of high serene inspiration, and secret efficacy to the soul of those who behold them, be they in spirit even thousands of miles distant from the number of believers.

Let the truth prevail. Religious sentiment has its root in the heart, in the intellect, in the imagination, and, in a word, in all the impulses of the soul. A heart without God is a heart without love, and will not love woman but for the brutal pleasure she procures, and, in consequence, not even the children that are the fruit of, and also a burden upon, his selfishness. He will not love his country except for the honours and the gain that can be got out of it, and will sacrifice it carelessly for a single moment of pleasure or interest, because a heart without God is a heart without love. An intelligence without the knowledge of God is wanting in a basis as starting-point for all its reasoning—it is without the light that should illumine the objects it takes hold of to examine. Such an intellect is circumscribed within the narrow circle of things perceptible to the senses, where, finding nothing but aridness wherein to quench its burning thirst, which is always insatiate for goodness and truth, it ends either in a fierce desire of suicide, or as a vengeance of nature's own in that saddest of nights, madness. An imagination deprived of the splendid visions of the supersensible, loses even its true functions, because, not seeing or divining through time and space, through life and death, in the stars and in the atoms, anything but a casual mechanism, it is cruelly condemned to inertia, and with clipped wings can no longer sustain its flight—those wings which so potently upheld Dante as he passed from planet to planet, leaving the earth down in depths far beneath him. The eye accustomed to matter is besmeared with mud, and can no longer bear the bright light of the sun and the planets, which seem as if they were the eyes of God.

Religious sentiment has existed in all times, amongst all people, and it exists in the conscience of man independent of all education and example. The immense vault of the heavens; the innumerable planets resplendent in light; the sun that illuminates, warms, and fertilises the earth; the expanse of the waters of the sea; the prodigious variety and beauty of animals, plants, and fruits; the loveliness of colours, harmony of sounds from everywhere, and for all our senses,—come to us as the proof of God. But more even than from exterior things we feel it within ourselves. The blood shed by the martyrs fighting for the faith; life given in large profusion for the defence of country, liberty, and honour, or our women and children; active indignation against tyranny, cowardliness, and injustice; the tender charm we feel for innocence, admiration for virtue, and charity towards the poor, orphans, and those in trouble,— all these are signs that God has placed within us a part of His very nature. We feel within us the impulses of charity, and in prayer we feel our heart. expand with hope; out of frailty we fall, and faith renews in us the strength to rise again. Religious sentiment makes the heart glow, illuminates the intellect, fertilises the imagination, and creates not only the good citizen and good father, but also the artist.

Our hundred basilicas, the paintings and statues of our Christian artists that Italy and the world is so rich in, bear witness to this tribunal of truth to which anxious humanity, even from its earliest days, appeals. Phidias, Homer, Dante and Michael Angelo, Brunellesco and Orgagna, Raphael and Leonardo, Donatello and Ghiberti, and a hundred others, prove that religious inspiration is of so large a source that one can always draw from it; and although in the application of it the form may in a measure vary, yet it will always be great and admirable, because the mind that lifts itself up, though it may deviate more or less salient in curves, will always remain elevated. Correggio and Bernini, Guido Reni and the Caracci, were under the bad influence of their time as to method, but the intention was always good. And coming down to our recent fathers, and speaking always of artists, were Canova, Rossini, and Manzoni not great, for the very reason that they took their inspiration from religious subjects?

As the venerated name of Manzoni has fallen from my pen, I shall describe the visit that he made to my studio. When his visit was announced to me, I had but just finished the bas-relief for Santa Croce and the " Pietà." He was in company with the Marchese Gino Capponi, Aleardi, and Professor Giovan Battista Giorgini. After having seen several of my works, he stopped before the model in plaster of the bas-relief for
. Santa Croce, and said—

"I see here a vast subject that speaks to me of lofty things ; it seems to me that in parts I can divine its meaning, but I should wish to hear the artist himself speak and explain his entire intention."

It is always unwillingly that I act as cicerone to my very poor works—and to say the truth, I only do so most rarely with my intimate friends in order to ask some advice ; but the abrupt request made by such a man as he was did not displease me, and I began my explanation. But after I had been talking a few minutes, Marchese Gino Capponi began to stammer out something full of emotion in his sorrow not to be able to see the things I was explaining, and had to go out accompanied by Giorgini, if I mistake not. And here was another of those great souls that warmed itself in the rays of that faith which broke asunder the chains of the slave— opened the mind and softened the heart of the savage— restrained the flights of fancy within the beaten road of truth and good—willed that power, justice, and charity should be friends with each other, and made one taste of peace and happiness in poverty—and that enlarged and extended the confines of the intellect, of morality, and of civilisation.

I beg pardon if I have enlarged too much on this subject, but I do not think it can be superfluous to endeavour to correct the tendency of the day, when from every side one hears repeated that, for the future, in art the study of religious subjects is at an end, as if society of to-day was entirely composed of unbelievers or free-thinkers, who, by way of parenthesis, amongst other fine things have never thought that thought itself is not at all free. It seems to me that thought is an attribute ' of the soul that is moved with marvellous rapidity by means of a strength and impulse superior to itself, which .

depend upon physical constitution, education, and example. Thought, with all its freedom, all its flights, is subject, dependent, and, as one might say, formed by those forces and those impulses.

In the infinite scale of human thoughts there are some good, but a great many more are bad. In the moral order of things, those contrary to good are evil; as in the intellectual, those contrary to truth—and in the ideal, those contrary to the beautiful.

Now thought moves inconstantly from the beautiful to the ugly, from the true to the false, from good to evil, until our will, which is really free, either repulses it or takes possession of it according to the power, more or less, that reason has over the will. It is clear, therefore, that thought is not free, but, on the contrary, is subservient to laws independent of and superior to itself. How this happens is quite another pair of sleeves; but the fact is this, our thought is moved, and so to speak, subject to this power. Will comes and accepts it, weds it and makes it its own, good or bad though it be, with or without register of baptism, and snaps its fingers at the syndic or the priest. Once stirred, thought moves the will, and the will assenting, commands it as with a rod. And now, for the second time, let me really beg pardon.

After my "Christ," his Imperial Highness the Grand Duke Constantine of Russia gave me an order for an angel that he wanted as a present for a German prince, whose name I do not remember. This angel was to be the Guardian Angel; the subject was determined upon, and I don't know if, in the mind of the giver, it was to guard the prince or the principality. If it was the prince, I hope my poor angel will have done the best he could; if the principality, I am afraid that he has been overcome by cunning and force. His head is crowned with olives, and his lifted right hand points to heaven. Will the prince feel any consolation looking at the statue? I hope so; and in any way, he will be persuaded that true peace is not of this world.

It is now the time and place to speak of Cavour's monument. As I before mentioned, I was one of the judges on that committee. My vote had been for Professor Vela's design, but the prize was obtained by the architect Professor Cipolla; and as he was an architect, he naturally could not carry his work into execution: he therefore went the rounds, and it was not difficult for him to find several sculptors who assumed, each and all of them, certain parts, either a statue or bas-relief. For the principal statue of Cavour, it was the intention, I know not whether of Cipolla or the Giunta Comunale, that I should make it, but their reiterated request I did not think well to accept.

In the meantime, in Turin there began to be a sort of persistent, dull warfare against Cipolla's design. All sorts of possible and imaginable doubts were raised as to its general character, meaning, proportions, and effect. That excellent artist, Professor Cipolla, proposed to put an end to all this talk by setting up in relief, in largish proportions, a model of his so-much-contested design. Would that he had never done so! The aversion to it grew beyond bounds, and pronounced itself by means of the press to such a degree, that the Giunta thought it best no longer to intrust him with the commission for the work; for, by virtue of an article in the programme for this competition, the committee were not in the least tied down to commit the execution of the monument to the gainer of the prize at the competition, having left itself full and entire liberty of action. From this began a sequel of remonstrances and appeals on the part of the artist, and answers backed by law on the part of the commission, which was then broken up and another formed, for the purpose of studying anew the whole affair.

I hurry over these things quickly as they come to me and as my memory has retained them after many years, without searching amongst letters, newspapers, or elsewhere, wishing, as I have done until now, to make use only of my memory.

The new Giunta, presided over by my illustrious and lamented friend Count Federigo Sclopis, took up this tangled affair, discussed in so many ways, and came to the determination of not having any more competition. They decided that the best thing to be done was to choose an artist, and order the work directly from him, leaving him free to determine the rendering of the subject, the size of the monument, the materials to be employed, and choice of the site, and all other matters, except, naturally, as to price and time,—which latter could be but short, owing to the two years that had passed in competitions! The choice fell on me, who was a thousand miles away from thinking of such a thing. However, before saying a word to me, and much less, writing to me, I was interrogated by a most estimable person if I would accept that work, and I answered at once that I would not: in the first place, because the subject was a difficult one, on account of its purely political significance,—so extraneous, not to say tiresome, to my nature and studies; in the second place, because, having been one of the judges on that commission, it did not seem delicate to accept it; and finally, because I thought Vela's design most praiseworthy. But neither my refusal nor the reasons I put forth availed

to alter the resolution they had now taken to make
me accept the work, which, for the matter of that, if
it presented great difficulties, and even rather rough
ones, in the rendering of its great conception, yet
offered a most rare opportunity, that would have flattered many other artists of more ambitious hope than
I, who have always been temperate. With all this,
however, I should always have replied in the negative,
had not a gentle and most noble lady begged me to
accept, touching on certain family affections that have
always found in me an echo of assent.

I accepted this commission, therefore, not blinding
myself to the great difficulties that I was going to en-
counter, or the many little annoyances that I should
undergo on account of the disappointed hopes of those
who had competed for the work. I saw and felt all the
seriousness of my undertaking, and thought of nothing
else but carrying it out most conscientiously. I asked
for eight years' time, which will not appear much, to
execute the work ; but I was begged to be satisfied with
six, and I wrote my adhesion, still declaring in the contract that it would be impossible for me to complete it in
that short time. Although I worked with all possible
energy, and provided myself with additional workmen
besides my own usual ones, yet the monument could not
be finished and put in its place until after the eight years
that I had asked for.

My composition of the architectural part of the monument was a quadrangular base, with two spherical bodies
on each side, whereon reposed another base, with the
corners cut off, that sustained the principal group of
Italy and Cavour. In front, on the lower base, is the
half-reclining figure representing Right in the act of
rising, who leans with the right hand on a broken yoke,

and clenches the left on his breast in a menacing attitude. His head and back are covered by a lion's skin,
signifying that right is strength. Opposite is Duty, in
a quiet attitude of repose. His head is crowned by a
wreath of olives, signifying that in the fulfilment of duty
peace is to be found; his right elbow rests on a block,
where, on the two sides exposed to view, are sculptured
in bas-relief the two extremes of human activity. On
one of these there is a king distributing a crown and
prizes to a virtuous man, whilst behind him there is a
chained delinquent undergoing his penalty; and on the
other there is a husbandman ploughing the ground. On
the two lateral sides there are two groups. That on the
right is of Politics, with two little genii, Revolution and
Diplomacy. Politics is seated, but alert, and almost
in the act of rising : her head is turned to the little genius
of Diplomacy, who has unfolded the treaties of 1815,
and is gravely showing it to her with his right hand,
whilst with his left he hides behind him a sword and
olive-branch, demonstrating that he brings with him
either war or peace. The other little genius of Revolution, in the act of wishing to dash forward, is held back
by Politics, who keeps her eyes on him, and, with a caressing expression, tries to temper his ardour ; one of his
feet rests on a fragment of medieval architecture, and he
holds in his right hand a brand, the symbol of destruction. The group on the left is of Independence, tightly
clasping in her embrace the little genius of the Provinces,
at whose feet still lies a link of his chain of captivity.
Independence has Roman sandals on her feet, and a
warrior's helmet on her head; her right arm is uplifted,
and she holds a broken chain in her hand, in the act of
dashing it from her. The other genius is that of Unity,
crowned by an oak-wreath ; he holds the fasces, to show

that union is strength. The principal group stands up
on the top, and represents Cavour, wrapped in his fune-
real mantle. Italy, at his side, in the act of rising from
her prostration, is offering him the civic crown, with expressions of gratitude, more decidedly expressed by her
left arm, by which she holds her great politician tenderly
around the waist ; whilst he, with kindly act, shows the
people a chart, on which is written his famous formula,
"*Libera Chiesa in libero Stato*," or free Church in free
State. On the two façades of the great base are two bas-
reliefs in bronze. In one of these is portrayed the return
from the Crimea of the Sardinian troops, who, by Cavour's
advice, took part, in union with France and England, in
the war against Russia, to put a check to the ambitious
designs of that Power in the East. The other bas-relief
represents the Congress of Paris, where for the first time,
on account of Cavour, Italy's voice was listened to.

The architectural part is made in rose granite of
Baveno; the ornaments—that is to say, the arms,
cornices, and trophies—and the statues are in clear white
marble of Canal Grande, which withstands all attacks of
weather. The entire monument is elevated on three
steps, and surrounded by a garden enclosed by railing.

The inscriptions are : On the front, "To Cammillo
Cavour, born in Turin the 10th of August 1810, died
the 6th of June 1861." On the side over the Politics,
"*Audace prudente ;*" over the Independence, "*L'Italia
libero ;*" and behind, "*Gli Italiani, auspice Torino.*"
These inscriptions are by Professor Michele Coppino.

385

CHAPTER XX.

ALLEGORIES IN ART—THE MONGA MONUMENT AT VERONA—OF MY LATE
DAUGHTER LUISINA—HER DEATH—HOW I WAS ROBBED—MONSIGNORE
ARCHBISHOP LIMBERTI'S CHARITABLE PROJECT—ONE OF MY COLLEAGUES—
NICOLÔ PUCCINI AND THE STATUE OF CARDINAL FORTEGUERRI—CESARE
SIGHINOLFI—CARDINAL CORSI, ARCHBISHOP OF PISA.

 SHOULD now feel inclined to speak at length of the troubles, the thoughts, and of the opposition that I had to encounter during eight years, the grimaces and the miserable enmities, of fickle, unstable friends and un-generous enemies; but I must keep silent, as I have been thus far on all such matters, because my intentions and my works being known to all, others may judge them. Then I also remember a wise warning that was given me when I was quite little, which is never to satisfy any desire or impulse to give vent to personal resentment, and I have always found myself the better for it. In such cases, silence has two advantages, —that of leaving one's own soul at peace, and of not satisfying those who would take pleasure in hearing us complain.

Only on one thing I will not be silent, because this does not concern me, but is a principle in art. I was reproved for having used allegorical figures in Cavour's monument, it being asserted that as the subject was entirely a modern one, and could not bear allegory, it was inopportune and improper. To which I answered, that when the subject permitted, it was well not to think even of allegories. If they had said to me, "A memorial of Count Cavour is wanted, make us a statue," nothing would have been easier. A portrait-statue dressed in the clothes he wore, one or two bas-reliefs on the base, and a brief inscription, would have been enough; and, I repeat, nothing would have been easier. It was not this, however, that the commission required for Cavour's monument. The commission desired that the whole of his character and intentions, the tenacity of his will, the greatness of his propositions, and the benefits obtained therefrom, should be portrayed. Now, how to explain this with real historical figures, or, as they say, in living art? As if a complex idea expressed by one or more figures, as is the case with allegory, is dead art! Oh, do me the famous pleasure, you irritating æsthetics, to go and prattle to babes! But don't speak to them of Phidias, Zeuxis, Alcamenes, and others, of that dead art that is now more alive than it ever was; nor of Giotto, nor of Giovanni and Andrea Pisani, nor of Raphael, nor of Michael Angelo, and many more, for they might find you out in your error. I repeat, this does not concern me or my work in the least, but it bears on a principle, and is a question that has been many times ventilated and resolved by the best thinkers in the way of argument, and by artists, who were not blockheads, in their works.

From the noble Signora Augusta Albertini of Verona, through my friend Aleardo Aleardi, I had an order for a monument to her family, an extremely painful subject. The Signora Albertini had lost, one by one, all her family—father, mother, brothers, sisters, all—and she had alone survived; alone, but with the bitterly sweet memory of those she had loved so much, and the desire to erect a monument to them. Some time before, she had given the commission to a young Veronese sculptor of great promise, Torquato della Torre, and they tell me that he had already made a sketch ; but shortly after, the young sculptor died, and after a long time had gone by I undertook to make this monument. Here is the description of it. On a quadrangular conical base there is placed a group consisting of the Angel of Death seated, and prostrated at his feet the only survivor of the family, waiting, as it 'were, after the havoc made by that angel in her family, for her turn to fall a victim. The angel, seated on a fragment of an antique frieze, to denote that he is superior to time and the pomps of humanity, is crowned with cypress, and has a pained expression, as if he deplored the office that Divine Justice had ordered him to fulfil ; the exterminating sword is still in his hand, but the point is lowered. On the base is a bas-relief representing the dead members of that family ; and as they died at brief intervals the one from the other, as if Death had blown them down with her breath as the wind overthrows the trees in the country, so they are laid out, shoulder to shoulder, by each other. A little angel hovers in the air near them with hands clasped in prayer, and in the background, on the horizon line, one perceives Verona. The bas-relief is in bronze, and its colours add seriousness and sadness to the scene. On the sides, and again in bronze, are sculptured two wreaths of cypress, so that this first base on the plinth seems as if it were entirely made of bronze ; the upper part, on which the inscription is engraved and the group stands, is in granite. This monument is at the end of the first nave on the right in the cemetery at Verona.

I said in the beginning of these memoirs, that I wrote

not only for young artists desirous of knowing something
of my life, my works, and the principles that have been
my guide in art and my intercourse with my fellow-
beings, but also to leave to my family a remembrance of
my feeling and affection for them.   And now that it
behoves me to speak of one of our greatest sorrows—
that is, of the loss of my most beloved daughter Luisina—
I know that I am doing what my dear ones desire, however sad it may be ; therefore I warn those not caring for
this theme to pass on.

I would that I could divest myself of all my defects
to speak of Gigina.   I would that this page which I
consecrate to her memory breathed a little of the
sweetly chaste love that showed itself in every act,
every word, and every look of hers.   I would that I
could simplify my style, temper and purify my words,
that they might sound sadly sweet, pure, and serene,
as were her words, her looks, and her mind.   But I
greatly fear that I shall not succeed in giving even a
feeble idea of that dear child; I fear, because purity
and chastity of imagery and simplicity of words have in
some measure vanished with my youth and ambition—
the passion and love for renown have perhaps clouded
the clearness of mind wherein was reflected the true
and the good.   I shall also not succeed, because the
innate beauty of that sweet creature was not fully revealed to me, for the confidence existing between a
daughter and her father is always modified by respect ;
and so it is bereft of those intimate and delicate traits
which are its sweetest perfume.   My family will read
these words on our beloved Luisina, and supply with
their loving memory where I fail in my littleness.   My
son-in-law, Antonino, wrote of her with the intelligence
of love; and several of my friends in condoling with me

rendered her image more beautiful and more amiable. Yet notwithstanding all this, I feel a desire to return to that dear little angel, were it for nothing else but to rejuvenate and sanctify that sorrow.

From her early girlhood my Luisina was as vivacious and playful with her little sisters and with her mother as they would allow her to be; with me she was more serious, and sometimes even sad, perhaps because she saw that I was serious, and because at that time my health was not good. As she grew older she was more confiding in me, and displayed great love for her mother and sisters. She took pleasure in helping them with such little household affairs as no one else could or can do. She also drew, seeing her sisters draw, and could draw from memory faces and persons of our acquaintance. I have also amongst her papers extracts copied by her from books that had pleased her. She loved flowers, and in the morning, together with her sisters, she gathered them in the garden of our villa, and, making bunches of them, placed them on the altar in the little chapel. Those days were delicious ones, but they were brief! There is no happiness on earth, or it lasts but a very little while. True it is that memory remains to make us taste of a bitterness mingled somewhat with a sweet sadness, because the dear person taken from us lives again in our mind and responds to the beating of our heart. We remember the movements, the modest look, the words, the gentle affections, and all the virtues by which she was adorned, rendered still more visible and clear without the encumbrance of the body, by whose veil the light was subdued. And then—then there remains for us that sweet, most consoling hope of seeing her again for evermore, leaning on that faith that " is the substance of things hoped for, the evidence of things not seen."

O my good Gigina, my beloved little angel! I remember all that relates to thee—thy obedience, thy
affection, thy anxious delicate care of us, our walks on
the delightful Fiesole hill so dear to thee, almost a pre-
sage that the body should one day have rest there, and
now the little chapel in the cemetery there contains also
that of thy dear, tired, and martyred mother! Oh if
I had strength equal to love, I would also write of her!
I shall do so in time, but now I return to thee. The
remembrance of that morning lies buried in my heart;
it was in June 1872, two days before thy *fête* day, San
Luigi. For several days thou hadst felt ill, and could
not dissimulate as in the past. That morning, before
going down into Florence, I went into thy room, and
seeing that thou wast determined to get up, I ordered
thee to remain in bed; thou wast obedient as always, my
angel, but wept, because wanting, as I afterwards knew,
to be up on thy festal day. The illness was felt by thee,
but with hope to overcome it, at least for two days, re-
signing thyself to all suffering thereafter. Thou didst
obey, but weeping. Perhaps this aggravated thy disease.
This is the thorn I bear within my heart.

As soon as Bendini, the medical man from Fiesole,
saw her, he thought her case most grave, and wished to
consult her own doctor, Dr Alberti, who had treated
her at other times. I went at once to beg him to come,
and brought him back with me, as he has always had
great kindness and friendship for us, and from that day
he always saw her in company with Bendini. But the
disease increased more and more, and she already
breathed with difficulty, but preserved in her thoughts
and words serenity and resignation. Then began those
most painful alternations of disease—a little better and
then a little worse—and always the same story over

and over again. There is no pain more cruel and stinging than the delusion of a hoped-for good; the heart that
opens anxiously to hope is as if crushed and torn from
one's breast by implacable delusion. He who has ex-
perienced these painful alternations knows that they are
more cruel than even death itself. O Great God of
Israel, sustainer of all faithful souls, look down upon the
affliction of Thy servant! oh assist him in all things to
come! This affliction that came to us by God's will
broke down my pride, and spread over my family a veil
of sadness; it gave a shock to my beloved Marina's
health, and perhaps accelerated her death. .

Luisina expired in the first morning hours of the day
of the Ascension of the Most Holy Mary. She had,
whilst living, the semblance, the thoughts, and the affections of an angel; and she seemed to fall asleep in the
Virgin's arms, and fly away with her to heaven. In this
belief I find comfort and a sweet peace that not only
compensates for her loss, but even more, makes me taste
of so pure a pleasure that no words could express and
no worldly care could disturb. Her body rests in our
chapel in the new cemetery at Fiesole, and there my
daughter Amalia has erected a little monument to her.
The sepulchral urn is placed in a niche with a flat background, and on it lies sculptured the dear child in peaceful slumber, holding the crucifix in her right hand.
Everybody could see, and none better than I, how much
poor Amalia suffered in completing this sorrowful work.
I attempted to dissuade her from this most painful duty
she had imposed upon herself, but the strong affection
for her dead sister suggested perhaps to her that in offering this tribute of sister and artist the pain would be
somewhat softened.

I know that this remembrance, and the thoughts that

have dictated it, may make some smile; but in time they will think better of it, and will know that sadness is worth more than laughter, for the heart becomes better for the sadness in the face. And with this I have finished talking of my Gigina, keeping her memory always in my heart.

To narrate the death of my Luisina, I have omitted a circumstance, and not a trifling one in my life—that of the theft that occurred to me of fifty thousand *lire*. I hasten to declare that until that day (it was in 1866) I never had been the possessor of such a sum, and as soon as I was, it was stolen from me. This is how I came into possession of the money, why I kept it intact, and how it was stolen from me. I had only begun on Cavour's monument a short time before, and in accordance with the form of the contract, had received the first remittance of fifty thousand *lire*. At the same time, I was arranging to buy a house in the Via Pinti that I thought I should be able to adapt and make into a spacious studio, such as was necessary for me in modelling the colossal figures for the monument. As the sale of the house was to take place from day to day, I was persuaded also, by the advice of my lawyer, not to employ this money in any way, so as to have it ready to give in payment for it. And as I had kept the little sums of money that I had had in hand up to that time in a secret drawer of the closet in my own room in the studio, I placed this also there.

At this time I was working on the marble of a statue, the "Tired Bacchante," which had been bought by the King of Portugal. I had a young Roman girl as a model, and she came accompanied by her mother. This woman also had a son (so, at least, it was said; then it was no longer so; in fact, there was some mystery that I don't remember, because naturally such things were of no importance to me). The boy came also for a model, and appeared to be a good fellow, as well as the girl.

One morning (I was still in bed, but about to get up) my poor wife came into the room and said—

" Here is Bardi, who wants to speak to you."

" What can he have to say to me ? Does he not know that in half an hour I shall be at the studio ? He could wait. Let us hear what is the matter."

Bardi was one of my studio men, the rougher-out, whom I had brought up from a boy, and he had been with me twenty-three years. He was a thin, white-looking man, with a black beard, and dark lines under his eyes in his normal condition. That morning, as soon as I saw him, he really frightened me, for he looked absolutely like a dead man, or as Dante says, *cosa rimorta*. He took me aside, that my wife should not hear, and he told me that he had found the door of my room open, and having waited and listened awhile to ascertain if by chance I had arrived before him and was inside, but not hearing a sound after having called me, he entered the room and saw the closet open, the drawers on the ground, and the papers scattered about. He asked me anxiously if I kept anything of value there.

" All, my dear Bardi ! all that I possessed in money was there." And having almost no breath for words, I went out with him, rushing through the street. It is easier imagined than told how I felt on seeing all the drawers upset and empty, and the papers and thousand little objects they contained scattered about the ground. All the men of my studio gathered about me, and pitied me without even suspecting that it was a matter of such a sum of money. My good friend Cavaliere Raffaello Borri, being told what had occurred, came to me at once, and with rare generosity offered me his purse and his credit, and accompanied me home, with my heart full of anguish to be obliged to give this news to my poor wife. My friends rivalled each other in consoling me, ´some with offerings and some with affectionate words ; and I can never forget the charitable proposition made by Monsignore the Archbishop Giovacchino Limberti, to collect a certain sum for my benefit amongst those who were best able to give, and who knew me and loved me. All these I truly thanked from the bottom of my heart, saying that for the moment I was not in straitened circumstances, and if I was no longer in possession of that money—for which, thank God, I was not in debt—yet it was not lawful for me to accept help of any kind, for in substance I could not call myself strictly in need, and I remembered in the past having really been poor and not having accepted or asked for anything, because my principle is that every one ought to be sufficient for himself.

How the thieves were discovered, how some escaped from justice, how one was taken and condemned, and how, finally, part of the money stolen was saved, the sum of 12,400 *lire* returned to me, besides the gold medal that I had obtained at the Universal Exhibition of Paris in 1855, and which was shut up in the same place with the stolen money,—all this appears in the judiciary chronicle of that time.   Nor do I feel inclined to mix in such mire, and the reader could not follow me without disgust.   It was well that in the part of the theft recovered my Paris medal was found, not only because by this the reality of the robbery committed on me was proved and the restitution instantly made, but still more because it silenced some, I don't know how to qualify them, who seemed to doubt the misfortune that had befallen me, as if almost I had invented it—as if I had been a vulgar impostor, and had invented this fable to avoid payment . . . of what? I had never had debts before that time, then, or since ; and that I had no engagements to meet is proved by the refusal I made to those who so kindly and willingly offered to come to my aid.

But yes, once I had a debt, but merely by chance, or I had better say by forgetfulness. When this happened I was very young—at the beginning of my artistic career, if I mistake not. Then I was making the " Cain." In order to put it into marble I went to Carrara, found the block that suited me, and said that I would pay for it when the marble itself arrived. The trader answered, " All right ! I shall send the marble at once ; and as to the payment, I shall draw out a promissory-note for the first of the month." I had before me some twenty days' time. My mind being entirely possessed by the marble, I took no note of the day when the money became due. I knew that I had to pay, but the date escaped me, and one fine day I suddenly beheld before me a man from a bank, who came to receive the money that I had not got in full. I stammered out something, as a man might do about to be hanged. " Oh, don't hurry yourself much," said the man ; "suit your own convenience—I will return later; there is time until three," and he went away. How I felt can easily be imagined by those who know me. I became whiter and harder than the marble that I had then before me on the ground. I must find there and then, in the beat of a drum, the three or four hundred *scudi* that were wanting; and where to find them, I, who had never before asked for anything in loan? A good inspiration came to me. " Yes," said I, " Sor Emanuele can do me this favour ;". and putting on my coat, I ran into the square to the

Fenzi bank. Sor Emanuele was there at the back in his study, and you could see through the open glass door that fine jovial witty face of his.

When he saw me he exclaimed, "How are you?"

"Sor Emanuele, this and this is the matter," and I told him everything.

He gave me a slightly frowning look, and then burst into a fit of laughter that made his subalterns who were behind turn round, and he said, "Look here, we will do so;" he tore off a cheque, wrote the sum on it, and continuing to laugh, added, " Pass on there to Bosi and give him this; and *au revoir* until this evening" (I used to frequent his house); but when he had turned he called me back again and said: "Listen—I want to give you a counsel. You must never again sign any promissory-notes if you can help it; or if you do, make a note of them and look at it every day,"—and he began again to write, smiling to himself.

Will you believe it, Sor reader, I have never again signed any bills, although more than thirty-six years have gone by? Yet (to return to the robbery), amongst those who doubted my misfortune there was a colleague of mine, who, listening that day with an incredulous air to the account of what had occurred, and hearing that the sum in question was fifty thousand *lire*, with a smile on his lips and bad feeling at heart, came out with these words—

"Fifty thousand *lire!* that is rather too much !"

This colleague of mine was not the only one, nor one of the worst. Some few years ago a little thing happened which shows the uprightness and generosity of another of my colleagues !

. Cavaliere Nicolô Puccini, in dying at Pistoia, left orders in his will that a statue of Cardinal Forteguerri should be made and placed in the Piazza del Duomo of that city. Cavaliere Puccini's idea was, as every one can see, a wise and generous one, and belied reports, which made him out odd and unfriendly to the priests. This statue was to be assigned by competition, and with the obligation of presenting a model in plaster respresenting the Cardinal in his robes, with the insignia of his office, and the size of life. It is evident to all that this obligation was a serious one, and would cause many to withdraw from the competition, as really happened. One person, how-ever, went in for the competition, and this was Signor Cesare Sighinolfi of Modena, who, having left my teaching but a short time before, set himself to model this statue in too trivial a way—without a model, without the necessary robes, and without even caring a pin as regards asking me anything concerning the composition, or the requisite means for not making a jackanapes instead of a cardinal! Vivacious and careless as he was then, he had the pretension of being able to model a cardinal's statue life-size by only consulting some prints or pictures of cardinals, and the result was—as it should have been—that the statue was a very bad one. An article in the programme for this competition provided that the adjudication of the prize should be given by the Florentine Academy. I was not present at the meeting, to avoid giving a vote against it, as I was not unaware how the work had turned out. The poor statue, therefore, was judged and condemned without mercy. Then, after the first ebullition of juvenile impetuosity that had made him run on so foolishly was over, he returned to his senses, remembered me, and as at the same time though he had so much youthful light-heartedness, he had also a certain tenacity of will and self-love that had been wounded by the rejection of his work, he ran to me and entreated me to intercede with the commission that organised the competition, and obtain for him the concession of another trial.   I willingly agreed to do so, seeing the despair he was in, and appreciating the no small amount of courage required to recommence from the very beginning a difficult, expensive, and uncertain work; but I had to say to him, ". . . that is, if you are only in time, because the commission having just fulfilled its duty, and the competition turned out null, is now free to give the statue to whomsoever it likes without the obligation of competition."   It was therefore necessary to make an appeal to the commission to obtain its consent that another competition should be opened, and this was done by Sighinolfi, accompanied by a recommendation from me; and that it should have more value, and the second trial be conceded, I advised Sighinolfi to have this appeal signed by all my other colleagues.   He did so, and hurried by rail to Pistoia to present his request to the commission; but what was his surprise when, on his arrival there, and just as he was going up the stairs to present his paper to the secretary of the commission, he saw coming down one of the professors who had backed and signed his appeal!   The poor youth divined all, but still wished to make the attempt; and he did well to do so,—in fact the secretary in the most polite manner tried to persuade the young artist that now there was no longer time, that the competition had resulted in nothing, and that another trial would only draw things out to too great a length ; and finally, that as an offer had just been made to the commission in shape of a request for this work whereby its own responsibility was covered, so that it would come out of the affair with honour, he thought the commission would not accord the petition, but that he would take it, and officially present it, so as to give it its due course. As soon, however, as that excellent gentleman had set his eyes on the paper, and had seen the recommendation and signature of the same individual that only a short time before had made a request for the work for himself, he was so filled with indignation that, turning to Sighinolfi, he said—

"Go back to Florence, make another trial, and as you are recommended by Professor Duprè, he will assist you, and the commission will trust, I am certain, to the words and help of your master."

These, or words to the same effect, were reported to me by Sighinolfi on his return, and I saw myself doubly pledged that the young man should really this time succeed.

Here I am met by a reflection. Was it not perhaps quite lawful for an artist to present himself and ask to have that work to do himself, which, by reason of an unsuccessful competition, any one was free to ask for and obtain? Lawful it certainly would have been for any one who had not recommended the young man for a second trial, but certainly it was not praiseworthy in one who had made this recommendation ; so, at least, it seems to me.

Therefore, as matters stood thus, I thought it my duty to advise and direct the youth to follow a sure road, and the only good one by which to come safely into port. And, satisfying myself first as to his firm will to do all and follow in everything what I advised, I ordered him to make a small sketch, enough to get lines grateful to the eye. Then, remembering the kindness that Cardinal Corsi, Archbishop of Pisa, had always shown me, I wrote him a letter nearly in the following terms: "Eminence,—Signor Cesare Sighinolfi,

my scholar, is the person who presents this letter to
you. He has to make the statue of Cardinal Forteguerri
for Pistoia, but could not possibly make anything good
without having the robes appropriate to that high office.
See, *Eminenza*, if it would be possible for him to obtain
them from you—as, for instance, if your Eminence had
a robe, even a worn-out one, that you could let him
have for a short time—you would be doing a great act
of charity; for I repeat, without this neither he nor any
one else could succeed in doing anything. I am here
to guarantee that the sculptor will take the greatest care
of it, and return it as soon as possible," &c., &c. Sighinolfi, although he is not, I believe, one of those many
would-be devourers of priests, yet was, and still is, a
most decided Liberal, and the dignity and the face of
a cardinal must have had the same effect upon him as
coming in contact with a most antipathetic person would
have upon you or me. But, as the proverb says, one must
make of necessity a virtue, and having crossed himself, he
presented himself before his Eminence. Great was his
surprise to find that prelate most jovial and pleasant, and
quite ready to grant his request ; and that worthy man
pushed courtesy and amiability to the extent of making
him sit down at the table while he was taking his breakfast. It is as true as the Gospel that I have seen some
democrats more aristocratic than his Eminence Corsi.
He then called his secretary, Codibò, and told him to
have a whole suit of his best clothes, from the hat to
the shoes, given to Sighinolfi, and dismissed him with
kindness. I don't know if Sighinolfi offered to kiss his
hand ; but even if he had, it would have been the same
thing, for Corsi would not have allowed him to kiss it,
as I well know, for he would never allow me to do so.

With this precious bundle of cardinal's clothes he was

able to dress one of our models, who, although somewhat ridiculous, lent himself admirably to being dressed
in that way; and this is the only means of doing serious
work. The model was made under my direction, and
exhibited to be judged by the Academy, and declared
worthy of being executed in marble. So ended the
difficulties arising from the light-headedness of a young
artist, and made still harder by the intervention of an
artist who was neither generous nor just.

CHAPTER XXI.

T is now necessary for me to speak of the Universal Exhibition at Paris in 1867; but first, I wish frankly to give my opinion on the utility or non-utility of such exhibitions, monstrous agglomerations of manufactures, machinery, raw material, food, liquid for drink, sacred utensils, machines for war, &c., all exposed by the different nations of the world at the same time and in the same place. It has been said that this serves to create rivalry and emulation in the people of the different civilised nations, by placing their industries in contact with each other, to be judged by special men named for the purpose to give them their merited reward. The idea seems to be a fine one; in fact, it is so much too fine that the excess deforms it. On the contrary, I believe that all this assemblage of things in an immense edifice, with thousands and thousands of visitors, on one of the

pleasantest and most smiling sites, in the most beautiful part of the year, in one of the great metropolises
of the world, answers admirably to the economical and
political aims of the State that assembles the exhibition ;
gives an opportunity to travellers and exposers to see,
to divert and enjoy themselves, and make acquaintances,
sometimes good, but oftener bad; brings money into the
pockets of intriguers and swindlers in proportion to their
dexterity, and gives or increases the renown of Tizio or
Caio, to the detriment of Sempronio, in the opinion of
some with justice, and in the opinion of others with
great injustice. But who has the rights of it? The
rights of it are at the bottom of a well, and need the
grappling-irons of time to drag them out.

I should believe in the utility of these world exhibitions if they were by sections—industries, manufactures,
machinery, and agriculture — everything separate ; and
separated always absolutely from all the rest, in time
and in place, the Fine Arts, to which I should wish to
see prizes awarded, not by a medal, but rather by the
purchase of the work itself, or if this be already disposed
of, by the commission for another.

It may be somewhat useful to artists to see the works
of others, their variety, and the different modes of feeling
and seeing of their authors ; it may infuse into them new
life, new strength, and stimulate them to search within
themselves for what they find in the works of others :
but if this examination, this comparison, this stimulating
fever be of assistance to some, to the greater number
it is a stumbling-block, and the cause of their going
astray. It is useless to have any illusion. The greater
number of young artists allow themselves to be taken by
the bait of novelty, only because it is novelty, without
being able to discern the hidden reasons for which good

sense and experience concede or deny merit to such novelty. To but few belongs the power of examination and criticism,—to them alone who, having by nature the sentiment and cult of art, exercise themselves by constantly holding up the mirror before it; for they find in it always something new and varied, and on this very account do not ignore the reasons and laws that willingly give consent to these varieties and novelties. But the others allow themselves to be dazzled, and accept the novelty whatever it may be, choosing by preference the strangest and most unusual, which for that very reason is sure to be the least true; and so they fall into double error—into imitation which lands one in mediocrity, and into oddity which has affinity with error. As with both—that is to say, amongst those who do not depreciate novelty, and amongst the others that are seduced by the false attractions of mere novelty—there are some who are capable of appreciating the good only so far as the means for being able to manifest it is made apparent to them. To these, great exhibitions are of use; but to the first named they are not of use, as they have no need of them—and to the others even less so, for to them they can do harm.

When, now many years ago, Vela and others of the Milanese school taught a new and totally different way of looking at and treating drapery, flesh, and more especially hair, they would never have believed, I think, that their imitators would have gone to such lengths, and have so exaggerated that method as to have rendered it supremely false, ridiculous, and incomprehensible. In fact, things have got to such a pass to-day that hair looks like anything but hair—more like stalactites or beehives, salad or whipped cream; and this last the hair made by some of the imitators and exaggerators of that peculiar way of seeing nature particularly resembles. At the great exhibition at Paris one saw both master and scholars; or it would be better to say, the initiator and the imitators. Vela with his sobriety of purpose, full of life, here and there with rough-and-ready touches as art and taste counsel, and nature and harmony teach—the others, with little taste, great self-reliance, and equal audacity, striving their best to muddle up everything together in a topsy-turvy fashion. Taste, which is an individual sentiment, was reduced to a system, or rather a manner; sobriety was transformed into hardness, and a studied neglect of certain parts, exchanged for a systematic and excessive carelessness; and on the contrary, as if in contrast, an affected imitation of little folds, bands, lace, and polished beads and necklaces, the delight and admiration of women and children, little and big.

At the exhibition in Paris, amongst the fops and the milliners this alluring kind of work was received with enthusiasm, because a novelty always makes a greater impression on the frivolous; but serious people of good taste, as well as the judges, did not allow themselves to be attracted by such superficiality. It is true, however, that they were too severe with works of merit, and if it had not been that the limited number of prizes prevented them from being more liberal, the jury that I belonged to would have been to blame. But it is not requisite for me to repeat here what I said on sculpture, and what I wrote officially on that exhibition.

I became acquainted at that time with the best French artists, and they showed me almost brotherly kindness. I sat at their meetings at the Academy, of which I had been a member since 1863, and was afterwards raised to the rank of corresponding member, which is the highest

honour the Academy can confer. Although unworthy
to do so, I had Giovacchino Rossini's seat.

Rossini's house was the genial meeting-place of all
there was of most distinguished then in Paris, not only
of the musical class, but of the artistic and literary.
He had music, and often sat down to the piano and
accompanied his inedited songs. I remember two of
singular beauty; one most sad in subject, words, and
notes, of a father from whom his little son had been
stolen. It was a lament, refined, delicate, and touching,
and at the end of every verse came the *ritornello*—" *Chi
l' avesse trovato il mio piccino !*" The words, I was told,
were by Castellani of Rome. The other song was brilliant, strong, thrilling. It was an outburst of love, where
a Tyrolese *jodel* was interpolated and sung by that brilliant
imaginative genius Gustave Doré. Here one met with
choice conversation, fruitful, instructive, amiable, and
vivacious, from which one came forth with the mind
more elevated and a greater warmth at heart; but . . .

To that exhibition I sent a plaster cast of my bas-
relief representing the "Triumph of the Cross," the
marble group of the " Pietà," and the model for the base
of the Egyptian Vase. For these works the great medal
of honour was conferred upon me. In painting, Professor Ussi had the same great medal for his picture "La
Cacciata del Duca d'Atene." Domenico Morelli for his
"Torquato Tasso," and Vincenzo Vela for his " Dying
Napoleon," obtained the first-class gold medal, but they
also deserved to have had the great medal.

A fine genius is Domenico Morelli, as well as a loyal
and generous friend, for he greatly rejoiced when Ussi
obtained the great prize for Italian painting; and I
remember that he said, "As long as there is the great
prize, be it awarded to myself, Ussi, or any one else,

it is of small consequence as long as Italy does not fall behind. Long live Art and Italy ! "

For the matter of that, one art (I speak of painting) was most worthily represented, and brought forward a virgin element—subject to discussion and confirmation, it is true, yet fruitful of good result, such as recalling art to its fundamental principle, which is the imitation of nature, and relieving young men from the conventional trammels learnt on the benches of the Academy (I wish I could say learnt in the past), making them breathe a more ventilated, healthy air, placing before their eyes that infinite variety and beauty of which nature is composed in all its parts, in all its effects, and in all its forms—in the heavens, in the sea, on the hills, in the plains, in the forests, in the animals and in men—and every one of these things always varying according to light, according to the quietness or the emotions of nature, according to temperament, to the habits of animals and men ; all of which things are so well taught by nature to those holding a constant firm will to study her. This element, I say, appeared with but slight deviations at the world's exhibition in Paris, and did good. It rejuvenated art, and lifted it out of some conventionalities, whilst it placed others in bad repute. But enough of this for the present; let us speak of something else.

One of the reasons that spurred me on to write these memoirs is this: Allowing that my works may with time not be entirely forgotten, I have wished to register them all in this book, that it should not occur after a certain time that some copy, some imitation, or unknown piece of sculpture, more or less praiseworthy than mine, should be attributed to me. For this reason, from the first I have mentioned even such works as are of no great size and importance, and will continue to do so, excluding, be it understood, reproduction, which would carry me to too great lengths. · The Signora Maria Galeotti, *nata* Petrovitz, ordered from me a life-size group of her grandchildren, sons of Prince Trabia.   This group reminds me of that most unfortunate robbery that I have spoken of further back, and this is why I am reminded of it.   In the closet where I kept the money shut up that was stolen from me, there was a little of everything, papers, designs, tools, books, medals, and various little trinkets, that were respected —that is, not taken away, for they were scattered about on the floor.   In this closet I also kept my clothes ; and for convenience, or out of carelessness, amongst other things I had left a straw hat there.   This straw hat of mine the thieves had put on the head of one of the little ones in the Trabia group, and it would have been really ridiculous to see the statuette of that little boy with my great straw hat hiding half of his head, had it only been at another time, because even now (and a good many years have passed), only to think of it — no, indeed, it does not make me laugh !   And to think that of those gentlemen thieves, for there were several, some escaped the claws of justice, and some must have come out of " college " by this time, and if by chance they meet me, may smile to themselves under their beards at my simplicity.   So goes the world ; it is so fashioned, and has always been the same, even from the so-called prehistoric ages, and no instruction, either more or less obligatory, will change it one atom.   As for me, when I am Minister of " Justice and Mercy " (devil take it, why not?) I will have engraved upon all the corners where one now reads " Stick no bills," the eighth commandment, " Thou shalt not steal ; or if so, the whip will be administered

and plenty of it;" and to my colleagues in favour of
progress who rise up in arms against me I will answer:
"A little luxury as regards the whip, my good gentlemen,
will bring about great economy as regards the prisons
and domiciliary compulsion, and what is more, will
bring about a considerable rise in the funds—of public
security. But it is said the lash degrades humanity.
Perhaps it is degraded less by theft? In times not
very remote, theft was punished much more severely
even when it was not a very grave matter; but if it was
grave and accompanied by the breaking open of drawers,
the thieves were hanged outright. Certainly this punishment was excessive, Draconian, and in a word barbar-
ous; and yet, in those days Arnolfo built, Giotto painted,
and Dante wrote his immortal poem. Be it as it may,
this is most certain, that thieves were then conspicuous
by their very scarcity, whereas to-day they shine by their
frequency; and *vice versâ*, Arnolfo, Giotto, and Dante
then existed, *e questo è quanto*, as Marchese Colombi
would say."

Count Antonio Pallavicini, a man cut out after the
old-fashioned stamp,—one of the few who in their
hearts keep to the religion of gratitude and affectionate
remembrance of their dear relations,—gave me the
order for a statue of his grandfather, Marshal Pallavicini,
who was in the Austrian service under the reign of
Maria Teresa. The Count told me an anecdote of this
excellent grandfather that I wish to repeat, so that one
may see how, though in a foreign service, the heart—I
will not say of an Italian, for Italy was hardly spoken of
then, but—of a Genoese and good republican beat.
Here it is: The Republic of Genoa—I know not on
what question with Austria—had become discontented,
and threatened to resist by force the pretension of that

powerful Empress, who, either because she was by nature careless and unmindful of public virtue, or because she thought of obtaining a better result, decreed that Marshal Pallavicini should move at the head of an army to put down Genoese arrogance. But this brave soldier—this worthy patriot—on coming into the presence of the sovereign, took off his sword, and placing it on the table, said with calm dignity—

"Your Majesty, it is impossible for me, a Genoese, to make war against my own country; and I therefore to-day give up this sword that I have so often used in the defence of your empire, that it may not be stained by the blood of my brothers." At which the Empress smilingly answered—

"Take back your sword, that is so well suited to you, and that you use so valorously; and as your service is denied us in reducing to obedience your dear but obstinate brothers, be at least our envoy to arrange the difficulties and treat of peace." And peace was concluded.

It must be agreed that the subject was a fine one and a worthy one, and the statue was made and placed in the cemetery of the Certosa at Bologna; but the above-mentioned anecdote, that I would have so willingly treated in bas-relief as portraying vividly the character of this personage, was not given me to carry out, because the base was entirely occupied by long Latin inscriptions that the Count would at all costs have engraved upon it, to set forth the whole family history, and the reasons for his gratitude and the erection of the monument.

About that time I had to make a little monumental memorial of Frate Girolamo Savonarola. The reason for my having this order was this,—that in Germany—

I do not remember in what town—a monument had
been put up to Luther, and one of the figures that
adorned this monument was Fra Girolamo Savonarola ;
and how much to the purpose, all, excepting those
good Germans, can see, for they know Savonarola as
well as I do the Emperor of the Mississippi. The
promoters of this work were Gino Capponi, Bettino
Ricasoli, Niccolò Tommaseo, Raffaello Lambruschini,
Augusto Conti, Cesare Guasti, and Isidoro del Lungo.
I assisted at their meetings, and the idea that prevailed was to make the statue of Savonarola and place
it in the cloisters of St Mark ; but this intention we did
not fulfil, because another commission had already been
formed with the same purpose of doing honour to Savonarola, and this had already asked for and obtained the
place in the cloister, the more readily as the statue was
already made by Professor Enrico Pazzi. We therefore
had to change our project, and after many propositions
it was decided that the monument should consist of a
bas-relief and bust to be placed in the friar's cell. This
was done accordingly, and there it is to be found. The
subject of the bas-relief is Savonarola before the Gon-
faloniere and Priori of the Comune, reading the Government statutes proposed by him for the Florentine
Republic. On one of the sides or flanks of the bas-
relief is the youth Savonarola in pensive attitude medi-
tating leaving the world and dedicating himself to mon-
astic life, and on the other one are represented the last
moments of his life when he is on the way to his
martyrdom. The bust is in bronze.

Six years have not passed since the honour befell me of
sitting amongst those famous men who wanted this work
to be made by me, and three of them are already dead.
Gino Capponi, Tommaseo, and·Lambruschini—they are

dead, but their names and their works live, and will live as long as Truth and Good are loved and revered.

In 1873 the Universal Exhibition at Vienna took place, and I was named on the jury in the Italian section on sculpture, in company with my dearest friend Giovanni Strazza, so early lost to his family, to art, and to his country, which he so honoured and loved. On an occasion like this I had the means of knowing the clear acumen and kind heart of my illustrious colleague, be it either in his judgment on works of art, or in his intimate relation of friendship with our colleagues.

I will not speak of that great gay city, nor of the works of art in which she is so rich, nor of the Pinacoteca, her galleries and magnificent library — for this is not what I have undertaken, and these are things that can be found in the guide-books; and even if I wished to make some observations about them, it would be impossible for me to do so, because at that time I was most unhappy in the recent loss of my dear daughter Luisina; and therefore, alone and far from my family, I felt a void around me, and a most vivid desire to see them again, so that I looked at everything most hurriedly and through a veil of sadness and anguish.

I was lodged at the Hotel Britannia on the Schiller-platz, on the fourth floor, up one hundred and thirty-seven steps, in a small room, even smaller than that of my own maid-servant; there was only one window, and this opened on an inner court. The furniture consisted of a little bed, too small, but soft and sufficiently clean; a table, two chairs, a wardrobe, a looking-glass, a dressing-table—and that was all. All this for the miserable sum of ten *lire* a-day. I will say nothing about the meals; but the breakfast, I mean the early one of coffee and milk, a roll and butter, was sixty *kreutzers*—a *lira* and a half; and with the little refreshment of ice in your water (it was in June), twenty *kreutzers* more— half a *lira*. A cigar was half a *lira*, the washing and doing up of a shirt one *lira*, an ice one *lira*, and so on to your taste. For the matter of that, if I had had a little of the good-humour that my Italian companions Petrella, Boito, Govi, Bonghi, Palizzi, Mussini, Cantoni, Colombo, and Mariani had, without counting Jorick, who had to give and to spare, I should have remained there longer, and should have amused myself—for the city is really beautiful, most animated and bright, especially in the evening, well lighted, with fine theatres and music. Oh, for music, you must hear it at Vienna! I do not mean by music German music—for on the contrary, I love our own Italian; but I speak of the execution, of which we have (setting aside exceptions) but a most imperfect idea. It cannot be otherwise. There the musician has an assured position. There there is an institute where he is trained to be a professor of music—that is to say, as far as execution goes—where music is provided for, and nothing else is taught. During the day he studies, and in the evening he plays, and the next day the same thing over again, and so on until the day comes for receiving holy unction. I defy any one, therefore, not to play well! I heard one Sunday, at the St Stephen's Cathedral, music so sad and so sweet that I was almost carried away by it, it seemed as if it were a sweet and loving lament of the angels. These seemed not to be the voices of the instruments of this world, but a something superhuman, celestial, that filled one with emotion. Oh, music comes directly from heaven! The harmony of sounds is something of a more intimate, secret, and mysterious nature than the harmony of lines and colours; for what constitutes the beauty, harmony, and attraction of exterior things, is not there alone in appearance, but radiates from the spirit within : there-fore it is that the beautiful, emanating from the divine harmony of sound, is more exquisite and more living, because it is the manifestation of the soul and the spirit without encumbrance. Our intellect grasps hold of it and falls in love with it, because it is itself also a part of that immortal beauty to which it feels an irresistible attraction to unite itself. But the impression of the beautiful, visible or invisible, we receive imperfectly, because the senses through which it is revealed to us are only so fitted as to enable us to receive it in part— that part which gives us pleasure, for its entire splendour would kill us. Harmony has laws of order and unity, and relations and affinities, inexplicable. We feel that certain combinations of notes express sorrow, others joy, others love, and so on ; but given without that order and unity, without those relations and affinities, they express nothing, and are only unpleasant sounds. Why is it so ? Oh, friend Biaggi, if I speak profanely, make the sign of the cross and correct me !

The same can be said of all things that have form and colour, that are animate or inanimate. There is in nature, in the configuration of certain parts of the country and certain places, a something, I know not what, of gloominess and melancholy, that, when we look at them, fills us with sadness. Others, on the contrary, are bright, happy, and joyous. It is just the same with one's self, and not by reason of the more or less fertility in this or sterility in that, nor by reason of the state of one's soul, but entirely from the effect of lines and colours. And so it is, again, with things animate. There are beautiful animals, and animals that seem ugly — some, in fact, absolutely repulsive—and why ? Perhaps

because they are harmful? Yet no; for there are
most beautiful animals that are really bad and most
dangerous—for example, the lion, the tiger, and the
leopard; whilst others, as for instance a spider, a
mouse, a tarantula, a black beetle, a worm, and a
scorpion, which do no harm, or very little, seem to us
so ugly, so repulsive, that we are obliged to turn away
from them.   Be it observed that this sort of aversion is
felt the most by those natures that have the most exquisite feeling and love of the beautiful—the reason
being that these animals have in their form a harmony
certainly necessary to the universal order of nature, but
most ungrateful to our eyes; whereas the lion, tiger,
leopard, and above all, the horse, are beautiful and
attractive to them.   Therefore, in nature, to our way of
seeing, there is the beautiful and the ugly—there are
beings that attract and others that repulse us.   "Certainly there are," I am answered.   "What sort of a discovery do you think that you have made?"   Very well,
I am delighted with this answer, because the above
tirade was made by me for the benefit of those who
affirm that all is beautiful in nature,—in fact, their formula is, *nature is beauty*.   Instead of which, I, with
what I have said and am about to say, would wish to
demonstrate that ugliness has a negative harmony all
her own, and only in conformity with her cold and
obtuse vitality; and therefore, nothing of it radiating
on us, we are not attracted by it, but rather repulsed.
In as far as the animal is perfect in living harmony,
so much the greater the light that emanates from him.
Man, who is the most perfect of animate creation,
radiates so much the greater *light* in proportion as the interior harmony of order, of justice, and of love makes its
impress upon and forms the body that encloses it.   In

the serenity of the brow one observes the majesty of order, in the erect bearing of the person and the temperate firm use of words the dictates of justice, and love is in the intense calm look of the eyes and almost happy expression of the mouth, which, with the eyes, are, as it were, the windows of the soul, from which that beauty radiates that attracts and impels to admiration and to love.

Man, therefore, is the most living manifestation of the beautiful, and he is also the being that most thirsts for the enjoyment of it. He looks for it everywhere—in the splendour of the heavens, over the expanse of the sea, on the high mountain-sides, in the mysterious shadows of the forests, and in the solitude of the valleys, when the dying sun casts languidly over them its violet light. At night, when man and beast rest after the fatigues of the day, and silence and quiet begin, he feels a tender harmony, delicate and mysterious, as the memory of the days of innocence, or as the hope of a future life. The harmony of night is, as it were, the breath of sleeping nature.

Look, now, into what a labyrinth I have been dragged by the music I heard at St Stephen's ! The campanile of this cathedral is pointed and very high; it can be seen from all parts of the city. One sees at once that it is the campanile of the *ecclesia major*. I wished to see it. The cathedral is always the first thing that attracts the stranger's curiosity when he arrives in a place, because therein is expressed the religious sentiment of the people who have built it, which is the first of all sentiments, and then follows that of the citizen. First the cathedral was made by the people of old, and then the town-hall, and in the same order I also look at them and think of them. I wished to see it, therefore ; but being at a distance, I stopped a cab and said to the driver that

I wanted to go there.   Bravo ! and without knowing a
bit of German !   I told him in three languages—in
Italian, in French, and in Latin (macaronic, of course) ;
but it was dense darkness to him.   I pointed with my
hand to the campanile in the distance, and this time
he understood !   He answered, "*Ja, ja,*" and whipping
up his horses, off he went for some time ; but as we
never arrived, I again pointed to the campanile.   "*Ja,
ja,*" and on we went, but away from the place I indicated.   Then I stopped him, paid him, and got out.
On the venture, I jumped into an omnibus, just to leave
the man, who was going who knows where, returned to
the centre, and got out at Oberring.   There I found
a friend, who took me in a short time on foot to St
Stephen's, where I heard that wonderful music, the remembrance of which still excites me to ecstasy.   This
does not often happen to me, but it does sometimes.

From there—that is, not from my ecstasies, but from
St Stephen's—I went to the Church of the Augustins,
where Canova's famous monument in honour of Maria
Christina is.   As to its being beautiful, I say nothing,
but an artist who was with me extolled it to the seventh
heaven ; though to me, with the music of St Stephen's
still in my ears, it seemed that Canova in other works
had arrived at greater perfection, both as regards general
conception and as regards sentiment of truth.   But, I
repeat, it may have been the music that made it seem
to me—and I say so in all reverence—a little conventional.   I was there in Vienna, however, to form part of
the jury on the sculpture of to-day, and not to criticise
the art of the past ; so that a little want of appreciation
or a judgment too lightly given may be forgiven me.
For the matter of that, Canova is Canova, and the braying
of donkeys, as the proverb says, does not reach heaven.

2 D

CHAPTER XXII.

HE Palace of the Exhibition was built on the Prater. It cost twenty millions of florins (fifty millions of *lire*), without counting, be it remembered, the sum expended by other nations on their special buildings. It is not my intention to describe this immense edifice, and all the smaller ones around it, in that large and most delightful Prater. I will not even speak of the Exhibition, excepting only as regards my department — that of sculpture.

Without expectations or merits on my part I was elected President of the department in sculpture; and this honour was most prized by me, because it enabled me to hasten on the work in our section with all the alacrity compatible with the number and importance of the works submitted to our judgment; and this, indeed, was not a trifling matter, for, between statues and groups, there were two hundred and fifteen, without counting large and small busts. There was a great deal of Ger-

man sculpture; but with few exceptions, it was somewhat hard and conventional. Ours, with some honourable exceptions,—and amongst them Monteverde's
group of Jenner, fine in the choice of subject, well
grouped, and admirably modelled — and a few other
works,—were like the usual old woman's tale, trivial
in conception and ungainly in form. It is painful to
say so, but the French sculpture at this Exhibition
surpassed, and more than surpassed, ours; and if it
proved possible to divide the number of medals between
the French and us, it is due to the condescension of
the French members of the jury, Dubois and Masson, to
the Germans, and to my obstinacy in upholding our art
as much as I possibly could.

Ugh! these blessed universal exhibitions! What good
do they do to art, to true art, to great art? None
whatever. I believe, at the best, they only bring about
the sale of some smart humoristic or coarse statuette,
and nothing more. I am aware that Vela's " Napoleon
I.," which was sold in Paris, will be brought up in
opposition to this. That is an exception to the rule;
and then—who knows?—if Napoleon III. had not been
on the throne, perhaps Vela's beautiful statue would
have come back to the artist's studio at Turin. Many
fine Italian statues returned at that time; and did not
the " Jenner " come back from Vienna? These universal
exhibitions—let us say it in plain words—are fairs and
markets, in which the merchandise most appreciated is
something odd, humoristic, or ridiculous. But of this
I have spoken elsewhere, and do not like to retrace my
steps.

I have said that the office of president was grateful
to me because it enabled me to hasten on the work in
our section; but I have not given the reason for this

hurry. The poor artists, the greater part of them
strangers, that had never seen Vienna, felt a longing
to do so; and when at mid-day, after three hours of
work, I suspended the meeting until one o'clock, they
said to me, "Mr President, have a little patience;
be reasonable. We have never seen anything of this
city. We will work as much as you wish in the mornings, but only let us be free the rest of the day." And
I answered: "Have a little patience yourselves. Let
us work now that we are at it: it is for this reason we
have come here. As soon as we have finished, we will
rest and amuse ourselves, and will enjoy all the beautiful
objects in the town and in the country; but now that
we are here, we must stick to work. Good-bye; I shall
see you again shortly—at one o'clock." And with very
long faces they went away. But why, wherefore, all this
hurry—this uninterrupted work, without rest? This is
why: I was there alone; and when I am alone, away
from home, without one of my daughters, whatever may
be the city or country, however beautiful and attractive,
everything bores me to a superlative degree. When, in
answer to my colleagues, I said that as soon as our
work was finished we would amuse ourselves and see
and enjoy all the wonders of the town, I repeated men-
tally to myself, I will take the fastest direct train, and
without leaving the railway carriage, in thirty-six hours
will get back to Florence; and I did so.

Notwithstanding all my persistence, we took, however, one or two half-days' rest, and each one of us went
the way he liked best to satisfy his desire of amusing
himself. As for me, I wrote long letters home, and in
the evening went to the theatre, where they were singing
(and really singing) Wagner's 'Lohengrin'; or joined, in
brotherly symposiums, the Italian, German, Hungarian,

or French members of our jury. The Viennese and
Hungarian members gave us a dinner, and it went off in
a most gay and friendly fashion : the toasts burst forth,
one after the other, in a bright rapid line of fire. There
is no doubt about it—Art fraternises all nations. Our
speeches, half French and half Italian and Hungarian-
Latin, were spoken freely, and without giving even a
thought that a phrase or word might offend the political
opinion or oratorical taste of any one. Everything was
good, everything applauded, and we drank to everything. I remember a Hungarian artist, who, drinking
to the toast of Art and the Italians, said that Italy had
always been great; and if, in days gone by, she had been
able to glory in Michael Angelo, to-day she gloried in
Garibaldi ! And we drank even to this, although the
comparison seemed to us to be very far-fetched. But
I repeat, when once we opened our mouth, it did not
much matter what came out of it. I also spoke, and
was applauded ; but if I wanted to repeat what I said,
I should have to draw upon my imagination, because I
don't remember a word of it.

We enjoyed other evenings of feast and merriment,
but none like this one. We were invited to a dinner
given by the Italian General Commissioner, which went
off most splendidly, but was naturally more dignified.
We were all Italians, but not all artists ; for, in fact, the
greater number were scientific men—and where there are
scientific men, all is at an end, and seriousness at once
walks in. The imaginative, frisky, and reckless words of
the artist do not venture to come out at such meetings ;
and the talk there gains as much in rhetoric as it loses in
living art, sincerity, and unexpectedness.

We were also invited by his Imperial Highness the
Archduke Ranieri to an entertainment, which was most

splendid, cordial, and brilliant. The Archduke talked
to every one in his own language; and if he expressed
himself with the same exactness and propriety to the
English, Russians, or Spaniards, as he did to us Italians
and to the French, he is really a wonderful polyglot. At
this *fête* something happened to me which proves that
the Viennese cabmen are more quarrelsome than ours.
This is how it was. I got into the cab at the hotel,
and said that I wanted to go to the palace of his Highness Archduke Ranieri, to remain there two hours, and
then return to the hotel; and for this the price of six
florins (fifteen *lire*) was agreed upon. Having stayed my
time at the *fête*, I descended to look for my charioteer.
He was not there. To be sure, the cab was there, and
the poor beast in harness seemed to be deep in thought
or sleeping; but the coachman was not there. He was
looked for everywhere, in all the neighbouring beer-
houses, but could nowhere be traced. So in a rage I
had to go up again, and coming down about half an
hour afterwards, I called him, but he was not there.
The poor beast stood with his nose nearly on the
ground, I do not know whether more from sleepiness or
hunger; and I in a rage, as may well be imagined, got
inside the cab to wait for him. Finally, after about half
an hour the man returned, and I abused him roundly;
but it was like speaking to the wall, for he understood
nothing, and off he drove. On arriving at the hotel I
put the six florins briskly into his hand; he refused to
take them, and I could not understand why. The porter
of the hotel intervened, and said that the cabman had
agreed to wait at the *fête* for two hours, instead of which
I had kept him there three hours. I explained to the
porter the whole thing, and what a rascal he was! But
not to discuss the matter any longer, I paid even for the

hour that I had to wait that *canaille's* convenience. Really I would have paid anything to have been able to say two or three words after my own heart in German to the miserable scamp.

My duty was now ended. I gave a last look at the beautiful Schiller Platz, where my hotel was, saluted the Academy of Fine Arts, then building, and with open heart, filling my lungs with a great breath of country air, I flew in thought to beautiful Florence, to my family, and to the studies I loved. I plunged into the most comfortable railway carriage that I could find, and never again turned to the right or to the left. I think that I was the first of the Italian jury that returned to our beautiful country.

At this time I was making the monument to Duke Silvestro Camerini that had been ordered from me by his illustrious and most noble nephew, Count Luigi. Senatore Achilli Mauri had first spoken to me of it on his behalf, and had shown me a design by Signor Gradenigo of Padua, in which there were to be two statues that the Count wished me to make. The design did not please me, and I answered that I would make the monument, but that I wished to compose it after my own fashion. The Count was content. I made a design; he saw it, it pleased him, and all was settled in a friendly way by a few frank words, without all those precautions of contract, seal register, witnesses, and caution that are invented by distrust to protect one from rascals. It is thus that honest men deal with honest men ; and of such is Count Luigi, and of such by God's mercy am I, and I can proclaim it loudly in the broad light of the sun. I am certain that, of the many persons who have given me commissions, not one has had any question with me, nor even the slightest feeling of unpleasantness ! The thought of this, and the certainty of being able to proclaim it *coram populo*, is to me a consolation so complete and grateful, that it forms, so to speak, my happiness.

Amongst those who have given me commissions, Count Luigi Camerini has been one of the most courteous—a true friend. Every time that I went to Padua or Piazzola on account of the work I was engaged on, besides the glad welcome that he and his amiable wife gave me, he managed to arrange some excursions for our pastime and pleasure—now to Venice, now to Passagno, now to Vicenza, and sometimes even farther ; and he pushed courtesy and friendship to the extent of taking us all as far as Turin, on the occasion of the inauguration of Cavour's monument. As I said, to do this, besides being amiable and kind, one must also be rich, and he is rich indeed. I remember that one day, during one of these excursions, we found ourselves in a first-class railway carriage with the Princess Troubetzkoi and her husband, Duke Talleyrand. We all talked together more or less about everything—all except the Duke, who gathered himself up in his corner, with his travelling-cap pulled down on his forehead, intent on reading a French newspaper. He had never lifted his eyes on us, so absorbed did he seem in his reading.

I do not know how it was that the conversation fell on the heaviness of the taxes. I am greatly afraid that it was I who started the subject, because on this key I am wonderfully eloquent ; I storm about the laws, agents, cashiers, everybody, and everything.

"Let them lay a heavy hand," I was saying, "on play, on luxury, on vices, on property, but leave in peace the labour, industry, and talent that are the bonds of civilisation and health, because the public conscience rebels against this."

The good Duke did not even move ; for him it was as if I was neither in the wrong nor the right. My friend Camerini, perhaps to allay my indignation, quietly smiled and said—

" You are right ; certainly these taxes are very heavy. But what can one do about it ? One must pay, and that is all——"

" Certainly," I continued, repeating his favourite word, " one must pay—and I pay; but it is too much —these taxes are too high."

" I agree, I agree. . . . Just imagine that I pay annually in taxes (beyond the indirect ones, you understand), two hundred and fifty thousand *lire !* "

At the mention of this sum the Duke turned slightly towards Camerini, looked fixedly at him a short time over his spectacles, then took them off very slowly, folded them and put them in their case, set aside his newspaper, and entered into a conversation with him that only came to an end when we separated. " Oh the power of gold !" said I to myself. . . . Let us return to the monument.

It is composed thus : on the first foundation a great urn, above which rises the base, on which is placed the seated statue of the Duke in a thoughtful attitude, dressed in the clothes he wore, and wrapped in a cloak. At the sides of the urn, which form two semicircles, are two statues. Beneficence is standing and offering money to a youthful workman, who, in an attitude of affectionate gratitude, wishes to kiss the hand that with such loving wisdom has lifted him out of misery, and ennobled him by the sanctity of labour, so that this payment is only the legitimate recompense of his work. This group

represents one of the virtues of Duke Camerini, who
made use of his very large rent-roll to alleviate the
misery of his fellow-beings, and give them encouragement and work; and certainly no one more than he
could feel the usefulness of work, because from being a
humble workman (although of a respectable family) he
elevated himself to the highest rank of society, and to
riches as honourable as they were great. Corresponding to this statue, on the other side kneels Gratitude,
who scatters flowers on the urn; and although gratitude
is one of the virtues that adorned that great man, as I
shall explain hereafter, yet this statue refers to that sentiment of affectionate remembrance by which his nephew,
Count Luigi Camerini, wished to honour the memory of
his munificent uncle. The lower base is ornamented by
a bas-relief, representing Duke Camerini when, during
one of the inundations of the Po, an immense population
of that desolate country were left without a roof to their
heads and without bread, he rescued them, encouraged
them, and helped them, giving bread and work to all,
ordering the work of new embankments immediately
to be undertaken, avoiding most wisely by so doing
greater disaster, and saving from misery and hunger
that wretched population. This bas-relief is an admirable work of Professor Luigi Ceccon, of Padua; and
this, as well as the execution of all the architectural and
ornamental parts of the monument, Count Camerini and
I intrusted to him.

The moral character of Duke Camerini is worthy of
being remembered and honoured. It is certainly not
my task to relate his life, but I cannot pass by in silence
a most notable instance in it, the knowledge of which
strengthened the study and affection that I put into
the modelling and chiselling of this monument. When

the youth Silvestro, in the capacity of simple labourer,
worked at I know not what improvement of land in the
neighbourhood of Ferrara, he used to go during the
hour of rest to a small eating-house to recruit his
strength with his usual temperance. It happened one
day that he found himself without money, and as he
was a daily customer, frankly, with an honest man's
conscience, he said to the host, "I will pay you to-
morrow." But·this man, who was hard and brutal,
answered that "when one has no money, one should
not order anything to eat;" to which the youth was
about to reply, when a young gentleman, who happened
by chance to be shooting in those parts, and had come
in to take some refreshment, seeing the embarrassment
of the young labourer and the hardness of the host,
tossed a bit of money on to the counter, saying to the
latter, "Take your pay for what this man has eaten
here." The host took the money and returned the
change; but the excellent gentleman said, "No; give
the rest of the money to this youth. He seems to me
to have the air of being an honest man, and he can
use it another day when his own money fails him."
It was not such a small matter either, for the money
he had given to be changed was a golden *Genova*. Then
on one side excuses were made and restitution offered,
whilst on the other a mild but determined insistence,
which ended in the shaking of hands and leave-taking.
From that day forward Silvestro Camerini had no more
need to go on credit, not because the remainder of that
piece of gold could place him for ever beyond necessity,
but because those insulting and brutal words had been a
lesson to him, with his high and noble spirit, never again
to place himself in a similar position. Camerini went
out from that house much moved in spirit and full of

gratitude towards the gentleman, whose name he inquired and ever kept in his memory. In the meantime,
by good conduct, economy, and work, he was able to
save something ; and as by nature he had a mind much
superior to his condition, he was able to take upon himself the direction of some works, and always advancing
in his activity, economy, and good administration, he
gradually made a considerable fortune, all of which he
put into land. But the noble gentleman who had so
opportunely helped him, either through bad administration, too much liberality, or some other reason, lost his
fortune, and was obliged to sell all his lands to pay
his debts. One day the last villa belonging to him, and
the one he cared most for, was about to be put up to
auction ; and that day, so full of sadness for him, turned
out perhaps the brightest and happiest of his life.
Camerini, who had already become rich, bid at the
auction for it, and having obtained it, went to the unhappy gentleman and presented it to him. His surprise,
joy, and incredulity are more easily imagined than described. He said, " What is the meaning of this? In
what way? Wherefore? Is it perhaps a restitution?
So much has been stolen from me that——"   " Yes,
really," answered Camerini, " it is a restitution, but not
of anything stolen." And he then told him, or rather
reminded him, of the youth that he had benefited so
many years before. The worthy gentleman at first held
back, and wished to refuse the gift ; but at last overcome
by emotion and admiration, he wept and embraced his
friend—a true friend indeed, for all the others he had
known in his prosperity had disappeared with it.

This anecdote deserves to be told, because it draws to
the life the lovable, grateful, and most liberal character
of Duke Camerini. It was told me by Count Antonio

Pallavicini of Bologna, the friend and contemporary of Duke Camerini and the other gentleman, whose name, I regret to say, I do not remember. The anecdote that I have just told, and many others that illustrated the character of this great man, as well as the nobility and generosity of his worthy nephew, who intrusted to me the execution of this monument, spurred me on and facilitated my undertaking.

If the reader has a good memory, he will remember that elsewhere I have spoken of my offers to execute works for their mere cost—that is to say, my proposals to give my time, work, and study *gratis et amore Dei.* He will remember, also, that these offers were not accepted, and that having been taught by so many lessons of this kind, I advised young artists to abjure and chase from their mind these Utopian ideas that experience had fully shown me could not be carried out. To confirm them in this opinion, I must now add a new and more striking instance of a work offered by me that was not accepted; and I trust that the account of this new fact will not be wanting in importance, and will serve as a good lesson.

When my excellent friend Commendator Giuseppe Poggi had finished the beautiful Piazzale Michael Angelo, and before the inauguration of the monument designed by him, with the statues of the divine artist himself, had taken place (and this occurred before the centenary), he proposed that the statue of Michael Angelo should be placed in a commanding position under the middle arch of the Loggia that fronts on the Piazzale ; and it was his intention (for which I thank him from the bottom of my heart) that this statue should be made by me. Knowing, however, that on account of its colossal proportions, as well as the importance of the subject, it would require no small expense, and as even then the municipality foresaw its present straits, he said to me, in a pleasant and friendly manner, that it was his hope, as well as that of others, that I would make the statue for its mere cost. "I am ready," said I to myself. "I like the subject, and I can satisfy my friend in his legitimate pride of citizen and artist, and also place there a sign of my veneration for Michael Angelo, and a testimony of affection and disinterestedness to my country, but at no slight sacrifice, it is true—that is to say, by working at least a year *gratis et amore Dei.*" I am mistaken; there is something else I should add—that is the income-tax and tax on the exercise of my art, &c., that the tax agent would naturally have insisted on exacting, even if it had been proved to him that I was working to gain nothing. But I had given my word, and said I am ready; and when I say I am ready, I stick to it. In the meanwhile time passed, the centenary drew near, and the municipality decided nothing about the statue; and, so far, all was well—it meant that they found it inconvenient to give even those few thousand *lire* required for the marble and the roughing out of the statue; and wished to save them. About this I say nothing, for, in fact, I am in favour of saving; but now comes the best of it. When the day for the famous centenary arrived, the festivities were conducted admirably, with an exhibition of all Michael Angelo's works, a visit to his tomb in Santa Croce, to his house, which is a most precious museum, and, at last, to the Piazzale, where the monument was inaugurated. There was music in the great hall of the Cinquecento at the Palazzo Vecchio, illuminations on the great Piazzale and on the Colli, and everything was done with the utmost order and decorum, thanks to the exquisite tact of our president of the committee for organising the centenary festivals, Commendatore Ubaldino Peruzzi. Among these festive meetings one was arranged to take place in the old Senate Hall, which had for its object the pronouncing of eulogies on the great artist ; and to all, the Academy of Fine Arts and the Della Crusca Academy were invited, as Michael Angelo was not only to be honoured as an artist supreme in the imitative arts, but also as a philosopher, literary man, and poet. This was splendidly done by the two Presidents of the Academy of Fine Arts and the Della Crusca Academy, Commendatore Emilio de' Fabris and Commendatore Augusto Conti. They were surrounded by the members of these two Academies united in solemn assembly, and the semicircle was filled by a crowd of distinguished artists, literary and scientific men, foreign and native, and was honoured by the presence of his Highness Prince Cazignano. My friend De' Fabris spoke of Michael Angelo as an architect, and my friend Conti enlarged upon him as philosopher, citizen, and poet. They had begged me to read a few words on that occasion ; but I, being aware of my insignificance, and, to speak frankly, my incapacity to think and speak on so great a subject, at first refused to do so; then I tried jotting down something in writing, and made my friend Luigi Venturi read it—and as he did not dislike what I had written, I accepted, and on the day before mentioned I read my little scrap of writing, in which I treated particularly of Michael Angelo as a sculptor.

That day the idea of the statue was again brought forward, and some of the gentlemen, in the name of the committee, came to my studio and asked me if I would agree to make the statue of Michael Angelo for the mere cost and expenses. I answered that I would, and added that I had promised to do so once before, but that no-

thing more had been done about it.   In the meanwhile
a subscription list was sent the rounds, and my illustrious
friends Meissonnier and Guillaume, who had come to
Florence for the centenary festivals, put their names down
each for a hundred *lire*.   And then, after all, as God
willed it, nothing more was done about it ; and in fact, on
the spot where the statue was to have been placed, there
is now a *café restaurant*, very clean and convenient,
and of a summer's evening it is enlivened by concerts of
a band of music.   Looking at the thing from this point
of view, it is certainly much more comfortable and amusing than to see a statue of Michael Angelo standing there.

The fact is, that there are sometimes fruitful enthusiasms and sometimes barren enthusiasms : the fruitful
enthusiasms are those in which one finds the quickest
and most perceptible enjoyment.   In these days (it was
1876) there were people running in crowds to see and
hear Signora Adelina Patti—spending an amount of
money that they would have had great difficulty in
spending on an object less sensible, or, rather, less en-
joyable, such as in fact a statue might be, that promises
to give you the rather meagre enjoyment, it is true, of
making its appearance two or three years after it has
taken the money out of your pocket.

It is true, however, that the enjoyment of song and
sound passes in a moment—its waves die upon the air,
and our ears catch their last echo—while the view of
a statue, with all its beauty and meaning, remains, so to
speak, to all eternity.   But this is a rather subtle and
abstract consideration that not all can understand.

Thinking over it well, I do not believe the *fiasco*
about the statue of Michael Angelo occurred for want of
enthusiasm for art or statuary, or much less for the subject.   The deuce take it ! Michael Angelo is out of the

question ; besides belonging to the world, he is a Florentine,—and then, too, enthusiasm has not been wanting in
any town in Italy, and certainly not in Florence, even
when it has been a question of immortalising in marble
men oftentimes very unlike Buonarroti. Besides, did one
not see about this time, and in fact during these very
days, several thousands of *lire* got together for a bust of
Gino Capponi? And why was this? If I had asked to
make that statue, it might have been supposed that the
artist was not liked, and that no confidence was felt in
him ; but it was not so : in fact I was looked for and
even begged to make it, which is natural when one
desires to have work done for nothing but the pure cost
and expenses. Confidence in the artist, therefore, was
not wanting : there must have been some other reason,
and I have found it is this, that work asked for and
offered for nothing seems almost as if it had no attraction; no one wants it. One must, if one can, get as
much pay as possible. Listen to this other instance ;
they grow like cherries.

When I had made the " Christ after the Resurrection,"
for which my good friend Ferdinando Filippi di Buti gave
me the order, the idea came to the worthy syndic, Signor
Danielli, to erect in his village (which seemed as if it
ought to be sacred to Minerva, it was so buried in a
forest of olive-trees) a statue in honour of Professor del
Rosso, who had been such a worthy representative of
science and of his native place. The good and most
lively Signor Danielli was full of ardour to carry out
his project; and to obtain its success, he pressed me
to accept this commission at the smallest possible price,
almost for its mere cost.

I accepted. The subscription list was sent the rounds,
and I know that my illustrious friend Professor Conti,

an old pupil of Del Rosso, gave himself a great deal of trouble in getting subscriptions; but neither he nor any one else obtained the desired result, and the statue remains where it was—in the future. In the same way, it seems, ended the affair of the bust of Pius IX., that a pious committee in this city proposed to have cut in marble and placed in our cathedral.

So, as I have said, these instances grow like cherries.

Let us remember, although above I have spoken about the necessity of getting well paid, yet at times, either as a matter of duty, friendship, or gratitude, one can and one ought to work for little. I remember a young scholar of mine who enjoyed a little pension, given to him by a gentleman from his village, who, to enable the young man to work from life, went so far as to allow him to model his head, and, to encourage him, desired that he should put it into marble, —but before giving him the commission, wanted to know what the expense would be. The youth, in telling me this, asked me what he ought to ask for it. I answered, "You must ask nothing; the gentleman is over and above good to give you the pension. Would you also ask him to pay for the bust? You will give this answer: I have asked my master about the expense of the marble and the roughing of it out, and he has answered me that one hundred *lire* is necessary for the marble and two hundred for the roughing it out ; as to finishing it, I will finish it myself, and so learn to work on marble, because no one can call himself a sculptor who does not work on the marble himself."

But the youth showed no judgment, did not follow my advice, and asked the gentleman a thousand *lire*, and the avidity and ingratitude thus shown by the person he had benefited so disgusted him, that he did.

not let him make it.   When I heard how matters had
gone, I did not fail to call him an ass, and he really was
one.   Born and bred a peasant, he had learnt nothing
in town by mixing with educated young men.   He was
tall of person, and endowed with uncommon strength ;
he used to exercise himself—making it more a business
than a simple pastime—at the game of *forma*, and,
challenged or challenger, was always the winner.   He
died from breaking a blood-vessel in his chest ; and for
the matter of that, as no one was left behind to weep for
him, for he was an orphan, and as he had no talent or
judgment, it was better so.

Let us therefore understand each other.   One must
always get one's pay, excluding the case or cases of
gratitude like the one I have mentioned above, and even
between friends, there must not be one that gives and
the other that takes.   I remember now, many years ago,
that Luigi Acussini made my portrait, and I his ; and
later, Cisere painted my portrait and that of my wife,
and I made a bust of his wife, *amici cari e borsa del
pari*.   Presents don't answer well, and therefore it is
rare to find those who make them ; and if any one with
heart and no head does so, he makes a *fiasco*.

A singular taste, and one that I can enter into completely, is that of preparing one's own place of burial
whilst living ; and for those who can, besides the burial-
place, also the chapel and monument.   It does one
good to see, whilst living, the place where one will
sleep the last sleep.   Amongst those who agree with
me in this, besides Marchese Bichi Ruspoli of Siena, and
Signor Ferdinando Filippi di Buti—whose monuments I
made some fifteen years ago, and who are still living,
hale and hearty, so that I even think that the thought
of death and the sight of the monuments prolong their

lives—is the Baroness Favard de Langlade, who also wished to have her monument made; and after having had the illustrious architect Giuseppe Poggi construct the beautiful chapel in the park of the villa at Rovezzano, which is adorned by the beautiful paintings of Annibale Gatti, she ordered from me the monument wherein her body is to rest.

The difficulty of this kind of work is not to give umbrage to the modesty of the person who gives the commission. At first sight it seems like vanity and pride to order one's own monument; but besides the fact that he who orders a monument does not order it for himself alone, but also for his family, the artist composes his work in such a way as not to give the least offence by adulation and flattery, which is the more contemptible in the person who offers it in measure as the adulated person is in a high position. The artist, however, who has a proper respect for his own dignity, and wishes that of the person in question also to be respected, will find a way of making his work, even though it be grandiose, so as to enable both him and the person who is to die to look at each other in the face without blushing.

The subject that I treated for the Favard monument was the Angel of the Resurrection, who, poised on his wings, offers his hands to the dead woman, who is in the act of rising, to lead her to heaven. She has half lifted herself up on the sarcophagus where she was laid out, and her expression shows her happiness in awakening to eternal day. The only adulation—excusable, I think—that I offered to that lady was having made her appear younger than she was,—not more beautiful, for one can still see that she must have been most beautiful. I regret that this work of mine is almost hidden—first of

all, because it is far from town, as I have already said,
—at Rovezzano; for although the noble lady has given
orders to have it shown to any one who asks to see it,
yet the double difficulty of the distance and the asking
prevents many—those who are lazy and who are luke-
warm, who are the most in number—from being able
to see it. It is still worse as concerns my "Christ after
the Resurrection," which is on a hill in the neighbourhood of Buti, a little village, nearly hidden from view
and out of hand, between Pisa and Lucca.

CHAPTER XXIII.

NARRATED, all in its proper place, how it happened that I was not enabled to make King Victor Emmanuel's portrait; and it is necessary for me now to explain how I did not obtain the concession to make a bust of Pius IX. Marchese Pompeo Bourbon del Monte, the President of the Working Men's Catholic Association in Florence, had the intention of giving me an order to make a bust of the Pope, to place in a niche in our Duomo, with an inscription commemorative of the great pontiff's passage through Florence, and his consecration of four bishops there. Naturally the Pope was first asked whether he was willing that his bust should be made and should be placed in our Duomo. With both of these propositions the Pope showed his great satisfaction, and he was therefore asked the favour of giving some sittings to the sculptor; but on hearing my name, he refused to do so, because, having made Cavour's monument, he did not wish me to take his portrait. To speak the truth, this species of censure on the part of the Pope

was most unpleasant to me. As long as some of the prejudiced journalists of the extreme party, in blaming me for having executed this work, assailed me on the ground that some of the nude allegorical figures (just imagine, children of seven !) were obscene, I let it pass ; but the condemnation of the Holy Father was a great vexation to me. As Monsignore Archbishop Cecconi had been the intermediary, I wrote him a letter expressing my regret, and went over the story of the monument, and how I had accepted it, and what expression I had given to it, saying that I had not thought I was doing any harm, and that I was extremely pained to have met with the Holy Father's displeasure, and begging Monsignore to make known these sentiments of mine to the Pope. In fact the Pope heard of my letter, or at least a part of it, and answered that he had never doubted my sentiments or my good intentions, but for all that he was not willing to have his portrait taken by me ; and that, to prevent the matter from appearing *ad hominem*, he would not give permission for it to be made by any one else.

A few months after this, wishing to go to Naples to see the Italian Exhibition, I stopped on my way in Rome, and saw the Pope, but not in a private audience. Nevertheless, he spoke benevolently to me, and said, " Dear Duprè, what fine works are you doing now ? " I who, I must admit, never find myself embarrassed by any one, stood there perfectly nonplussed, and was not able to utter a word ; and that poor saintly old man, to put an end to my embarrassment, continued, " I pity you ; the political vicissitudes and the noises of war distract the mind of the artist, and are, in fact, opposed to the development of his genius." Then turning to my daughter, he said, "And you, too : well done, my sculptress ; I bless you together with your father."

It really gave me pleasure to see him again, and listen for the last time to that vibrating, and, at the same time, benevolent voice. Something within me told me that he would soon be missing to us; and in fact, barely eight months after, he died, and but a few days after the king, to whom, during his last moments, he had sent his benediction ; and report has it that he even said he would have gone himself to comfort the king, whom he personally loved, during his last hours, had he not been really so ill himself. These words of his gained for him the goodwill of those who were not his friends.

Now I must speak of the Exhibition at Naples, and most particularly of the naturalistic element that manifested itself there in sculpture. It deserves being studied with attention, so as to enable young artists of good purpose, and for whom I have most particularly written these memoirs, to acquire something that may be useful to them. Naturally the vast question of realism and idealism rises again to the surface. Those who know me, know that I am neither a realist nor an idealist, be it understood, as is generally intended and practised.

Idealism, in my opinion, is nothing else but a species of vision that the artist creates by strong love in his mind when he thinks of a given subject. Idealism is therefore the idea of the subject, and not in the least the idea of the parts of the form. It is true that even these are associated pleasantly together in the mind, but it is wrong and false to believe that we can grasp hold of them only by the help of memory, and without having nature before us. The idealist, as I should understand him, seeks in nature for the models appropriate to his idea and his subject. He does not content himself with one alone, because he does not find in one, or even in two, the multiplicity of parts by which his idea is com-

posed. From one he takes the several masses and movement, and will take great care in these never to change
from his model; from another he will take the head, or the
hands, or other parts of the body in which the model for
the general masses may have been defective, and will
be careful that in age and character they be not dissimilar from the principal model—that is to say, the model
that he has used for the general form. If he departs
here or there from this simple method, the idealist will
fall into academical conventionalism, or into the vulgar
and defective. Corrections of the model's defects made
from memory bring us to conventionalism, and the
exact imitation of the model alone drags us down to
the vulgar and defective, because it is humanly impossible that one model can have in himself, besides the
whole, all the perfections of parts that constitute beauty,
which is the aim of art. Such, and nothing else, is the
idealist; and so am I, and such has always been my
teaching.

Now let us see the realistic. The naturalistic, to
my way of seeing, is simply intolerant of long study of
the many rules and dogmas of the academicians that
teach one to make statues in very nearly always the
same way, with the same measures and with the same
character—be it a Virgin or a Venus, a Messalina or an
Ophelia, and so on. He is in love with his own subject,
and wishes to give it expression in its true character and
with its own individual expression, and even with those
particularities and imperfections that distinguish it from
others. Bartolini did so in his "Ammostatore," in his
"Putti" for Demidoff's table, and in almost all his works;
and so did Vela with his "Napoleon I." and his "Deso-
lazione"; and lastly, although in a much more minute
manner, did Magni with his "Reading Girl"; and up to

this point I am naturalistic, and stand up for it.   But in these days there is another species of naturalistics—better call them realistics—who love truth and nature to the extent of accepting even the ugly and bad in form and the useless and revolting in idea.   And truly here I am neither with them, nor can I advise any one to hold in esteem this school, that I should rather be inclined to call the hospital or sewer of art.   But what I have said so far is enough, for elsewhere I have touched upon the same subject, and do not want to repeat myself, but only to mention the question again, because at the great show in Naples the naturalistic school appeared in sculpture in all its audaciousness, and, I must frankly say, in all its power, worthier of a better cause and better intentions; and this, it is presumably to be hoped, may be at last more easily recognised by the young men who look for the truth, even wallowing in ugliness, than from those who fill their heads with the idea of looking for the beautiful in their memory and conventionalism. From this it is evident that I have a predilection for the naturalist who caresses an idea and the idealist who is a faithful and not a timid friend of truth.   The artist is not a servile copyist of nature—of ugly nature; not the imitator of statues, even though they are beautiful; not the slave of the name and teaching of the masters, ancient and modern.

I like the artist to be free in his imaginations, free in his feeling, free in his way of expressing himself and in his method, but yet strongly and tenaciously bound to nature and the beautiful.   By this means we could have more good artists and fewer mediocre ones; but as long as there is official teaching it is useless to hope for it.   Government schools, in spite of the difficulty of admission and advancement from one class to another, will always have too many scholars, amongst whom some—the very few, those who are really destined by nature for art—will have lost too much time in long academic courses; the others, the many, will have lost it entirely, because it is difficult with official teaching for any graduate to be expelled from school on account of tardy development or want of talent.

I do not say, indeed, that young men ought not to study, or ought to study only a little. Quite the contrary. They ought to study very much—study always; but with freedom—perfect freedom in their way of seeing and feeling and expressing the multiformity of nature; and as this freedom does not and cannot exist in official teaching, young men ought to select a master after their own taste. Certainly masters who do not belong to these academies will accept but few scholars, and will retain still fewer—that is to say, the best, those who give promise of succeeding—and the rest they will send away. And here is the great gain, because the minor arts— subsidiary, so to speak, to the fine arts, will take possession of these young men, who, instead of becoming mediocre artists, will become good workmen. Official teaching in the fine arts ought to be confined to architecture; in fact, there it ought to be amplified by the study of mathematics, engineering, and its mechanical application. The purse and the safety of citizens must surely be protected.

This little digression on teaching, which I have elsewhere treated more at length, has sprung up and been jotted down here after having seen the exhibition of the works of art of the Neapolitan school. I say the school, and not the academy—I should better say the grades of the naturalistic school of Neapolitan sculpture. It is undeniable that various works in sculpture, exposed to the solemn trial of the Neapolitan Exhibition, show that the young sculptors have emancipated themselves outright from the trammels of academical teaching, and have entered with full sails into the interminable sea of nature.   This sea is beautiful, full of agitation and life, and in its greatness rouses the desire of research into the unknown; and to him who navigates therein with strength and purpose, promises unknown lands, rich in supreme beauty.   But it is easy enough, by steering one's boat badly, or missing one's direction, to get stranded or dashed to pieces against the rocks.

Signor d'Orsi exposed a group in plaster representing the Parasites.   Nothing could have been better imagined than those two (I don't know how to call them) creatures.   Brutified by food and wine, they sleep or drowse on a *trichinium*, leaning against each other. They are a literal imitation; and in this is all the merit of the work.   It is not minute imitation, that battle-horse of small minds, but really the true expression of the conception and intention of the artist; but the idea is hideous, enormously hideous, so that to many it appeared disgusting and revolting; and I felt on looking at the work two opposite feelings—one that drove me from it, and another that kept me fixed to the spot.   The ugliness of the subject and its forms repelled me; the knowledge and art by which it was expressed attracted me, and forced me to admire the talent of Signor d'Orsi.   "This man," said I to myself, "has not come out of the academy; he is looking for a passage through the vast sea of nature, and a shore to land on. Will he find it?"

A group in plaster of "Cain and his Wife" is the subject exhibited by Signor Giov. Battista Amendola.   Considered from the point of view of expression, it is of wonderful truthfulness. This man, guilty of fratricide, cursed by God, stands there transfixed to earth; the anguish that oppresses him overcomes his arrogance; and not even the sweet words and caresses of his companion are able to appease that sullen brow and ferocious look. But Signor Amendola, who has so well entered into the human sentiment of passion, pain, and rage that agitates the heart and upsets the mind, has made a mistake in the physical character that he has, with intention, given his·figure. For since Cain and his wife are of a savage ugliness, more resembling the family of the orangoutang than the human being, he seems to be a follower of Darwin's theories, which, if they are desolating as regards science and human dignity, are absolutely revolting when represented in art. The truth is, that I think the primitive type of our race, although fierce and uncultivated, was much more beautiful than it appears to-day in our young men and young girls, who are with difficulty built up by preparation of iron and sea-baths. Then beauty was undoubtedly coupled with vigour and strength; but bad habits, mistaken education, effeminacy, and vice, have so diminished its vigour and physical beauty, that if one desired nowadays to make a "Cain," an "Abel," or an "Adam," it would be difficult to find amongst our young men a model who even distantly resembled them in their splendid strong beauty. It is also strange and absurd to look for them amongst the savages of New Zealand. I admire Signor Amendola's strength of conception and expression, but I blame his application of it in the selection of his types. He also is an artist that does not seem to be an academical student; and if to originality of subject and truth of expression, of which he has given proof in his group of " Cain and his Wife," he adds study and love in the research of the beautiful in nature, he will get on and be an artist, and what counts more, an original artist, but otherwise he will not. To make Cain, and even his wife, one must not, therefore, look for a model amongst the anthropophagi or amongst the young men who live between Doney's and the Piazza del Duomo. First of all, the type of such a subject, like any other, must be clearly in the mind of the artist, and then, with a great deal of study and love, he must seek for it in nature, abandoning in part or entirely those places where such types have no existence.

When I made my "Cain," I had the good fortune to find the model without the slightest difficulty; and the model I used was a strong and beautiful man, and what was more, he had feeling for action and expression, so that I copied him to the best of my ability, without even giving a thought to the classical style so much recommended by Academicians, although not copying with servility all the little accidents of veins, wrinkles, and so forth (nowadays some people even imitate the corns and glands). I answered the Signora Laura Bianchi of Siena in these same words, or something like them, when she asked me, at the instance of Thorwaldsen, who was in intimate relations with the family, and made the monument to her husband, Cavaliere Giulio, what style I had used in making that statue, which he had not yet seen. Later I became personally acquainted with this distinguished artist, at a ball in Casa Larderel at Leghorn, in 1845, and explained this by word of mouth, modifying my expression, because dignity of name and years must ever be respected by young men, and he being an Academician, might have been offended by the harshness of my words on the classical style.

I will continue my examination of the naturalistic Neapolitan sculpture. Signor Raffaele Belliazzi exhibited a group in plaster, representing the Approach of a Storm, and a sleeping Calabrian, each the size of life.   In these works the artist shows a real sentiment for truth in the expression of the woman holding the little girl firmly by the hand, both of them with their heads bent down, eyes tightly shut to avoid the sand that the wind is blowing with great force into their faces—their quick step and close clinging garments blown about them, showing the violence of the wind and approach of the storm.   It is, if you will, a common subject, not very attractive, and at best more suitable to be rendered in small proportions than in life-size ; for nothing that has great movement and lightness of touch can well be reproduced in large size in statuary.   Now there is nothing more full of movement than clothes blown about by the wind ; the eye can hardly see them, much less retain an impression of them, and therefore the artist is obliged rather to indicate them as they possibly might be, than definitively or accurately to reproduce them, as he should in a large work.   I repeat, these momentary impressions are excusable, and may even succeed in being praiseworthy, if they limit themselves to expression in small figures with rapid touches, after the manner of a sketch ; but in great dimensions they are not.   The other work of Signor Belliazzi, " The Sleeping Calabrian," is a very beautiful study from life, most accurate and pleasing.   Signor Belliazzi is of the naturalistic school ; he loves nature, but he does not feel, or does not care to devote his thought to, what there is in nature of choice, attractive, and great, be it either in conception or in form.   It is, however, also true that neither of his works can be put down as bad and ugly.

One who loves, feels, and reproduces nature with refinement and grace, seems to me to be Signor Constantino Barbella, as it is shown in his little *terra cotta* group called "A Love Song." It consists of three young girls singing as they walk along, their arms interlacing each other. They are dressed in the rich and peculiar costume of the Abruzzi mountains; and this dress on these figures, so young and so beautiful, flexible and lifelike in their movement of walking, the joy expressed in their faces for the charm and virtue of song, make an admirable composition which one can look at with ever new pleasure. Here the small size of the figures, and the material in which they are made, is all forgotten, and it seems as if one could hear the song,—the very breath and joy of those young girls. This peaceful work seems to be one of the most beautiful of the Neapolitan naturalistic school, and in this measure I like the naturalistic.

The study of nature, so felt and understood, draws the artist nearer to the ideal conception—that is to say, to the reproduction of beautiful nature in all its most varied forms ; it opens the mind to ideas and serious thoughts of loveliness and grace, for which Phidias, Giotto, Orgagna, and Michael Angelo were celebrated, and will remain so to the end of the world. The study of the material imitation of nature, especially when it is defective and ugly in conception and form, besides rendering these particular statues disagreeable, drives the artist away from the ideal conception of monumental works, to which sculpture should be specially devoted. The design for the monument to Salvator Rosa, the work of Signor d'Orsi and Signor Franceschi, go to prove the truth of my assertion.

These few words on Neapolitan sculpture are said to prove how much and how far the naturalistic school is to be accepted; and I have selected these examples because in them are demonstrated the power, audacity, and error, as well as the beginning of a healthy and fruitful innovation, provided it be upheld and sustained by the sentiment of the beautiful.

Delightful Naples, rich in vineyards and orange-trees, with her splendid sky and enchanting sea, in which the city mirrors itself, and ever rejoices and sings, recalls to my mind the beautiful school of Italiañ melody of Scarlatti, Pergolesi, and Bellini. Bellini, a name beloved and venerated by all who value beautiful melody—whose song is so passionate and graceful, expressing in its suave sweetness passion and love, rage and remorse, and creating dramatic situations from the very notes themselves, more than from the words; Bellini, a master without pedantry or artifice, clear without being common, profound without being abstruse, and really of the future (because I believe that both thought and ears will soon be tired of being obliged to listen too attentively to catch, here and there, *rari nantes* in *gurgite vasto* some half phrase obscure and *slegato*);—Bellini, I say, who is indeed a great man, is soon to have a monument erected to him. ' This monument was to have been made by me, and God only knows how willingly I would have worked to have made a statue of that graceful and strong genius! That work, however, has fallen into excellent hands; for Giulio Monteverde, whom I love and esteem, is to be the fortunate artist.

But if I am glad that this important and most sympathetic work has fallen into good hands, I am none the less sorry not to have it to do myself, the more so that the way it was taken from me seems inexplicably strange. This is how it was. Some years back I had a commission from Marchese del Toscano, of Catania, to make the bust of the Maestro Pacini. At that time I was also asked by the same Marchese, who was then syndic of the town, if I would be willing to make a great monument to Bellini, that the city and province proposed to put up to their great fellow-townsman. Naturally I met such a request with pleasure, although it was accompanied by considerations of economy that, whilst they were not in the least to diminish the grandioseness of the monument, in view of the place where it was to be erected, and the dignity of the subject, led him to suppose (and in this the worthy gentleman was not mistaken) that the artist would have to be discreet in his demands, so as to facilitate the work of the organising committee. I answered as a disinterested artist who was desirous of doing the work should. "Tell me the sum at your disposal, indicate the size of the place where you wish to erect the monument, and I shall make you a sketch for it which, I hope, will give you satisfaction; for I shall not look in the least to my interest, as this great man is so dear to me, and I highly approve the idea you have had of doing him honour."

In the meanwhile things proceeded very slowly; the sums of money collected were not sufficient to make the monument of the proposed size, and to this effect they wrote me after some time had passed; when at last, one fine day, a letter arrived from the secretary of the municipality, saying that the sum had been collected for the Bellini monument, that the municipality intended at once to have the work begun, and that, with this object in view, the syndic would soon forward the order of the commission to me. Naturally, I looked for the letter from the syndic, which did not keep me long waiting; but I leave it to the reader to judge of.

The Marchese del Toscano was at that time no longer syndic of Catania, and in his stead there was another,

whose name I do not remember; for I have the good fortune to forget the names of those who treat me badly,
and so bear them no resentment. I say this merely for
the sake of truth, that no one may suppose me possessed
of a virtue that I have not. I have read somewhere,
but I do not remember where, that the person offended
engraves in porphyry the name of the offender, and
the nature of the offence; whilst on the other side it is
but traced in the sand, that the slightest breath of wind
cancels. This may be true; but as regards me, I must
confess candidly that the very reverse occurs: and I
thank God for it, and so live on most happily, and my
blood gains in colour and vitality every day that I grow
older.

Here is the sense, if not the very text, of the Signor
Sindaco's letter: "It is some days since my secretary
wrote to you, to ask if you would accept the order for
Bellini's monument for this city. It must be finished
in eighteen months. Answer at once, for I have no time
to lose, and otherwise we shall appeal to Monteverde."
One cannot deny that this epistolary style is of an
enviable brevity and clearness. I answered that I had
received the letter from the secretary, but as he had
announced to me that the syndic himself would write,
I had waited for this letter so as not to have to answer
both, because I also had no time to lose. I said that
I could not accept under such close conditions, and with
such limited time; and as to appealing to Monteverde,
he did well, as he was a most talented artist, but I
doubted whether even he could accept for the same
reason—want of time. Monteverde was given five years'
time, and the price increased not a little from what was
proposed to me. My best wishes to the artist are that
he may be well inspired and make an excellent work;

that the good Catanese may have reason to be satisfied with their way of proceeding; and that the monument to Vincenzo Bellini may in its lines recall the passionate phrases of melody of the divine master.

Here my memoirs come to an end. Those who have followed me with open trusting minds, know me as if they had been with me from a child. They know my humble origin; they remember my early years when I wandered here and there with my father in search of work he found little of, and that with difficulty; my attempts to study, to satisfy an inward yearning that I knew not how to appease; the difficulties in my position of satisfying that craving; the efforts that I made to content it, and the dangers to which a quick nature abandoned to itself is exposed. They have learnt how I chose for my companion a young girl as judicious and good as she was gentle and beautiful, who was my providence and my angel, the educator of the family, and an example of temperateness, patience, and faith to me (who am so intolerant and easily angered), and whose loss I feel even more heavily to-day, when I think that by God's mercy I could now have made her life more peaceful and easy.

I wished to explain my principles on questions of art, on teaching, and on the relations that the young artist has with his colleagues, with his masters, and with his subjects. I wished to prove that justice and temperance, in judging and sentencing works of art, are the foundation of urbane and friendly artistic life.

INDEX.

THE END.

PRINTED BY WILLIAM BLACKWOOD AND SONS.